SICK AND FULL OF BURNING

SICK AND FULL OF BURNING

by Kelly Cherry

THE VIKING PRESS ❪ NEW YORK

ACKNOWLEDGMENTS

god tunes: From *Starship* by Paul Kantner, Grace Slick,
Marty Balin and Gary Blackman (page 53). © 1971 by god
tunes. All rights reserved. From *Sunrise* by Grace Slick
(page 52). © 1971 by god tunes. All Rights reserved. From
Hijack by Paul Kantner, Grace Slick, Marty Balin and
Gary Blackman (page 53). © 1971 by god tunes. All Rights
Reserved. From *Have You Seen the Stars Tonight* by Paul
Kantner and David Crosby (page 55). © 1971 by god tunes.
All rights reserved. All reprinted by permission.

Harcourt Brace Jovanovich, Inc.: From "Mr. Edwards and
the Spider" from *Lord Weary's Castle* by Robert Lowell.
Harcourt Brace Jovanovich, Inc., and Faber and Faber
Ltd.: From "The Waste Land" from *Collected Poems
1909-1962* by T.S. Eliot. Reprinted by permission.

CONTENTS

PART ONE

PART TWO

PART THREE

PART ONE

Rev. 8:5 And the angel took the censer, and filled it
with fire of the altar,
and cast it into the earth. . . .

1. THE ANGEL OF EXPLANATION

After Bernie left me, I enrolled at Mount Sinai with a view to becoming a gynecologist. One of the doctors not too long ago asked me how I happened to choose this particular field. "Oh," I said, having been alerted by his hand on my thigh under the table, "no special reason. An impulse toward the wholesome in life."

"Hah! So you admit there's something else that moves us!" My glasses slid down as his hand slid up. "I am speaking of . . . darker forces—" At fifty, he was himself curiously ambiguous.

"A death wish?" I asked, as ingenuously as my age allowed. "No," I said. I slapped his hand. "Why would anyone wish for what's inevitable."

It was a rhetorical question to which I never expected an answer, much less the one I later received. I am careful now to grasp the rail whenever I descend the steps outside my door. Where once, observing life's liaison with death, I shuddered in existential prurience, I now worry about cancer. I examine my breasts before I enter the bath.

❧ A young man I'd known casually over the course of five years had looked me up in New York on his way home from Canada.

"Do you recall," I mused, "that it was you who introduced me to Bernard I. Stein?"

"I saw him yesterday," Adrien said. "He hasn't changed at all. You'd think anyone would have in five years."

Adrien had changed! His yellow hair hung longer, curling around his nape like an ascot. His blue Catholic eyes reflected a new interest in me.

"This is narcissism," he said. My skin rippled under his touch. "You could be my sister." He was stoned.

A curious thing had happened when we turned on. I'd seen his words flow out of his mouth, streaming through a narrow channel of air like the colored crepe ribbons my sister and I used to buy for a nickel apiece in the Triangle Book Store on our way home from James K. Polk Elementary School. But I have learned to mistrust such sentiment nearly as much as Bernie did. "That's silly," I said. Adrien and I looked nothing alike.

"Maybe it is, maybe it isn't. If you want to be serious," he said, "come spend the summer in New Hope."

Then he got up to leave. "Aren't you going to sleep with me?" I asked. It had been a long time since anyone did, and Adrien, I had learned, was intelligent enough for me to think he might be the man.

He laughed. "That would be stupid," he said.

I didn't argue. In a way, I was flattered. I rang for the elevator, and while the elevator operator eavesdropped, Adrien said, "I'll be in touch." He tightened the straps of his knapsack. From a side pocket poked the long handle of the wooden spoon which he carried everywhere, not because of any effect it might have had on taste but because in the cooking of oats it made a mystical marriage of grain with grain that purified his organic system. That's what he told me. "Before summer comes," he added. It was absolutely amazing how like an angel he seemed, his skin all pink and white, his hair in yellow flames.

❡ If there are readers, they will forgive that exercise in poesy. I am on the whole rather a straightforward woman, inclined, as I have said, to deal in facts. When I fall in love, which is something I do less often these days, it is invariably with a scholar. Adrien, of course, is not a scholar but a poet of French extraction, and if he brought angels to my mind, it is only because grass will usually make one more suggestible: "I believe," he'd said, delighting in my perplexity, "that at certain unpredictable moments, people act as angels do toward one another. I know *I've* been visited by an angel now and then." His language both intrigued and discomfited. In his letters, postmarked from New Hope, he wrote, "I'd like to plow you in a field of flowers," enclosing a dried violet by way of underscoring the contradiction. I had six to sixteen weeks in which to wring what definition I could out of that, before summer came. I decided to distract myself. I had had, understand, practice in the discipline of self-distraction, going (infrequently, because they confused her) to movies with my good friend Maxine, to the weekly meetings of my Women's Lib group (alone), making lists of the women whose psychology I planned to dissect in *Sexual Inmates: A Cellular Study,* my longish reply to Norman Mailer's *Prisoner of Sex.* Lulu, Cam, Willa Mae, Max, myself. Veronica? I had a lot of time on my hands and crossed out Lulu Carlisle and put her in again. Time gave every appearance of passing. I sold the article. In February, Maxine drove in from Long Island to bring me a tee-shirt with TRIUMPH splashed across the front in bright blue; it was her way of expressing acceptance of my affiliation with Adrien, whose big red bike had won her admiration as easily as that of the younger doormen at the Park Avenue building I was sometimes wont to pat myself on the back for living in. I continued to live there because Lulu let me, and having no money of my own beyond what I'd earned tutoring her daughter (not counting the Scholar Incentive Award and the federal loan), had spent some of that time, fall and winter, in my room, figuring how I might use the money someone would surely advance me after the bulk of the essay was completed. Since so many of the versifiers and English majors I'd gone to college with had published books, I was confident someone would take mine (which was only an article, after all, and a raunchy one at that), even if the recession continued, as it seemed bound to do. If this was literary prostitution, wasn't sex almost always sold for a worthy cause? My tuition, I reminded myself, was a worthy cause.

Occasionally, I even studied toward this end, though certainly less often and less intensely than civilians would like to acknowledge. I was only in my second year, and no one dares ask a great deal of a second-year med student. We've scarcely learned how to take histories and haven't begun to master the theory behind it, being at this point in our careers considerably more intimate with the corpse—ah, that first brave assault on the axilla (i.e., armpit)!—than with the living organism. I was taking a program in Reproductive Science Interdigitated with General Endocrinology, but the fancy name was attached to a few general platitudes about social disease and contraception and a few basics that every doctor was supposed to know about the relevant organs. There were other courses and some of them required some work—"required" is the operative word, because there *were* those students who lived in the labs and the library (just as there were the ping-pong addicts who hung out in the lounge every evening and during every class break)—but except for anatomy the first year and the organic chemistry class I had had to make up the previous summer, our work was shockingly simple. My biggest problem was that people kept giving me a rough time about choosing gynecology; it was not a feminine field.

I didn't let anyone know the real reason was that I knew I'd be a washout as a brain surgeon—unless clumsy brain surgeons were lately in demand—and didn't mean to become a pediatrician like every other woman doctor. "You'll change your mind," they said, "you don't have to make up your mind yet." I said nothing.

Instead, mimicking my old man—meaning my father, since I

was just a little too dated myself to figure among those who meant somebody different by the same slang—I kept a prayerbook which no one ever saw. "Dear God," I wrote in it, "I'm thirty years old already, and if You don't send me somebody soon, the kind of somebody that makes permanent commitments, I could die without ever having a kid, and wouldn't that be a dumb waste!" He doesn't mince words with me, so I didn't see why I should mince mine with Him. But as a rule, all I got by way of answer was silence. Came the hour when I would be writing in my prayerbook, Lulu had turned off the television in her room downstairs, the incense she used to gloss over the perfume of grass was gone, sucked out into one of the quieter districts of nighttime Manhattan, and I had only the company of the pink pansies on my wallpaper to contend with. I was lonely. I thought (fleetingly) of taking to the "personal vibrator" which our housekeeper, Lulu's housekeeper, Willa Mae Wood, had procured for me in an excess of pity for all us white women. She'd come in one day back in November, bearing a Whelan's paper bag, her diamond earrings bobbing like yo-yo's under the beehive wig, and said, "I ain't goin' to let no nigger clerk intimate me! No ma'am, no *way*. 'Sonny,' I calls him, 'I'll take *two*. I am a *big* woman.' Blush? Sweet Jesus, you never seen a black'un blush so fine. Now how he goin' to know I don't have no pain in my neck?" She massaged her aching neck.

"He knows you don't have two heads," I volunteered.

Willa Mae chortled. She could afford to, countering Lulu and me, as we knew very well that she, to *our* discredit, possessed both husband *and* lover. "Honey," she said, parceling out the packages, "soon as I grows two heads, just you remind me so as I'll put the extry on your needy shoulders."

I smiled. She indulged me, did Willa Mae, because I looked to her for advice and comfort. But she had made it clear that there was a limit I was better off not exceeding: Willa Mae was one of the Survivors, and as such, assumed, when all was said and done, that we all could "cope" if only we would make up our minds to.

Lulu's difficulties, for example, she attributed to the "changes of life," conceding, with a nod of condescension, that even she herself had suffered from dizzy spells in weak moments, and, once, admitting (but I was not sure I believed her) that, appearances to the contrary notwithstanding, she too relegated sex to the role of a minor nuisance which intelligent middle-aged women tolerated as a fair trade in return for their "propers." Her favorite propers were diamond, so when, at dinner on the following day, Lulu gave her a butterfly with ruby-tipped antennae and a sparkler in each wing, explaining, "I haven't any use for it, and one does get nervous having jewels around the premises," Willa Mae was being no less than logical in inquiring after the vibrator.

Lulu said she'd experienced quite a pleasant sensation as she lay on the lounge, tool in hand, watching "Gunsmoke": "Matt Dillon," she said, "reminds me of my dead father," and returned to her room, leaving us to make what we would of that.

My own father is an unbelieving religion professor with a happy knack for confusing the Heavenly Kingdom with the foothills outlying the city of Knoxville. While we had not discussed the subject, I felt safe in thinking he would have been more or less appalled to learn that my Women's Lib group counseled autoeroticism as liberating. Insecure as my grasp on modern technology was, I confined the wisdom of my women friends to my prayerbook and went in search of a more primitive means of satisfaction. "Peter," I said to the only man around, an ex-lover from pre-Bernie days, "how's about a li'l ol' roll in de hay?" He combed his moustaches.

"Masturbation," said friend Peter, "is liberating. Haven't your girl friends explained that to you?"

And later in the year, still hoping to get some kind of rise out of him, I told him I was waiting for Adrien and the summer to come. But he only smiled pseudopaternally and said he hoped I would be happy. Then I nearly called my father long distance to ask his advice but on second thought, bearing in mind my overwhelming—to me—phone bill, wound up detailing the situation in my prayerbook thus: "After Bernie left me," I began, "and after I enrolled at Mount Sinai, I found a job as a latter-day governess to a lovely fourteen-year-old retarded rock freak named Cammie Carlisle. We shared a community of interests. Pretty soon I was divorced from the male sex. Indeed, pretty soon I was having nightmares in which the mother, Lulu Cameron Carlisle, discharged me from my position. 'But you can't do that,' I cried, 'I love her more than you do.' Lulu's drugged speech evaporated into bad breath when I awoke. The dreams, though, were oddly reassuring, because Bernie, bowing out, had sworn that my longing for motherhood was altogether too feverish and sentimental to be trusted. The dreams showed it is at least deep-seated."

Following that paragraph, I knelt by my bedside. I am as superstitious as the next person, and wouldn't be surprised if housemaid's knee wasn't more efficacious in praying than writer's cramp. "Dear God," I said, "teach me not to dress up the truth to the point where reality will fail to recognize it." I tugged at the hem of my nightgown till it covered my chilly feet. I waited until my back began to ache—a kind of confirmation that I was praying, if not that my prayer was being heard—before continuing. "Teach me not to exaggerate all the time," I exaggerated. Cammie was not retarded; she limped and stuttered; and all sense of our relationship was going to be lost to That Big Shrink in the Sky if I couldn't say, "Look here, this girl was short and stubby and had furry brown eyes and a complexion I envied and freckles I didn't and she poked her way through this cavernous but neglected duplex like a war orphan turning over rubble with that peculiarly disinterested movement of the wrist which belies so disturbingly the bathos the cameraman has so painstakingly captured on her face." Right from the beginning, from the first day I met her, she seemed to be in possession of a degree of control I'd never dare aspire to. I'd gotten the interview on a tip from a teacher I worked with on Saturdays. "Ask for ten," he whispered; "they can afford it."

"It will be ten dollars an hour," I said into the phone, and blinked when Mrs. Carlisle said, "Yes, of course."

Of course I dressed in my best skirt and blouse, cursing the myopia that condemned me to glasses, and then tripped over the step up to the marble foyer. "My shoe," I mumbled, trusting the doormen to elaborate my excuse at their leisure. I was less eager to trust my own ability to speak in complete sentences. "Mrs. Carlisle?" I asked. One of the doormen disengaged himself from the group and called up to see if I was really wanted.

I could hardly be sure I was until Cameron led the way into her room, explaining what would be expected of me. I was to tutor her in all of her subjects. "I don't know geography," I panicked; "I don't *know* French."

"That's all right," she said. "I don't either."

Then she introduced me to her mother. "My father's dead," Cam had announced earlier, stumbling over the *d*. "Same accident that fixed me up."

I had begun to relax. "You seem cheerful enough," I remarked.

"Every day for lunch," she said, "I eat a laughwich." When I scanned her smile for sarcasm, I found none—a dimple, yes, but nary a downturn of the lower lip.

And then the two of us found Mrs. Carlisle in her bedroom, munching Hershey bars. She had on a pink quilted robe that went nicely with her cropped red hair. "How do you do," she said, turning off the television set by remote control. "Cameron's grades are terrible."

"You know that it will be ten dollars an hour. . . ."

"I don't see why not," she sighed. "It's only a fraction of what the Black Panthers take."

❲ At that time I was living in a renovated brownstone next door to the Broadway Hotel for Transients. Across the street was the *bodega* where I bought cat food for The Prune and bologna and mustard and Wonder Bread for myself, bologna sandwiches being all I ever ate, as I figured that with my luck I was going to need all the money I could save. Back before Mount Sinai, I'd applied to half-a-dozen med schools, but scholarships were suddenly tight, much tighter than they had been during the fifties; and evidently no one in this town had any crying need for a hick chick riding on one ten-year-old degree that had itself been achieved only after six transfers to five schools. Memories of that now long-gone spring dampened my first year: I reckoned Bernie (my post-collegiate roommate) had split in the nick of time and the rest of the world was on the verge of joining with him in an adverse judgment as to just how timid my intelligence was. I fed Prunella and sat in the window and read anatomy. I closed the textbook and the window and watched television with Prunella. As the evening wore on, I got drunk, wrote a suicide note, got stoned, and called my parents in Knoxville to let them know that I was moving to Majorca. "Wait a minute," my father said, "I'll look it up in the atlas."

"He wants to see how far it is from Paris," my mother said on the extension.

My sister lives in Paris.

My father came back to the telephone. "It's not so far," he said.

"It's closer than Knoxville," I agreed.

"Do you think your mother and I might like to retire there?"

"Your father and I," my mother said, "have decided to start a new life together."

"You don't understand!" I said.

My mother came alive instantly. "What," she said, "*is* it that we don't understand."

I could hear my father coughing in the background.

Rather faintly, I pointed out that there weren't to my knowledge many foothills in Majorca. Of course, there might be foothills I didn't know about.

"In that case," my mother said, "we won't go. You'd better not either. I doubt if such a backward place has medical schools."

"But I'm fed up with med school," I said.

"In that case," my father said, "hadn't you better come home for a while?"

I was so close to doing just that that when the phone rang an hour later I jumped at the offer Mrs. Carlisle made me. "My best friend?" she asked, tentatively, urging me to wonder whether I was supposed to say yes. "Gladys Brunner? She always came with us, but this time she has to go into the hospital instead." If I had thought about it, I might have thought there was something vaguely threatening in her tone, as if to imply that Gladys Brunner, in going into the hospital, had somehow failed to do right by Lulu.

I wasn't sure I had understood her correctly. "I don't see how I can afford"—I stalled—"to go to Jamaica for three weeks."

"I always paid for Gladys," she said, a bit plaintively, I thought. "Cameron thought it would be fun to have you along this time."

Actually, I now had at least a margin of money, although I would never have blown it all on a trip to the Caribbean. With true *petit bourgeois* anxiety, I was tutoring Cammie twelve hours a week, teaching Saturday mornings at a school for emotionally disturbed children, and free-lancing at whatever turned up in odd hours. My one extravagance was twice-a-week psychotherapy with a Sullivanian named Veronica, who fudged the bills on my behalf so that between us we managed to take United Equitable for most of what I owed her. I had *not* told Veronica that Mount Sinai offered its own elaborate coverage to students, including free prescriptions and psychiatry: it all came under the heading of "professional courtesy." A rube right to the core, I couldn't quite bring myself to take advantage of their services —the setup was elitist; on the other hand, there was something sporting in devising new ways of ripping off big business. But I was afraid that if I explained to Veronica that what she thought was good common sense was actually compulsive hairsplitting, she might think I was—you see—sick. So I let her arrive at her own conclusions. "You'll need your money," she rationalized, "for Mount Sinai."

"What," I asked, drinking my coffee, "do I need Mount Sinai for?" One of the pleasanter facts about Veronica, in sweet contradistinction to the authoritarian shrinks I'd submitted myself to in the past, was that her answering service rang me at six in the morning to wake me up. It was the only time of day I could fit her in, and she always had coffee ready when I got there. Today she'd gotten a strand of her hair into her cup, and was fishing it out while I went on to say, "I'm illiterate and unmethodical. Also defensive."

"That's why," she said. "Doing something you believe in will bolster your ego."

My ego was indeed a shaky construction. "Knock, knock," I used to say, rapping on my head.

"Who's there?"

"Me."

"Me who?"

"Mimi La Bohème." I liked to think I was a tragic heroine with a hacking cough and a fine soprano. The Asian internist at the out-patient clinic that Veronica had insisted I visit soon enough squelched that fantasy. "The cough is good," he said, "very good. Now may I hear your voice." I sang "Don't Pluck My Peaches." He had fierce black eyes and I could tell he was torn between recommending a laryngectomy and asking me out. "I was brought up strict," I warned. "My father is a religion professor."

The black faded to misty gray. "I was raised by a most beautiful young woman," he said, "who read from the Bible to me every afternoon. A beautiful young woman, she was truth to say highly partial to the story of Ruth. If I so miss her now," he asked, turning on me, "please to think how shall I miss her when I become older!"

"Sorry," I said, chastened.

"You need a rest," he said, "I know. I quite indubitably know what you are going through."

"You do."

"It enervates one's energy. Med school." He looked tired.

"It does," I said. There would be no date.

"Depart the Saturday job," he advised me, which I did, and in August Cam, Mrs. Carlisle, and I flew Pan Am to the West Indies. At last, I thought, I was going to get laid.

❈ When Prunella was in heat, she sprayed everything in sight, and when she finally zeroed in on my anatomy text, I decided it was time to do something about it. A sexist Japanese vet on upper Broadway fixed her for thirty bucks, five off the usual fee, and a lecture on why only male (tom) cats could be said to spray; but I, having neglected to think things through, hadn't realized she would have to return the next week to have her stitches removed. Peter said he would take care of this for me, since I would be in Jamaica. The day before we left, I left her with him. I don't mean to be maudlin in what follows, but one must understand that Prunella was a calico with a checkerboard face in which the minuscule nose flared and receded according to the optical play of the sly planes of color that crisscrossed it. Now she had an enormous bandage pending from her middle and meandered dopily around Peter's place in the west 40s. "She only likes chocolate milk," I cautioned him. He smiled wanly at his dark-skinned girl friend. "Let it pass," he muttered, "let it pass."

"Well, Prune," I said, "this is good-bye."

Prunella purred.

"This is good-bye," Peter said, shaking my hand. I smiled wanly at the dark-skinned girl friend sitting on the floor. "Live it up, kiddo," he said (too loudly and punching my arm besides).

"This time," I affirmed, "I'm going to," and meant it, not knowing beforehand that no one was going to approach me except a big black beach boy, pushing forty, who sold straw hats over the counter and *ganja* under. I ran in and told Mrs. Carlisle and

Cameron about his amusing but, I reckoned, unrealistic proposition. It never occurred to me that Mrs. Carlisle, whom I still thought of as a distant and rather uncommunicative employer (although I had seen her pale and freckled body as I'd never seen my mother's, gritty with sand as she removed her bathing suit), would whip out a bill and tell me to score as soon as I could decently manage it. I did as I was told. The beach boy met me at the shed where lounging chairs and blankets were stored; and after a small skirmish, he handed over the two largest joints I have ever seen. They were rolled in tobacco leaves. "I only do this," he said, "for the mostest special guests. Do not you know many rich Americans marry Jamaican boys? Oh, yes, we love you very well!" I gave him the Panther fist and strolled back to the hotel with the joints nestling in the top of my bikini, where, unfortunately, I had plenty of room.

The hotel sprawled across an unconscionably large tract of prize real estate like a pink bird with two outstretched wings so grand in conception that they kept it from ever getting off the ground. Cameron's room was situated at the end of the left wing, overlooking the beach, and I shared the adjoining room with her mother. Each morning I garnered the breakfast orders and then called them down to room service. Mrs. Carlisle was shy and did not like to do such things. Still in our nightclothes, then, we sat on the terrace in the sparkling sun, sniffing salt from the sea and the fragrance of tropical flowers that climbed the trellis to our balcony, watching the underwear we'd washed the night before bleach to a state of pristine glister against the wrought-iron railing. For breakfast we ate watermelon, grapefruit, bananas, pancakes, and coffee. After breakfast, we went swimming; and after the swim, we showered. For lunch we ate filet mignon or lobster in the breeze of the outdoor dining room. Then we swam and showered. Dinner was roast beef or sirloin or native dishes in the indoor dining room, where every evening I silently said thanksgiving and prayed bologna sandwiches might prove a thing of the past for evermore. At ten o'clock the hotel presented a floor show in its night club, and, rousing with difficulty from the lethargy of our day, we three went. We must have seemed an imposing sort of party: we were one fiftyish redhead, still slender, shy, but given, I began to realize, to interminable complaints about the food or the water or the air conditioning; one lame teen-ager who hoped for the loss of her virginity as an alchemist hopes for the philosopher's stone; and one governess in the throes of a belated identity crisis. I tutored Cameron throughout the vacation, seeking to maintain some semblance of authority over her even when she informed me point-blank that bras were old hat and I should throw mine away. I admitted I didn't wear it for support. "I need it for illusion's sake," I said.

"Be honest with me." She turned from the mirror before which she brushed her honest strawberry mane a hundred times a day and confronted me with a grimly set jawline.

"Okay," I said brightly, "if you'll agree to do some studying."

"It's a d-d-deal." But I had gotten the worst of it, because she went to a la-de-da private school where all she ever had to study was poetry and painting. The academic subjects, I'd discovered, were for show. Even so, it was my place to take the best advantage of the bargain, so I conjured an anthology from my suitcase and let it fall open at random. "Here," I pointed at the page: "Memorize." It was something—this—by Robert Lowell.

On Windsor Marsh I saw the spider die
When thrown into the bowels of fierce fire:
There's no long struggle, no desire
To get up on its feet and fly—
It stretches out its feet
And dies. This is the sinner's last retreat;
Yes, and no strength exerted on the heat
Then sinews the abolished will, when sick
And full of burning, it will whistle on a brick.

"Jesus please us," she said, "how dumb can you get."

"Memorize," I repeated, a little less adamantly after I'd read it through myself. She bent her head over the book, two silky lengths of strawberry, draped from the center part, closing over her face like a curtain. I wished I had so handy a way of hiding from Lulu Carlisle.... She dogged my steps, swam when I swam, read what I read, never went out alone at night, peered over my shoulder at the spiral notebook as I amused myself by writing long letters to Peter in New York and Adrien in New Hope. I gave her the issue of *Harper's* in which *The Prisoner of Sex* had not so very long ago appeared. "I once thought I might write," she said, "or do something useful. Take care of people. Be a nurse. But it's so tedious. Taking care of people. Especially if you don't have any talent for it. Writing." Her complaints left little room for contradiction. Yet everything else about her was completely contradictory: her red hair, so much more definite than Cameron's softer shade, framing a face far less established; the youthful body too tightly strung to be believed in; eyes that reflected nothing of the sensitivity her skin attested to. Whenever I looked away from her, I had trouble recalling what she looked like. Until one day I realized she looked like a flower on fire, or a rosy-tipped match waiting to be struck. She lit a cigarette, looked at the magazine open on her lap, and looked at me—or, rather, looked almost at me. Her gaze, resting lightly on the tip of my left ear, caused me to feel slightly unfocused. When I tried to move my eyes directly into her line of sight, she looked quickly away, back to the magazine, closed its pages and rolled it into a makeshift telescope through which she could pretend to view the horizon. "Norman Mailer!" she said, so that I felt a little as if the telescope had been intended for a megaphone: just one more cross-purpose contributing to my sense of dislocation. "Norman Mailer!" The bottom of my bathing suit had fused to my seat; I got up and snapped the fabric loose, letting the sea air in (in my suit). "There's another example for you," she said. I wondered what she thought my bathing suit stood for: Macy's? "Even think-ing," she said, "is tedious. Even when they're about sex, ideas bore me. But I suppose I never had any talent for thinking, either." Did she mean to imply a flair for sex?

"Everyone has a right to express herself," I said, choking on the liberalism I seemed compelled to second in her presence.

"No one would want to read what I think."

I felt it would be an invasion of her privacy to ask why not, but she slapped the magazine against her knee and went on to say: "I think my father was a . . . male chauvinist. He once caught me in bed with Sam. Before we were married."

"Oh." I glanced up to make sure the door between our room and Cammie's was closed.

"He wasn't much good at it, you know—Sam wasn't. Or at least I never enjoyed it much."

Her voice was soft and girlish, sharing confidences, a little eager. I said, "Oh."

"Of course, nowadays things are different. Nowadays you can look around until you find one who is. Good at it."

"I guess you can."

"Oh, not me," she said, "but I hope Cameron looks around a bit before she settles on one."

"I guess you don't have to worry about that yet," I said, help-fully.

"She's fourteen!" she said, as if time were slipping by far too fast.

I didn't say anything.

"Now if *I* were to have an affair"—she jabbed her cigarette in my direction as if she were asking me to light her fire—"don't get me wrong, I'd never marry again, of course, but if I had an *affair,* it would be with a black man. They're a lot handsomer." She thought for a moment. "On the whole."

I scarce knew how I was expected to reply, whether she was baiting me or being candid. I used to lie awake nights thinking of things I could say to her, conversations we might carry on the next day, but there was no way to divert the course of her ideas without exposing my own emotions, and she was not overly interested in what I felt about things. She'd ask me a question, and two nights later, she'd ask the same question again. At the same time, the way I felt about things was, I wasn't ready myself to get too deeply embroiled: you meet someone and live with him and then he splits; you find a friend and then the friend marries; you make up your mind to do something useful and trailblazing, such as be a gynecologist, and no one really wants to take you seriously. I'd grown cautious, and keeping an eye out for trouble whenever I began to invest in somebody, I would refer to a scrap of paper Max had kindly made pertinent notes on. It was torn from a Stuart memo pad, headed at the top with their product's description: *Dialose, dioctyl sodium sulfosuccinate 100 mg. and sodium carboxymethylcellulose 400 mg.* "You have a lot of constipation on Long Island?" I had asked her. Ignoring me, she had in laborious longhand headlined: "One-to-One Relationships."

"They're the best kind," I had said, but she went on stolidly drawing up her list:

"(1) *Symbiosis*—Mutually beneficial; (2) *Commensalism*—Though only one benefits, neither organism is significantly harmed, as in the case between the shark and the remora; (3) *Parasitism*—The parasite gives nothing in return to the host, with the result that the latter ultimately is injured or even destroyed by the former. Remember Bessie Smith."

I was unsure what Bessie Smith's fate had been. In fact, reading over the list, I decided it confused me more than it did anything else. The only conclusion I could draw was that I definitely felt safer keeping a certain distance between Mrs. Carlisle and me. "Call me Lulu," she yelled from the back of the bay in front of me; "Mrs. Carlisle makes me feel so old," and I felt I had to, but resented the encroachment just the same.

"Lulu," I hollered, "this horse is killing me." We were riding in the middle of the afternoon, Cameron up front with the guide, Lulu in line behind Cameron, while I struggled (valiantly, I thought) to bring up the rear. Tennessee might be my nickname, but I'd been nurtured in academia, nowhere near bluegrass country, and this was my first time on horseback. I hoped it was my last. Gallumping along, trying to keep within my line of sight those two thoroughbreds and their guide sitting tall in the saddle, listening to the clop-clop-clop my reluctant pony made come to an emphatic stop every three feet in silence, waiting for the guide to turn around and start me up again, lurching forward and back as the pony and I repeated our clop-clop-clop-thud-stop, I knew it had been sheer malevolence which had prompted Lulu to say to him, "Give her an easy one, she hasn't ridden before."

"Let's go back," I whined.

But Lulu's saucer of hair spilled over her face with glee—this was one thing she'd learned to do at finishing school and still did well. She dug her heels into the bay and charged off, skimming past the shanties that lined the hot road, past the women with baskets on their heads, the boys with donkeys on their ropes. That evening I told her I'd had enough of sport. "Let's see the tourist attractions," I said, so in the morning we were off to the famous grotto.

"It's damp," she said.

"Caves are damp," I said.

"Why ever did you drag us to a *cave*," she said, launching into a series of complaints that continued long after we were back in the hotel. She turned the air conditioning up. "It was so *hot* in there," she said.

Cameron came into our room, sat down, and took off her left shoe. Her heel was bleeding. "You should have said something!" I said, recalling all at once her mother's gripes of that morning and mine from the afternoon before. I had held Cam's arm while we hiked through the grotto but she had said nothing about her foot, that it hurt or was being rubbed raw. I went to the hotel drugstore for iodine. Returning the length of the long hallway, I reflected that though she made her likes and dislikes known and was never to be bullied out of an opinion she held, she very carefully refrained from infringing on anyone else's personality, particularly her mother's. It was unnatural. "Let's see," I said.

She thrust her foot in my face.

"You'll survive," Lulu said, as I applied the iodine. Cameron's foot twitched and I told her to hold it steady.

"This time," I told her, "it's your turn to decide what we'll do." She laughed and said she felt like turning on.

I laughed to humor her, and was going to say it was time to dress for dinner, but Lulu had already lit the first one herself, inhaling with the expertise of a woman who has smoked more cigarettes and drunk more drinks than the bags under her eyes could easily forgive. The skin on her face looked soft and deep and warm, like a thick towel, and might have been wholly attractive were it not for the few places, beneath the eyes and around the mouth, where it folded over as if to conceal some small indecency. She passed the stick to Cammie, who, I was then informed, had been smoking in school for several years; and Cammie passed it on to me. The smoke was harsh. I pretended to take a heavier drag than in fact I did. We went around like that for quite some time, until the air in the room grew uncomfortably thick. Lulu threw open the door to the terrace. "Somebody will smell it," I objected, thinking of the watchman who patrolled the hotel grounds at night.

"Nonsense," Lulu said. She was swaying back and forth in her red slip like a Chinese lantern.

"I wish we had some music," Cameron said. "I wish we had some boys."

Lulu danced.

I was amazed by her strange behavior. I was glad I had not gotten stoned with her and Cameron.

Cameron stood up. "I'm going to recite a poem," she announced, and proceeded to fling herself down on the rug, acting the part:

There's no long struggle, no desire
To get up on its feet and fly—
It stretches out its feet . . .

She stretched her legs, the bruised and painted heel glowing red as if in reflection from her mother's bright slip. Dying, she lay immobile, soundless, for what seemed like hours. "Cammie?" I asked. "Cam?"

"For a governess," she said, "you're pretty dumb." She giggled. "You must be crazy, talking to a dead spider!" I reached out my hand and hauled her up. Lulu went on with her private dance. "I wish," Cam said, "I wish I had a boy friend."

"Good lord," I answered her, "you're much too young."

"You only say that because you're afraid you're getting too old." I would have let her have it for that, except it was said very simply, and might be true. I would have to think about it. "Mama too," she said.

"It's not what it's cracked up to be," Lulu said.

Cameron lay down on her mother's bed. "I'd like," she said, wistfully, "to find out for myself."

"Now look what you've done!" Lulu was standing over her. They seemed to be moving about at a great speed. "If you have to lie down, why don't you lie down in your own bed instead of mussing mine up?"

Suddenly the room was charged with electricity. I tried to defuse the situation. "Why don't we play cards?" I asked.

Lulu stared at me; Cam turned her face in my direction; but I had the feeling that neither mother nor daughter saw me. I brought out the deck of cards and began to deal them out.

"I never win," Lulu said. "Unlucky at cards and unlucky at love too."

I held my tongue. The plaintive wail of her grievances against the world—"It's unfair, no one loves me, I do all the work, write all the checks, I have nothing to do with myself on these unending days that I am made to suffer for the sake of a child who thinks I'm passé to begin with"—wearied me beyond telling. If they flowed forth in so continuous a stream, they could be stopped, I thought, only at their source. I admitted to myself that I was curious about the source of her complaints.

"Must you deal so slowly," she muttered.

"It's not me, it's the dope."

"Well, it *seems* as if you're dealing very slowly."

Cameron said, "Time is an illusion, Mama."

"My little girl," Lulu said to me, "thinks she's a Hindu."

"I *was,* once." There was sweat on Cammie's face from the attempt to be taken seriously. "Do you ever meditate?" she asked me.

"No," I said. "My mind wanders."

Lulu laid down her hand. "Cameron can read fortunes with these," she said, the note of pride sounding discordant in the atmosphere.

Cameron reshuffled the deck and arranged the cards face up in six-by-seven lines. I fell silent. "Well, come on," Lulu said.

"I never finished my poem." She scooped up the cards.

"You're trying to psych us," I said, prepared to chew her out for playing on our nerves when everyone was already keyed up. Lulu interrupted me.

"Did I hear the telephone ring?" She looked first at Cameron, then at me, as if one or the other of us could tell her what she had heard.

There was no one in the whole of Jamaica who knew us, or knew our room number. We waited. Then the telephone was ringing, and I lifted the receiver to my ear, and the other party hung up. "They hung up," I said, listening now to my own voice in the silence of the room. The sketchiest of breezes had stolen into the room through the sliding glass door that opened onto the terrace. Now I knew we were in for trouble, that this extraordinary decadence I'd been dallying with, dope and the full moon and two women I pitied perhaps but didn't even know well enough to like or dislike, who supported me in a style to which

I was not accustomed and for reasons which I couldn't pinpoint
... that this romance had to be paid for as dearly as any circum-
vention of the reality principle. I knew there was no hope of
explaining all this to *them*. So I said, "I'm scared."

"Tennessee's afraid of the bogeyman," Lulu taunted. She replaced the cards in her nightstand drawer. "You'd both live in
pigsties if you could."

"I can feel how afraid she is!" Cam said, pointing at me. "I can
see the vibrations."

Lulu looked at me, reaching out her arm spontaneously as
though she meant in fact to feel my fear, but then she let it drop.
"She's probably afraid," she said, "that the beach boy is going to
come get her. I don't believe anyone ever rises above their origins."

I remember that I got up then, ready to defend the Southland
at last, and don't remember anything after that until Cameron
confronted me in the bathroom, where I was crouching beside
the toilet, and I saw her unlined face approaching mine with
amusement and not a little dismay. "This," I said, "is the sinner's
last retreat." She laughed. She seemed incredibly young and I
was pleased I had made her laugh. I didn't want to alarm her,
didn't want her to know yet all the possibilities for evil that
existed. And I too laughed aloud, peering, from my vantage point,
at the peculiar world that now insisted upon revealing itself to
me: the porcelain and tile, shiny and slick as the armor secreted
by some mean, self-preserving creature uncommitted to land or
sea; Cameron's face, virginal, as open to suggestion as I wished
I still was; the frosted Plexiglas so-called shower curtain climbing from the rim of the tub to the stucco ceiling like a miracu-
lously convenient blank screen upon which I might project all
the odds and ends of my memory bank.

It was Maxine who had gone with me on a Saturday night to
Ninety-seventh Street to see what we had thought was to be a
wonderfully lush and weepy exposé of life among the rich and
shady. We were munching popcorn, the bags propped against

our chests, our legs propped against the seatbacks in front of us, chagrined at the utter absence of nudity, annoyed at being duped for two-fifty per. The teen-age heroine was as wholesome as Young America and the sunshine boys surrounding her looked like frat-party freaks. Only one was at all interesting, a Caligulan sort of fag, and our fantasies about him were necessarily going to be cut short. Caligula swished across the Riviera's wide screen, breathing to his male costars suggestions that were plausible enough, hinting to the heroine at possibilities Max and I were surprised she didn't simply laugh at. Then Caligula decided to throw a little party, by way of pepping things up. They took a few drinks and popped a few ampules. Their spirits rose; our spirits rose. But just as he'd bound his lantern-jawed muscle-bound blond counterfoil in chains, Max leaned over to me and went into a little number of her own: "I'll tell you," she whispered, uninvited, "why perversion is so dull. It's a mask for lassitude. When you get right down to it, nitty-gritty-wise, perversion is effete, 'cause real sex—*real* sex—requires one helluva lot of energy. Can you dig it?" Caligula had swiped a sword from the suit of mail in his baroque bedroom and was brandishing it about like a child with a toy gun, and I was digging Maxine's speech, when then he abruptly and most inconsiderately severed his lover's head. Max had spent the greater number of her twenty years fighting her way out of communes and jazz cellars and mental hospitals and had learned to hold the enemy at bay by erecting what I had thought was an admirably firm fortress around certain areas of her brain. "Oh no," she said, "that's sneaky, that's unfair." Leaning forward, she spilled her popcorn on the floor of the auditorium: it rolled down the slant. When she brought her feet down, the little balls crunched underneath. There was blood spurting all over the screen. Caligula, crazed by some unspecified drug, was now murdering everyone in his unhappy mansion, by knife, by gun. "By god," I said, "we're going to walk out on this." Max was crying. I nudged her and then her eyes blazed and she said: "Boy-oh-boy, the pigs who shot this flick, they should drop dead already." Two old women behind us leaned over and asked us please to lower our voices. "Or we'll have to call the usher," they said. I left and Max followed, ranting up the aisle, ranting all the way up upper Broadway. I knew she had to talk and listened, but the more she talked, the sadder I felt. *"Okay,"* I said.

"Wanna Eye-talian ice?" she asked, switching horses in midstream. Her working acquaintance with madness made her unusually receptive to any disturbance in wavelength. But I knew only the ordinary neuroses that everyone in New York knew, and, unwilling to acknowledge in public my own puny phobias, hadn't learned to wall them off with words the way she did. I was stuck with the visions in my closed-circuit skull, and couldn't stop seeing that blond, startled head dangling from Caligula's prissy grasp, or the great wound its vacation had rendered, like a second mouth crying "Come back! Come back!"

"Hush, little girl," Cameron said, immensely pleased, I could tell, with the turnabout. "You can come back into the room with us now. There's nothing to be scared of."

"Nothing! I can think of at least four," I shouted, ever ready to fulfill my duties as a tutor. "How about the Four Horsemen of the Apocalypse?"

"What's the Apocalypse?"

It felt good to know more than someone else in the world did, especially then it felt fine, and a warm content suffused my arms and legs, which had begun to cramp in their awkward position next to the toilet. I said to Cam, "I'll be all right now," and followed her lead back to the bedroom, where I remembered the terrace door had been left open, and shut the door.

"You must keep a dozen locks on your door in New York," Lulu said. "Are you hoping we'll keel over from the heat in here?" Then, reverting to the locks, she said: "Unless you have a . . . roommate?"

Cam was still reciting her poem:

. . . I saw the spider die
When thrown into the bowels of fierce fire . . .

"I wish I'd never told you to memorize that," I said. She was still high, pointing at her mother as she giggled and stuttered through the final line:

This is the Black Widow, Death.

Only the way she said it was, "This is the Black Widow, D-D-D-Death." Lulu's face, paling, seemed even paler by virtue of the red slip beneath it. I was sympathetic to others who suffered from superstition as I did and made an effort to redirect her thoughts.

"No," I said, "I don't have a roommate."

"Do you get lonely?" Cam asked.

But Lulu said, "Who doesn't?"

"Then why doesn't she move in with us? She could have the room upstairs that Gladys used to live in." Cameron and her mother had a way of referring to me in the third person, as if I weren't quite all there, as indeed I may not have been. "Please! Mama?"

I'd have guessed that Lulu Carlisle would find some way out of what seemed on first thought to be an impossible situation; but then, I didn't know her. "Why don't you?" she asked.

"Well, I—"

"You're there a good part of the time anyway. It's closer to Mount Sinai." And then, the *coup de grace:* "And Lindsay has asked everyone to make use of all available space, the apartment situation is so impossible."

"Well, I—"

"Please," Cameron said, and I, nearly as stoned as my poor misguided Caligula had been, consented, considering her, her wide eyes and hopeful tone, the bread I'd save, and the nights I'd lain awake wondering whether the footsteps and scratchings I heard originated from the roach-infested hallway outside my door or were confined safely within the Broadway Hotel for Transients where they belonged. I trusted this would bring the evening to an end. It did. Cameron retired to her room; Lulu swallowed a sleeping pill and fell asleep in her bed with a cigarette in her hand. I took the butt from her hand and put it out and stayed up reading until the grass wore off and I could go to sleep without bad dreams.

❡ It was a hot, sticky day. I sat by the truck Roosevelt Jones had rented with my money, reading, swilling water from his canteen, while he and the kid he'd roped into this moved my things downstairs. "Good girl," he said, when I gave him the rum I'd brought back from Jamaica for him. Rosie was a window-washer by trade, and in his leisure time, a frequenter of the bar old Peter used to hang out in. The bar was the Recovery Room, a watering spot for doctors, med students, and—as Rosie and Peter had each in his own time discovered—nurses. I'd known Rosie off-and-on for quite some time. It was through him that Peter had met his current girl friend, and through Peter that I had met him. I used to believe there were really only about two hundred people in New York and Rosie knew all of them. I myself knew fewer black people in the city than I had down home, but the ones I did know, Willa Mae and Rosie, frankly enjoyed taking me under their wing in a sociological reversal that no white Northerner would recognize but which every Southerner is familiar with and not ungrateful for. Rosie was a kindhearted soul, a stocky, broad-beamed, middle-aged, hard-working soft touch, who, drunk, collapsed into the kind of nostalgia for the South that I had to beware of in myself. That didn't stop him from taking full advantage of the privileges of the North. When we'd made our way crosstown to Park Avenue, I introduced him to Lulu. "I could go for that chick," he said after she showed us to my room and left. I blinked but chose to ignore him.

"What's eating you?" he asked. "Why so glum and silent?"

"Nothing," I said. "I feel funny without Prunella."

"Well, lookit. . . ." The Carlisles' two dogs tore by, chasing the family cat up the stairs to the Sun Room and terrace that took up the opposite half of the floor I was to live on. "Speaking of cats, here's a cat. And dogs. And it's a doggone penthouse. Cheer *up,* for crying out loud."

But The Prune was gone for good. "She vamoosed the first day she was here," Peter had explained, tugging on his ear with embarrassment. "It must have been the drugs. She was woozy, remember? All I did was turn around and she was missing. I didn't mean to leave the window open!"

"Sure, Peter, I know that. Curiosity killed the cat. It wasn't your fault." I knew he felt guilty enough. But he couldn't know I felt guilty too: I had abandoned her when she needed me most, and in the back of my mind, I had realized life with the Carlisles would be simplified if I didn't have to introduce my cat to theirs. I set my typewriter and textbooks out on the table, studied the flowered wallpaper with something akin to despair, and experimented with shutting the door. It was going to be all right. When the door was shut, I might have been miles away from anyone. "You're a dum-dum, Tennessee," I told myself. I'd gotten into the habit of talking aloud to myself when I was alone, it made for company of a sort. "You always worry about how the lilies of the field are going to make out, and now here you are on Park Avenue." I put things in order, and late in the day, opened the door. I heard a low wail climb the staircase. It was a cat, it wasn't Prunella, it was Clio. But it wasn't Clio the cat, it was Cameron. I ran downstairs. She was in her room, crumpled on the sofa bed, her mother standing by the door. Inanely, I asked if there was anything wrong.

"Gladys Brunner died," Lulu explained. "In the hospital. Today."

"It's not fair, it's not fair." I'd never seen Cammie like this. Her mother left the room. I excused her, thinking her grief must go even deeper. But that left me with the task of consoling her daughter. I went to the bed, put my hand on her back, and wished almost bitterly that I wasn't so self-conscious or so timid about touching people. "Hey," I said. "It happens, you know."

"I warned her against eating that shit. . . . Sugar and instant rice and soda and shit."

"What are you talking about?" I had visions of botulism. Ruptured gallbladders. Emaciation.

"It was cancer! Cancer, you dodo." She was fairly screaming.

"That's out of date," I said. "Try dum-dum."

"Well, dum-dum—" She was sitting up now, glaring at me with eyes bloodshot from tears, and in the light of the sun setting over Central Park, I saw her as she might look twenty or thirty years hence: weak and worn out from struggling to swing with one bum leg and a talent for empathy that couldn't prove much use or afford much pleasure in the world she lived in. "You should know, being a tutor and all, that you get cancer if you d-d-don't eat right."

"I noticed you ate plenty on our trip. Five pounds' worth, at least." If it was cancer, Lulu Carlisle must have known Gladys Brunner was dying before we had ever left for the West Indies.

"It's not how much, it's what, and you have to eat certain kinds of things in moderation." Her patience was infinite. "You just have to be careful, you don't have to be a nut."

That was before we had all heard about DES in beef and preservatives in bacon, and I thought maybe you did have to be a nut. But I grasped her meaning more clearly that night at dinner. The Jamaican feast was over. Willa Mae served raw hamburger patties, brown rice, lima beans, and tap water. Afterward, I went upstairs to the room the dead Gladys had apparently occupied at some point in her life. Although my desk at the hospital would be waiting for me, registration was still a way off; and even if some of my classmates should happen to be there already, the probability of my having to walk back by myself to an apartment which, while safer (I thought) than the one crosstown on the

Upper West Side, was in a neighborhood both darker and less friendly—so unnerved me that I planned on doing most of my studying throughout the year in my room. I sat at my table for a fruitless hour, reading all about hormones whenever I wasn't veering off into recollections of my father's homiletics. "Life and death," he liked to say, "are two sides of the same coin." Gladys had tossed and lost; but I had won, and here I was in the penthouse she had walked away from (why?). First, I worried that if I was filling her shoes, I might take the direction she had gone. Then I thought I could feel her presence in the room, the presence of death; I thought I could smell it and that it smelled ever so faintly like the pathology lab. The room was hot, it was as still as a tomb. First I felt trapped; then I thought it might be the other way around, that I had pushed her out of here and into her grave the way I had elbowed Prunella out of my life. I thought of Prunella wandering in a drug-induced daze out onto the fierce streets where some mean-spirited kid kicked her in the belly and opened her wound until the blood gushed onto the sidewalk and she couldn't meow any more. The room was silent, too silent. I could hear nothing except the jagged edges of soft music as it scraped itself sneaking under the crack of the second door to my room, the one that led out the back down the stairs to the lobby nineteen floors below. The music was getting on my nerves. I had to talk with someone, so I called Dial-A-Prayer.

"*Hel*lo," it said. "Thank you for calling the Dial-A-Prayer Fifth Avenue Church. Let us pray. O Lord, help me to overcome my loneliness, my sense of alienation. Help me to open myself to others, seeking Your Presence in meaningful re*la*tionships with others, that the work of Your Son, Jesus Christ, may be renewed and made meaningful by our en*count*ers on Earth. Sometimes, living in this great city, this busy, bustling city, I feel . . . left out, I feel, for I know I can speak frankly to *You,* just a little bit insig-*nifi*cant. I feel, well, as small as a . . . sparrow. Help me to know that You are watching my fall. Help me to know that You are there to catch me. Help us, O Lord, to reach out with Your Word, so that all of God's creatures in the Greater Metropolitan Area may straighten out and fly right. Help us to just, well, *chirp* that hymn of praise that in our hearts we hear. In Christ's name, we ask this. Amen. Do *you* sometimes feel lonely? *I* do! Why not call the Hot Line at CIrcle 6–4200 and let's us rap about it to*gether*. 'Bye now!" What I most enjoyed was the way the voice ran— scurried—up and down the scale, encompassing octaves in a vain attempt to sound spontaneous. There was no hope for anyone, not even ministers. I grabbed the Harvard bookbag I used as a purse —I'd bought it in the Hunter College Book Store, though Hunter and Harvard shared the distinction of being among the few places where I'd never taken an undergraduate class—and pressed the button to the upstairs elevator entrance in the Sun Room, said thank-you's at the top and at the bottom, and hailed a cab downtown to Peter's place. "You must be maybe eighteen," the driver said, his voice thick with an accent I was at a loss to classify. "I have a niece—she's, oh, eighteen too—very pretty. Not see her, oh, uh, ten, twelve years."

I asked him where she was.

"Algeria. All my family, Algeria. Oh, yes, is a pretty country. You think it is hot? But is very nice, is on same, you know, *line* of New York."

"Really?"

"Really, I do not kid. You are eighteen?"

I thought he was being fresh. "No," I said. "Thirty."

"Oh, I'm sorry to hear—I am very sorry, how could I know."

"It's not the end of the world."

"But thirty— Have you a husband?"

"No." It didn't seem right, given Dial-A-Prayer's prayer, to cut him off altogether.

"Oh, I'm very, very sorry. Well, I shall give you my advice. Just a little. Not too much advice!"

"Right on."

"When I was a young man, my friends and I, we wanted to have a, you know, social life? So each weekend we give a party. And each weekend we ask lots of people. Then when all the people came, if they use drugs or drink too much, we take their names, and make a list, and don't ask no more. Pretty soon only nice people come to the party, and each weekend we have a satisfactory time indeed."

"That's nice."

"One man, he was my friend, he was Italian, he was fifty years old already and still no wife. Well, at the party he meet a nice, very nice girl, and now they live in New Jersey, and are very happy. Oh, no big money, no big house, but a little money, a little house, and bi-i-g happiness."

"It's a regular fairy tale," I said.

He'd pulled the cab to a stop in front of Peter's building. Now he turned around to face me. "You think I'm kidding you? You take my advice. Find a *good* man. No drugs. No whisky. Then you and he, you fit one another, you make like the, you know, the mountain and the valley. Is no good," he said, "a woman alone."

PART TWO

I Cor. 7:9   It is better
to marry than to burn.

2. THE BLACK-AND-BLUES

On the very day on which I was born, the country of which I had just become a citizen entered World War Two. It was a responsibility one felt one ought to try to bear with grace if one could not manage quite without groaning, and though Bernie may have sidetracked me, I would not let him keep me off course forever. I was going to be a gynecologist, selflessly treating female America for the wounds unavoidably inflicted on her in the battle between the sexes, soothing and succoring and healing her, that she might, repaired, go forth and successfully restore the male population that I, kicking my way out from my mother's womb, had so carelessly and so cruelly kicked clear across the ocean into that holocaust that I was as yet ignorant of. As for how I came by the megalomania necessary to assume this cross, or where I found the gall to rail against a burden I had, after all, helped myself to, anyone's analysis will, I feel sure, be as simple as my own. I find all such analyses tedious and banal and should remark only that, with the possible exception of my father, men, left to their own devices, would soon desert this world in favor of the next. Women were a different matter—or had better be, and might so become, under Tennessee's tutelage.

I had a dream for women. They would grow up whole and well

and live their lives in a state of health bordering on holiness. "Cleanliness," my mother said, "is next to godliness," and I was never one for ignoring anyone's cliché. To ignore the common is to bypass whole realms of experience rich with pearls of wisdom. "We are all figments of our imaginations," my father insisted, but neither my mother nor I believed him, and my sister wouldn't say what she believed but left home as soon as it was feasible. I saw even my sister raised up under this regime, transfigured from her role as apprentice to a violinmaker at the Sorbonne to a player of violins herself, in harmony with the higher craft of self-expression, for the woman-soul actualized should surely be at once the most intrinsically beautiful and necessary of instruments, as if the disembodied scale itself, sounded at last with an unheard-of perfection, gave birth to all the lesser, lovely chairs of the mortal orchestra. Naturally, it was I, Mary "Tennessee" Settleworth, in whose moist palm the baton, the scepter, the speculum rested. It was I through whose palm the nail might be driven.

Should I seem to mock my own ambition, the reader is advised to chalk it up to self-consciousness. The dream itself was as serious—in fact, as humorless—as a dream ever was, and could not be otherwise when I was daily confronted with the reality it operated in reaction to. In the middle of November, just when I was getting caught up in the pathophysiology of the genitourinary system, Cameron had transferred to a special school in Maine, leaving me behind to deal with her mother by myself, or generally by myself, because Willa Mae worked days only and went home to her husband, or sometimes to her lover, promptly at seven each evening. I had never fully understood why Cammie wasn't in a school for exceptional children, as they say, to begin with, and she'd wanted to be off on her own in any case and had finally worn her mother down. Her chief argument was that it was time she got laid and that there was no way she could accomplish that at home, since the boys in her school there (here) were all snobs and wouldn't sleep with a handicap. She'd talked Lulu into asking a doctor to prescribe birth-control pills for her, packed her albums of The Doors and The Rolling Stones and her boar's-bristle brush, and, waving good-bye, drove off with a suspiciously long-haired teacher to an experimental institution that had been operating in the red until her mother had discovered it, or until it had discovered Lulu, and left me without job or rationale. I now needed the free rent. Yet I assumed I should leave, and was planning to, when Willa Mae cornered me in the kitchen, whispering: "Don't you be fixin' to leave us, now! You ain't fixin' to leave? Mrs. Carlisle, she be heartbroken. . . . I reckon, 'cause she done told it to me her*self.*" She paused to embrace the kitchen, the duplex—the diamond ring on her pinkie drawing and mesmerizing my glance. "Such a *big* old beaten-up place without our li'l Cameo to play her songs all the time." Then Willa Mae winked and I knew I'd have to be utterly without feeling in order to move out. I asked her why Mrs. Carlisle hadn't given me the message directly. "Our madam be *right* shy," she said; "you know it." So I sat through dinner with them at the rusted patio table which functioned as our dining area, had coffee with Lulu in her bedroom in front of the newscast until half past seven, and introduced my friends to her. "You have so many friends," she said, querulously, "that I can't keep them straight." She called Max "Veronica" and Veronica "Max" and recalled with clarity only the one friend who was both male and black, Rosie Jones, whom she'd met the day I moved in. "She's interested in you," I told him, but couldn't bring myself to set up a date, as she was not about to go out with him alone, not having dated in thirty years, which meant I would have to conduct the trio we made in a concert that threatened to be painfully tuneless. She couldn't herself enter into a dialogue: when you spoke with her, it was like two runners loping along the same race track, and if it went well, you found yourselves side by side at the finish line, saying, "Good night. . . . See you tomorrow." I usually said my good-night just about when Dave Brinkley said his. Then I'd dump our coffee mugs into the sink, beat it upstairs, close my door, and wonder how on earth I could establish some sort of friendship with a woman who evidently didn't want one and yet seemed to expect it.

That she did expect it, I took for granted as the corollary to my sense of obligation. That she could on the contrary fear I might not want to be her friend came as a revelation one evening when I opened the mail to learn that I had sold *Sexual Inmates: A Cellular Study* to *The Male Bag*, a highbrow nudie magazine with intellectual, even philosophical pretensions. I was ecstatic and showed the letter of acceptance, signed by Ace Winters himself, to the two of them. "That's nice," Lulu said, her enthusiasm knowing no bounds.

Willa Mae overcompensated. "Honey!" she said. "How come you ain't told me you a typewriter?"

"I'm not," I said modestly. "I just did it to earn some money."

There was a silence.

"My friend Peter helped me," I explained. "He's the one who submitted it to Mr. Winters."

Lulu scowled. "I suppose you got a lot of money for it."

I found myself feeling nervous. Conspicuous. "Not much," I said. My voice was leaving me and I cleared my throat to bring it back. "A little," I said.

"I suppose you'll be getting an apartment of your own."

I thought maybe she was hinting I should. "I could," I said. "But—"

Suddenly Lulu rose from the table, her small round head flaring up in the dim room like a match struck into flame. We heard her walk away and heard the door to her room shut. I looked at Willa Mae. "She ain't heard from Cammie in the longest time," Willa Mae said. She fixed her gaze on me.

"I had a letter from Cameron today. She's fine."

"I done said to her to call up that crazy school she in and ast what in hell be goin' on up there."

"I don't hear from Cameron very often," I said, wondering why I should feel guilty about hearing from her at all. "Just today."

I could understand how Lulu would be upset about not hearing from her: I had been plenty hurt myself when she had gone off.

Willa Mae started scraping plates. I helped her carry them to the sink. "Teen-agers!" she said. "Ain't got a brain in they heads."

She had one of her own, so I figured she should know. "But Cameron means well," I said. "She's probably busy and just forgot."

Willa Mae turned toward me with her hands on her hips. "See here, Tennessee, honey. You want to know how come that girl have a messed-up leg like that! They was all three drivin' around in one of them foreign cities in one of them foreign cars and Mr. Carlisle, he be drunk, and the sky, it be dark, and all around it be rainin' cats and dogs, and the madam she gets a hind of the wheel and the rest I reckon you may guess your own self if all that studyin' you be doin' be doin' any damn good at all!"

I wondered if Mr. Carlisle had been killed instantly or lingered.

"Jus' like that," Willa Mae assured me, snapping her fingers. She crossed herself.

"Why are you telling me all this, Mrs. Wood?"

She was a good deal taller than I am, and the wig added another four inches. She had shoulders like a football player. "The madam," she said, in a tone calculated to render me helpless, "think she have rooned her own chile."

She handed me the coffee cups and told me to take them in. I knocked on Lulu's door. When she didn't answer, I went in anyway, slowly, giving her time to tell me to get out. She didn't. I placed the cups on the little table between the two chaises longues we lay on, and she pointed to the television screen as if telling me to focus my attention where it belonged. On Vietnam. After a few minutes, I sneaked a look at her. She was weeping.

"Well," she said, "it just gets so confusing when people keep moving in and moving out." I waited for the explanation. "Like Gladys Brunner," she said.

"I thought you liked Gladys Brunner."

"I did!" She stirred her coffee. "I can't help it," she complained, "if I complain a lot!" She was crying openly now, fumbling as she reached in the drawer of the table for a tranquilizer. The drawer stuck. "It won't open," she said, panic creeping into her voice. I opened it for her and handed her the transparent vial. "I've had a really rotten life, that's all."

Again I waited.

"It's bad enough being lonely all the time, but what would you do if you had a handicapped daughter on top of that?"

"She's pretty and she's smart," I said. "The accident wasn't your fault."

"I *know* it wasn't my fault," she said. "That's what I'm complaining about!"

"Oh."

"I just don't know why this had to happen to me." Lulu laughed. "You've been listening to Willa Mae Wood, haven't you? That woman is a sentimental old witch."

"I guess so," I said. It was clear now that Lulu never had wanted me to stay on; that had been more of Willa Mae's sentimentality.

I got up to leave. But then she stopped me. "Don't go," she said, rubbing her thumb over the lipstick that had come off on the rim of her coffee cup. I was too embarrassed to look at her except out of the corner of my eye, though from there I saw that she wasn't looking at me either. Even when I turned around, she wouldn't look at me. "I mean," she was saying, "it does seem empty around here when I'm alone." She put the cup down on the table and blew her nose. I could tell she was trying to clear the whole room of the congestion her plea and apology had created. "I must look," she said, "terrible."

She had short red hair and a small face with regular features and a shape more or less like my own; I was perhaps an inch taller, a few pounds lighter, and, of course, wore glasses. She said, in fact, that I was just the type her husband had gone for, though she hoped he rested now in peace, and in time admitted he had gone for my type fairly frequently. She certainly didn't hold it against him—seemed even to enjoy the memory she had of him as a man-about-town. I supposed her memory of him somehow complemented her image of herself. They had done a lot of drinking together; and once—she said this shyly, like a young girl owning up to her first kiss, or as a young girl used to admit to her first kiss in the generations before Cameron's—once, she had dived naked into the Firth of Forth, or the Bay of Fundy, or some other sea that sadly diminished any antics that had ever taken place in the fountain of the Plaza Hotel on Central Park South. I had trouble at first believing that these tales were true: Lulu had long since renounced alcohol for sedatives, sex for politics, and now her politics were largely the lonely business of check-writing, usually to organizations or private persons that hadn't even bothered to put up a decent front; they were all, as Max said, ripping her off, including, I was positive, Cameron's new school. Cameron had written me how very groovy the school was, e.g., when the disturbed son of a famous couple entered the lounge, plunked himself down in an armchair and undid the buttons on his striped bellbottoms, neither staff nor students blinked an eyelid. I'd have asked her what her friend would do if he had to live in the real world. She anticipated me and wrote, "This is the way the real world should be—free and loving," but I noted (with relief) that she didn't rush to inform her mother just how the grass grew in this greening of America. But there were those institutions and persons—the Unitarian Church Lunch Subsidy for Negro Children in the Louisiana State School System, the Biafrans, a sculptor-nephew in Munich—who turned Lulu's money to good account, and anyway, she needed to be able to lavish her wealth on something, and had no interest in spending it on herself or on the apartment. It was an enormous duplex, its size accentuated by the absence of furnishing or ornament. "What's the point," she said, "when there are dog hairs all over everything, and besides, who cares?" In her bedroom, the room she lived in day and night, just to the right of the main entrance downstairs, there were two chaises longues, a television, and a king-sized bed. The bedspread was pink, the rug was dark green, the walls were blue dimming to gray, the lounges were black, the curtains were pale yellow, and there wasn't a painting or a photograph in sight. We lay on the lounges just inside the room, a secondhand night table between us, the presence of the great bed at the far end of the room as unremarkable and essential as a categorical imperative, drinking coffee, watching the evening news; and because she flicked off the commercials by remote control, I struggled one minute out of every seven to think of something to say. The only subjects which elicited any reaction at all were politics and sex, and as her dearest political expression was "Off the pigs!" I found myself loath to pursue the subject in any detail. "I had a letter from Adrien," I'd say, to fill up the vacuum the commercials created (and if she didn't know who he was, I was already beginning to think I might like to know him better); or at dinner, when I'd say I wouldn't be taking coffee, didn't have time that night, I'd catch myself explaining, "I'm seeing Peter tonight," simply because the silence demanded it.

"Maybe Peter be the one!" Willa Mae rejoiced.

"One what?" Lulu snapped.

"Mister Right."

"I can't imagine why anyone would want to get married," she said, looking at me. "You know it isn't necessary any longer."

"Now don't you 'spose Tennessee like to have a li'l one like you and me? . . . I wouldn't trade my Stella for nothin'."

"How is Estelle?" I asked. Willa Mae always gave us the low-down on her friends and family—and never brought them around.

"Oh—" Willa Mae sighed. "She all right. *She* sure ain't goin' to get married now or never. Queer as a two-dollar bill. I doesn't mind, I doesn't mind. 'Stella,' I says, 'just don't you try and jive me. Who *do* you think you jivin'?'"

Lulu made a face at the mashed potatoes on her plate and pushed them aside. "Is she truly a lesbian?"

"If she ain't, Mrs. Carlisle, I can't imag' what she and Jewel is up to all the time . . . calling each other up any disrespectable hour of the night. What does youall 'spose they have got to *say* that can't wait till mornin'?"

"They could be talking about school," I suggested, "or boy friends."

"No, sir, no way. Stella don't date no boys. I know. I reads *Cosmo,* they tells you these things. She ain't never played with dolls, not from the day I birthed her. It's all right, honey, so long's she ain't shootin' up on heron—"

"Heron?"

"Don't you know nothin'? Heron. Smack. So long's her arms look good when I checks them out, and she ain't goin' to have some illegit'mate brat I'se got to raise up, I ain't complainin'."

"After all," I said, viewing the situation with as much sophistication as I could muster on the spot, "men aren't everything."

"Don't you get me wrong, now, I likes men, myself."

"I can take them," Lulu said, "or leave them."

"Anyway," I said, "Peter's just a buddy."

Willa Mae pursed her lips. "Well, if you ast me, you has got only yo'self to blame for that."

I asked her what she meant.

"A man, he likes a woman what will ease his soul and comfort his bod."

"What do you mean, ease his soul?" I asked.

"What do you mean, comfort his bod?" Lulu asked.

"If you got to ast," Willa Mae said, "I ain't goin' to be able to 'splain."

"That's a cop-out," I said.

Willa Mae chortled. "I tells you what. You get Peter to take you to one of them movin' pitchers on Times Square like the one Doak done took me to. My god, Mrs. Carlisle, they ain't nothin' these days they daren't show! They showed this thing—cross my heart and hope to die if it weren't ten-foot long and in Technicolor—pretty as you please. Doak, he was feelin' his oats all right, and I reckon old Willa Mae be feelin' right fine too."

"And what did they do with it?" I asked.

"Hunh! Don't you jive *me,* Tennes*see.* This"—she gestured—"and that." She licked her lips.

Lulu made another face at the potatoes. Then she said, in a very small voice: "When I was a girl, that was something you did once a year out of a sense of duty to your husband. I suppose," she went on, in the forlorn vein that seemed to thread its way through all these evenings, "I suppose I missed out on a lot of things."

❦ Willa Mae was at least as sorry for Lulu as I was. That was why she had bought her the vibrator. The reason she'd bought mine for me was that somehow none of my dates ever turned out to be "Mister Right." A few hours hanging around in the emergency room at Mount Sinai was enough to convince anyone that there were no Rights in the world: when men weren't beating up on each other, they were beating up on their women. These women showed up, hair still in curlers, right on time every Saturday night, meek and tentative, bowed down under the assumption of guilt, apologizing for their lacerated limbs, fractured skulls, and bloody parts. Fascinating as they were, I was happier during the time I was allowed to observe at the pediatric clinic, where one of the major jobs was dispensing contraceptives to black and Puerto Rican adolescents. Most of the kids were required to show for a check-up every three months. I watched the pelvic examinations, listened in on the group discussions, and picked up elective credit for making a nuisance of myself. After a while I forgot about dating altogether, gave up on it, and settled down to studying and daydreaming, sometimes wondering whether Adrien would ever haul himself out of New Hope and come to visit me, sometimes wondering in what ways I had failed to ease Bernie's soul and comfort his bod. (He had the soul of a Flatbush revolutionary and the bodily instinct of a carnal conservative, and was it any wonder I got confused between the two?) I'd have been perfectly willing to do what Willa Mae said they did in the porno flicks but I had thought it was a thing done only for the sake of what one of my texts called foreplay. It didn't seem sensible to remain in the dark about such a basic concept when one was already thirty and would in another short ten or twenty years find oneself staring straight into the face of the "changes" Willa Mae warned me of. I asked Max what her experience had been.

"Yeah," she said, "they do it." She shrugged. "And sometimes it happens, and sometimes it doesn't. So what can I tell you?" I asked what it tasted like. "Christ," she said, *"I* don't know."

"You're a big help."

"Well," she said, "I don't dig dirt."

But I did! And should have thought men would appreciate that in me. So why didn't they? As Bernie always said, there were two possibilities; I wrote them in my prayerbook, the better to confront them: *"Either* all the men I have known are gentlemen *or* I am the world's lousiest ———." (In a prayerbook, there comes a point where one *has* to mince one's words.) I stared at my choices; they were a bad dilemma for a girl to be on the horns of, and in an effort to unseat myself immediately, I stated my problem at the next meeting of my Lib group.

FIRST WOMAN *(she was twenty-two, but we were careful to refer to ourselves as "women" during the meetings):* The first time it happened to me, I didn't know what was coming off. *(General laughter.)* You can laugh, but I thought I was going to have a baby.

SECOND WOMAN: The corners of your mouth get tired.

THIRD WOMAN: After a while, you're thinking, Come *on,* fella, get it off.

FOURTH WOMAN *(a lean blonde in paisley trousers and see-through body shirt):* Aha! One more manifestation of the slave-master relationship that perverts our politics.

I: Who said anything about politics?

FOURTH WOMAN: That's where you always slip up, Tennessee. Your political I.Q. must be about ten. *(Not that it would have made any difference to her, but right away I could see that life with her would have been very like life with Bernie had been.)*

SECOND WOMAN: It's not exploitation if you make sure you get your own back. *(I thought the "propers" concept kept turning up in the unlikeliest places.)*

I: An eye for an eye, a tooth for a tooth, a—

FOURTH WOMAN: There! You see? You aren't as naïve as you pretend to be! Right, sisters? How many of *us* live off unhappy millionaires? How many of *us* go around exploiting the wealthier members of our own sex? *(I started to advise her to renounce politics for an examination of her own semantics, but out of the corner of my eye saw someone else's tears splashing on the cheeseboard.)*

THIRD WOMAN *(stroking First Woman's shoulder):* Lay it on us, kiddo.

FIRST WOMAN: He dropped out of school right after that. He never even bothered to call me. *(Cries.)* It's just one big rip-off, that's what sex is, one big rip-off.

I told her *she* should cry—no one even *wanted* to rip me off. She cheered up immediately, but I went home in a funk. One doesn't, however, subscribe to depression save as a last resort, and so one decided to ask one's old friend Peter what the score was. His eyes lit up. "Terrific! Super! Magnifico!" My face fell. "You must have led a very sheltered life," he said. At that point a person might have got truly depressed, but the spark in his eyes had given me another idea. "Wouldn't you like me to do it to you?" I asked. "Experimentally, that is."

"What?" he said. "And destroy a perfectly good friendship?"

"What'll I *do?*" I wailed.

"Do what everyone else does," he said, unwaveringly reasonable. Now I *knew* what he meant: he meant I should liberate myself. I had known Peter for ages already, and we'd already had this conversation any number of times. I went to him frequently for advice on these matters, taking him for an authority as an Ivy League graduate who, ever since he got, first, divorced, and second, sacked, had been living on unemployment insurance with the compliments of *U. S. News and World Report* and exploring all the ins-and-outs of life in Fun City. "It's not true," he had told me, trying to make me feel better about myself, "that the chicks in this town spend all their spare time swinging." I had said, "But you make out all right! You have girl friends!"

"That's different," he said. "I'm a man."

I started to cry, but then he said, "What's wrong?" in that pinched voice men squeeze all their anxieties into when they think a woman's getting ready to pressure them into whatever it is they don't want to do, and I wound up giggling instead. "Nothing," I answered, leading him out to the elevator in the Sun Room. "I have this tendency to become waveringly unreasonable." How could I explain to him what no one had ever even acquainted him with, that women climb the walls with a desperation every bit as athletic as his own? Not even most women knew that, which was one more useless pearl of wisdom I'd fished up in my role as every gender's favorite buddy. Every pore in my skin was screaming, I could've orchestrated all those downy little mouths into Super Symphony and come unstrung. I rolled a couple of joints and waited until I'd heard the door downstairs open and shut and knew Lulu was returned from her Tuesday night group therapy, where, punching pillows to release hostility, embracing in ecstasy the computer programmer she was eyeballing according to the leader's instructions, she swore she'd found bliss. She may have been trying to show me that she was capable of something other than complaint; or maybe—I was generous—she was sincere, on those few occasions when we went out together, to a movie or shopping for Cameron's Christmas presents, as she stopped every so often to admire the small children we passed along the way (they filtered down to us from El Barrio) or stopped to admire the sun sinking in a soft haze of pollution behind the lower-income housing developments between Amsterdam and Columbus avenues, both safely on the other side of Central Park. Her beatific smile was accomplished only by wrenching her face so profoundly out of shape that the result was a scattering of lines and wrinkles, muscles shooting out in aimless directions, that belied any integrity of person. Oh, but I'm callous too! for I know that in her group she must have encountered a freedom of self-expression I deprived her of, feeling, as I did, that she so thoroughly limited my own. Though come to think of it, I may be doing Lulu Carlisle an injustice of sorts in assuming she might have been in any way answerable to my moods; after all, while I found myself growing less and less capable of speaking my own mind, of revealing my own attitudes without first checking to see whether they coincided with hers, she maintained a very real power over me, one which broadened every day. With a word—to Willa Mae, perhaps, not even directly to me—she could alienate me from my surroundings and friends. She could deprive me of my *modus operandi*. She could take away my room which, such as it was, was my home. And each day that room was a little more seriously my home, simply because I had passed another day in it, read another letter while lying on the bed in it, told someone else the number of the telephone I had had installed in it; and if the strain of holding a conversation with Lulu, the emotional entrapment I felt in her presence, increased, that unease served only to heighten the sense of sanctuary I experienced whenever I was able to remove myself to my upstairs room. I waited—hid—until the lights downstairs had gone out and the television was off. Lulu knocked herself out with chloral hydrate promptly at eleven, and nothing on earth could wake her. I sat at my table. Itchy! Itchy! The bushes that rose from outsized window boxes planted on the terrace outside my window scratched against the screen, and the moon, highlighting those black leaves, might have fooled the least imaginative among us (meaning me) into thinking she sat not at her desk but in the country she yearned after on her bluer days. In the distance, a siren swelled and sank and gathered steam; from the apartment outside my back door, fragments of a song broke the silence in my room. It was a lady who lived there; we'd never met, and never would, but this one knew that one by the unrestrained sobbing she indulged in late at night and by the songs she played on her phonograph, tunes from the twenties, songs better suited to edgy, half-empty German *Bierhallen* than to Park Avenue. One night there was a great slamming of doors and opening and shutting of bureau drawers and I thought my neighbor might be looking for sleeping pills to do herself in, but the next night, she was quiet again, spinning her songs, nostalgic and bitter and stuck. One night I held a glass to the wall and my ear to the glass, struggling to make out a conversation she was holding with what I thought was a man, but old buildings have thick walls. I might have stepped into the back stairs that led down from my room, but couldn't in any case eavesdrop for very long, being far too fast overcome with a flush of remorse that forced me to wonder what people would say if they saw me in that compromising position. Whenever I do feel guilty, I flush. It's unfortunate, but I have thin skin, and the capillaries, some of which lie close to the surface, have already begun to break, forming little bugs of blood that lie lifeless below my left eye and next to my nose, as if they'd been squashed there by someone who then forgot to sweep them up. Veronica said I set too much store by appearances, and she was right, of course; but New York is populated with the most necessary men in the world—the ones upon whom economy and culture depend, or at least the ones who do their best to support that illusion—and it is a buyer's market. "Lately," I had told Veronica in one of our sessions, "I can't even give it away." She was picking the polish off one of her nails, and flicked it into the ashtray at her side before she suggested, the furrow between her eyes pronounced to show her sympathy, that I look into the singles' bars over on Third Avenue, or try one of the mixers advertised in the *Village Voice.* "You really think I should?" I asked.

"Why not?"

"I hear those places are meat racks."

"I thought that's what you wanted." She smiled. "To be a sex object."

It wasn't, though; I didn't want to end up crying like the girl in my Lib group. So I dropped in at the Recovery Room from time to time for a drink with friends but late at night found myself alone in my Park Avenue penthouse. I washed the vibrator in hot water, laying it on the chair next to my single bed, and lit the first of the reefers. I put the Jefferson Starship on my phonograph, sending neighbor's Berliner *Lieder* into the oblivion they sprang from and testified to (a favorite theory of mine, subject to speculative embroidery, was that both mass and energy were in turn translatable into space), and turned off all the lights, leaving only the glow from the amplifier to take my bearings by. The music streamed out in several directions at once, buoyed and channeled by the sweetest grass to be found north of the Mexican border, while Grace Slick's drawn-out *sunri-i-ise,* her arrogant dismissal of *civili-i-ized man,* made a beeline for my swimming head. No devotee of popular lyrics, I! but listening to Sister Slick singing about *two thousand years* of lies, and glory, I was awed by her prescience. That was exactly how old I felt. And why not? Exaggeration is one of the minor vices, and there was no one around to say I wasn't civilized and wasn't old. And the heavy, urgent beat of the music swore that after all these years the Apocalypse surely *was* upon us, and thinking that in the final analysis only God and Norman Mailer were going to be around to judge what I was about to do, I rubbed some patchouli body oil I'd bought in a Head Shop into my skin, and an aroma of lemon and cream and sugar rose from my flesh to mix with the scent of pot. You could almost see those two currents of smell meeting and mixing in the air about my head, pressing me down to my bed the way I remember any ordinary Southern sun will push you right into the latticed straps of a lawn chair, but the only light came from the moon and the amplifier and the filter indicators showing two abbreviated spots of red and green. I struck a match to the second joint, inhaled, coughed, sucked air with the inhalation, and laughed to think that little over a year ago I'd been a novice at blowing pot. ("Blow is a metaphor, dear," said

the man to his wife, concluding a dirty story I'd never understood.) How foolishly shook up my companion had been when I
insisted on getting out of bed to cover myself in a white nightgown and then paced the room next door to the Broadway Hotel
for Transients, stoned, wasted, saying, "I've got to get myself
together," and feeling unbearably frustrated because it sounded
like a catch phrase when what I meant was that my mind was
floating around up near the ceiling while my body went on pacing the floor. Now I knew that a mild attack of paranoia was par
for the course. I listened for sounds. The dogs and Clio must have
been asleep, the little dog always slept with Lulu; the wind was
lowered; Slick's voice was stringing two or three notes out like a
cat in heat, there was a nice sullen ferocity to it which played
well against the energetic choirboy background of her band. *Hijack the Starship* indeed: of that group, only Grace would've had
the guts (she named her son "god," and even that was a lower-
case *g)* and she had no grounding in astrophysics but only threatened inappropriately to let her *babes wander naked through the
cities of the universe.* Poor babes, I'd catch them up and rub
Witch Hazel on their diaper rash and pet them. I stroked my
arms with the oil, my elbows and chest and the crevices between
my toes, as the music went *ahh-ba! ahh-ba! ahhhhhhhh-ba-ba!
ahhhhhhhhhhhhhhh-ba-bop-de-ba,* and shuffled through my
thumb-worn fantasies, searching for one that fit the mood,
finally settling for a Hell's Angels Gangbang, figuring that if
there were indeed no one man around at all, one might as well
conceive a superfluity. It seemed likely that if Norman Mailer
held the action I was about to engage in in such unmitigated
contempt, as the ultimate of solipsisms, he'd have to take my
fantasy of a gangbang into consideration as a sign of good faith,
that he might even, Mailer might, take pity on me and supply the
lack in my life, which was another favorite daydream of mine.
His girth was growing, true; but I wasn't any prize either, and he
had beautiful eyes and a vulnerability that wasn't easy to come
by among the men of my own generation. If the women in my Lib

group tagged him for a male chauvinist, I, trying every trick I could think of to locate my "best possible mate" that I might "conceive the best possible children" toward the furtherance of the "best of all possible worlds," reckoned he was merely short-sighted and hadn't yet seen how the odds were stacked against the sex he swore he worshiped. *Genesis is not the answer,* sang Sister Slick, but she was already pregnant even then and every-one knows it's easier to reject what you have than deny what you don't. "Worship me," I'd beg, but with captivating self-irony, when Norman finally met me and saw what soulmates we were. "Worship *me*. Not the whole female race!" I sent telepathic mes-sages to his townhouse in Brooklyn Heights and to Provincetown, but he never answered them, and let that at least be on his head, for if he had, I might not have sunk to my present state. I felt low-down, I felt rejected. Veronica said I was hypersensitive; Max said we'd drive to Provincetown and check out a place she'd heard of called Piggy's and maybe my Mailer, blind-drunk though he'd be, would turn in his chair and move himself to his feet and reel from the sobriety of my nearsighted gaze, a temper-ance he'd looked for all his life and given up on but still longed for with a secret slice of his soul that he never dared to spread out on paper or never wanted to butter his bread with. "There's no sense waiting around here," she had said. "Norman Mailer isn't comfortable on Park Avenue." She was fingering a minia-ture booklet of Mother Goose rhymes that I'd got in a Cracker Jack box. Putting it back on the windowsill, she'd added, "And what you gotta do, you might as well get done, since you'll do it sooner or later anyway."

I'd fetched her a Pepsi from the icebox in the Sun Room. "All your pragmatism," I said, a little nastily, "keeps you on the go?"

"Yes," she said. "I deliver foreign auto parts to foreign auto part repair shops."

"Since when!"

"Since last week. My father knows a man in Levittown, and I needed a career."

"Who doesn't? It's the defection of the men," I said, bringing my fist down on my desk, "that's brought us to this pretty pass."

Doggone if she didn't always take me at my word; it was unnerving. "You," she said, not troubling to disguise the envy in her voice, "had a career in mind *before* Bernie defected."

I started to say it wasn't Bernie I was thinking of but the whole sex but wasn't sure I had a right to and said instead: "Nobody has a career without society's consent."

"Baloney. . . . Think of all the careers society doesn't consent to, think of whores and thieves, hoboes, rumrunners and madams."

I thought of whores and madams. "Oh, Max," I said, "I wanted so much to dye my hair and run away to New Orleans. I wanted to wear a flower-print slip and stand on hot nights in the doorway of a smoke-filled cathouse in the French Quarter. I wanted—"

"Have you ever considered," she asked wryly, "that you could use to see someone more professional than Veronica?"

"I did! I did! I asked everyone I met where I could find a pimp. . . ."

There weren't any; pimps belonged to Introductory Soc. 101A, there were never any in my life. But I didn't need them now, or so Sister Slick assured me: *the glow of the machines'll get you on.* I flicked the switch on the vibrator and tuned in to the buzz slicing through the music; but the music, barely beginning to work itself up, dropped the beat and skidded off onto an unstructured sideline: *Have you seen the stars tonight. . . . Have you looked at all the family of stars?* You had to be very young and hopeful to listen to that. "Grow up, Gracie," I said; "grow, Paul! Leave philosophy to the physicists and physics to the philosophers." I was distracted, disinterested, eager and blue, hungry and dying of thirst. I wished I had a Pepsi, but Maxine had drunk the last can. I licked my lips, gnawed at the flecks of peeling skin at the corners of my mouth. That's not neorealism, it's a well-known phenomenon among heads: your lips shrivel and peel like a plum that's been picked but not eaten. When the telephone rang, I felt I'd just stumbled into an oasis after six months in the Gobi. "Hello?" I said, though what I meant was, "Rescue me, please, from this desert. Take my hand and ply me with goodies and this time I'll keep it all down, my stomach's stronger than it was when Bernie was around to upset it with his demands that dinner should be served smack on time every livelong time, I promise not to regurgitate any of it the next time around." What miracles occur when least expected! The person on the other end of the line knew just what I meant, how much I had to offer. "I want," he said, his voice low and scratchy, his respiration like a little storm, "some Pepsi."

"But— Baby! I'm all out of Pepsi."

He was silent, he was going to hang up on me because I couldn't give him what he needed. "I would if I could," I said quickly, trying to make myself clear, but the words slid out sideways, I was too stoned to speak plainly. "Maxine drank the last one."

"Who is Maxine?"

"Oh, well, she's just a friend."

"Will you let me be your friend?"

I stopped. "You are, aren't you?"

No answer.

"Who are you?"

"A friend."

I breathed a sigh of relief. One man's cliché is another's reality, and I for one find myself very often breathing a sigh of relief. "In that case," I said, "you know that if I had a Pepsi to give you, I'd give it to you, even if I *was* just wanting one myself just now."

"I didn't ask for a Pepsi," he said, enunciating carefully, "I said I want your *pussy.*"

"Oh. That puts a different light on matters."

"Indeed."

"I thought at first that we were wanting the same thing. I mean, had the same aim in life."

"That's all right," he said, "anybody can make a mistake." He added: "Even me."

He seemed surprisingly well-spoken for a phone phreak. "I guess you talk with a lot of people?"

"You're evading my question."

"Oh yes, you mean about—about—"

"Pussy."

He was becoming impatient with me. I didn't want him to, never wanted anyone to. "It's too bad you're male," I said.

He cleared his throat. "Are you some kind of a dyke?"

"No. Oh no, man. I was thinking of your own best interests. I mean, what I meant was, if you were a woman, you could use a vibrator too. Then you wouldn't need any—any— They're called neck massagers. Ha! Ha! Ha!"

"My first obscene telephone call," he said, slowly, "and I have to get some kind of a nut." I held my breath. "Nut!"

That was too much, of course, and I said (pretty haughtily, I thought), "Sir, I'll take offense—" but he hung up, his ungentlemanly *click* resounding in my head like a slap on my face. Was I sore? You can bet I was sore! Then when I went to slam the receiver down, it slid out of my hands—all that patchouli body oil—and dangled from its cord and began making a noise like *tsk! tsk!* like the noise my father makes when he's grading papers, until finally I managed to grasp the thing with both hands and place it back in its cradle. I wouldn't have minded being returned to my own cradle then. But I was no more likely to make my way back to the womb I'd so eagerly and ignorantly shot myself out of thirty years before than that immature music was going to avoid its own resolution. A fine teleology! It was climbing again, getting it together now, and I reached for the vibrator, which was still humming away as blithely as my mother while my father read her the odder pages from his students' blue books and ran my fingers up and down the grooves in its shaft. Here I neglect clinical details not only out of a distaste for them—there's that too, so I do have something in common with practicing gynecologists—but because when one is high and lonesome, when one's riding on dreams, one couldn't care less about one's pulse or plateau or one's labia majora. Minora? Minoan? Well, I am not the only medical student with a gap in her education, nor the only woman in the world to confuse her construction, the blueprint of her particular build, with the ruins of ancient Cretan civilizations. Besides, although in my first year I'd taken an elective on The Physiology and Sociology of Sex, which included a two-hour seminar on Coitus, the teacher had omitted any discussion of Sexual Compatibility With and Adjustment To Self. And the dope was confusing me. And the buzz—ah, yes, the vibrator was buzzing, I was buzzing, the Starship was blasting off, I was blasting off, and if it took centuries to arrive at our destination, I wasn't complaining, no sirree, Lulu! no complaints from Tennessee. I was taking it slow and easy. "The trick in getting there," I had told Max, "is, you want to hypnotize yourself." She said I theorized overmuch. But who could argue with what was actually happening? The *thump-thump-thump* of the machine against—ah—*down there,* the buzzing in my brain, the rock rolling over and around the key of G, swinging up and down but always reverting to harp on that key of G, until the universe itself was one great long and sexy and capitalized G-string: *it's so fine ... starshine.* "Just fine, Grace, my sweet, yes, it's fine. Take me with you on your trip, on all your trips. Only let me tag along and I'll come." One was certainly hot and sweaty, one was certainly going to be glad to lie back and relax when the trip was over, one was getting there, certainly. Even the vibrator seemed to relax, however pathetic *that* fallacy might be, and the buzz dropped to a low, throaty thrum, pursued a sonar trajectory like a rocket homing in right on target, the bull's-eye in the center of the cosmic scale.

Then the batteries went dead. "Lordy, lordy, lordy," I cried—aloud, for it was no time to stand on ceremony. For half a second,

I could've sworn Norman Mailer was visiting me with the Divine Wrath, but I've a good mind in crisis situations, and without thinking, used it to sit up and throw the vibrator down on the table, and as the vibrator cracked apart, fell over and hit my head against the edge of the table, and picked up the bottle of patchouli from the table and held it over my head and poured it over my head until the fires were doused. I lay down again. I was as slippery as a rock in a stream, gushing oil and juice from the gorge that God knew was a no-man's-land, but when waters flow, pools are emptied, and I was emptied, and tired, and fell instantly asleep to the laziest, easiest of lullabies.

At first
  I was iridescent
Then
  I became transparent
Finally
  I was absent

but dreamed of dog-eared poets and their bad rhyme and wondered how they sang so innocently of sin. Sinners! That's what they were, and I knew myself for one of the crowd, knew any attempt to rise above it or vanish far from it was the most prideful sin of all and punishable by death. I would be meek. When the sun fell into my room, traveling all those light years simply to shine on my face, I was terribly grateful. It sparkled on my face, on the sheets white and wet, on the record still spinning on the turntable. I turned the turntable off. When the telephone rang, as it promptly did, the sun sparkled on it. I thought it might be the party from the night before, and reaching once again for the receiver, vowed a proper meekness. The receiver was sticky. I said hello—or thought I was going to say hello, but when I opened my mouth, a wave of pain hit me with a brilliance that bid fair to outshine the sun. I remembered knocking my jaw against the edge of the table the night before. "Hello? Hello?" The voice was Maxine's. "Tennessee?" she asked. "You all right?"

"No."

"So what's not all right? Has the cat got your tongue?"

"You're warm," I said, holding my jaw as immobile as possible. I was weeping. "Do you know," I said, "I'll *never* be able to do it to anyone now?"

"Do what?"

"Fellatio."

"That doesn't sound like a problem that can't be solved," she said. She paused. "But what is the problem, exactly?"

"Lockjaw," I said.

3. INSIDE MOUNT SINAI

He held me in his arms. I leaned back, resting my shoulder against his, watching, beneath lowered lashes, as his jacket creased and crumpled beneath my weight. "Now," he said, "open wide."

Returning with the X-rays, he wore a sweet look of bafflement. He said I seemed to have some sort of joint trouble—in my jaw. "Leastways," he said, "we don't seem to have any cavities this time."

"But it hurts."

"If you say it does, I guess it does," he said, making what I should have thought was rather a dangerous assumption. "Try these."

"Demerol?"

He nodded, unwilling to implicate himself further. I figured I could make enough on the black market to pay his bill. As soon as I left his office, I took one, and then floated over to the hospital. "Wanna score?" I asked, cornering this classmate and that. I had put on my best underworld-connection stance, sidling up and down the corridors.

"Not now," said the classmate I'd latched on to—someone I'd seen doodling rocket ships during anatomy the previous year.

"Goldberg's doing a laparoscopy in fifteen minutes."

Sinai was a small school, a new school, and though we weren't officially involved in O.R. procedures until third year, we could, as I knew from hearing other students talk, usually sneak in to watch whatever we wanted to. Acting on my classmate's advice, I checked the name on the list and got the nurse to let me look at the patient's history, donned mask and gown, and crept in to stand on the sidelines. Goldberg was the last to enter. With his arms outstretched and bent at the elbows, palms turned inward, his bald head gleaming under the spotlight, his goatee glistening with the anticipatory sweat that even the most casual of surgeons is subject to, he looked less like the fiftyish though splendid gyne he was than like some ageless apparition of the Satanic power performing a black mass. I wondered how it felt to hold life and death in those hands, which were, after all, despite my fancies, human, requiring purification by Phisohex before they might minister to the patient on the table: a "twenty-six-year-old white female in good general condition" and an awkward position that was, I wagered, going to wreak havoc on her upper torso some three days hence. The circulating nurse finished her countdown. The anesthesiologist, unsung hero, finished his, and passed the word to Dr. Goldberg, who injected three liters of gas into the abdominal cavity via a needle. Then, through a quarter-inch incision directly below the navel, he inserted the diagnostic laparoscopic trocar, and when the gas was issuing freely from the trocar, he inserted a fibro-optic telescope. I heard him saying that the endometriosis was extensive. I knew that the purplish lesions on the ovaries would have to be biopsied for confirmation. In this instance, since there was no obvious malignancy, surgery was felt to be undesirable, but the usual alternative of hormonal treatment also had been contraindicated. Dr. Goldberg followed up the diagnostic trocar with an operative trocar inserted into the abdomen via another tiny hole, this one closer to the pubic hairline. Then biopsies were taken, and the biopsy sites were cauterized to stop the bleeding ("secure hemostasis," we doctors say) and destroy the endometrial implants. As Dr. Goldberg removed the telescope to clear the lens of fog, a spiral of smoke escaped from the peritoneal cavity, releasing a scent of crisping tissue, of scorched flesh. I couldn't take my eyes off that "pillar of fire" (cylinder of smoke) and at first I didn't hear what the Doodler was saying. "Pssst," the Doodler said.

I raised my eyebrows.

"Plan B," he whispered. "There's a new chick who is perfect. Meet us in the lounge at three."

"Silence!" Goldberg hissed. I flushed and moved away from the Doodler, but Goldberg said nothing more to us. "Beautiful," he said, "beautiful." He was humming and grinning. "We have burned the bloody hell out of her insides! Sew it up." He stalked out of the room, leaving his subordinate to finish. The Doodler said, "Don't forget," and left. I was weak from the Demerol and the smell. I trailed them out the door, stopped outside the Recovery Room (not a bar) across the hall, and slid my back down the wall to sit on the floor. I put my head on my knees. Someone tapped on it. I looked up.

"There's something I think we had better discuss right now, Miss Settleworth." Dr. Goldberg, seen from the bottom up, loomed as large as a giant. I trembled. "Step in here, please." I followed him into the unoccupied O.R.

"I'm sorry," I said.

He wrapped his arms around his back and stooped over me. I wondered how tall he was.

"Let's get down to brass tacks. I want to know whether you'll have an affair with me."

I was still dizzy. "How tall are you, Dr. Goldberg?"

"Maury," he said, "my name is Maury. What's my height got to do with the price of onions?"

"Nothing," I said, bracing myself against the left stirrup. "Your height is fine."

"Well?"

"I'd like," I said, "to think it over."

"What's to think?"

"I thought you were going to bawl me out for talking while you were going in."

"I suppose I should," he said, stroking my hand.

I removed my hand and walked around to the other side of the table. "Suppose someone sees us in here?" He followed me. "You know people, they could start a lot of talk."

"Talk? Talk doesn't bother me."

"You mean you weren't upset by the talking I did when you were going in?" I was now at the head of the table.

"It's bothering me now," he said, lunging. I reached up and switched on the two-thousand-dollar nonshadow beam over my head.

"Hot damn," he said. "Our Miss Settleworth is a little spitfire!" I was exciting him, which was just the opposite of what I meant to do. I started to cry. "Oh, now," he said, "now, now. Wait just a minute here. Tell the old man what's wrong."

"You're married," I explained.

"They're all married," I had explained to my Lib group when they said I of all of them shouldn't have any difficulty finding men.

"So what?" asked the Fourth Woman.

SECOND WOMAN: I know what Tennessee means. There's no future with a married man.

FOURTH WOMAN: That's what we're fighting for—the right to define our own futures.

I: How can you communicate with a man if your definitions are idiosyncratic? Singular means singularity!

FOURTH WOMAN: Cut the philosophic crap, Tennessee.

"Cut the crap," Maury Goldberg said. "My wife doesn't mind."

I ran for the fibro-optic light parked under the tourniquet clock. "One more step," I said, "and I'll let you have it right between the eyes."

He looked at the "snake" writhing in my hands. Suddenly he smiled. "All right, Miss Settleworth. If that's the way you want it," he said, menacingly, "I'll *court* you." Then he ducked out the door.

I let the snake coil itself back up. I wondered if, when Cammie was a Hindu, she had been a snake charmer. I was a snake charmer! Hadn't Dr. Goldberg been charmed into courting me? Wasn't Dr. Goldberg a snake? I sighed and wished Adrien would court me. Not a word out of him for over two weeks. The last letter had said he was curious to know whether I still saw Bernie. I wrote him no—my hand shaking, because Adrien had no reason to ask about my relationship with Bernie unless—eternal hope— unless he contemplated initiating some relationship with me. "Bernie's married," I wrote him, "didn't you know?" I asked Adrien if he corresponded with Bernie, but Adrien hadn't written back to me. I was becoming confused. I was still dizzy. The room smelled of antiseptic. I took off the gown and picked up my book-bag and went to pick up a book from my work-study desk in the lab. Each of us had his own: desk, bookcase, armchair. Some of the students, usually but not always those with an interest in research, practically lived in their work-study desks. We had one girl—in fact, we had a number of women, and while I had no way of knowing to what extent Mount Sinai was nobly nonsexist and to what extent it was merely expedient, let the record show that there was no discrimination against female students as such— we had one girl who read her text as she walked to the cafeteria, read her text between classes, and spent every spare moment standing at the bench in the lab, examining histology slides. (Fran Dabrowski was reserved but friendly and wore thick lenses that magnified her eyes and gave them a watery, slippery look which cruelly mis-characterized her, since she was cer- tainly one of the most dedicated students I ever met: her father had been a G.P. before going off to serve in a Naval hospital in the Pacific Theater, and though she never got to know him, she remembered everything her mother had ever said about him. I wondered if she was competing with his memory for her moth- er's affection, in which case she was running a fixed race, and it served me right when she pointed out that her mother had long since been remarried to one Mr. Spadory, a calm and gentle man who had been even a little flattered by his then eight-year-old adopted daughter's delight in telling him to go to hell so she could run to her mother to announce: "I cuss Spadory! I cuss Spadory!")

I used my work-study desk as a place to read in during the day; I kept certain texts there, my dissection kit (in our second year, we did dogs), slides, and my microscope. "My" microscope was one I rented from the school for a yearly fee. I did sometimes dream of owning my own but it wasn't really that important to me: I was more interested in my observation periods at the pediatric clinic and in our ongoing class in Physical Diagnosis, and if there was one instrument that more than any other, even the speculum, symbolized medicine to me, it was the stethoscope. Of course, the white lab coat was an emblem we all got a kick out of—a long time after we were pretending to ignore the symbolism of the white lab coat completely; and probably the women students got a greater kick than the men, because all our coats were marked with our student numbers, and we dropped them into hampers located at various points and then lo and behold! they reappeared, white and fresh and clean, in the locker room. Even with Willa Mae to wash mine at the apartment, it gave me a feeling of power (rare feeling) to have an entire institution so intimately involved with my laundry.

A med student is less likely than an anthropology major to sport an Indian headband or peasant blouse, not because the anthropologist is that much more radical but because the doctor comes in daily contact with Middle America, not to mention both extremes. If I wore skirts and sweaters to class, it was in order not to offend the patients (though they may have been in toreador pants, if they were lucky, and throwaway robes, if they were not). But no one was rigid, no one was compulsive, no matter how straitlaced television may portray us as. We had most of our lectures in a little room off to one side of the mezzanine in the

Basic Sciences Building, but with the detailed syllabi we were given, we could manage a certain amount of cutting and still do all right on the exam that wound up each systemic study (at that time, if I remember rightly, we were engrossed in Blood). Most of the mezzanine was taken up with coffee machines and ping-pong tables and the Activities Bulletin Board, on which someone (not I!) had tacked a notice offering "Free Pussy" in red skin pen (a pencil used to outline the area of incision; it was one of our dissecting tools). At the bottom margin was the word "cats" and a phone number. I took down the number in case the person responsible for the note turned out to be my telephone pal. Well, Adrien had written me, on the basis of the descriptions I wrote him in my letters, that med school sounded very juvenile. Sometimes I tended to agree with him, and sometimes I thought—but only half-thought—that Adrien expressed a funny kind of pontifical attitude, even an evangelical one, which might go undetected among the younger generation but had a way of pulling me up short. He wrote me that he and Linus Pauling recommended ascorbic acid in high concentrations, and when I replied that that was very interesting but Heisenberg and I remained uncertain on principle, he wrote back that I was sometimes amusing and sometimes lacked a . . . "felicity." Felicity? I decided that if Vitamin C was a tricky subject, literature would be downright dangerous; so I didn't let him know that I'd written and sold the article to *The Male Bag*. Maybe, I told myself, when it came out—

But that would still be some time off. I crumpled my Mintmallow wrapper and pitched it from behind the line we had chalked on the floor into the trash bin and returned to the lab, where Fran was busy giving herself a test on slides. "Is it true," I asked her, "what they say about you?"

"That depends on what time it is."

"Lunchtime." Her microscope was gorgeous, a gift from her stepfather. "I ate a Mintmallow."

She put her equipment away. There was a grundgy hamburger

place nearby where we occasionally went together. With a green woolen scarf pulled over her forehead and tied tight under her chin, with her huge eyes swimming in their pools of glass, Fran looked very much like a frog. But a nice frog. "What are people saying about me?" she asked.

"That you sleep on the couch in the lounge."

"Sometimes."

"It's probably safer than going home at night," I conceded, "but you really shouldn't study so much."

"You shouldn't live on candy."

I told her about Adrien and ascorbic acid. She wasn't even a close friend, but I needed someone to talk with. Max just didn't understand what med school was all about—she had different ambitions (getting married, being a blues singer, and winning the Grand Prix). Fran asked me how my work was going. I told her about the pediatric clinic.

She asked if she could try on my glasses. We swapped. Hers were a good deal heavier than mine and I had trouble keeping them on.

"I have a pronounced nose," she said, trading glasses back.

I was leery of getting into any discussion of noses. I lifted the top of my hamburger roll and looked inside. "It looked better through your glasses," I said.

She leaned over and looked at my patty. "No," she said, in a tone of quiet reasonableness, "even through my glasses it looks pretty bad." I felt I could trust her, after that.

"Fran," I began, "did you know that thirteen thousand women die each year of cervical tumors?"

She had called the waitress back to ask for a slice of raw onion but my question stopped her. "Have you got any symptoms?"

"Sure, kid," the waitress said. "How do you want 'em, pan-fry or hash brown?"

"Very funny," I said to the waitress.

"Are you all right, Tennessee?"

"Nothing that a swift kick in the pants wouldn't cure," said the waitress.

"Would you please bring my friend Fran a slice of raw onion?" I asked, icily.

"Her I'll bring. You should sprout onions through your navel." I giggled in spite of myself and made a note to ask Max about that one.

"You haven't answered my question!" Fran said.

"I'm fine! Physically, I'm fine."

We ate our hamburgers.

"What I'm getting at," I finally said, "is that gynecologists are desperately needed. By women, anyway."

"I'm going into general practice."

"To each her own."

"I don't think anyone wants to argue with that," Fran said. "If you want to be a gynecologist, nobody's going to stop you."

"Some of those kids in the clinic . . . Fran, they come in there, they've been, you know, *active* for years, since they were in pigtails and braids, and they don't know which end is up. If you get my meaning. You wouldn't think so much could be accomplished in a state of ignorance."

"You wouldn't?"

"*I* wouldn't."

"Maybe," she said, "you should fill me in on what gets accomplished."

"Bobbi Jean Rodriguez," I said, "is fourteen years old." Precisely Cameron's age. "That's Bobbi-with-an-*i*-on-the-end-of-it because her loving, immigrant parents would like only the best for their daughter, and that means American all the way. Only their daughter thinks 'Bobbi Jean' is déclassé and insists on being called 'Roberta.' "

"Gee, Tennessee, that's tough."

"Score one for Dabrowski," I said. She laughed at her own joke until I began to be embarrassed for her. "Roberta Rodriguez, as she likes to be known, is just *fourteen years old.*"

"You said that."

What I had failed to say was that Roberta, at fourteen, looked thirty-four, from a distance: she had skin the color of coffee with only a drop of cream in it (made the men want to lap it up), a toughness to the texture that gave it the illusion of durability (made the men want to bite); she had pierced ears, neon features (colorful, turned on), hips that never stopped moving, not even when she was standing still. The thing about her, though, was that when you got up close, you saw the paint, the acne, and her nervous habit of keeping time with one foot to some never-shared song which she played over and over to herself in her head. It was the foot-patting that agitated those hips, though this was apparently the one artifice which was completely natural, as it were. Thinking of oppositions reminded me: "Did you know that some of our Latin patients believe in hot and cold medicines? Sort of like yin and yang." I corrected myself. "Not really like yin and yang, though."

"She doesn't have cervical cancer, does she?"

"No," I said, "nobody does. Except thirteen thousand women who die from it every year. I just think that's an interesting and appalling piece of information."

"There are a lot of pieces of information like that, Tennessee. I don't think you ought to go around collecting them."

I explained that I didn't really but that sometimes I needed to remind myself why I was in med school. She looked at me as if this were a shameful thing to have to admit. "You have never questioned your decision?" I asked her.

"I never made a decision. I just always knew."

"And you know absolutely positively for certain that you want to go into general practice?"

"I suppose. Sure, that's right. I want to help people with their everyday problems." She was abruptly expansive; I had the feeling that she wanted to make sweeping gestures to illustrate her points but that the habit of personality restrained her. "I want to send them to the right specialist when they have to see one and send them home when they don't. Tell them they can't have a penicillin shot every time they catch cold."

"You can recommend ascorbic acid," I said. "Adrien does."

"There was only one moment I've ever doubted myself," she went on, passing up the chance to reply to my crack. "That was right at the beginning, when we found out that the smart students steered clear of female cadavers. You know, all that extra fatty tissue to slow you up?"

"Hey, Fran," I said, "I didn't know you were a Women's Libber."

She smiled quietly, even proudly. "We're everywhere," she said. "Are you in a group?"

Was I in a group! I tried to tell her what my group was like. "Like, I told them I was going to specialize in OB/GYN. I even let them in on one of our biggest professional secrets. That the correct pronunciation is not *gyne* but *gin.* As in rummy."

Fran suppressed a smile.

"Women should have some control over their own bodies," I had said, quoting almost word-for-word from a Lib pamphlet.

"That's beautiful, Tennessee," said the First Woman.

I *(humbly):* Thank you.

FOURTH WOMAN: *Thank* you!

I *(sincerely):* You're welcome.

FOURTH WOMAN: Cut it out! *Thank* you! Are you going to accept praise for doing what we are *all* doing in one way or another?

I: Shoot, I'll accept praise for just about anything. Even that.

FOURTH WOMAN: No doubt. Some Schweitzer you'll make. I'll bet you don't even know the Hippocratic Oath.

"Oh, you must!" Fran said.

Of course I did. I'd had it down pat when I was eleven. Like every other medical student.

"It's starting to rain," I said, looking out the window. Across the street, mothers were throwing their children into yellow slickers and yanking them away from the slides and swings. A traffic jam was in formation (an interesting progress, involving the contagion of annoyance from the pedestrian caught off guard to the driver in sympathy to the driver behind him who was definitely not in sympathy with the pedestrian caught off guard). In a matter of minutes, the sky was as dark as five o'clock, but it was still noon (the sun was only hidden, not removed to some far corner of the universe, however much it might appear so). The headlights came on, pair after pair. Fran and I felt cozy. We were chatting. I asked her who her favorite teacher was. "What do you think of Goldberg?" I asked, cleverly.

The whole school must have known about it. "He's stuck on you," she said.

"Stuck?" I said. "Isn't that a little old-fashioned?"

"I'm an old-fashioned girl," Fran said. "Maybe he is too. Old-fashioned, that is." She was getting ready to go back. "We're going to be late for class," she explained, a note of anxiety disturbing the placid voice. She had her scarf, but bad weather always came as a surprise to me. Barreling through the downpour to the main entrance, I had my head down and bumped into a world-famous gastroenterologist, knocking him to his knees. "Oh my," Fran said, "oh my."

He said, "Why don't you look where you're going?"

I said, "I didn't see you looking where *you* were going."

He said, "Dammit, woman, that's what I said! Haven't you got bat brains?"

"It was an accident," Fran said, stepping in to apologize for me. Meanwhile we were all getting soaked, and besides, the son of a gun had almost gored me to death with the spearhead of his umbrella. I started to say something about that but Fran was tugging at my sleeve. We trudged on back to the main entrance but it kept bugging me, the way Fran was coming on as if she were so much more "mature" and "forgiving," a stance which probably wasn't justified but which, if it was, was only exacerbating my bad conscience. Just before we entered the classroom I said to her, in great sadness, "Arthur's very low today. . . ."

"Who's Arthur?" she asked.

"Arthurmometer." Then I beat it to my seat. By the time class was over I was feeling penitent, as well as uncomfortable because my jaw was beginning to ache again. I bought a bag of peanuts from the machine and stopped by the lab and, seeing that Fran was somewhere else, left it on her desk as a peace offering. Then I went back up in search of the Doodler. It was three o'clock and I found him in the lounge.

"Got it?" he asked.

I handed him the Demerol. "Ten bucks," I said.

"Not that," he said. "The leg! The leg!"

"What leg?" I thought he was pulling mine.

Someone else said, "She's not the one. Here it is."

"Oh yeah," said the Doodler. I followed his gaze to see a student enter with a large package slung over his shoulder.

"What's up?"

"Plan B," said the Doodler.

"Will somebody please tell me," I begged, "what Plan B is?"

"There's this new chick," said Someone Else, "and we're going to put Roy in her bed."

"Who's Roy?"

The student with the package slung over his shoulder said: "This is Roy. His right leg, anyway. The rest of him is in Autopsy."

"Youall wouldn't do a thing like that!"

"We-all sure would." Someone Else chuckled. "This chick is just perfect."

"Do you always do it to a chick?" I asked.

"Always," the Doodler said. "It's part of Plan B."

I was curious. "How come you didn't do it to me?"

The student with the package set it down and told me how it worked. "She's first-year," he said, "and our guess is, she's as squeamish as they come."

"I'm pretty squeamish too," I admitted. "I practically fainted today." Of course, it wasn't every day that I was vouchsafed a vision of the burning bush, even transplanted from Midian to Manhattan, from Mount Horeb to Mount Sinai.

"That's different," he said.

I asked how I was different.

The Doodler grinned at me. "*You* didn't pull down an A in anatomy last year."

I was stung. "Did you?" I asked, sarcastically. Officially we were graded "Pass" or "Fail"; unofficially, we knew who deserved an A and who didn't, and graded each other accordingly. "Did you pull down an A?" Talking almost to myself I added, "Did you ever really want to?"

"Good God, no," he said. "That's the point." He dropped a dime into the coffee machine. "To tell the truth, if I don't look out, I'm going to flunk the National Boards." We all had to take Part One of the Boards at the end of the year.

"Then why are you wasting your time making some poor little first-year coed miserable?" Speaking of miserable, my jaw was sticking little penknives of pain into my nerves.

"Look who's preaching," he said. "Why are you wasting yours pushing downers in a place crawling with downers and uppers and anything else you could want?"

"That's a good question," I said. "How are you going to get into this girl's apartment?"

"We've got it all figured out," he said. "Are you with us or not?"

"Not," I said. "I have to sell this stuff today if I'm going to be able to pay the dentist who gave it to me."

"I know the super in this chick's building," Someone Else put in. "He's got a little thing going on the side—come with us, we'll help you unload it."

The Doodler kicked the machine that had swallowed his dime, and the student with the package, who had set it down, picked it up again. "Are you coming?" they asked again. I needed bread. "Okay," I said, but with misgivings. It had stopped raining but the sun hadn't wanted to come out again. I tagged them up the block to the girl's building. She couldn't afford the regular building that a lot of the students and some faculty lived in. She lived three flights up over a Greek restaurant. My classmates rang the super's bell. "Look," I said, thinking that if the girl who was going to suffer this prank could live on nothing, as she so evidently did, then I was well enough off and should leave well enough alone, "I think I'll go." They glared at me. "Here," I said, "you can keep the money." I thrust the little package of pills into the pocket of the student with the larger package slung over his shoulder.

"Chicken," said the Doodler.

"It's not that," I lied, just then realizing how apprehensive I was also that the pass Dr. Goldberg had thrown might yet come in for completion. I wondered why people always had their own plans for me—and what plans the first-year girl had that these people, with their Plan B, might be about to disrupt forever. Hearing her screams in my head, I knew it ached on her account. "It's just that I just remembered I've got to see my adviser at four," I said, and backed away and hurried home to Lulu and Willa Mae, but couldn't shake a feeling, at once tenacious and elusive, that the home I was headed for was no refuge from psychic or somatic trauma. By the time I got there, my jaw felt like it was on fire and I could have kicked myself for giving away all my Demerol. The pain was killing me.

4. THAT CO/MOPOLITAN GIRL
WILL BE THE DEATH OF U/ YET

Lacking that deviousness which the female early learns, Bernie had viewed self-pity simplistically as a hostile and destructive force bent on undermining all his good intentions; but it was more than that, was a way of life, was a summation of energy in the name of survival. As long as I went on weeping, I knew I existed; and if, shedding my tears, I thereby increased the seas of negation in which I was drowning, well, that was just another of those ironies with which so artificial an ontology might wisely pretend to interest itself and which one was in consequence as mightily thankful for as amused by. I acknowledged, then, that my unseen neighbor wept for reasons not dissimilar to mine, and knew too that Lulu was no less entitled to the excuse I gave myself than my neighbor was. But when Lulu asked me if I knew "what it's *like* to have no reason at all to go on living," a question that justified itself in my own mind at three in the morning proved intolerably trivial in the midst of the body count on the seven o'clock news.

"But you used to picket," I said. "March! You believe in politics."

"If they shot Martin Luther King," she said, lighting a cigarette, "what's the point?" Though she chainsmoked, she'd never use the burning butt of the one to fire the next, as I did, but always flipped the lid of her lighter before she tapped the tobacco down and placed the cigarette between her lips. It was an insignificant habit, but a feminine one, which I tried, from time to time, to adopt.

"*I* didn't shoot him—" I started to say, flushing under the heat of her gaze, but didn't. I said, "Maybe if you'd go to some of the fund-raising parties you're always being invited to, you'd meet a man you liked."

She answered me with a question, and for all the lazy nonchalance she put it with, there was an anger in her voice which told me how she expected me to receive it. "Would you," she asked, "come with me?"

No, I didn't know how to explain to her that when we went out together we were taken either for mother and daughter or for worse. "I'm shy at parties," I explained, condemning myself to self-hatred when she said, as I knew she would, that she could understand that, that was why she had found it helpful to drink in the days when she used to go to parties with her husband. I asked her, not, believe it or not, untactfully, if he had done anything besides drink and chase women. "Shoes," she said.

"Shoes?"

"He designed shoes. Sam," she said, "was a very aesthetic person."

I allowed as how I was a shoe-freak myself.

"Don't get the wrong idea," she cautioned, quickly. "He was a war hero too."

I was impressed. My own father had been disqualified for having flat feet, and Adrien was a Conscientious Objector. Bernie, of course, might have seen duty during the Korean War *if* he hadn't had a ten-year psychiatric profile on record at the Downstate Medical Center in Brooklyn, not to mention the fact that the older he got the farther left he moved (I would bet that even now that he was married his first love was still the mimeograph machine). As it was, the closest he ever got to war was stickball on Avenue

J, and the closest I'd come to it was overhearing Rosie's drunken conversation with Peter in the Recovery Room last Christmas Eve. "Poke Chop Hill," he had said; "man, tha's wha' life be *all* about."

And Peter had been as impressed as I was. "I envy you, man; boy, do I ever respect the living daylight out of you for that."

"Ah, ya shoulda been there. . . . Far as th' nekkid eye could see! The Yellow Peril!"

"Terrific!" Peter said. "Super! Magnifico!"

Then Rosie had passed out in a pile of peanut shells. "Let's go," I said, tugging at Peter's sleeve. "It's Christmas Eve."

"Go where? Where would we go? It's Christmas Eve."

"Well, let's just go somewhere where we can have us a quiet little holiday celebration."

The irises of his eyes kept sliding up beneath the lids, leaving the bloodshot whites to glare balefully at my tentative smile. *"Home,"* he said. "I don't wanna go home, wild horses couldn't drag me home. I don't *have* any home any more." He raised Rosie's head and let it drop again. "President Roosevelt," he said, "he had the right idea." And he laid his own head on the table and started to snore. Overhead, I-V bottles filled with "blood" hung from heavy beams, and a model skeleton danced at the end of a length of catgut. Scalpels and spatulas, dilators and curettes ranged from the back of the long, skinny bar to the stained glass diamond pane up front. On my way out I passed the shadow-boxed bedpan into which countless pennies had been chucked. If you could chuck your penny in, you were still sober. Peter and Rosie had failed the test. I left them there, left them to sleep together, two of the gentlest, most peaceable men I knew dreaming such gloriously violent dreams as only they could tell, and schlepped uptown on the subway alone, promising myself, assuring myself with a fury designed to keep the tears back, that next year, now this year, I would have a pleasanter Christmas. "If you won't come to the party with me," Lulu was saying, "why don't you bring your friend what's-his-name, the black one, you know,

Roosevelt Jones?—Why don't you bring him around and we'll have a party of our own right here."

I said I was going to Knoxville for the holidays.

She stubbed her cigarette out.

"But I'll ask Rosie over sometime soon," I added, feeling guilty, and realized, when she whipped open her compact and lipstick, that sooner or later I would have to do that: she counted on it as completely as I counted on the visit I hoped Adrien would ultimately make—penultimately, as it developed. Adrien, insofar as he constituted one area of my life which was effectively secluded from Lulu's household, was becoming, letter by letter, ever more important to me, though there was no way *he* could know that— or maybe the reason I began looking forward to his visit so was simply that, since our relationship remained undefined, there was a promise (but not a promise "made" by anybody) of a kind of intimacy which Lulu and I could never share, or would never have dreamed of sharing. Every day at noon, I descended the steps to search out the mail before Lulu could go through it, reading return addresses to pounce on the telltale "New Hope." (I ran home from school and ran back in time to grab a candy bar and drink a cup of coffee for lunch.) I didn't want her to do my waiting for me; she now had, I told myself, her own waiting to do—for Rosie—and she did it. In the mornings, she splashed lipstick across her face, and when her skin had sponged it up, she freshened it in the evening while we watched television. She combed her hair religiously and cleaned her teeth with a vengeance. But with what fear she crept out to buy a new dress! and never dared go for a walk in the park, not even with the dogs, which Willa Mae took out twice daily. I took her to the movies several Saturdays in a row, and then gave it up, because afterward she'd say, "That was nice," or "That wasn't much good, was it?" As if she and the film, coming together in the darkness of the Fine Arts on Fifty-eighth Street, made only the most formal, and judgmental, of connections. Where Cameron, undisturbed by if not incognizant of the hesitancy with which the world at large approached her, assimilated the whole of it, Lulu considered herself unworthy and dared let nothing impinge upon her consciousness lest whatever did so should inform her of its dismay and revulsion. I wasn't entirely without sympathy and could by now recognize in this the source of that dismay and revulsion she countered with, and if at first I wondered why her analyst failed to help her, I soon saw that he considered her as hopeless as she considered herself, thought her not much worth working with, confirmed her low opinion of herself and doped her with tranquilizers and sleeping pills in lieu of recognizing her as a patient with valid claims and complaints. "Of course not," Veronica agreed when I reported the situation to her; "in the minds of most of us, only a young man is an acceptable patient." She grinned. "Male supremacists, that's what they are."

"But what about the tranquilizers?"

"I'm addicted to them," Lulu would say with a small laugh; "he tells me that without them I'd go into shock." I found myself laughing with her, as if that were comic indeed; but when she told me she was copping extra drugs from a chemotherapist, I was obliged to say she shouldn't.

"Don't worry," she said, "I know what I'm doing."

There were times she didn't, times when she came to dinner and did a nod that moved Willa Mae to roll her eyes up to the ceiling and shrug her shoulders. "You got to keep a eye on her, honey," she'd tell me; "our madam don't know shit from shinola when them *pills* has got her feelin' so good like that." But it was only the lack of choice in Lulu's condition that made me loathe it. Veronica had said there was nothing I could do, nothing anyone could do, and I, revolted, more often than not would raise my own spirits with a reefer or two when I could get clear of Lulu's oppressive world and get up to my room and close the door. Yet if I, stoning myself into a state of paranoia, took the bad with the good and told myself it was an intelligent compromise because I had opted for it freely, Lulu, as another case in point, proved the opposite, finding in marijuana a surcease, even an exhilaration, which not merely held no terrors but held at bay the ones that normally sat on her shoulder and whispered in her ear. I knew they were there, and called them the Crazies; and while anyone might have deduced their presence, I am forced to admit that I once actually saw them, saw them snarling her bright red hair, tangling it, three crazy crones shrunk to the size of ashes, while all unaware she sat at her French Provincial nightstand lit by tensor lamp, writing checks to charities. I figured she had got used to them. Of course I would sigh and couldn't stop sighing. I was stoned. "Have a good session," I would say, dredging good humor up from the slough of despond her edginess dropped me into, and every time she returned from her analyst or her group, would cast a quick glance at her shoulder to see if the Crazies had been exorcised at last. "Have a good session," I said on the Tuesday before Christmas, when she left me alone with Cameron to decorate the tree.

"We'll do it tomorrow, Mama."

"Oh," she said, wrapping her cloth coat around her as she waited for the elevator man, "go ahead without me."

Christmas made a fool of me once every year—as if I wasn't foolish quite frequently enough anyway. In a rush of sentiment I said Cameron and I would have more fun if we waited till tomorrow, when we could all do it together, but Lulu insisted she would just as soon come back to find the chore done and out of the way.

Cammie blinked back her tears. "Buck up," I said, as the door closed behind her mother.

"I'm all right," she said. I took in her teary brown eyes, the freckles, aflame with insult, standing out against the pale complexion, the suede vest with a torn fringe, the injured leg clad in bleached blue jeans as if it might, so costumed, achieve a conformity with the other that, bare, it lost. "I can take care of myself," she said. Then she looked straight at me. "But I can't take care of Mama any more."

I sighed. "What makes you so precocious?" I asked.

She asked what the word meant. "I'm not," she said, after I'd told her, "but I-I-I have to try."

I wondered if she had to try so hard. On her first trip home from Maine, she'd thrown herself in my arms and announced she was a fallen woman. "So at least somebody is getting something," Maxine said, when I relayed the news during a late-night call to Levittown. "She's one in a million," Max said, "if you're the random sample."

"You've been hanging around with me too long, it's affecting your thought-processes. The kid is only a kid!"

"Things have altered since your generation, Tennessee."

"I just don't want she should be jaded."

"Tennessee," Max said, "you've been hanging around with *me* too cotton-picking long. About Cameron, the thing is, sex isn't something that sticks in your memory. You can't store it up so you can't suffer from a surplus."

"Well. I mean, well. I hadn't realized the Aquarian Age was dawning over Levittown too."

"*Look,* Tennessee. . . . How well do you remember what your darlink Bernard I hear so much about was like in—"

"Camelot," I mused, sitting with her by the nude tree in the living room, "have you noticed how conversations keep taking a wrong turn of late?"

"I can't help it," she said. "Sometimes my mother gives me a pain."

"You don't mean that."

She giggled. "Did you really think I did?" She was going through the box of ornaments and avoided looking at me when she said, "I know I don't have any right to think things like that."

"Don't be silly." I wanted to reassure her, to allow her a little leeway for living. "People have to think mean things sometimes, it's part of being human." Perhaps I only wanted to reassure myself, thinking "mean things" so compulsively that in my prayerbook I'd written: "If I can't think happier thoughts, maybe You shouldn't let me think at all. Maybe I need a lobotomy." Clio the cat had crawled onto my lap, rubbing the side of her face against the fiber-point pen in my hand. I shooed her off, thinking how inferior she was to The Prune, how devoid of personality. Important ideas! "Maybe," I wrote, chastising myself, "I have yet to *have* a real thought, good or bad, kind or cruel, true or false." I felt in fact that my responses, since moving into this penthouse on Park, were more instinctive than intellectual. Lulu Carlisle provided me with room and board, and I, reflexively as if some witless muscle in my mind had been tapped, was instantly jerked into a posture of responsibility. Receiving payment, however unsolicited, I felt myself required in all good faith to hand over the soul that seemed to have been bought when my back was turned. It was, again, a matter of "propers," and perhaps that was why I welcomed every word I drew from Adrien. He committed himself, I was beginning to see, to nothing, gave nothing, and demanded everything—or nothing. "I may come to see you," he wrote me, "and I may not. If I go up to visit my friends in Canada, I'll come to see you in New York on my way back to New Hope. If you want to see me, you'd better be there—but I won't tell you when. You probably think," he went on, "that I'm being unreasonable, but I don't believe reason serves much use in these matters. I want what I want, and if it's not what you want, that's tough luck for both of us. Don't cry over it, though.... Please don't cry. There's nothing to cry about as long as the sun shines." I didn't cry, I waited. I waited for Adrien all the time I was studying and reading and getting to know the regulars at the clinic and tutoring Cameron during the holidays and trying to write another article for Ace Winters and writing in my prayerbook and all the time I was warding off advances from Dr. Goldberg. He sent candy, he sent a beautiful book on the care of the patient in surgery; as a joke, at Christmas time he sent me a child's doctor's kit with a toy stethoscope and three little vials of multicolored candy-coated sugar pills that I wished had been the right shape and size to substitute for Lulu's tranquilizers when she wasn't looking (if it wouldn't've sent her into shock). He called me up so often, promising to take me here or there, wherever I wanted to go, that I began to depend on the calls and was chagrined whenever a day passed and the phone failed to ring. "No," I told him, unrelentingly, but I felt neglected when he forgot to ask. Almost, I asked Fran Dabrowski what she would do in my shoes, whether she would go out with a married doctor. But I had had trouble looking Fran in the eye ever since the day I came home from school and took out the phone number proffering free . . . kittens. The ring had hardly got going good before someone answered. I was all prepared to deliver my speech in throaty tones screened through the sock I had slipped over the receiver (in a house full of women, where was I going to find a handkerchief?), but the party I had reached was saying hello in a strikingly familiar voice. That gave me pause. "Hello?" said Fran Dabrowski, again, and that slight edge of anxiety that I'd noted before was back, and suddenly I realized who it was and that she had hoped her ad would bring a call from a man, and rather than embarrass her—or disappoint her—I hung up on her. Upset, I told myself that probably she thought she was being liberated, but, discovering how my image of Fran was irremediably revised, I strengthened my resolve. Bless Fran. "No," I wrote in my prayerbook, holding in my other hand the Clairol Air Brush aimed at my compulsively clean, but haughty, hair, "I won't give in to Goldberg and I won't let Adrien bamboozle me either. I'll wait, but won't let him know I'm waiting." Like my mother and my sister and everyone else from Tennessee, I still thought that if a man cared he could be made to propose, but I didn't let my Lib group know that was what I was angling for. Only Maxine knew. "Right on," she said, approving. Admiring. Even so, I wondered if she hadn't herself capitulated too thoroughly to what she called the "Long Island School of Thought." As a nulliparous female, I had to watch out for *all* the ways in which time could pass without my finding a man willing to make a grown woman out of me by knocking me up (you can see the problems and contradictions I was up against). I, after all, couldn't deny to myself that I had read Adrien's letters and she hadn't, and part of me wondered somewhat fearfully if Adrien might not mean what he said he thought. "I don't like myself," Cam interrupted, bringing me up short, "when I think mean things about Mama. It's not her fault that everything is all screwed up."

"She knows it's not her fault."

She looked at me sharply. "What do you mean by that?"

"Well," I said, trying to weasel my way out of waters that were suddenly over my head, "nothing is anybody's fault. The fault," I laughed, nervously, "is with the stars."

"Hey, that's groovy! What's your sign?"

I didn't tell her I had lied: I told her I didn't believe in nonsense.

"I do," she vowed. "Nonsense is the only thing I b-b-believe in."

"I gather that's what that school of yours teaches, all right."

"Oh, Tennessee," she said, "you're so old-fashioned."

I winced. "I'm trying," I said.

"Let's see you try to get this up there!" She dangled a cardboard angel in front of my nose and pointed at the top of the tree.

"The wings are loose. . . ."

"I'll get the Scotch tape," she said; and while she was away, she put a record on her stereo.

"Maybe when your mother gets back we'll pop some popcorn."

"You're kidding."

"I'm kidding," I said. We both knew it would be too much trouble, too messy, and too fattening for Lulu. She weighed at fifty-two no more than she had weighed when she left for her junior year (1938) abroad.

"My sister loves Paris," I said, making small talk.

"Georgette says I'm cheap," she said.

"Who's Georgette?"

"You're worse than Mama," she said, repairing the angel's wings. Her cheeks began to quiver. "You don't understand anything."

"Uh-oh—" Now I was full of sorrow for her disillusionment. Hadn't I prophesied it myself? "I warned you!"

"It's not that," she snorted. "Jesus please us, Tennessee! I d-d-don't care what Georgette thinks. I just wish you could remember who my friends are."

"How could I?" I asked her. "I'm not even sure who *my* friends are."

When she laughed, it was like the unrolling of a string of laughs. I was tied up in knots. I climbed the stepladder to lean out over the branches and place the angel at the top of the tree. Peering down at Cameron, I asked her if she had ever played King-of-the-Mountain. "My sister and I used to play it," I told her, "on a rubbish heap on the far side of the school playground." Remembering, I removed my red coat and hung it over the monkey bars and rolled up my sleeves. The "king," my sister, waited at the top of the mountain for the rest of us to plot our strategy. Then, while the others shrieked and giggled and moved *en masse* head on, I charged in from the flank and pushed her over. I hadn't meant to split her head open on the knifelike lid of the tin can, but that's what happened, and after the ambulance came and the principal called my parents, I was permitted to go home early. I sat over the furnace grate in the dining room, reading a Tom Corbett space mystery, until I decided I had better take the bus to the hospital and face the music. Then I put on my red coat and walked up the hill, stopping in the tavern at the crossroads for a Pepsi and a Zero candy bar, because the bus was county-run and couldn't be counted on to run very often. When my sister's fourth-grade teacher drove by, she slowed the car to a stop and said, "Get in," and I didn't know what to do with the Pepsi and the candy bar except to go on eating, swallowing as fast as possible, praying I'd be through before we got to the hospital. Finished, I tucked the candy wrapper in my purse and buried the empty bottle in the pocket of my coat and followed the teacher to the room where my kid sister, her shorn scalp turbaned in gauze and adhesive tape, with glittering eyes looked up at me from the narrow cot she lay in and said: "Uneasy lies the head that wears the crown!"

I chewed my lip and shuffled my feet. My mother and father and the teacher had huddled together, unmistakably proffering me both the opportunity and the inescapable duty of speaking with my sister in privacy.

"It wasn't your fault," she said, absolving me. "It was an accident." Thus it made, under the circumstances, more sense to agree than to argue. But I had known an argument could be made and this arcane knowledge continued to tease my thoughts until, nearly twenty years later, when Maxine, waxing pensive over the telephone, assured me that "it's all an accident, everything," I discovered myself inclined, even determined, if not predetermined, contrarily to mistrust a philosophy of chance that had mushroomed in popularity until it covered the whole range of contemporary morals and mores like some putrid weed slowly sucking up the little fresh air that remained and giving off a vile, stinking, noxious, carbonated gas that was, I suspected, going to suffocate us all before it might blossom into a lovelier maturity. "You're a romantic," Maxine said.

"You're reactionary," Cammie said. "King-of-the-Mountain!"

"I'm a sucker," I said to my parents, when I'd finally got home for the holidays, sitting on the deacon's bench at the kitchen table, playing three-handed Hearts, the spare deuce of clubs pitched to the side, propped against the cocoa pot. "You can't imagine what that family is like," I told them. "You'd have to see it to believe it."

The tree was up and lit when I walked in, trailing my father. It was impossible to stop him from carrying the suitcase. The bald spot on the back of his head lighted my way like a beacon through the falling fog. I love Knoxville, love the chill gray of its winter afternoons which never entirely erases the softer hues of summer, love my city's utter uselessness on the grander scale of things and am thankful that my father has also liked living there. "There is some mail for you in your room," he said, heading there with the suitcase while I greeted my mother. "Here it is."

"Bring it into the kitchen," my mother said. She started the cocoa and I leafed through the letters.

"A card from Adrien," I said.

"Who is Sylvia?" my father asked.

"Someone special," I answered. I sniggered. "You really should be able to keep my friends straight by now."

My father, amiable old man, sniggered right along with me. "Does Adrien," he asked, "send us anything to remember him by?"

At that time I still hadn't seen Adrien for a space of almost two years, not since the split-up with Bernie, but we had established an intimacy in our correspondence that I was leery of sharing so long as it did not yet exist in reality. "Nothing much," I said. "He says he's a bit blue about the direction his poetry isn't taking, but to keep the faith, and someday he'll show me his . . . stuff. *Merry Christmas,* it says here. *Someday we'll all sit down to lunch again: Swiss cheese and lettuce. . . . Jesus brings it in.*"

"He sounds," my father said, "like a sensible young man."

"Your father," my mother said, "is getting senile." She poured the cocoa. "Isn't it wonderful?"

"The cocoa?"

"Senility."

"I wouldn't know! Don't rush me. . . ."

"There, there, don't fret," my father said, leaning across the table to pat my hand. "You'll find out in plenty of time." He reached for the deck of cards, made them, and began to deal. "Now," he said, suddenly businesslike, "tell me how my Little Fruitcake is?"

It was one of his nicknames for me, and I had learned long ago that the more I objected to it, the more he used it. He was a religion professor at the University—a fact which I like to think accounts for his ability to disregard more mundane matters— and if I chose to pester him with my more immediate concerns, my mother quickly ran interference. It was not that she felt duty bound to safeguard him from my problems and inquiries but that, over the course of their marriage, she had adopted his habit of pedagogy, and lacking her own lectern to exercise it from, applied it to me. "Civilization," she was wont to say, "hit its high point with Thomas Hardy; from here on out, it's all downhill. The survival of the fittest, Mary, is only an illusion to sustain the courage of those of us who do survive."

I said she could at least smile when she said that, "pardner."

She smiled. "You have an amusing mind," she said, "though it is not perhaps so serious in intent as your sister's, which is brilliant but for its predilection to Francophilia."

"Franco?"

"Funny you should say that," she said, "but you don't have to play dumb with your own mother. You know what I mean. We all know that France is a nation of perverts."

"I suppose when I laid her head open I crossed the wires that carry these lively little currents of prejudice."

"Speaking of wires, she called today."

"Oh?"

"To wish us a Merry Christmas."

"And?"

"And she said she was getting married come spring to a Spanish bassoonist."

I was distressed. For want of a logical rebuttal, I pointed out that the elder daughter ought to marry first.

"I think she's tired of waiting."

"Me too," I growled. "Where will they live?"

"France." She sighed. "I don't understand it." She hitched her arms around her knees, holding the hand Dad had dealt her far enough away to read it without her glasses. "I'll tell you something, Mary, all kidding aside: I think the time comes when a person begins to appreciate having death to look forward to. As a reprieve, a relief. It just looks like the older you get, the harder it becomes to adjust to the way things change. It gets too exhausting: trying to keep your mind open." She plopped a marshmallow into her cocoa. "You know Mrs. Trumble? Next door? We were talking and she told me that she remembers that her own father refused to believe there could be such a thing as a sound barrier. Mrs. Trumble is no fool. Even if it's on presumptive evidence, her father was a smart man!"

"Not so smart as your husband," my father said, laying the Queen of Spades on his daughter's trick. *"Nay, do not start! She is no agèd hag, but beautiful and dark,"* he quoth, and threw me thirteen points I didn't want. But sometimes he tried to slip the Old Lady to my mother, also a very sharp cookie, and then, more often than not, he would have to eat her, which amused him just as much as anything else did. "For heaven's sake," my mother said, "control yourself." His shoulders shook up and down, his head bobbed, and he winked at me as soundlessly he laughed. "I only hope," my mother said, "that we reach retirement age before your father enters his second adulthood."

"In Majorca?"

"It's England now," my mother said. "We've been reading up on their National Health Service. France isn't far at all—just far enough. And you can't imagine how much cheaper it is to die in England than it is here."

"You weren't really planning," I said, "to die?"

"It happens," my father said, his pent-up laughter exploding as he added, "Why, some of my best friends are . . ."

But when I saw him with my mind's-eye, saw him stripped of skin, his skull bearing into eternity the grin he showed me across our kitchen table, I was disheartened, and to change the subject, said, "Why don't I open Lulu's gift now? It doesn't really go under the tree with the rest." I didn't have to explain why.

"What is it?" my father asked, balling up the torn paper and clearing the table.

I laid the marbled egg on my palm. My mother said, "I think it's a paperweight?" She patted me on the head and wished me better luck for the next day's game, the next Christmas, and the next man.

"Well," my father said, startling me with the word I always

forgot myself to connect with Lulu, "what else would you expect from a millionaire?" It wasn't until after they had gone to bed that I found, rummaging among the scraps my father had thrown away, the card which let me know that my poor paperweight represented a contribution to the disadvantaged whites of the Appalachians, and I knew what expense of spirit had gone into Lulu's first brave trek back over the color bar on my account. She had certainly as much feeling for me as I for her.

"Lulu," I had said, sentimentally imagining we were some approximation of a family when she returned from her session, "why don't we all pop some corn?"

"I can't hear you," she said. "Cameron, turn that infernal racket down."

"Why can't you just *ask* me?" Cammie cried.

"I have a splitting headache."

"Well," said Cam, in the only reference I had heard her make to the way she felt about her handicap, "I have a lousy stinking rotten lame leg."

"That will be enough out of you!"

Then Cameron hobbled into her room and scraped the needle over and off the record and slammed The Doors against the wall. "I hate you," she wept, "I hate you," and all the time she went on breaking her records, as if she hated them rather than her mother. "Camille—" I began, but she said, "I hate you too, I hate everyone."

"Do you hate Willa Mae?" I asked.

"Yes," she said.

"Do you hate Maxine?"

"Of c-c-course."

"Do you hate Georgette?"

"Her especially!"

"And everyone at school?"

"Well—"

"How about my friend Peter?"

"He's all right."

"And the memory of your father?"

"No-o-o-o," she said, wiping her eyes with the back of her hand.

"I guess," I mused, "that the exceptions just go to prove the rule," and was fairly bowled over by the pride I felt when she sank onto the edge of the sofa bed, eyes dry, and looked up at me with a kind of rueful self-mockery. Bernie could go hang, I thought, I would make a terrific mother! But then Lulu brushed by me at the doorway and ran over to put her arms around her daughter. "Oh, my poor baby," she said, "I'm sorry, I truly am." I thought Lulu was crying too.

"It's all right," Cammie said, patting her mother's back.

"It was my fault," she said in a plangent wail that rose and fell as she rocked that strawberry head in her lap, "it was all my fault," and because I felt left out and didn't know whether she meant the argument or the automobile accident, I left them and put the leftover ornaments back in their box, put the leather watchband and love-beads I'd bought Cameron and the paperback on home-cultivation of marijuana which I thought would tickle Lulu under the tree, turned out the living-room light, and went upstairs. My jaw was still too sore to risk another reefer. For a while, unwinding, I read from *The Waste Land,* wondering if it would do to read with Cam before she went back to Maine after the holidays. We had to do something, didn't we?

> *O the moon shone bright on Mrs. Porter*
> *And on her daughter*
> *They wash their feet in soda water*
> *Et O ces voix d'enfants . . .*

When the floor below was quiet, I went to sleep, waking in the middle of the night with a small cry of my own. After I'd got back from Knoxville, I tutored Cameron, and after she'd gone back to school, I carted my nightmare off to Veronica. "It was a case of mistaken identity," I explained. "The judge in the dream insisted I was this Carla Quinn and said he was going to lock me up. But

I knew who she was and the resemblance was only skin deep. I told him that. I told him I wasn't at all like her, she mainlined and had short, stringy hair and she was a butch. Look! My hair is *long* and stringy!"

"When was the last time you made it with someone," she asked, nibbling at the eraser of her pencil.

"I don't see how that's relevant," I objected. "Anyway, I don't remember, it's been so long. . . . Well," I said, my voice running scared, "you know how it is. You spend hours getting ready for a date, and then you get down to business, and your hair gets plastered to your head and you sweat and your makeup comes off on the pillow, which brings the blood-bugs out into the open, and then no matter how exhausted you are, before you can go to sleep you have to get up and take out your lenses that you have suffered untold agony with in an effort to impress whoever-it-is, and if you're a good girl, you put your bite plate in then, and so help us all, by the time morning rolls around, you feel like an *impostor.* An impostor who's been found out."

"What did you say was the name of the woman in your dream?"

"Carla Quinn," I said. She smiled and spat the bits of rubber into the wastebasket. I gave up and let myself fall back against the shiny black headrest of the ersatz leather armchair. "Okay," I said. "Harlequin."

5. CRUISING

Then things began to change. Cameron went back to school for the long haul till Easter. Lulu said it was too cold to go out during the day so we watched the Saturday night horror flick on Channel Five instead. Willa Mae borrowed my back issues of *Cosmopolitan* and read through the long winter afternoons in her quarters behind the dining area, absorbing advice on how to domesticate the New York bachelor. Peter seemed preoccupied. Adrien stopped writing. I was depressed and removed all the mirrors from my room.

Rosie called to ask when he could come up to see Mrs. Carlisle. "Sometime," I said, "soon. When things calm down." But things were as calm as the eye of a hurricane.

"Have you heard from your friend?" Lulu asked. "The one that moved you in? Roosevelt Jones?"

I wearied of all this groping after one another and said so to Max when she came charging off the elevator, stamping the snow from her cleated shoes.

Her face was red. "It's snowing," she explained.

"That's not surprising," I said. "There's more and more weather around here lately."

"What's eating you, Tennessee?" Fixing me with her almond-shaped, anthracite-bright eyes (a trick she'd learned in Bellevue, where whoever could stare the other down moved toward the top of the pecking order), she made it clear that she knew the answer in advance. I was in no mood to say what there was no point in saying.

"Nothing," I said.

"Nonsense."

"No one," I said.

"I see."

"Nonsense," I said. "It's an unspecific malaise that's been gnawing at my innards since freshman year in college."

"That was a long time ago."

"Why rub it in?"

"Hasn't Veronica helped?"

"Let's be frank," I said. "You've had some experience with head-shrinkers. You know she can only explain my life away, she can't make it amount to anything."

"You sound like Mrs. Carlisle."

"Proximity."

"Then what you need," she said, "is to get away from it all."

❨ At five on Friday morning we stowed our gear in the trunk of her dark red Fiat. (She dreamed of a silver Stutz.) The world was pitch black minus that streak of it the headlights showed, though by extension that same streak revealed the sleet and snow slapping invisibly against the side windows, unless—as was possible —our deductions were illogical, and the sounds sideswiping us emanated from other sources, ill winds or easy riders or demons along the shoulder of the road. But then, with the rising of the sun, our spirits rose also. While neither Max nor I had ever visited Provincetown before, her parents had, some twenty years previous, and she cheered me with the story of how her father had flown her mother on a surprise second-honeymoon to dine by candlelight at Gino's. Love was lucky, even in January, even in retrospect. "Maybe some of it will spill over onto us," I said.

Maxine insisted she'd rather have a new car.

"I refuse to believe you," I said, "on the ground that it might tend to incriminate me."

"That's *your* problem," she retorted, shifting gears. "Maybe a new car isn't the solution, but it will do as a metaphor." I pointed out that she was talking to someone who didn't know how to drive. "Tell me something I don't already know," she said, exchanging blue-tinted glasses for prescription sun-lenses. "It would help if you'd learn!"

"Teach me," I challenged. "But it'll be hazardous to your health. I'd be a lousy driver."

"I know, you are. Speaking metaphorically." She sucked her breath in, inflating her already-outsized chest with the hot air I knew she was about to expel in polemics. I was pleased to grant her the authority of her own experience but grew uncomfortable when she tried to dictate to mine. "Life is a piece of machinery," she said, "and you move from one day to the next by adapting to the mechanics of the process. That is the Long Island School of Thought on the subject." Defensively she added: "Dig it?"

"It's dug, Maxine. . . . Only, then what happens when the other driver decides to throw a wrench into the works?"

She raised her right eyebrow above the disconcertingly dark lens to acknowledge the reference to Bernie. "All right," she said. "That's when you gotta check out the latest models."

"What do I want with a new damn car," I pleaded, "if *I* don't run so hot no more? My birthday was last month, you know."

"If you'd been born just a few days later," Max mused, "you'd be a whole year younger."

"Cold comfort."

"Well, it's all an accident," she explained. I could tell she was being patient.

"Nonetheless we have to *try* to drive in a straight line, no matter how unpredictable the course may be, and it seems to me that this discussion has gotten off on the wrong track. We started out to discover whether love came before life."

"Life," she said.

"You *mean*, a person's got to be *whole* in order to *give* herself without making hy*steri*cal demands. Speaking as a Southerner, I'd say that's liberal garbage."

"Love," she said.

"You mean, a person's got to *re*spect himself or herself, as the case may be, before he or she has got a foundation"—I paused to draw breath into my own rather underdeveloped rib cage—"a foun*da*tion on which to build love for an*other.* Speaking respectfully herewith as a pietist, I should say that's self-serving bull."

"Then maybe," she said, "what comes first of all is a new car, and screw the metaphor."

❡ We had seen the sun come up this side of Massachusetts, tinting the snowflakes red. "By golly," I muttered, "a sunrise will do for a start."

"God must have had the same idea."

"Great minds think alike," I said, and waited for the lightning bolt, but the snow only slackened, and I could see it was going to be a fine day despite all our blasphemy. We stopped for scrambled eggs at a Howard Johnson's, stopped for gas in New Bedford, turned the radio up for good sounds, down for the news. I liked New Bedford, which, Max told me, was economically depressed, and felt like crying from sheer homesickness—that was how at home I felt amid the paint-peeled, weather-stripped, ceiling-cracked frame houses perched precariously atop rocky hills. We drove past the church where impressionable young Ishmael had been preached to, and the whaling museum, but the church was closed for the off-season, and the museum, with its harpoons and buttermolds and oil lamps and whittled ivory, was too dangerous to stop for: we both feared it might banish forever certain illusions about Ahab we'd retained since adolescence. "Too much reality," Max said, "can get in the way of more important things," and though I changed my mind later, I was then inclined to agree with her. I considered whether I could do extracts from *Moby*

Dick with Cam if she came home for the break between semesters, but she was a city child, whereas I . . . if I were not from the South, I'd have claimed New England, a long-lived if declining home on Cape Cod, wanting only a screen door to the kitchen and a porch on the front to rest contented, although, I reminded myself, the lot of a sailor's wife was bound to be even lonelier than that of a farmer's helpmeet. "Quick!" Max mocked me, "the Seltzer! From such sweet daydreams you could get sick to your stomach."

"Go on," I said. "Don't tell me you don't yearn after the ghetto."

"I'd never admit it. My mother would shoot me."

"They Shoot Horses, Don't They?"

"Oy," she said, her hokey wail wonderfully in tune with Janis Joplin's transistorized "Crybaby" which was in its own turn a miraculous conjunction of redneck rhythm, pop orchestration, and acid harmony. My mind, such as it was, was rocking right along, cruising along the highway; my mind was free to roll. With my liberation from the duplex on Park Avenue came an elasticity of the mental muscles, stiff from disuse, yanking present perceptions out of shape into an elongated association that stretched all the way back to Knoxville, Tennessee, where old Sue Carol, exiled in the way of all memory from time, still went on combing her peroxide hair by the flash of the car mirror and still at this late date had not stopped saying, "I declare, some men are just about too immature for *words.*"

"I'll bet we could think up some words if we really put our minds to it." I was thirteen, Sue Carol fourteen. "Backbiters," I said, "haters of God, despiteful, proud, boasters, inventors of evil things, disobedient to parents, without understanding, covenantbreakers, without natural affection, implacable, unmerciful, mother—"

"Mary!"

"Yeah?"

"Where did you ever . . . you know that's not ladylike."

"I ain't no lady, I'm a kid."

"You certainly are," she said, "you're very immature."

"You can't get through life on one stupid word," I said, sullen. That was, after all, a conclusion I'd come to much earlier, which was how come I'd set about learning others, drawing up lists against the day a dialogue such as this one might ensue. "Like for instance, what are you going to say to Chuck Pryor? He's on his way over here right now."

We watched him bounce on the balls of his feet from the other end of the drive-in stand. "Oh, Christ," we heard him say, as one of the carhops grazed his shoulder and sent the straw from his milkshake flying. "Oh, Christ." He had the slickest ducktail in school and was high-scoring guard on the varsity basketball team. The newspaper said he shot the eyes out of the basket.

"Hello," Sue Carol said. I gave her a passing grade for that: I was tongue-tied.

"Hi," said Chuck.

"Hi," I said.

"Hi," said Sue Carol.

I poked her in the ribs. "You're repeating yourself again," I whispered.

"Hey, no secrets!" Chuck said. He leaned on her side of the car. "What's up?"

"What's up, Chuck?" I asked, snickering.

"I just *love* strawberry," Sue Carol said, helping herself to a sip. "We saw you play today! My, you were terrific."

"Good grief," I said. "He knows he was terrific."

"Mary, Mary, quite contrary," Chuck said. I reached down to pull up my socks. "Going to the Sadie Hawkins dance?"

"You bet!" said Sue Carol.

"Who you taking?"

"Well, now, I don't rightly know," she stalled, her voice growing throaty, the overhead cabin light glancing off her steel-blue eyes like flame from a flint. "You're all so adorable, it's hard to choose."

"You're pretty popular," he allowed. "What about you, Mary?"

"What about me?"

"You going?"

"I'm not pretty," I said. "Just popular."

"You taking some fella?"

"I might could, if the fella was to want me to."

"It's a deal," he said. "See you Saturday." He sauntered off, leaving me to face Sue Carol alone.

"You little brat—" she began. But I was smiling as I saw Chuck Pryor fling the shake she had sipped from into the parking lot. I knew Marge and Gower Champion would have nothing on Chuck and me, come the night of the Sadie Hawkins Sock Hop. "You little good-for-nothing brat—"

"What'd I do, Susannah Carol? . . . I haven't done anything. Not anything . . ."

"Nothing! Not one little itsy bitsy thing, huh?"

"I haven't done *any*thing," I said, tears of guilt, shame for my own sense of pride, tears of cowardice starting to crowd my short and colorless lashes.

"What in heaven's name is *wrong?*" Max asked.

"Nothing," I said, "not one itsy bitsy little thing!" I laughed. It felt fine to be on the road, out in the open, carried along by the swift surge of energy pouring out from both engine and radio. I thought it was incomprehensible that the great moments of history had ever taken place without musical accompaniment in the background. Where would our Dark Angel Death be without The Rolling Stones to imbue him with that terrific irony Max and I delighted in? Skulking silently through unseen and subconscious corridors of the all-too-human mind, noiseless and ruinous and ridiculous and untrustworthy as a termite. Where was Christ Almighty without Bach and Beethoven? Speechless in a profane world. Where, oh where was I without the songs of Janis Joplin and Grace Slick to incorporate in sound all the ambitions and meanings of the bodily urges I was unable alone to collect and order into act or statement? I loved them all for what they gave me. I was obliged in return to stumble toward some expression of sympathy for the world they spoke to. I would begin by being honest with Maxine. "Do you ever," I asked, slowly, picking my way, "mistake the memory of a fantasy for a fact?"

"Not while I'm driving."

So much for compassion, I thought. I shut up.

"I can't help it if you're always leaving yourself wide open, Tennessee." She was apologizing. "I know what you meant, I do the reverse trip sometimes."

"I don't know what *you* mean," I said.

"Like, look. Once I had this date with a rock drummer and we went to this discotheque on the Island and we were dancing—"

I danced the way I drove: never.

"—but it was, like I was thirteen, and my old lady said I had to be home by midnight and I thought maybe I could turn this to my advantage, be a little shrewd, that, you know, this guy, he would really be turned on if I came on sweet and innocent, kind of."

"You weren't?"

She snorted. I said, clicking my fingers, *"That's* right, *you* belong to the *post*-Pill generation."

"You wanna hear my story? Or you wanna make stupid wise-cracks?"

"Go on."

"So I did this song-and-dance about how if I didn't leave at twelve I'd turn into a pumpkin."

"Original!"

"Maybe not, but my drummer was charmed. In fact," she said, "he was so charmed I felt lousy about being such a hypocrite and to make up for it when I got home I went into the kitchen and ate myself blue in the face and before the year was out I was as fat as Cousin Herbie."

"Who's Cousin Herbie?"

"Forget it," she said. "Think of him as a figure of speech."

"You'd look right peculiar thin," I assured her. "But it's obvious that you still think of yourself as a very hefty chick, which you are not." She would walk with a stolid step, wore hiking boots for her weak arches, clamped her chest in a black leather jacket. "You could have all the guys you wanted if you wanted them."

She drove for a while in silence. "You say things like that, Tennessee, you put me uptight. It reminds me of being in school, which, believe it or not, I was for a while before the hospital scene started. It's like flunking a test after you have studied your head off. Better you shouldn't study already. Like, suppose I really tried and none of those cats materialized?"

"We'll go shopping in Provincetown," I said, "I'll help you choose some clothes."

"Aha! What would your Women's Lib group say about *that* if they knew?"

◖ FIRST WOMAN (*in man's sweatshirt and blue jeans*): I like clothes just fine, I really do, I just don't like the way men lock us into them.

SECOND WOMAN: Or the way they unlock us.

THIRD WOMAN (*judiciously*): They do keep you warm.

I: Men?

SECOND WOMAN: It wouldn't matter if you could wear whatever you felt like, but you put on whatever you think you're expected to, a dress to go out in, bellbottoms for work. It's not you.

I: But doesn't it just knock you out when you remember that underneath the clothes everyone is naked as a jaybird?

FOURTH WOMAN (*pacing regally in a caftan she'd brought back from a parent-sponsored trip to Tangiers*): Think, sisters! Think it through. . . . If it's just a matter of expressing ourselves or keeping warm, why are we made to feel so insecure about our appearance?

I: If you mean our collective appearance, you don't look too insecure to me.

FIRST WOMAN: Well, I am. My mother wanted me to be this very classy chick, Vassar and a high color in my cheeks and short fingernails. Like that. But I have these big boobies *(glancing down at them and quickly away)* and no matter how I try to disguise them I look more maternal than she does.

THIRD WOMAN *(solicitous):* Have you tried a no-seam bra?

FOURTH WOMAN *(who, I'd learned from the Third Woman, was a radical painter engaged in "making" art):* A man designed that torture device.

FIRST WOMAN: You can say that, you've got a nice-size bust. Without a bra I feel like there are two of me, the clumsy one in front and the real one behind.

I: Things could be worse, you could be in my shape. Without a bra, I'm not all there, there's a communication gap between me and the fabric.

SECOND WOMAN: I never wear bras. I haven't even shaved under my arms or on my legs in over a week.

(Group is thoughtful, mulling over new information.)

I: How does Sweeney feel about that—

SECOND WOMAN: He spends a lot of time smelling me now. Believe me, he really flips out on it.

FIRST WOMAN: Isn't it uncomfortable?

SECOND WOMAN: No, man, it's great, odor is an important dimension of life, it's one-fifth of your capacity for sensual perception.

I: She means the hair. Doesn't it scratch?

SECOND WOMAN: It's very soft, silky, and the only thing is, it collects moisture, and that's what makes the smell.

FOURTH WOMAN *(smelling Second Woman):* Beautiful, baby!

I: But *Cosmopolitan* says the natural look is dead, we're supposed to be into the forties' look now.

FOURTH WOMAN: How can you read that trash, Tennessee!

I: In a consciousness-raising session, you're supposed to offer testimony, not lay your value system on us. My view is, who wants to look like a freak? You've got to keep up with these trends.

FIRST WOMAN: But sometimes you just can't. If you've got big breasts, you just can't look classy.

I: Class is not the trend.

FIRST WOMAN *(tearful again):* Then why did Jerry tell me I'd make a great two-dollar whore?

FOURTH WOMAN: I wish this group could keep its eye on the ball. How the hell did Jerry get in here?

I: You didn't really think it was her mother that was behind this complex?

FOURTH WOMAN: If you'd stop reading *Cosmopolitan,* you might find time to read a little Freud.

I *(angry):* Radical schmadical. Siggy was an incorrigible romantic with a literary flair and a great need to justify man's ways to God.

FOURTH WOMAN: You really think you're hot stuff, don't you! Don't you think we all know that? But the point is that women have been compelled to look at themselves from the viewpoint of the male establishment, and consequently, all mothers undervalue their daughters.

I: Sure, but that's only the beginning. What happens then is that every daughter comes by her revenge willy-nilly, which is by watching her lovely mother grow old and die, and that's where the guilt comes in that makes us hate the way we look. Our own beauty is an ill-gotten gain. And we can't even refuse to get what we got. *(First Woman starts to weep.)*

THIRD WOMAN *(rising, stepping over the coffee mugs on the floor, and putting her arm around First Woman's shoulder):* Go ahead and cry if it makes you feel better.

FIRST WOMAN: I feel so ashamed. . . .

THIRD WOMAN: Oh, don't be, we're all your sisters, we'd all cry if we knew how.

SECOND WOMAN: Right on.

FOURTH WOMAN *(looking at me):* Some of us don't seem to understand the purpose of consciousness-raising. Some things are better left unsaid.

❡ No kidding. Even I knew that. Even I knew that was one of the reasons I tried to make a joke out of everything, though come to think of it, lately the jokes were turning sour. But in this great organic equation (riddled with variables) that I had got hooked up with, wisecracking was the factor that saved me from an untoward reaction, a chemical combustion, a fatal confusion of my specificity with the makeup of all the other women I knew. If I am spelling this out at too tedious a length, make allowances for a med student: my bent is practical, or even philosophical, before it is psychological. And this fact, and factor, was not something I had learned from my crash course in carbon compounds but was too hard won (introspection is not what I like to do most) for me not to be impressed with it. It was, however, much easier to apply to my "peers" than to Lulu Carlisle, who held so much power over me, not least of all the power she derived from the pity I felt for her; and even where it was easy to apply, this salve of joke, snack of retort, this mathematical constant, even there it was apt to rub the wrong way, go down the wrong way, or result in the wrong answer. Only half seriously, I asked Max what she would do if someday she had the option of earning a couple hundred thousand extra a year just for performing abortions. "You know what I say whenever I gotta pay some stupid doctor's bill?" she said. "I say, *Check enclosed,* and sign it, *Yours for socialized medicine.* Tennessee," she said, laughing at me, "I have to tell you something. You are never going to earn that much money, not if you live to be as old as my Uncle Moishe. Something, or if you get lucky, someone, will screw you up." She grinned. "As a Long Islander, I can tell you that moola like that just has never been programmed into your Appalachian genes." I laughed too. "I kid you not," she said.

❡ At the first motel Maxine waited outside while I went in to ask about the rates, but the lobby held half-a-dozen honeymoon couples, so we drove to another. We had turned the radio off, and now, at the edge of the Eastern seaboard, the silence was the silence one would encounter at the edge of the inhabited world, if there were still a point at which it came to an end. "This *is* the end of it," Max said, though I was not yet convinced. The second motel, set back from the sea, overlooking a marsh, was cheaper and emptier. The lady who signed us in had curlers in her hair and that made me feel secure but Max said I was too class-conscious for my own good. We let ourselves into the room and I hung my clothes in the closet while Max, exercising the Long Island School of Thought, unrolled a napkin full of silverware and brought in thermoses of orange juice and coffee. After inspecting the three dresses I'd packed for two days in Provincetown, she handed me a long-sleeved undershirt, explaining that she'd thought an extra might come in handy. I asked her if she'd forgotten the chicken soup, and she got mad and went in to take a shower. The bathroom was clean, the water hot, the room nice, but now that we were here, there, we didn't know what to do next.

"We could go to a movie," I said.

"The last time we did that it freaked me out."

"It doesn't have to be that kind of movie."

"What about Norman Mailer?"

"He's probably not sunbathing," I said, looking out over the ice-sheeted marsh. "He's probably at the movies."

"Movie," she said. "There's only one. Throw me a towel."

"The town may have grown since your parents were here."

"I checked it out with my travel agent."

"The Long Island Approach to Life is stifling me," I said. "I'm going to take a nap."

"Do me a favor," she said, slamming the bathroom door in my face. "Forget to wake up."

¢ When I woke up, Max was sitting cross-legged on her bed, fiddling with the guitar. "I'll bet you couldn't play 'Come to Jesus' in whole notes," I said, intending to be funny, but shocking myself by the abrasive timbre of my voice.

She looked at me. "There's a lecture tonight," she said skeptically, "at the Fine Arts Workshop." I'd heard about the Workshop in a letter from Adrien; it's a center that underwrites young (immature, Adrien thought, but then, Adrien always thought that) artists and writers for a year at a time. "Who's reading?" I asked.

"Horace Hathcock."

I tried to think what underground magazine I might have seen his poetry in. Adrien had sent me to several—unpublished himself, he was constantly letting me know what he thought (usually ill) of whoever was getting published. The name didn't ring any bells.

"Not a poet," she explained. "Oceanographer."

"Of course," I said. "That explains everything."

"Norman Mailer might be there. The sea is the next big frontier after space."

"It's not as phallic," I pointed out.

"No," she retorted. "Just amniotic."

"You win," I said, extending my hand.

She shook it. I went into the bathroom to take a bath, insert my contacts, make up my face, put up my hair, perfume, and dress. "Tennessee," she said, observing my toilette, "this is not Tennessee."

"I know. Nobody dresses up in Knoxville."

"That's not what I meant." I found out what she meant when we went outside. It was snowing to beat the band and the tempo of the wind, I swear, would have shamed Toscanini himself. The streets were deserted except for the main thoroughfare, where the wind collected a few hip kids like dust in a funnel. Blown about, their bellbottom levis acting as sails, they turned up the collars of their pea jackets and headed into the harbor of the coffee shops. Max pulled the car around to the front of the Fine Arts Building, and, getting out, we followed signs down the street to the small hall where the lecture had been booked. Near the entrance my heel slipped on the pavement and I nearly went down but caught at Maxine's sleeve so that we entered arm in arm. It was a small hall, crammed with wooden folding chairs. Max wanted to sit in back. I wanted to sit up front. "If Mailer is here," she argued, "you don't want to miss him."

"If Mailer is here," I said, "I don't want him to miss me."

"You do your thing," she said, unzipping her jacket in one practiced pull, "okay? And I'll do mine. Besides, my hands are acting up." She grimaced eloquently. "I may have to split from this joint if the pain gets to be too heavy." I thought that was really sinking low: I had made up my mind long ago that the recurrent pain in her hands was psychosomatic, an excuse to fly youth-fare to Frankfort for acupuncture before CBS found out about its news value, and the reason she dug acupuncture was that at the conclusion of each treatment she was given an herb which she brought home so her mother could burn it, according to instructions, in a pretty Oriental ("Made in Japan") jar behind her daughter's neck, fanning the fumes around front toward her knowledgeable nose. The herb smelled suspiciously like grass, but even if it wasn't, imagination and memory were the way Maxine—and her mother—could take a trip now and then without getting uptight about the whole drug scene. I didn't want to take her special little racket from her, but did she have to remind me that it was also her car and her willingness to drive it that ever got us anyplace? As if I were an obstacle in the road. I didn't answer. She chose a chair in the back and I moved down front. The place began to fill up, the men mostly middle-aged and weatherbeaten, their women still liable, I was sure, to the Mann Act, long Indian-print skirts straggling beneath yellow slickers. I had wanted to be such a girl but bore a closer relation even now to Sue Carol than to them, was born uptight, and, uptight, wondered whether Max was so peeved as to leave the lecture while my back was turned and leave me stranded among aliens. I tried to look back at her without her noticing it but when I peeked around she was staring straight at me, dark eyes bright as black sunspots. I looked away. If Norman Mailer was there, he was not coming over to me. Someone turned off the overhead lights and someone else made a cute introduction studded with inside jokes I couldn't follow and Horace Hathcock emerged from the slide projector to place both hands on the lectern as if by not letting go he might pilot the evening's passengers safely between the Scylla of his stagefright and the Charybdis of his compulsion to explore and extol the coast he so transparently loved. Alas, Horace was no Greek. Bandy-legged and grizzly-haired, he seemed instead that Ahab of my heart and captain of my fate who drew my deepest and most secret sympathies, not Gregory Peck, not Norman Mailer, but the tough and wise and single-mindedly farsighted father-lover whom this age of technology and the nuclear *Nautilus* had so brutally discarded, erecting in his place the make-do figure of an overweight Jew with classical education and the naïveté of an American with which I must needs content myself and indeed on honest days admit was almost as inaccessible as the richer romances of an even deader culture. Here I was, as ever, humble, and longed for my paunchy, aging amalgam and was resentful of Horace Hathcock's mythical detachment, the definition that straightened his backbone and steadied his voice, the knowledge of a life energetically lived and not unpleasantly got through and the serenity of a sex that was source now only of some philosophical amusement that precluded me from any importance. To old Hathcock's eyes I must look a child, the tides and movements of my mind made no claim on the climate of world opinion, lacked the depth and breadth of the Gulf Stream that showed schematically in thin white lines against the blue of the slide on the screen, smarting my sensitive lenses. Yet I knew, whether the world did or not, that there were storms in my soul which required some accounting, and talent for navigation, and demanded some attention, if only in necessitating the search for a yellow slicker or black raincoat with which to shield myself from myself; and without, I think, undue self-aggrandizement, I endured such submarine upheavals with a certain calm, a little humor, a clever acquiescence to their turbulence ("riding with the waves"), and derived from them a kinship to my fellows in

Atlantis which a few of them at least appreciated me for acknowledging. "You do, don't you?" I would pump Maxine, when we were through with our little spell of bitching at each other; "you do appreciate me?" It was this self-seeking, self-serving, never-satisfied question I was projecting against the immediate future that my anxieties aimed toward when a member of the audience, raising his hand in the fluorescent light that had a second time (I knew and resented) usurped the pink from my wilting cheeks, asked if bad weather in the sky churned up the insides of the sea the way it screwed one's logic and stomach: "Does atmospheric disturbance," he asked, "have an effect below the surface?"

"A good question," Hathcock said, making me feel at once that I had fallen short in not thinking of it but only of more petty matters such as myself. "We might say," he said, making me think indeed I was doomed to drown in a flood of irrelevant statement, "you could say that whatever happens in the atmosphere is paralleled undersea. But whatever occurs within, say, a day in the sky, roughly speaking, requires three days to come to completion within this vast body of water." He snickered in manly fashion. "Which is so seductive to we sailors," he added.

How could a woman compete with an ocean?

"Well," Max said, as we were leaving, "too bad."

She meant it was too bad Norman Mailer hadn't shown. "All the same," I said, "it wasn't a total loss. We learned something."

"Yeah?"

"For one thing, now we know why human beings are always a little slow on the uptake, wisdom-wise. It figures," I said, "if a month on the outside lasts three in the mind." It was an attractive notion, only slightly removed from what Horace Hathcock had actually said. "Do you realize, Max, if that's the case, a person beside himself is one up on the rest of us!"

She threw a spitball at me and watched me squirm as it plummeted down the neck of my blouse. "Anyone who's ever done time in a bughouse," she said, "coulda told you that."

❡ On the Craziest Ward, you were not allowed to brush your teeth because you might harm yourself with the toothbrush or the tube of toothpaste. She told me she had dreams of O.D.'ing on Crest. I said she was making that up after the fact but she swore it was the truth. The proof was that she had had to eat out of paper cups because no utensils were allowed, and was awakened in the middle of the night for a compulsory and unnecessary trip to the bathroom, where her escort stood guard. If that is a humdinger, the story that got to me was the one about occupational therapy: how they were returned from insanity to society as useful citizens by stuffing piece of paper upon piece of paper into envelope after envelope, and all the pieces of paper were blank, and all the envelopes were without address.

❡ In the morning we went back to the Fine Arts Workshop, where, we thought, the bulletin board might tell us something about Mailer, his comings and goings. A kid came into the front room and without ceasing his business, which, near as we could tell, was a matter of shoving some canvases around and gathering up the tools of his trade from various tables, said what could he do for us, nobody else was there. I told him we wanted a list of the visiting authors scheduled for the spring session. He asked if I was published. "I'm a med student," I said, "and my friend here is an auto part deliverer." I couldn't resist feeding his sense of superiority.

He said we were barking up the wrong tree.

Affronted, Maxine turned inward; I saw her slink away, as with all her solidity she could come and go like a shadow, another of the tricks she'd learned in Bellevue. "I sold an article recently," I said, "to a magazine called *The Male Bag*. But you probably wouldn't be familiar with that publication."

Smirking, he said he knew it very well.

He had pimples on his neck and slanted eyes that reminded me of a mongoloid child who'd lived next door to us before my father was promoted to full professor and we moved to a better neighborhood. I'd never know whether she died or the parents finally gave up and placed her in an institution but could testify that she was a gentle little creature who liked nothing better than a smart push on the swings, provided it didn't send her too high. "Look," I said, suddenly sorry, "let's not play this particular game."

Max moved all the way outside.

"The secretary is on vacation," he said, pompously—as if the secretary were his. "You'll have to check with her." His eyes were opaque, shuttered.

"Thank you very much for your courtesy and cooperation and I hope you stab yourself to the death with that chisel," I said. When his mouth twitched I felt I was victorious. I went outside.

"Hey," Max said, "look what I ripped off while you were chewing the fat with that friendly son of a bitch." She held up a spool of thread.

"What's that?" I asked.

"Thread," she said.

"I mean, what's it for?"

"Your button," she said, pointing at my coat. Little mother! The third from the top was truly dangling loose, ready to spin away like a forgotten folk tale with the next good blow off the beach. I sighed. "I am without charity," I said, "you know that?"

"No man, you'd be a boss mother. I know you well enough to know that."

"I like to have wrung his neck, Maxine!"

"So? Look at it this way," she said. "Just because you'd make a good mother, that doesn't mean everyone else necessarily is going to be a good *child.*"

❡ Although I didn't normally lay my school life on Max, that was all the encouragement I needed to talk about the clinic. Most of our kids—the older ones, which were the ones I saw—were black; there was only a sprinkling of Puerto Rican and there were even fewer middle-class white kids who needed free contraceptives and didn't want their parents to know. We ran group sessions, dispensing advice and the contraceptives, but left group therapy per se to private practitioners: there was no room for it in our clinic, and anyway, the kids seldom needed it as badly as they needed the more immediate guidelines for survival we provided, tips on how to apply for a job, caveats to steer them clear of the drug culture, and an ongoing sales pitch for dental floss inter-digitated with advice on general health and hygiene. When I say "we," I really mean the nurses. The nurses were phenomenal. I sat in on their lectures and took their advice to heart, discovering that even for myself the street language it was couched in made it much more comprehensible, when I could get used to hearing it, than the diluted Latin in which such matters were spoken of everywhere else in the hospital complex. *Morning drip* and *the clap* were—almost—music to my ears, because then I knew I would get to watch a G.C. (gonorrhea check), though I shied away when one of the doctors, responding to one teen-ager's complaint of a sore throat, got set to run yet another G.C. (That teen-ager knew something I didn't.) I backed away, plunging my hands into the pockets of my white lab coat, which I never failed to wear whenever I was in the clinic since it made me feel as though I were actually a responsible member of the team, when pretty much all I did was poke my nose into this and that. Some-times I was permitted to take a kind of cursory physical, but the doctor always did his review. It was during the physicals that I sometimes got to talk with the kids, and got to know some of them, and got attached to Roberta Rodriguez. She was on the Pill, and had to report every three months so we could make sure she was taking it faithfully and had not developed any untoward side effects. Also, the Pill, at least more often than not, increased the alkaline balance of the environment that the gonococcus might find itself in, and might then thrive in. Roberta would lie down, and I would make a preliminary palpation of the thyroid, breasts, and inguinal glands. I had done this kind of thing (physi-cal examination) so rarely that I was still amazed at how little relation to reality our transparent classroom models bore. One neat little item in the female sexual store was regularly missing from those models, I suppose because it paid out to the wrong person, or maybe just because it played no necessary role in reproduction and wasn't too likely to exhibit any pathology, not so anyone but a gynecologist would notice, anyway. After a while, I got over the shock of seeing real live naked women other than myself. (I never got over the shock of seeing myself. I no longer had a mirror in my room at Lulu's and had disregarded our Lib group's suggestion that we learn to look at our own bodies. "As women"—what else?—"we need to get acquainted with our physicality," the Fourth Woman said—repeatedly—with matchless eloquence. Suddenly I had visions of Anna and the King of Siam singing "Getting to Know Yourself." A nice movie that would make.) But the tough part was only beginning. Roberta would be lying there, an incipient Miss Subways, popping her chewing gum and tapping her foot in the stirrup, utterly self-controlled, until the doctor walked in to do the pelvic. Then every time it was the same thing, even with Roberta, who by now knew better: the Puerto Rican kids, no matter how sophisticated, were terrified that spirits would enter into the womb and take over (over what? the government of the menses?). I never did learn exactly what the story was—only received excited chatterings about spirits and demons and how the IUD was a trick of the devil. For this reason many of the Puerto Rican girls opted for the Pill—the pelvic was only once every three months, but the IUD haunted the uterus all year round and ought to be self-checked weekly, a schedule which would involve enormous risk to the womb-spirit avoider. I might not sound so heartless or seem so lacking in understanding if one of the kids had ever explained to me what the deal was; I couldn't even get Roberta to tell me, she said she didn't like to talk about such things. For the same reason they rejected tampons, though they caught on quick enough that one way to alleviate cramps was by practicing a bit of that liberation which Peter and my fellow feminists endorsed.

Roberta, calmed, got dressed, filling me in on her love life while pulling on open-crotch panties. Her dreams of class were still superficial. I wasn't about to abet her social grandiosity by clueing her in on her *faux pas*. Rising above mere class distinctions, I asked her where I could buy some *faux pas* for myself. But I never did, because I had no one to wear them for, and, coming from Tennessee, caught cold easily; instead, I stocked up on Vitamin C tablets. Roberta was as healthy as the horse of another color (coffee-and-cream). She never did get any kind of V.D., at least not as long as she was visiting the clinic. But when *Cameron* thought (proudly) that she needed a Wassermann test for syph, she refused to go to "Tennessee's h-h-hospital," and I had to take her in a taxi down to St. Vincent's on Twelfth Street. Smiling up at the lab technician, she stumbled and had to be helped into the chair. I rolled up her sleeve. Her biceps were just a smidgen overdeveloped to compensate for the leg, while the crook of elbow, turned upward to the needle, revealed vulnerable thin skin and made her seem as defenseless as a child, but her blood was fine. Lulu had let us put the test on her Master Charge.

❡ Maxine, lip curled, shoulder hunched, chin up, gaze direct, seemed only sporadically ten years my junior. Every so often, when I was too plainly wishing I had a man beside me rather than Max, she turned defensive. "This is a stupid town," I said, hugging my cup between my hands. We were sitting in a fake-o coffee shop that had benches instead of chairs and beer barrels for bar stools and was crowded in the corners with little groups of hip he-men, guys with movie cameras in tooled leather cases and blue eyes rimmed red from dope. We were waiting for one of them to mosey over in our direction. "Nobody is very aggressive here."

"I like Howard Johnson's better."

"You would." I frowned at her lack of upward mobility.

"I'm also hungry and they only serve clam chowder in this joint."

Someone who could have been Roman Polanski's second cousin from Cracow was ostentatiously ignoring us. "Somehow, the thought of Gino's depresses me."

"Maybe it's because we're not on our second honeymoon," she said, and I realized I'd better pay her some mind and suggested a steak.

But the steak house was nearly empty, and as we took our seats at a wooden table in the center of the room, gazing at each other over the candlelight so rudely caught in the old-timey kerosene lantern, our speech dwindled to a whisper. Max tucked her napkin into the neck of her blouse; I placed mine in my lap; and the waitress, when she finally chose to wait, looked us over with violet-fringed eyes, revealed a dimple, flicked her ash on the floor, and said, "Have you two got a place to stay?"

"It's interesting," I said, pleased to find we had a friend in Provincetown, "that you should ask that. I was just thinking—"

"You were thinking—"

But the planes of her face were smooth and variegated, and I was surprised that the waist-length hair wasn't violet to match the lashes.

I harrumphed. "I was thinking," I said, to prolong the conversation, though I had been thinking nothing of the sort, "that you might know, being as how you are evidently a person who lives here, it seems, how a person would go about finding a place to live here, year round, that is, and what your average rent would likely be. Would you?"

"You're a painter?"

"Yes," I said, not wishing to attempt another sentence in the presence of so perfect a judge.

Max snorted.

"New York?"

"Yes."

Max snorted again. She picked up her water glass and drained it.

"Femme?"

"What?"

"Femme."

Max was staring hard at the third diner in the room, a young man.

"I'm sorry," I said, "I can't seem to catch what you're saying." Max was making it no easier for me.

"F-e-m-m-e."

"Oh," I said, experiencing a certain *déjà vu.*

"I'd like mine rare, miss," Max said.

"Because if you're not," Miss said, "the friend I have who rents cheap won't rent at all."

"Well done," I said.

"I'll bet you're from someplace else originally." She stamped out her butt with her sandal-shod foot and helped herself to a cigarette from the pack I'd put out on the table.

"Down South," I explained, still whispering, "we're squeamish about eating anything that might still be alive."

The pretty face pulled itself into a moue. Turning to Max, I saw that her own face had screwed up tight, the black eyes become burned-out fuses. "Turn on the lights," I said.

"Huh?"

"Let me see what's passing through your brain."

"I was thinking that that is a nice-looking fellow over there," she said. "He seems lonely."

❡ Peter had told me that a guy who looked sad invariably was. (The same does not hold true for women.) I went over and introduced myself to Jonathan and he seemed relieved to be able to join us for coffee. He was twenty years old, hailed from Harvard, had come to Provincetown on a whim. The collar of his shirt was immaculate, the macramé belt was brand-new. I asked him what he wanted to be. He said, "Rich." I wished him well. Maxine said she knew just how he felt.

"It's agony," she said, trying to sound like a coed, "feeling poorly."

"Poor," I said.

"That too," said Jonathan, annoyed that I had made a joke at Maxine's expense. He was decent—but wrong. I was thinking of Lulu and her wealth. "It's not money I'm after," I said.

"It's Norman Mailer," Max explained.

"Oh, do you know him?"

"No," I admitted.

"I hear there's a place called Piggy's," Jonathan said. "We could check it out, maybe Mailer hangs out there."

"Jeez," Max said, "how'd you know about Piggy's?"

Jonathan cleaned his fingernails with the toothpick. "You dig sound?" he said.

"Right!" she said.

"Bessie Smith?" he asked.

"Yeah!" she said.

"Coltrane?"

"Whoo-ee!"

"Is that what they're teaching at Harvard these days?" I asked. "Jazz?"

"The way I figure it," he said, "there's going to be a renaissance in jazz, and if somebody were smart, they'd start reissuing the great ones. With just a little capital, you could make a pile."

"Wow," Max said, "you are all right, Jonathan!"

He blushed.

I flushed: Jonathan was turning out to be a formidable fellow. Maxine's black eyes shone with the reflection of the candlelight. I started stacking dishes on the table.

"Did you think it over?" the waitress asked, approaching with the check.

I had forgotten her, yet, nudged, was reminded that her brows were so beautiful that there had to be worse things to look at on an idle night. They were raised in an attitude of disdain that let me know she knew it. "Think what over," I said.

"What I said," she said.

"Oh," I said, "yes."

"And?"

I saw Maxine's hand dive in the direction of Jonathan's knee.

"Do you know how to get to Piggy's?" I asked.

❦ Piggy's, it developed, was a roadhouse that looked for all the world just like the roadhouse at the end of the road we'd lived on when we were living next to the mongoloid idiot and I was still in grade school. My kid sister and I used to walk up there after school for Zero bars and potato chips and Pepsis, which we'd bring home to eat while sitting on the furnace grate that divided the living room from the dining room. It kept us warm and cozy and we made it through the Nancy Drew stories in record time. But sometimes when we went up to the end of the road the tavern would've already begun filling up with its nighttime customers, and Peg, the henna-haired divorcée, would be sitting on a stool, nibbling at pickled pig's feet, or Ike, the innkeeper, would be talking with his wife, whose name I never learned, while the wife, sitting on a stool, listening, would be casually crushing beer cans with one hand and piling them up on the counter, and one of them, Ike or Peg or the wife, would give us an extra dime to play Shoot-the-Bear. We took turns with the dime and kept a running score on a little pad of paper that my sister carried around in the drawstring purse she'd woven of white rope in Vacation Bible School one summer. She was a strange kid with an early inclination to mysticism, not to mention a very fast trigger finger. "It's my turn," she was quick to say, hefting the rifle to her armpit. I dropped the dime into the slot. "Son of a gun," Peg said, "that little girl is goin' t' be a real tiger of a lady." My sister took aim and started shooting at the little bears as they sped across the lighted backdrop; one by one, they keeled over. Peg patted the kid on the head and Ike gave her a free piece of dried venison. I thought it was a bit much when my sister continued to capitalize on her success at home; she told the folks, and after that, she was known around the house as The Tiger Lady. "Shucks," she said, modestly, "I didn't do nothin'."

"You didn't do anything," I corrected her.

"I did too," she said. "You can't shoot half so good."

"Well."

"Well, nothing. You can't and that is all there is to it."

But there was more: the killer was that she looked like an angel, so that no matter how cloying the cuteness got, I had even then to recognize something celestial that transcended mere sweetness. You had only to look at her to see that here was a child whose physical connection to the earth was indeed tenuous, the body almost insubstantial, the mind aglow, and the will one which brooked no interference from outsiders, nor even, actually, from her own family. At the age of five, for example, she'd decided she should have a new hat for Easter. "Don't be silly," my mother said, snapping at us after a long morning of trying somehow to obtain a little more for a little less, "we're Pelagians, not Presbyterians." My sister went into the store anyway, and since she was only five, we had to follow her in.

"Just where do you intend to wear this thing?" my father asked.

"To church." She had found the one she wanted. It was a straw sailor with a yellow ribbon that circled the brim and trailed down her back and would flutter in the breeze.

"You don't need a hat for Sunday School," I said, envying her exemption from the eleven o'clock service; I was old enough to go to both.

"I know," she said, "I'm going to church." Then she set $1.19 in pennies on the counter. I shrugged and said there were some things a kid sister had to learn through firsthand experience. One of them was that the Settleworth family was looked on by its neighbors with a suspicion which was only strengthened by the inability to prove its heretical inclinations. The preacher shook my father's hand every Sunday, but when my mother said, "Good morning," the preacher's wife barely nodded. No one made a special point of complimenting my sister on her new hat; no one even asked her first name. She was in tears on our way home.

"Well, Tiger," my mother said, "that's what comes of associating with full-fledged Christians."

"Easy does it," my father said; "you may think it's funny to tell the girls we're Pelagians, but the truth is we're hypocrites. And so long as the state of Tennessee pays my salary, we can't afford to forget that."

Tiger wiped her nose on the long yellow ribbon. We understood: the conversation was now between our parents. Without saying a word, she left by the back door. "Leave her alone," my father said, settling down to read the paper, "she'll get over it." But by suppertime there was still no sign of Tiger. "Where could she be?" my father asked, working hard to keep his tone professorially dispassionate. "Call the police," I said, hungry for drama. "Check the roadhouse," my mother said. Sure enough, we found her in the tavern, sitting on a bar stool, wearing her sailor, supervising Ike as he swept out the floor for the coming week. "What are you doing up here on a Sunday?" my mother demanded.

"I'm in church," she said, "and the cong'ration admires my Easter hat. Don't you, Ike?" There was a beer can on the counter in front of her. I was sore as a scab that my kid sister should get to taste the stuff before I did.

"Sure as shooting, I do. That's a fine hat."

"If I am a P'lagian," she said to my mother, "I gotta have a church to be it in."

Ike turned to my father. "Listen," he said, whispering so Tiger wouldn't overhear, "the kid's a little tight, but it weren't much, and darn it all, she was crying up a storm!"

"I can imagine," my father said, he and Ike commiserating as if they were both powerless in the presence of the Eternal Feminine. After all, I thought, she's only five! Evidently, Mother was thinking the same thing, because she scooped Tiger up from the bar stool and said we were going home.

"First you gotta tell me one thing," Tiger stalled, and while everyone else was looking at her, waiting to hear what the one thing was, I sneaked the practically full beer can into my coat pocket.

"Ask me anything," I said, doing the vamp via my Gloria Grahame voice (with the novocaine lips). "You wanna know what a hypocrite is?"

It was depressing to have a kid sister whose mind was always on profounder matters than one's own was. If it hadn't been for the hidden beer can, I would have felt downright defeated. She slid down my mother's length and stood in the center of our quizzical circle. The expressionless stare she answered me with said she already knew what a hypocrite was. "But what's a P'lagian?" she asked.

❦ "Pelagius was an Irish apostate of the fifth century"—I could reply now, if I didn't know my sister had probably long ago researched the question in depth—"who, like dissenting Irishmen ever since, in time forsook the Oulde Sod for points south, wending his way first to Rome, thence to Africa and Saint Augustine, and ultimately eastward where he was never heard from again." Messages he might have sent undoubtedly were intercepted and destroyed by the Perplexed Penitent himself; and if I overstate my case against the Bishop of Hippo, it does no one any harm, least of all the institutional church, since my hyperbole should be easily dismissible by the orthodox as sour grapes. On the other hand, I may not have exceeded the truth by so far as you might think. Sanity, as history shows, is seldom welcomed, and Pelagius, as lone spokesman for moderation in all things mystic, had been barely bidden eat and sleep and eat again—a late breakfast—before being urged on his way. It was a humid morning. "Mystery is everything, all is mystery," Augustine said, splitting the word into sharp syllabic splinters meant to prick and pinch the voice of reason. "The miracle of Christ cannot be denied lest the love of God reduce to a system of checks and balances." (Of course neither Pelagius nor Augustine caught this reference to political democracy, but we will.)

Pelagius clasped his wrist with his hand. These talks made him nervous, particularly when they took place in the hot sun. He found it quite sufficiently mysterious to find himself in this alien land, beneath this tremulous palm, its fat leaves sweating in the heat, to find himself stubbornly admitting ignorance of the noetic illumination which could have allowed him to say, compelled him to say, "Augie boy, you are *so* right." He could say only: "Father, forgive me, but I believe you may have mistaken my point?" If he sounded stuffy, it was because he had never learned how to be impolite.

But Augustine would point out that he, Pelagius, was hardly the *Rationes Aeternae*. What made an Irishman want to tax his poor brain so?

"If evil proceeds from the supranatural," said Pelagius, "man's moral autonomy is imperiled. . . . Surely it is illogical if not unethical to plead an inequity in nature as the excuse for imbalance in the sphere of human choice. With the dogma of original sin, you say that we who die do so because we are, alas, morally imperfect, but that through Christ there is redemption and resurrection. And when my soul ascends to Heaven, shall I then be free from biological blemish? Why not? You have confused your categories!"

Augustine narrowed his eyes. "Moral philosophy is the province of Jews, Stoics, and Skeptics, my son. I too should prefer to see good come to the good and punishment befall the wicked but God in His mysterious wisdom has seen fit to foreshadow our life in the next world by life in this rather as figures cast by children in a lantern-play dip and curtsy indistinctly on the screen of a sheet." The Bishop stopped for a moment as he thought unwillingly of certain sheets he had lain on, but there were times when self-castigation was an indulgence, and this was one of them. "The same distortions hold," he explained. "To project the understanding we arrive at in our earthly voyage forward to the City of God, to equate the Divine Mind with the human, to assume that what is temporal is more than temporary, is the grossest error of pride. In delimiting God's Being, you violate the first of the Commandments you are so touchingly concerned to justify with this pragmatic eschatology of yours. *God* doesn't need your paltry affirmations!" I had to admit this last was an impressive point, but wondered if I would have been as wowed had I been more familiar with the Catholic line. I wondered if Adrien, for example, would agree with Augustine when he said, "Salvation is by grace."

"Works."

"Faith."

"Good works," Pelagius said, correcting himself with that intellectual caution which was his salient characteristic. Instinctively I sided with him, if only out of sympathy for the underdog, and, fifteen hundred years later, suspected Saint Augustine of being guilty of condescending to us both in charging his colleagues not to assume "that heresies could have arisen from a few beggarly little souls. Only great men have brought forth heresies." It was a cheap puffing-up of his own position that the Bishop accomplished, and I, arguing for the privilege of responsibility, would remind him that the atheism he feared Pelagius might encourage in his followers, or I in my fellows, was only a mood, a given temperament like "sanguine" or "phlegmatic," a humour that might be opposed to an inherited predisposition to religiosity, an aggravation of blood and bile that might be easily remedied with a little hardship or tempered by a little humiliation, but Pelagianism rightly comprehended was the advocacy of Act and as such deserved better than this sly refusal to take it seriously. "Bring him back," I'd tell the Bishop of Hippo; "hurry, before it's too late." But Pelagius was even now receding into the distance, head bowed beneath the freight of free will, the large questions of good and evil, right and wrong, life and death buzzing around his brain like a fly in the desert sun around carrion, continuing, after fifteen hundred years, on his way, motivated, I thought happily, by a sense of direction no less accurate for being less dependent on his vision than on a desire to keep his feet on the ground. I hoped he had reached his destination, however far from the Celtic hearth. I hoped Byzantium had embraced him in her bosom. I hoped he'd found friends special enough to compensate for the loss of family.

❪ "Nobody's home," I said, peering through a crack in the boarded-up window. The place was deserted; there was a sign on the door that said the owners had gone to Florida and would return with the summer season. "I guess your travel agent forgot to check out Piggy's," I said to Max; and if she would normally have reacted with anger, she was now too attentive to Jonathan to work up any hostility. This was a new Maxine. "You might as well drop me off at the motel," I said, "and go to a movie. Or something." Jonathan thought he should make some objection and hemmed and hawed. He was obviously a well-bred boy. I felt I should be pleased to see him holding Maxine's hand, but instead I felt old. Left out. At last I understood why it was bad manners to coo and bill on public streets. Maxine, too young to share the prescription for behavior I had grown up with, must still have sensed my uneasiness, because she said, "Come on, Tennessee, you know I don't groove on flicks."

"So go fly a kite," I said, "I would just like to be alone for a little bit." It was true that I hadn't been really alone in months. So after they'd left, I locked the door (a hangover from the habit of fear I'd picked up in New York) and bundled myself in blankets like an Indian, having first capitulated to the warm undershirt Max had had the foresight to bring, and poured black coffee into the red plastic cup that came unscrewed from the thermos jug, sat up on the bed (again, like an Indian), and settled down to take stock of where I was and where I was going. But I was out of practice and couldn't think cogently but only found myself turning again and again to recollections of Bernie which against my will merged with my daydreams of Adrien, until I was helpless to stop myself from being carried along the course of Expectation

to the great ocean of Deliverance. I don't mean anything dirty. I
mean I discovered I had submerged all serious reflection in im-
ages of white satin and lace and meeting Adrien at the altar. I
thought, wryly relishing this pose I had adopted, warming my
nose in the steam from the coffee cup and wringing my metaphor
dry, that I was drowning in my daydreams. Had I been a woman
of will, I'd have thrown up sandbags and blockades, a logistical
barricade, against my wishes, the better to review that long-lost
relationship with Bernie. But then I thought, dropping my metaphor, and almost my coffee, in precipitous enlightenment: that
was *why* I had so much trouble trying to reason out the past. It
was past, and how on earth was I going to get it to flow backward
and uphill into the dam I'd finally gotten around to constructing?
On a paper napkin torn from the roll Maxine had brought, I
made a note which I meant to transfer to my prayerbook when
we got back. "Having a kid can give meaning to the future, but
only the future can give meaning to the past." I would have liked
to discuss this subject with Maxine, but she had something else
on her mind. "Shut the door," I said, "it's freezing in here."

Max slumped onto her bed; she was still wearing her black
leather jacket.

"Coffee?"

She shook her head no but reached for a cigarette from the
pack I'd left on the nightstand. "Hey," I said, "you never smoke."

"Now I do." She had started to turn green.

"Oh brother. Your folks will think it's my fault."

"Don't worry, my folks think everything is *my* fault."

I thought we'd horsed around long enough. "Look, Maxine," I
said, "you just met this boy tonight. There hasn't been time for
a trauma!"

"I'm not upset, Tennessee, I'm just down. Don't I have the right
to be down once in a blue moon? You think you are the only
person in the world that was ever down?"

I admitted that I had known many depressed persons in my
time.

"I'm just down, that's all," she said.

"Okay, okay."

"Jonathan Zucker, in case you'd like to know, is an okay dude."

"A little young," I said.

"From your point of view."

I said I was pleased she'd found somebody she liked. The sobs that shook her then caught me off guard. "What's *wrong*, Max?" I entreated her. She was a strong young woman and even cried heartily. "This isn't like you. . . ."

"Yeah, well maybe you don't know me as well as you think you do! Like maybe I'm scared Jonathan Zucker will forget all about me as soon as he gets back to Harvard Schmarvard!"

"Maybe he won't," I said. "Forget."

"It's not like Long Island is crawling with cats who know what jazz is all about, you know."

"I know," I said, nodding my head. Maxine knew I hated jazz, so if she didn't feel my sympathy was any the less on that account, I assumed it was enough.

She stuck out her tongue and said, "Yecch," and stubbed out the cigarette. "We might as well turn in," she said.

"Right!"

I wanted to ask her whether she'd gone to bed with Jonathan, but she volunteered nothing and I knew better than to pump her. She kept these matters to herself and I knew only in a general kind of way that she considered herself reformed but felt she had to keep herself under constant surveillance to ensure that she toed the line which in her youth (!) she had complained was never straight enough for an ordinary eccentric like herself to see. "Crooked, crooked, crooked," she had said to the nurse on the Craziest Ward, and when they refused to listen to her, she escaped to California with a friend she'd made in the asylum but who had been released first. They probably never would have found her but she turned herself in, after riding Greyhound all the way back to New York, and the doctor thought this was a sign of sanity and let her out again. Max said it was a sign of compulsive cleanliness because the reason she hated California was that it was full of pigs and she'd had to spend all day cleaning out the commune, including the barn, since no one else there cared whether or not there were rat droppings in the dinner. "Not that Bellevue was much cleaner," she said, "but at least in Bellevue I didn't feel it was my responsibility." I switched off the lamp on the stand between our beds. I was feeling pretty confused myself, as if my life was slipping gradually out of control—and had been for several years, at least from the time I met Bernie. I wanted to know whether that was a sign that I should sign into Bellevue. "Go ahead," she said. "You're crazy if you do."

❡ The local stores were open on Sunday. We loaded everything in the hatch so we could leave as soon as our shopping expedition was over. First, though, we stopped at a diner where Max watched me try to eat a stale doughnut; she had already met Jonathan for breakfast and seen him on his way. "He said he'd look me up on Long Island," she said.

"It beats chasing Norman Mailer around Massachusetts."

"Hey, man, I'm sorry that didn't pan out."

"Oh, well, that's all right," I said, soothingly, "these things never turn out the way you expect them to anyway."

She flinched, as if I'd struck her, and then said, with ostentatious stalwartness: "I guess not."

I would have had to be sadistic as well as dense not to know that she wanted encouragement. I paid the cashier and carried my doughnut out with me, shredding it into tiny pieces that I dribbled along the sidewalk for the winter birds. "We'll buy you those clothes we've been talking about," I said, "and then all you have to do is sit back and wait until he sees you in them." And by golly at my insistence we found a sweater that had a couple of very real advantages over the black leather jacket, although she was still worried about whether it was right to make use of them, and a crocheted skirt, and even a dress. Bitching about the money, she blushed and forked over her Master Charge. Her nonchalance unnerved me. Unlike Max and Cam, and in spite of having taken out an educational loan, I couldn't stand living on borrowed anything. Certainly not at eighteen percent. I was proud of it, and that, of course, was a laugh, since *I* was living on borrowed everything, my status—and independent intelligence—about on a level with that of an indentured servant. The only thing *Lulu* had borrowed was time, though we didn't know that yet. And Willa Mae never borrowed anything at all; she waited until it was given to her and then accepted it unconditionally (a great gift, to be able to receive). The clerk stamped the ticket with Max's card. Max hadn't said a word while we were at the check-out counter. "Suppose he doesn't look me up," she said, finally coming out with it.

I tried to make a joke of her anxiety. "That's a risk you have to take," I said, "when you live on Long Island."

We dumped the packages in the back seat of the Fiat, strapped ourselves into the front, and left, neither of us laughing, each thinking her own thoughts. Some time later, approaching New Bedford, Maxine said, "Would it be like horrendously uncool to invite him on down? I'll just bet he'd really dig seeing Mr. Five-by-Five at the Half Note, for example. Don't you think he'd dig that, Tennessee?"

I nodded. "Let's eat here," I said.

She turned into a district of warehouses and discount stores pitched steeply toward the harbor. "Or there's Slug's. I haven't been to Slug's since the early sixties, but with Jonathan along, it'd be okay."

"You really want my advice?" I asked.

She nodded. "Watch out!" I shrieked.

"Don't yell at me!" she yelled.

"Why are we doing this?" I said, still shrieking in spite of her warning. We were speeding down the hill and had just missed riding up on the sidewalk.

"The brakes are gone."

"Maybe Jonathan will come to the funeral," I said, bracing my feet against the floorboard as if I might be able to will the brakes into working.

Max was rotating her hands on the wheel, one over the other in a rapid motion that explained why I wasn't any more frightened than I was. "I'm not *really* worried," I said, just in case she might feel I'd lost confidence in her expertise.

"Just worry about jail," she said, as we came to a halt at the bottom of the hill next to an abandoned warehouse. The siren at our backs blew up into a whistle and then thinned out again into silence.

The cop didn't like us. "Hippies," he said. "Let's see your license."

"The brakes gave out."

"Who's your friend?"

"Mary Settleworth from Knoxville, Tennessee."

"Cat got her tongue?"

"Please, Officer," Maxine begged; "she's just out of the hospital and doesn't feel too hot yet."

"Me neither. I thought for sure you two was going to jump the curb."

She smiled weakly. I growled.

"What's wrong with Mary?" he asked. I thought he was a nosey cop.

Max pointed her finger at her head.

"That the truth?"

"A bad trip. You know, Officer. Acid. She was in the hospital for months."

"I knew you two was hippies," he said.

"Oh no. Someone spiked her drink but neither of us would ever knowingly partake of any kind of narcotic, you name it, uh-uh." I thought Max was overdoing it.

"Yeah, well," he said. "I ain't got no use for hippies so you get them brakes fixed quick and get Looney Mary home, you see?"

"I see," she said. I looked at him and crossed my eyes. He tilted his head back and looked down at us, scratched the netherside of his shaven chin, shrugged, and walked away. We drove back to New York that evening and parked the car in a garage and went to Steak and Brew to avoid Lulu. I knew she would want to hear about our journey, and, more to the point, complain about my having taken it. I didn't need anyone to tell me that being alone in the city on a weekend could be a bum trip—I hadn't completely forgotten the bad time I'd had After Bernie Left and before I got acclimated to Mount Sinai. And I knew I was, if not the cause of, at least the spark which more and more often ignited Lulu's discontent so that it tended to flare up whenever I was around, though when I tried to cheer her up, she always contradicted me and said she felt fine, as if the center of all this confusion might lie in the simple act of contradiction and as if her complaining might be simply a methodology for self-definition, even, in a peculiar way, a kind of creative aggression insofar as it set her off from all the cheerful (Cam), unflappable (Willa Mae Wood), dauntless (Max), and half-witted people she was surrounded by. But what was I to do? Because of Max, I couldn't ask Lulu to come with us to Provincetown, not even had I wanted to. She would gripe about the car, its size and faulty brakes; she would demand air conditioning in the dead of a Down East winter; she would freeze when Jonathan Zucker spoke to her; and neither Max nor I would be in a position to talk back the way we did to each other. But when all was said and done, I still knew my absence hurt more than my presence rankled. I could sympathize with that feeling at least, having experienced it myself when I was living with Bernie and he was out all day and half the night hanging around Columbia in case of riot, or writing press releases for (innocuous) subversive newspapers on paper napkins in the West End Bar. I began to think living with anyone had to be like that, a contest between resentment and gratitude. I supposed, with sudden inspiration, that Adrien had sized it up in much the same light. Max disagreed: she said what it came down to was that anything she liked doing alone she dug even more with somebody else. She heaved a sigh out over my plate and I put my fork down and suggested we do something else, since brooding was one thing I preferred to do alone. We walked over to a King Karol to look at records and Max bought a couple and then we went into a White Tower for a cup of coffee. "Hookers," Max said out of the side of her mouth, tilting her head in the direction of a booth occupied by four attractive women whose ages must have run the range between Max's and mine.

"How do you know?" I asked.

"Footwear. You can always spot a streetwalker by what she wears on her feet." Sure enough, each of the girls had sought to outdo the next: gladiator boots and four-inch wedgies, backless clogs and open-toed saddle shoes. "Oh, Max," I groaned, "I didn't know! I always went barefoot in my imagination."

"Those chicks over there are for real," she said. "Hookers need coffee breaks just like everybody else."

"I wonder if Mr. Carlisle originated any of those shoe designs." By the time Max and I got back to the duplex, strolling, with magnificent abandon, the whole way up Third Avenue, trading comments with the cowboys and sounding all the parking meters we passed with the coffee spoons we'd snitched, Lulu was asleep. We entered an apartment that was thick with the odor of marijuana, dark as outer space and silent as the sea. "Listen," I said, "do you hear it?" Seeping through the wall to my room was the voice of Marlene Dietrich peeling off—one by one, as a stripper sheds her high-rise tight-fitting gloves and black silk stockings—the stanzas of "Falling in Love Again" from *The Blue Angel.*

"Meshugganah," Max whispered, when the tune came to an end and forced us to face each other in the feeble glow of the lamp I'd lit. She raised her voice. "Ah, you're trying to spook me!"

I laughed, feeling relieved, feeling . . . spared. From the premonition that had just then passed by so swiftly on the outskirts of my consciousness, though at the time I didn't admit even that much to myself. Max seemed to be having an even harder time shaking off the strange sensation. She shrugged her shoulders, spread her arms, satirized our uneasiness, and at last succeeded in severing it from ourselves and moving it out into the world at large: "So if I'm a traitor to my sex I apologize already," she said, "but sometimes you can't help but wonder whether all women are born crazy."

❮ FIRST WOMAN: I don't think so; society does it.

SECOND WOMAN: Doesn't it get monotonous to blame society for everything? After all, who *is* society?

I: I know who society used to be. Debutantes and little old ladies and Junior League volunteers. That was before society lost its class.

THIRD WOMAN: I don't want to be critical, Tennessee, but sometimes you seem to willfully misinterpret what we all say.

FOURTH WOMAN: Well, I *do* mean to be critical. This is a serious business. We are testifying on the topic of female neuroses, and anyone who isn't interested in getting at the truth can get lost.

I *(muttering):* Female neuroses! We aren't menopausal *yet.*

FOURTH WOMAN: Wait a while, you will be. *(Unable to resist the remark):* Sooner than the rest of us.

I: That's hitting below the belt.

FOURTH WOMAN: In your case, close to home, Tennessee.

I *(realizing that in the end she and I were going to have to come to a showdown):* Why have you got it in for me? Huh? Just tell me why!

FOURTH WOMAN: You're not on our side, Tennessee. Even if you think you are, you aren't. All you really want is to get married. Can you think of a single solitary bride who ever led a revolution?

I *(insightfully):* You underestimate me if you think that's all I want. In fact, I'm less sure of wanting marriage now than I was *(not if it would restrict me the way life with Lulu did)*—and surer still that change begins at home. *(All these squabbles were beginning to turn my stomach, I felt sick.)* I'm in *favor* of the movement, sister dear. But it's not enough. You want the truth, the truth is that every time I go away from these so-called supportive rap sessions in a state of severe depression.

FIRST WOMAN: I'm always depressed. *(Short pause until Third Woman, asking First Woman how come, nudged us all back to our primary purpose.)* I never felt I could do anything worthwhile.

I: What would you like to do?

FIRST WOMAN: Something worthwhile.

I *(doggedly)*: What would that be? *(Seeing her ready to say there was nothing worthwhile she could do)*: Assuming for the sake of argument that you *could* do whatever it was that you wanted to do which was worthwhile.

THIRD WOMAN *(gasps)*: Tennessee!

I: That's my name. What's my game? *(They obviously weren't going to let me stay in their group much longer anyway, so I had nothing to lose.)*

FIRST WOMAN: I'd like to do a dance or sing a song, or something. *(As a budding contemporary choreographer, she "did the dance," and as a child of our civilization, she wrote primitive folk songs.)*

I: But you *do* do those things.

FIRST WOMAN: I mean, a real dance or a real song.

I: Just one?

FIRST WOMAN *(in faint dulcet tones that could hardly be discerned)*: I'm not greedy. Just one song that would say something to someone.

SECOND WOMAN: Right on! Something that would communicate your definition of yourself to someone else.

THIRD WOMAN *(thoughtfully)*: Maybe that's the only way you ever find out that you're alive.

FOURTH WOMAN *(briskly)*: What a woman wants, then, is to be allowed to exist.

(Long pause while everyone ponders the profundity of this statement.)

I: That's not what I want.

FIRST WOMAN: What do you want, Tennessee?

I: Immortality!

❰ Even I knew it wasn't forthcoming. In fact, I was pretty sure that—just as Max seemed bent on plunging as far as possible into the conventional as a means of escape from that fictive commune that still loomed in her background—that my demand for life eternal, however cute, was an ordinary reaction to an ominously persistent sense that death was following me down every path I walked. I had thought that was only a metaphor for female paranoia. ("Rape don't bother me none," said the lady to the interviewer, "because I don't mingle. It has something to do with the company you keep, and me, I don't keep no company.") I didn't know how close on my heels death was. When the phone rang in the middle of the night and the operator told me to hang on for a transatlantic call, I thought it was my sister. It was my mother. "Hi," she said.

"What's wrong?"

There was terrible static; I asked her again—screaming into the phone loud enough to wake the dogs and start them barking but not, I knew, loud enough to stir Lulu—"What's wrong? She's not getting married so soon? What time is it over there?" I lit a cigarette. "What's wrong?"

"Your sister's had a skiing accident," she said.

"How bad—"

"She made it through the night." I realized it would be early morning over there. "She and Octavio had gone skiing on Mont Blanc." Static had turned to tears, and much as I had expected them, and as much as I knew I would shed my own as soon as we hung up, I found I was, ashamed though I was to recognize it, embarrassed . . . uncomfortable in the presence of my mother's lack of restraint.

"Is she still . . . in danger?" I asked.

"Fractures." My mother wept: "Fractures everywhere, legs, skull." There are two hundred and six bones in your typical skeleton. I waited while Mother got hold of herself. "Your father's with her now."

"Where are you, exactly?"

She told me the name of the hospital and the town. "When the worst is over," she said, injecting her voice with optimism as if she'd just noticed its pallid tone and felt obliged to pep it up on my account, "we'll move her to Paris. To the specialists."

"Is there anything I can do?"

"Study," she said.

"What about Octavio?"

"Octavio?" Her voice was getting vague again and I realized she wanted to be where she might be needed. "You'll call me?" I asked.

"We'll keep in touch," she said, the vigor of her voice almost convincing me (not quite) that she had recovered from the shock. Then she said good-bye. I put the receiver down and put out the cigarette and took out my prayerbook, copying into it the note I'd jotted down in Provincetown. Not wanting to tear sheets from the prayerbook, and, suffering a peculiar paralysis of life though not of limb, unable to reach for my Silver Bear Spiral Binder, I used the flyleaf of the book Dr. Goldberg had given me, which was near at hand, to start drafting a cablegram to my sister. All at once I observed that my fingers, gripping the ballpoint, appeared, in the lamplight, to have aged—without any advance notice that they were going to do such a thing. I felt they had double-crossed me. Here I was, running around in Mayor Lindsay's sandbox (no disrespect to him, only to his playground), still a student, still, in many ways, I thought hopefully, a girl, and yet my hands had gone and got all red, the veins blue, the palms penciled with numerous fine lines, the backs of them, once cushioned, now translucently onion-skinned. In a world fraught with every kind of terror, it did not do to trust even your own body. Defeated, I set aside the draft (the attempts at sibling humor) and called Western Union, where a young woman listened unmoved to my inelegant but heartfelt sympathy for my kid sister and plea for a rapid recovery and then correctly but without the slightest indication of interest read the whole of the cable back to me for confirmation. "You got it," I said.

"Fine," she said. "What number shall we bill this to?"

❡ My number was unlisted. I had even, acting on the advice of the gruffer of the two installers (he had a daughter of his own), omitted the number from the little round card at the center of the dial. "You never know what kind of sickening creep might could come in here and commit it to memory," he said, hitching the tester back onto his belt. Not until after he and his partner had gone did I find myself wondering what kind of men they thought I entertained. Luckily, Adrien had thought to write down the phone number I had sent him—I wasn't sure he would, but didn't want to seem overanxious by asking him if he had. (The sort of mental overkill one supposed no *man* ever needed to engage in.) When he called then, and said he was in town and would like to come up to see me, I was as disbelieving and unprepared as if I hadn't spent months waiting for him to do just that. I wasn't even sure, at this point (mid-January), exactly what he had in mind —whether he only hoped to restore the warmth to a friendship that had for a while been cooled by his more intense tie to Bernie, whether he was looking for the kind of pseudocommunal involvement that, in the absence of a political context, often foments poetry, or whether he wasn't looking for anything at all except a chance to chew over old times with someone who'd known him when. Or almost when. When I had first met him, he was a senior at Vanderbilt in Nashville, startlingly brash for the tubercular-type chest and pasty face that had since, I knew, acquired an authoritativeness—and vigor—that I was not alone in deeming attractive. He was a few years younger than I (but wasn't everyone?), so that back then he'd been really little more than a kid: the meager physique quite predictably elicited my maternal instincts—and every other girl's. It didn't take any of us very long to decide that the antagonistic manner sprang from an overweening sense of his own shortcomings. As the son of a druggist in Baltimore, third-generation, French-Catholic, and lower-income, he was so sure of his social inferiority that he assumed he was under par in every other way as well—well, almost every way. There were enough females around to reassure him on *that* score. But no number of scholarships—and he had them all, they rained on him—could convince him that he deserved them. He assumed that the scholarships, the grades, the awards could only be evidence of a gross injustice in the world which anyone who was at all shrewd (he knew he couldn't say "smart," for that would subvert the rationale underlying his entire lifestyle) would manipulate in his own interests . . . for as long as possible, though surely doom lay in wait around the corner. I had come to "know" all this by way of Bernie, and to some extent, through my correspondence with Adrien himself, and freely extrapolated from it to interpret other points of Adrien's behavior. I figured, for instance, that it was his fear of being stupid—or even just not quite brilliant—that compelled him to write poems. If you are a poet, you can always tell a critic, "If you know so much, *you* write one," or say to a doubter, "Look, that's what *my* aesthetic experience felt like," but a doctor sure can't tell his patient to get lost. Again, I figured it was his fear of wearing the wrong tie with the wrong shoes that had led Adrien to open-necked wool shirts and bare feet even before Jack Kennedy's inauguration and the advent of the flower children. I had indeed followed Adrien through several sartorial transformations already, the most recent—over two years ago—calling for a Borsalino hat and a fabulous, broad-shouldered, buttoned-up, self-fabric-belted trench coat that either had come from a thrift shop or, handed down, disclosed at least one thug in his totally typical American family. "Does your father remember the Valentine's Day Massacre?" I had asked him. He said I was sentimental. "Funny," I said, "Bernie used to say that."

But even if I misjudged the source of his literary impulse, even if I was wrong about the etiology of his dandyism—and I allowed for the possibility of each only out of politeness—I was positive that what inhibited him in both was some extreme sense of outrage, of anger, that neither sonnet nor style could contain. "What are you so *mad* about?" I asked him, when we'd run through the formalities, the pleasantries, and the gossip, and had begun to . . . feel each other out. The winter sun clarified every object in my room, the wallpaper flowers, the books, the telephone, each an island surrounded by cold clear white light. I simpered slightly, as if to say I wasn't making a *serious* (heavens, no) indictment of his temper.

He turned to ice, the features of his face hardening to a strange, forbidding smoothness. His eyes dazzled me. He was wearing, this time, black chinos and a white sweatshirt, tangerine boots he'd found in one of our city's public trash baskets and polished to a fare-thee-well, and he carried, in his knapsack, the fruit and Familia his Adelle Davis diet *(Let's Eat Right to Keep Fit)* demanded. He was into Health. "So am I!" I said, but he said, his voice distant, his glance mocking, "An apple a day keeps the doctor away," and reached for one and bit into it.

"Bernie always said you were an angry young man," I said, getting a little annoyed myself.

"Bernie never met anyone who wasn't."

"I guess," I said, "Bernie and I were alike in certain ways."

"The main difference," Adrien said, assenting, "is that you're a woman."

So he had noticed. "Is that why you're mad at me?"

He laughed, chomped on the apple, choked. "I'll bet you feel pretty proud of that crack, don't you? You've gotten pretty sophisticated living up here, haven't you?"

I was beginning to be afraid that he wouldn't, or couldn't, deny my accusation. But I'd known two or three of his girl friends in Tennessee; Bernie had known others in Maryland; and the flex of his wrist as he threw the core into the waste can was as streamlined as Wilt Chamberlain's. For all Adrien's loveliness, his altar-boy profile, there was a precision of line and an economy of movement that rescued him from effeminacy. The soft curve of cheek, melting into the small curve of chin, was lent a supportive cast by the set of bone beneath it, high and contemptuous—and I didn't like it. In my daydreams and fantasies I might be susceptible to the sadistic patriarchs, the sea-captains and obsessive-compulsive landed gentry who functioned as romantic models in this post-chivalric Western world, but up close, in real life, I felt something was missing—some simple fellowship that would equalize the emotion each of us was, or wasn't, investing. With a start, I faced the possibility that the letters Adrien had written were mere amusements, or a chance to play at involvement without having to lay his cards on the table—or his head on my shoulder. Maybe I was a fool to believe that any poet would ever tell the truth: his letters were never meant to be taken literally. Maybe I had let my imagination run away with me (to Nevernever Land). Most of all, I couldn't see why Adrien glared at me, as if he wanted me to know that nothing I could ever do would redress the (unnamed) offense that had, somewhere along the line, been dealt him.

"I'm not glaring at you," he said.

But I was convinced he was, and if he wasn't the source of my conviction, then probably I was myself. The only thing I could think of that might lead me to feel I deserved his anger was a sinking suspicion that my desires were stronger than his, therefore excessive, therefore blamable, therefore unattractive. I kept waiting for him to throw a pass but he just sat there, cool as the cucumber which, he had informed me in one of his letters, was not nearly as rich in nutrients as the cucumber people would like us to believe. He had written this with complete earnestness and with a warmth that I wished had sprung from a contemplation of my own garden of delights. His was very much on *my* mind, a tree of knowledge that I had mulched and pruned for months in my nighttime thoughts with the ultimate plucking yet to come. It wasn't fair for me to have to do all the tilling, to have to prepare the ground the whole way; the energy we put out was unequal, like positive and negative charges. Yet the tension *was* exquisite: painful in itself, it was a relief, a respite, even, paradoxically, a rest, from the uncomfortable but unchanging life I led with Lulu. "I was afraid that was how you would see me," he said. I asked him how I saw him. "The way Bernie did," he said. "In his own image."

I had waited too long for this visit to let it skid off onto the wrong track so soon. I tried to change the subject: asked him whom he'd been to see in Canada. "Friends of mine," he said, and this time I was sure I didn't *imagine* that his smile faded. "Draft-dodgers. Why in God's name can't we grant them amnesty?" It was the most concrete question I'd ever heard him put, no metaphor to cloud his meaning, no veil that seemed to have been draped over his mind solely in order to tempt morons like myself into trying, and of course failing, to rend it.

"At least you're out of it. This time, anyway," I reminded him.

He said, "I could never understand how they could ask anybody to kill anybody." I couldn't disguise the doubt I felt. "You think I'm fooling myself?" He leaned back in the chair, his slender feet in the tangerine boots propped on my table. "Maybe so," he said; "Bernie sure thought that if you dug deep enough you'd uncover murder in your soul. I don't think so, though."

"Do you recall," I mused, "that it was you who introduced me to Bernard I. Stein?"

"I saw him yesterday," Adrien said. "He hasn't changed at all. You'd think anyone would have in five years."

"I've changed," I volunteered, but when he asked me how, I didn't know what to say. I didn't know why I had been so eager to disown the past. "Adrien—" I said, but then I realized that I was afraid of rushing things: I didn't want to scare him off. And he glanced at me and then away as if he *was* frightened of me, although I couldn't see why on earth he should be. I thought he could be worried that I might trap him into marriage. Then I thought that was silly: I was thirty, he was twenty-six or -seven, and he knew as well as I did that marriage was perforce on my mind. It might even, I thought, be on his, since all his friends had been getting married, some even for the second time. Was it possible that he was afraid I *wouldn't* be interested in marriage? I thought, *Am* I indeed interested in marriage—as interested as I have always assumed I was? But I knew that whether I was or not (and I didn't really want to have to decide that, leastways not on the spot), I most certainly *was* interested in Adrien. I must have been gazing at him too intently. He asked what I was thinking, and I said, "Nothing," and he knew I was lying, and that set up another barrier between us. He reached into his knapsack and brought out a medium-sized Baggie filled with Familia. I went into the Sun Room and got the carton of milk from the icebox. The dust motes sifting through the streaks of lamplight, the shadowy terrace I saw as I peered through the French windows, called my attention to the time. "Adrien," I explained, hoping that he wouldn't jump up and run off, "I have to go downstairs and eat with Lulu." I didn't want to share him with her. He seemed, alas, glad to see me go away for a while but said he would wait and asked for a bowl to eat his Familia from. He was pointing his wooden spoon at the Baggie full of Familia. I got him one from the kitchen downstairs. "Hang on, girl," Willa Mae said. "Supper is served."

I said I would be right back and she raised her eyebrows at the bowl but let me go. When I returned, Lulu was squirting the juice of a lemon wedge onto her fish and complaining because she'd got some in her eye. "Oh," I said, "that means good luck."

She looked at me suspiciously. "I never heard that before," she said.

Neither had I. "Maybe it's Southern," I said.

"Speaking of Southern," she said, "how about your friend . . . Roosevelt . . ."

If I wasn't ready to reveal the reason for my good mood, I was more than willing to share the mood itself. "Rosie," I said. "I'll get him up here very soon." I picked a bone out of the fish on my plate while trying to avoid returning its perfectly round, glittery, baleful stare. "He's been out of town," I lied.

"If I was you, Mrs. Carlisle," Willa Mae cautioned, "I watch my step wi' this here stranger nigger."

I said Rosie wasn't any stranger.

"He might as well be," Lulu said, and I thought that was so low a blow that I felt fully justified in saying I was too busy to stay down for coffee. I beat it back upstairs and shut the door. It was dark out now. "I have some dope," I said to Adrien, who had stretched out on my bed. "Some really magical dope!" I half expected him to rise, state pleasantly but firmly that he intended only a platonic relationship, and leave. "Magical," I repeated, appalled by the timidity I could hear in my own voice—as if I were trying to bribe him and knew I should be ashamed of myself.

"Holy smokes!" he said, swinging his feet around to the floor. "I'm not going to eat you up."

I let that go by.

"Mary," he said. He had known me first by my true name but usually called me by the moniker Bernie had christened me with (if it's fair to say that Bernie ever christened anything and if I don't have to admit that every other Yankee had the same inversely eponymous inspiration). "Mary . . . we know something about each other, right? At least a little. If nothing else, from the letters. We aren't exactly strangers, so why are you so afraid of me? Why don't you just smile or something and come over here and kiss me on the cheek or something?" It would have been a lovely speech if he hadn't been buffing his boots with the hem of my Army-Navy store-bought blanket the whole time he was saying it.

But I thought, If he can't tell me why I'm afraid of him, we're in trouble. Because I was too afraid of him to tell him why. It was a cul-de-sac. An impasse. A dead end. I didn't see how we were going to get out of it, but, mustering bravado, tried.

"I'm afraid," I explained, "that nothing's going to go the way I planned it."

"How did you plan it?"

"I don't know." He looked impatient. "I don't!" I said. "I didn't *plan* anything, I just sort of—of—you know, planned it."

He sounded like my mother, didactic, saying, "You shouldn't ever plan anything; it's a bad business."

"I don't see how you can just make a sweeping statement like that, Adrien. I mean, there's the Marshall Plan. The Five-Year Plan. The—"

"The Plan to Keep Things from Going According to Plan."

"I already have a shrink," I said, "named Veronica. You don't have to psychoanalyze me."

"I won't," he said, "if you promise not to do it to me."

I promised.

"Not even secretly," he said, tapping my head, "in there."

"Knock, knock," I said.

"Who's there?"

"No matter."

"No matter who?"

"Wrong," I said, insanely triumphant. "No matter what."

He acted like my joking was a detour, definitely to be avoided. "Where," he said, ignoring me, "is that stash of which you spoke."

I got it out and sat on the edge of the bed while Adrien, sitting at the table, rolled a joint. He was practiced, deft. When he passed it to me, he knelt by the bedside, lifting the cigarette up like an offering, a token, a sacrifice. I felt as though I myself had been raised up. On a pedestal, I thought then, and laughing at myself, crashed from it. "You almost had me fooled," I told him.

"How?"

He was staring at me with dilated pupils, each black center a storm cloud threatening the incredible sky-blue of his eyes. He kept changing on me: hot to cool, cold to warm. "What are you staring at?" I demanded, fidgeting.

"Those earrings," he said. "I like those—these—earrings." He laughed. "*Your* earrings," he said, amending himself yet again, and I now noted, as he must've intended me to, the way he'd dehumanized me. I felt like a puppet. His puppet. "You almost fooled me into thinking you cared about me," I said, recklessly, not bothering to hide the bitterness, thinking all was lost anyway.

"And now you realize that I don't."

"You could at least have the courtesy to pre*tend*," I said. "For the duration."

"Duration?" he asked, and then dropped it. It was that—my using the word *duration* and his acceptance of it—which reminded me that we were stoned. He was shaking his head, it seemed to be rolling back and forth, this way and that, like a lightbulb being switched on and off, on and off. "But I do," he said.

"Do what?" I had forgotten what we were talking about, and I wondered what it was he did. Wrote poems. Letters. Talked in riddles a lot. Nothing so special in any of that, I thought, curling my lip.

He stroked my instep. "I do care," he said.

I didn't want to try his patience, but on the other hand, I felt he owed me an explanation. "Then why did you say you didn't?" I asked.

"I didn't say I didn't," he said, "you said it."

I thought it over. It *would* be like me, I admitted, to say something like that. "Okay," I said. "I'll accept that."

He laughed. "Good," he said, getting up and walking over to the table. He reached into the knapsack. "Apple?" he asked. I declined.

"You already had one for today," I said, taking care not to point out that it hadn't kept the doctor away.

"Oh that," he said. "That's just a saying."

"Like good luck for getting juice in your eye?"

"I never heard that before." He settled back in the chair and began to chew. The working of his jaw, slow, precise, grinding, grated on me.

"You chew just like my father," I said.

"It's true," he allowed. "I take a long time to eat."

"Why," I cried, "are we discussing your—your gustatory habits?"

"I don't know," he said, "they interest me. Everything I do interests me. I don't suppose, though, that they can be expected to interest everybody else."

"Adrien," I said, as he finished chewing, "I'm not everybody, you just said you knew that. In so many words, you did."

"It's true, you aren't everybody, you're somebody special." He reached out and touched my arm with his fingers but didn't budge from where he sat. "I don't know," he said, as if considering whether to stop right then, give it up as a bad joke. "This is narcissism. You could be my sister."

"That's not what I had in mind."

"Then come live with me and be my love," he said, "in New Hope. For a couple of months anyhow."

I was suddenly very frightened. "I don't know, Adrien, I don't know if I'm capable of living with anyone any more. A man." I almost explained that Bernie had been a man, but then, Bernie still was one, or at any rate had a wife who considered him one, and Adrien didn't need me to tell him so. I sighed, and forgetting myself, turned to Adrien. Later I realized I must have looked—would you believe—trusting. . . .

For a moment all the glintings and sparks and flashings fell away from his face and I saw how he looked when he wasn't fending something off, or counterattacking. "Yeah," he said, "I thought you might be afraid of that." Such simple concern took my breath away. "It's a risk we'll just have to take," he said. "You too."

I stood up. "It's the middle of the term," I said; "I have obligations here." Everything was moving much too fast. I didn't want to be hurried into relinquishing what I had unless he was going to provide me with something else. Not that the food he insisted on would be any worse than what I was already getting. But just living with somebody was a gamble. Suppose he walked out on me just as unceremoniously as Bernie had? I didn't want to talk about this any longer. I wanted to get something to eat. But bending down to reach for the knapsack, I saw, on the top of his head, like a tonsure, a small spot—about the size of a quarter—where the white-gold strands of his hair had already thinned, foreshadowing an early eclipse to the radiance that was, I lamented ambiguously, his. How sad. Did he know? Of course he knew, I chided myself, and erased the dolorous look from my face in case he also knew what I was thinking: that this revelation of his mortal fallibility only made him that much more desirable. He was to be cherished for being evanescent—evanescent and lovely. "And you know perfectly well," I argued, "that we don't look anything alike." I sat back down. "You don't even have a sister."

"Won't you permit me a little poetic license?"

"Poetry!" I snorted. "I'm a med student," I reminded him, remembering, as I did so, my own sister in a hospital overseas. I told Adrien about her. She was going to be all right—was going to be, my parents had phoned, after many months. "With your thing for angels," I told him, "she's the one you should be seeing." It had slipped my mind, for the moment, that the tree my sister had skiied straight into had knocked out her front teeth, so that she might not *want* to be seen. But then, by "seeing," I really meant "getting involved with to the point of possibly living with," and by "angels" what I meant was the unearthly beauty they both possessed, but I didn't know how to clarify either term. "She's more your type," I said, simply.

"There you go again," he said, seeming, strangely, rather pleased at being so exasperated. I think he enjoyed sounding off —it is, I learned later, something he doesn't usually feel secure enough to do. So, "There you go again," he said, his face lighting up once more, blue eyes shooting off little slivers of light like a child's sparkle-wheel (a toy that, now that I've grown up, has been outlawed in certain states as hazardous). "Psychoanalyzing me." But he couldn't deny, I thought, couldn't very well deny that his letters had supplied me with sufficient data for drawing certain conclusions about what he was looking for in a woman. Not to mention (even if I already have) the fact that I'd known one or two of his girl friends—and Bernie, others. I knew *some*thing about what he was looking for. He was looking for a girl—preferably bright and blonde; but she didn't have to be beautiful—for a *young* girl whose very innocence would infuse his intelligence with the energy with which to inspire hers. *If* he sought her in my eyes, all I could give to him was his reflection searching me. That would make me feel impoverished and ungenerous, but not in any real relation to my own worth. Unfair! I should have cried, and inwardly did. Of course he wanted to know why I wasn't talking to him. I said it was all a lot of talk (I didn't know just what *it* was). "Words," he said, picking his teeth clean of apple-skin, "are the most important thing in my life and you are the most important word in my vocabulary." Now who would've dared ask what word that was! Not yours very truly. He waited, though—he waited and waited until I thought he'd *make* me ask him. Just before I could, he pitched the core, the second core, away, and moved to my side and leaned over me, smiling, and whispered in my ear, whispered through my hair, brushing my hair with the sibilance of his scented breath: "Si-lence." Like that. Well, I heard a pin drop and had the sense to close my eyes. The trouble was, as I'd never gotten the question out, I didn't know whether he had answered it or not. A second time I started to speak, and this time he shut my mouth with his. Sure, if it'd been somebody else, I might have got the giggles then, but my sense of humor seemed to have left me altogether. So I was kissing him very seriously when he suddenly sat up and said he thought I had something on my mind that I ought to get off my chest. "Do you do this on *purpose?*" I asked, words springing into place. He was silent. Then his shoulders sagged and his wings folded and he said: "No."

I wanted to say I was sorry—to say I hadn't wanted to bring him down—but still worried that maybe when he'd spoken of silence he'd been telling me to . . . shut up. I decided it was safer not to say anything. I traced his cheekbone with my index knuckle and shivered with delight at the sensation of heat my skin drew from his. I felt he felt like he was on fire. I scrunched my shoulder a little deeper under his, moved toward him like, I thought (help-lessly), a moth toward flame, and, wrapping my hand in the warmth of the longish hair curling down the back of his neck, pulled his head back down to mine just as Lulu rapped on the door of my room. "Shhh," I said, clapping my hand over Adrien's mouth, though his instinct had been not to answer but to lie as still as if he were playing dead. The pounding at the door was determined, definite, loud, insistent, a polar opposite to the faint breathing of my name—"Tennessee?"—that was all Lulu could manage. I could imagine how uneager she was to act the part of idiot by calling out when no one was there to hear her . . . though who, then, would know she had been idiotic? But the part of her that remembered I had said I had work to do kept knocking, while another part of her told her that I must have gone out and that she should therefore cease to call my name. As Adrien and I lay on the bed, her knocking took on a rhythmic dimension, like the beating of an animal-skinned drum from far off, a danger signal in the slow, steady, savage code of short and long silences that antedated Mr. Morse's handy adaptation of it. There was a moon that night, and though Adrien and I couldn't see it from where we lay, it was by its light that we saw the demonic sil-houettes of the overgrown flora outside my window, a trans-planted jungle rife with Venus's-flytraps and African violets and Cameron's experiment in pot-growing at an altitude of nineteen New York storeys. I could use a pine tree, I thought, a spreading maple, baby's tears. Adrien's breath on my cheek was hot and sour, and cold though it was outside, indoors it was hellish; indoors, I half believed that any moment all our emotions would boil over into some huge cauldron of commonality from which the particularities of our various souls would rise and vanish like mere steam, leaving only the sodden, cabbagelike residue of the ordinary, the inescapable: loneliness, love unrequited, and death. Finally Lulu raised her voice to say, "There's a special on the television that I thought—" but, getting no answer, let the rest go and backed off down the stairs. Tomorrow I would make some comment about having gone over to Sinai "last night."

"You're going to feel guilty about it," Adrien said. "I can tell."

I denied it. "That would be silly." I was sillier than I knew— but still more time would pass before I found that out.

He got up, shrugging, yawning, carelessly stretching the elegant frame I so much admired. I wanted to warn him to watch how he used it, not to wrench or snap or break it or wear it out. Instead I asked him: "Is this just—*ahem*—a casual . . . well, is it just casual, Adrien?"

"Maybe it is, maybe it isn't. If you want to be serious," he said, "come spend the summer in New Hope."

He was fitting the knapsack to his shoulder blades, where wings had sprouted, even transitorily, when we smoked, before it dawned on me that he was getting ready to leave. I asked him then if he wasn't going to sleep with me. He said that would be stupid, or that it would prove to have been stupid if everything turned out to have been casual. I didn't argue. I had enough to think about already, without having to assimilate any heavier action for the evening. I showed him to the elevator: sneaking across to the Sun Room on tiptoe so Lulu wouldn't hear. She was shut up in her room below, undecipherable grunts and groans issuing from the television, past the closed door, up the stairs. The elevator arrived. I smiled at Adrien—and was relieved to see him smile back. He pecked my temple. "I'll be in touch," he said, "before summer comes."

❡ Meanwhile, two continuing courses in the second year at Mount Sinai, an introduction to medicine that included a consideration of community health problems and a course in history-taking, examination, and diagnosis, dovetailed only all too well with what I was doing at the clinic. When I slipped and called the Rodriguez kid "Bobbi Jean," she let me know that I was just like all the rest. "Who are they?" I asked.

"Phy*si*cians," she said. She made it sound as if the word itself was a private joke that I didn't understand.

I pointed out that I wasn't a doctor and wouldn't be for a long time yet.

"You are going to be a good one, then, on account of because you already think just like them. Can I have a cigarette?"

"Don't be silly," I said.

"See what I mean? Rules, rules, rules!"

"You'll stunt your growth."

She did a little shimmy into tight jeans and zipped them up, and shrugging into a wraparound blouse with plunging neckline, gave me the once-over from a frontal point of view. "Is that what happened to you?"

"That is an uncalled-for thing to say!" I sputtered, stung. "Roberta."

"My point is this, Miss Settleworth. You people think the Third World isn't no bigger than the tenements out there"—she waved her hand uptown—"but it is *grow*ing. We are going to take over! And then let's see don't you call me by whatever I want to be called."

I was tired that day. All I could answer was, "Right on."

She popped her gum. "You making fun of me?"

"No."

She thought. "You understand, there isn't anything personal in what I'm saying, Miss Settleworth."

I said I understood.

"God," she said, by way of letting me know that she didn't want to go too far and wind up by making me really mad, "just between you and I, I don't know how you can stand it."

"What?"

"The noise." The waiting room was overflowing with mothers shouting at the top of their lungs in order to make themselves heard over the shrieking and squealing of little children. The older kids stood around quietly, singly or in small groups, as if adolescence had robbed them of their voices for the time being. We didn't take emergencies and all were out-patients, of course, but tragedy turned up here just as it might anywhere else in the hospital complex. Not long ago one of the teen-agers, a sweet, rather withdrawn, rather elegant young girl named Gina, had developed cancer of the vagina. She didn't even weep, but the look of worry that she must have been born with, one which she wore perpetually and which made everyone want to reassure her in some absolute sense, that look etched itself even more deeply into her pretty face as we stood around awkwardly staring at it, or trying not to stare at it. Plastic surgery could reconstruct the vagina but not the uterus, and it couldn't reconstruct Gina's sense of herself either, not completely, not when that ego was so fragile to begin with. But I hardly knew Gina and might never see her again in my whole life; already I was learning that a doctor—or at any rate, this doctor-to-be—had to watch out for an inclination to adopt every child she saw. I would be stouthearted: each kid had special qualities and problems. Gina's particular tragedy was the result of her mother's having been given stilbestrol fifteen years earlier to enable her to carry Gina to full term, and one thing could be said in favor of it: that it was rare.

"What noise?" I asked.

Roberta couldn't believe what she'd heard. "Where's your *ears?*"

"Unlike some people I could name, by one name or two, I am not still wet behind them. Your grammar is atrocious."

She favored me with a look of exaggerated skepticism. "Miss Rodriguez," she said, "may be young, Miss Settleworth, but she don't be stupid by a long shot. You just wait 'til the revolution!"

"Sometime before then," I said, "I'd like you to meet a friend of mine." I walked out the door with her because my day was over too. "Her name is Cameron Carlisle."

"Why not?" she said. *"Ciao."*

"Buenos días," I said. Then on the way home I got to worrying that she might have thought I was making fun of her again.

❧ A few days later Cameron came home for the between-semester break. "Campy!" Max said, when Cam, swinging her bad leg to the front first and then catching up to it with a kind of hop, climbed the stairs and joined us in my room. "How goes it? What have you learned lately?"

"Oh," she said, "I don't read any more."

I asked her why not.

"No one at my school reads. Literature is linear."

I thought, The tedium is the message.

Max said: "That girl is getting too big for her britches." Actually, Cam had lost weight; but her hair seemed not only to have grown but to have expanded. She had frizzed it into masses of tight curls, which, since she was Afro-American by inclination only, wouldn't stand straight up but flared out in long ropes, like yards of pale yellow and pink ribbon with knots in it. She looked like a little girl from a story-book illustration.

"It's nothing to worry about," I told Maxine; I said it wasn't any more significant than, or likely to be any longer lasting than, my own junior-high-school preference for Odets over Tennessee Williams. Max was in a morbid mood. "You renounced your namesake?" she asked in horror.

"I wasn't named after him." Nor was I interested in performing for Cameron, but I could see Max was determined to clown around. Maybe she was trying to cheer herself up, though at the time I didn't know why she should be so depressed. Jonathan Zucker was phoning Levittown from Cambridge.

"Tennessee is a pretty name," Cameron said.

"It's rural, all right. I suppose your school approves of anything rural."

"Why fight ecology?" she asked, her face open and clean, the freckles glowing, glinting, as if the sun shone out from under them rather than on them.

"Because," I said, staring at the ice-slick leaves of the potted plants on the penthouse terrace, "because Old Lady Nature keeps on beating up on me."

"It's the wrong time of year," Max agreed.

"It's the wrong time of m-m-month," Cam said, giggling.

"That's something, anyway," Max said. "It should be that time of month all year round already."

Cam's dimple disappeared. Turning to me, she asked, "Who were you named f-f- . . . after?"

"Ernie Ford."

"Nah. I d-don't believe you, you're putting me on."

"How right you are," Max said. "She was named after Victoria Woodhull's sister, Tennessee Claflin, prostitute, financier, some-time spiritualist, and traveling medicine man who just happened to land on her li'l ol' feet as Lady Cook. My mother learned all about her at a meeting of Jewish Women for ERA . . . Equal Rights Amendment," she added for Cammie's benefit. "Personally, I think the whole Movement is a media rip-off."

"Max! What is *wrong?*"

She rolled over on the bed, lying on her stomach, pillow clasped beneath her chin, the black eyes narrowing. Then she laughed. "Hey, man, we've done this trip before, remember? Like, don't you remember like when you were freaking out. . . ." A note of cynicism crept into her voice, and I wondered if she were blaming me for something. "Wasn't that why we went to Provincetown?" she asked. "In the first place?" I nodded. "Can you dig it?" she asked.

"Sure," I said, "but why are *you* freaking out?"

I knew she wasn't answering me straight; she started picking lint from the blanket, balling it up and dropping it into the pil-lowcase. "Nothing much," she said, "I guess I'm tired of my job."

"What's your job?" Cameron wanted to know. The dimple was

back, she was determined to cheer everybody up.

Max told her: "Delivering foreign auto repair parts . . ."

I had nothing to say to that. I was busy crosshatching the amoebae in an old biology book with a Venus pencil and didn't notice, at first, that Cameron hadn't had anything to say to that either. When I looked at her, she was sitting on the floor in the lotus position. "You're cheating," I said, "you have to bring your foot back under there." She didn't answer, though, and I suddenly recalled Mrs. Wood's story about the foreign auto with which Mrs. Carlisle had, albeit accidentally, destroyed her own family. Cameron's brown eyes had gone muzzier than usual. I tried to change the direction we seemed to be going in. "Guess what!" I said, "I've been reading up on meditation. Edgar Cayce?"

"Who on earth is Edgar Cayce?" Max said.

"It wasn't Mama's fault," Cameron said.

"What wasn't?" Max said. "What did your mother do to Edgar Cayce?"

I went to work on the hydra. But even with my head down, I could tell that Cameron's answer was meant for me, not for Maxine, so finally I looked up and looked her in the eye. She was—I swear to God—smiling again. The smile wasn't just on her face: it was all around her, she was encased in a smile. I doubted if anyone had ever or would ever break through that smile. Lulu, maybe; or maybe she only *let* Lulu think she could get inside from time to time. "It wasn't Mama's fault," Cammie said. "I was seven years old. We had been to visit some friends of theirs and ate dinner. I don't remember their name. On the way back it was raining."

"When did it ever not rain, I ask you," Max said. "The weather stinks."

"That's what Mrs. Wood said," I said.

"I felt carsick," Cameron said. "I was b-bitching about b-being sick to my stomach. Papa, well, I guess Papa was pretty high. Maybe he wasn't, maybe he just didn't stop to think. We always kept a bottle of Pepto-B-B-Bismol in the glove compartment because I had what Mama used to call 'a delicate tummy.' Papa got it out for me and leaned over to spoon it out for me. I was sitting in the back. I said the hamburger we had had for dinner must have been rotten. 'Did you hear that, Lulu?' Papa said. 'She thinks the brains we ate were hamburgers.' His last words were, 'Cute, huh?' I threw up smack between them, all that pink Pepto-Bismol all over Papa's arm, and when he jerked his arm away, he hit Mama's elbow, and she lost control of the car. It all happened so f-f- . . . D-d-do you understand now?"

"No." I put the pencil down. "If you mean do I see that it's your fault, no, I don't see that."

She laughed. "I didn't think you would," she said, the inflection of her voice tinged ever so slightly with that sarcasm which had been missing when I first went to work there, and which never again exposed itself. "I didn't think you would," she said—and I felt as though I had failed her and felt angry that I was being made to feel that way.

"I thought *I* was the one," Max said after Cam had left, "who was supposed to be in such a swell mood. Too bad you took the mirrors down, you should see what that scowl does for your face!"

"If you had to eat brains," I said, "don't you reckon you'd be inclined to regurgitate?"

"Don't be dumb, Tennessee. I'll eat anything." She gave me the Bellevue glare. "Almost."

I suggested we both could use another weekend away from the city. "Maybe winter will leave before we get back," I said, the roach I had shared with Cameron—Max, of course, abstaining, but fanning our dope smoke her way—suffusing even the seasons with a degree of personhood which nevertheless yet eluded some of us who might have liked to consider ourselves more probable candidates for that autonomy than the inanimate and abstract world we seemed to be confined to.

❡ Lulu sort of semi-fell into her seat at dinner. Cam and I were still a little high too. Willa Mae knew nothing, or had the sense to act it. Lulu told Cammie to take her vitamins. She did, but couldn't resist making a face when she swallowed the yeast tablets. "Don't be disgusting," Lulu said. Cam laughed.

"I don't think I am b-b-being d-d-disgusting," she said.

"Well, I do."

"I d-d-don't."

"Well, you are."

"I am not," Cammie said, still laughing. Lulu's face was turning red.

"This here is the silliest fool argument I has heard in a coon's age, and that ain't just jive talk. I be gettin' on in years." Willa Mae said her feet were worn out from walking *Lulu's* dogs in the park and *I* could fill my own water glass. When I got back from the kitchen sink, Lulu had set her fork down. Her head was lowered but we could see that her chin was trembling.

"I just don't like it when you make faces," she was saying. "Do you have to make yourself look so—so grotesque?"

Nobody answered. I looked at Cam but couldn't even guess what she was thinking. Lulu's tears were making the soggy mashed potatoes on her plate more so. I said, "It's because you're high, Lulu; that exaggerates everything."

"Oh, of course," she said. Then we were all relieved that the tears had stopped before they had amounted to much. "But I haven't smoked a single joint today," she said, after a pause, as an afterthought.

❡ That seemed an appropriate subject for C-R (consciousness-raising): I told my Lib group that Lulu Carlisle's increasing vagueness troubled me. Like the suburban housewives we had all read about in Intro to Psych, she cried more and more easily, at nothing, and stopped with scary docility as soon as she was told to. The First Woman said she knew that was a terrible state of mind to be in because she often was. The Second Woman said Sweeney sometimes made her feel like that. The Third Woman said that when she had been married she had quite often felt like that. The Fourth Woman said it was time for "summing up." We had a "summing up" period at the end of each session, during which we tried to extract generalized truths from individual testimonies. It was a little like pulling teeth. This time the Fourth Woman said that what it added up to was that I had encouraged Lulu Carlisle to become dependent upon myself and deprived her of her autonomy. "What?" I said. "Just who is dependent upon whom?" I decided to discuss the situation with my friend and shrink, Veronica. Veronica said something ought to be done —or maybe I was the one who said that—and suggested that I discuss the situation with Cam. Cam didn't want to talk about it. She was busy listening to The Grateful Dead.

❝ I went up to my room to get away from it all. Looking for a weather report on my transistor (brand name El Cheapo), I came across a country music broadcast and stopped to feel a little homesick for Knoxville. But then I had to go and remember that my folks weren't anywhere around there, and face up to why; they were still in Europe. So I turned the radio off and started a letter to Adrien. I wanted to write him my new theory of disease. I didn't deny the existence of germs but merely questioned whether sufficient evidence had been garnered to hold them liable for the common cold. After all, I knew that when I went out into the "poisonous night air" or got wet feet, a cold was sure to follow; but none of the little fellows I'd ever seen under a microscope had ever actually turned on me then and there. I recommended amnesty for microbes—absolution, if it came to that. Aside from complicated questions of Germ Status, however, this hypothesis resulted in the simple and inescapable conclusion that the role of Vitamin C in the prevention and cure of the cold might be in line for some radical rethinking. Then I chickened out and tore the letter up and threw the pieces in the trash basket. There wasn't anything funny about germ warfare, I realized, nor about all the people in the world who couldn't afford orange juice for breakfast, and since the letter in and of itself fell somewhat short of humor, I was afraid Adrien might think I was making fun of him. I was afraid I might be. Maybe I thought I was safer that way—surrounded by a moat of mockery. And maybe no one was ever safe any way at all.

❦ Saturday morning I brought the early edition of the *Post* up from the kitchen after Willa Mae had finished with it—on weekdays she preferred the *Daily News* to the *Times*—and was in the middle of "Safety Hints for City Dwellers" when I heard the elevator man knocking on the door that led into the Sun Room. Among the hints: in case of new buildings going up in high winds, stay far, far away, else loose tools may rain upon your unsuspecting head; in case of strolling, steer clear of doorways and dark alleys; in case of purse-snatching, scream; in case of fire, avoid certain elevators (but the article didn't say which ones). By the time I crossed from my room to the Sun Room in bare feet to let Roberta in, I was anxiety-ridden, and it was still only one in the afternoon. The vibes were all wrong; the whole idea was a mistake; I wished I could call the afternoon off, but I was the one who had set it up.

"God, have you got it made," Roberta said, almost sadly. I was going to show her the view from the terrace but thought better of it.

"Would you like something to drink?"

She looked hopeful.

"Soft drink," I said. She shook her head. I smiled at her—with adult-type poise—and ushered her into my room. "Cammie!" I bellowed from the top of the stairs.

She had been waiting to hear that and appeared instantly. Looking up at us from the bottom of the stairs, she dimpled and waved and said, "H-h-hi."

"You're Miss Settleworth's friend?"

"Cameron Carlisle—Roberta Rodriguez," I said, cracking up.

"Miss Settleworth?" Cam asked, cracking up.

"I don't see what's so ——— funny," Roberta said, in her turn as alliterative as I had been. Her vocabulary was as poor as her grammar, as herself, in fact. She was daring us to answer her.

I said, "We might as well sit down, or something," and while they did, Cameron on my bed, Roberta on the edge of the chair by the table, I put the mandatory record on. I kept the volume low. Downstairs Lulu was watching television.

Cammie waited for me to get things rolling. Roberta looked as though she couldn't care less whether I did or not.

I sat on the floor.

"Well," I said, "how's it going?"

Roberta relaxed, sliding down on her spine, inspecting her long lime-green fingernails.

"That's p-p-p—" Cam said, waving her hand at Roberta's.

"Pretty?" I asked.

She dimpled again and nodded. "Uh-huh," she said.

Now Roberta thought the company was friendly enough to venture a question in: "Where do you go to school?"

Cam told her.

"I suppose that's a school for rich kids?"

"Not necessarily," I said.

"You could come up and see what it's like sometime," Cam added.

"Sure, kid." Roberta was precisely the same age as Cameron. That's why I thought they would hit it off. That, and the fact that each should be able to see from the other that the grass was no greener on either side of the fence. "I can't just split for the g.d. country anytime I feel like it, you know; I have financial obligations, you know. Life can get pretty hairy for we minorities." She came partway out of her slump. "Everybody's got to have their gig, dig?"

Cameron was wide-eyed.

"That's why I have to turn a trick now and then, see what I mean?"

Now Cameron was nodding her head as excitedly as a small child saying yes to an ice-cream cone.

"Come on, Roberta," I said, "knock it off. You never did anything like that in your life and it would make your parents sick if you did."

"Maybe they don't know about it." She got up and walked around the room, lifting one object after another up to the light that came through the window and then setting it down again. "Why, Miss Settleworth," she said, slyly, "if you went and rolled a John or did some number like that, would *you* tell your parents?"

The question wasn't as easy to answer as she assumed it would be, regardless of the many years I had debated it in my own mind. Finally I said no. "But I wouldn't do it in the first place," I complained, feeling misled.

"Would you?" she asked Cam.

And although she couldn't get the words out, there was no question about what the answer there was. The big brown eyes shone supremely, as if affixed to some rare vision of ecstatic religion. I guess it *was* a vision of love, in a way, in which, instead of her having to thrust her worst foot defensively forward, the boys came to her.

"You have good bones," Roberta told her, judiciously. Then she turned to me. "But if you would like my sincere opinion, Miss Settleworth, you would look a whole lot better if you cut your hair. I would be willing to do it for you. Supershort," she explained, lifting the hair off my nape as if testing her thesis. Cameron was shaking her head no. "I'm only sug*gest*ing," Roberta said. She went back to pacing the room. "I'm going to have to leave soon."

I turned the record off.

"Stay for lunch," Cameron pleaded.

"I have an engagement, but thanks anyway. Maybe some other time. You mind if I fix my face first?"

"You don't have to," Cam said; "your f-f-face looks great."

Roberta took a comb from the shoulder bag she was carrying. "How come you don't have any mirrors in here?"

"I needed a change of scenery," I said.

"Phy*si*cians," she said.

"Use this," I said, handing her a tiny plastic hand mirror I fished from *my* purse (the bookbag). We watched her fuss with her hair. She was standing near the window, to catch the light, her torso turned half toward us and half away. "Before I go," she said then, as if she hadn't had the courage to ask us straight on, "can I look at your clothes?"

"Sure," I said, nonplussed.

"Not yours." She returned the mirror. "Hers."

Cameron's wardrobe consisted of two pairs of ancient blue jeans and a suede vest, a bathing suit and a few dresses she never wore. She thought almost any kind of clothing was bourgeois, and was given to trundling around the duplex in her bright yellow knit bikini bathing suit even in February. But we schlepped downstairs to Cammie's room and she and I sat on the sofa bed that was always open, while Roberta went through the clothes in Cameron's closet. I was looking at those incredible hips: they seemed to keep on moving even when she was standing still. Cameron was entranced by them too, I thought, until I looked more closely at Cameron. *She* was looking at the indefatigable foot-patting which pumped the hips, the long legs which propelled their owner unerringly wherever she wanted to go. We saw her out to the elevator on the eighteenth floor. Next to the front door, the door to Lulu's bedroom remained shut. "She's very nice," Cammie said, after Roberta had left. There was a kind of catch in her voice, a small hook of wistfulness like the one that could sometimes be heard getting in the way of Lulu's complaining, so that what came out was torn in two and you could never be quite sure what the complaint was supposed to be about. I said to Cameron, "I'm glad you liked her." She smiled, elusively. I turned into the kitchen to see if Willa Mae had the makings for a bologna sandwich on hand.

❡ At the back of my mind was the thought that in caring about Roberta I was being disloyal to Cameron. Max said it was that kind of thinking which had sent her to the Funny Farm in the first place. "I thought that to be fair to everybody concerned I had to love everyone just the same. That meant my mother, my father, my brother, my uncle, my aunt, my cousin, my camp director, my orthodontist, my *bubba,* and thirty-five in-laws not counting the mixed marriage. You think I'm kidding? All I know is, I was going crazy from so much having to love everybody all the time already. As my *shiksa* sister-in-law used to say, *Oy vey iz mir!"*

❡ After further discussion, we decided we needed another vacation (weekend). But I had spent the money I'd gotten for the first article, *Sexual Inmates: A Cellular Study,* though it still wasn't on the stands, and hadn't finished the second, and Max was thinking of quitting work, so we were cutting the corners as close as we could, and, this time, took Max's outdoor grill and cooler with us to Provincetown, shoving everything into the back, dumping clothes and guitar and the book Max was reading on top. We wanted to be right on the water and again we tried twice before we found a place. The lady at the first motel said we could have a room for twelve dollars. I asked if it had two beds. She looked us over. "I don't allow any guests to bring in nonpaying visitors," she said. "I don't want my motel turned into a bordello."

"How about paying visitors?" I asked, probing her logic.

"No visitors."

"We weren't planning to have visitors," I said, the tightness in my chest squeezing the life out of my voice.

"Just so you got it straight now."

"Look," I said, "we don't even want to sleep with each *other.* That's why we want a room with two singles."

"I think you'd be happier elsewhere," she said.

Max turned and started to walk away.

"No, wait," I said. I said to the lady: "I'll bet you're going to refer us to the waitress's real estate girl friend, aren't you?"

"I don't know what you're talking about."

"All we want is a place to spend the night. We're just as American as you, lady." I laid it on the counter—and on the line. "This is American bread, uh, dough."

"I run a motel," she said, "not the U.S. government."

This was before Watergate and Max snickered.

"No, wait," I said. But the lady rang the tiny tin bell on the counter and immediately thereafter her strong-armed husband materialized in the doorway. Mumbling, I followed Max out to the Fiat. "Don't mumble," Max said.

"I was just thinking of some words Saint Paul neglected to include in his list," I said, speaking up.

❦ We lugged the equipment to the top floor of a Victorian frame house. The back of the house faced the ocean; we set the grill out on the little porch. Below us, winter birds, the first birds of spring, stepped gingerly across the clotted sand. There was a hush about the scene that made me aware of the murmurings of my mind, and prompted me to show Maxine just how silver the sea was, not blue at all, shaded with a touch of green and pink, not a trace of the gray lackadaisically ascribed to all oceans in February. She nodded. "That's very interesting," she said, clearly insulted, "but did you know that you can tell the age of a fish from its scales? Like telling the age of a tree from its rings? That the fish scales have rings in them, like the rings in tree trunks?"

"I didn't know."

Before she could gloat, the landlord, a bearded fairy (bless his everlovin' soul), said, "Whaddaya know! *I* didn't know that."

"Neither did I," I repeated, this time for the landlord's benefit. I was afraid he felt I was against him.

He stood up and made a show of straightening his spine. I had again insisted on singles before signing the register, and when he'd said, tittering a mite, "They *are* joined, but *act*-u-al-ly there are two of them—two beds," I'd said, "Separate them, please," as dictatorially as it was possible to, to so elfin a creature. He'd gotten them apart for the most part but couldn't sever them at the head. "We'll live with it," Max said. "For heaven's sake," she said, *"I'll* sleep with my head at the bottom and you sleep with *your* head at the top and that should do it."

I looked at the triangle the twin beds formed. "I just don't want anybody to get the wrong idea." It had become a point of honor.

"Who could get the wrong idea?" she asked, motioning slyly in the direction of our landlord.

"There," he said. "Just whistle if you want anything."

Then, before we could laugh at him, he revealed that the joke was on us. Stopping on the way out, he peered into the oval mirror which swung between posts rising from the top of the bureau. "That was very enlightening," he said, thoughtfully, "what you said about the rings. Like a woman, don'tcha know." He buried his hand under the beard, stroking, invisibly but unmistakably, the throat hidden there. "One ring at thirty, the second at thirty-five. Three and she's over the hill. You do know how to whistle?" he asked, darting out. "So many girls don't, really."

Max let him get as far as the top of the stairs and then she let out a wolf whistle that would have won her instant acceptance into the construction workers' union. But he was gone, disappeared into the dead of winter. So we grilled hotdogs on the porch, warming our hands by the gas fire, and drank Cokes from the cooler. Max turned the sound on, on her transistor. Late afternoon, the mesmerizing ebb and flow of wave over beach, the slow diminution of the sun—all these glazed room and view and atmosphere with a transparency, like the waxed surface which muffles the sound of a glass dropped, a fingernail tapped, like the one-way observation mirror through which autistic children may be so acutely remarked on and so safely distanced from sanity, like the small plastic amusement inside of which unreal snow falls eternally. Max was listening to her radio. I decided—again—to write a letter to Adrien. "Dear Adrien!" I wrote. "This comes to you from darkest Provincetown, where I am trying to figure out our relationship." It had occurred to me that he could be waiting for me to recover from Bernie and come to terms with the goneness of him, Bernie, that he, Adrien, required proof of my recovery, as of course there were many who diagnosed that attachment as an illness, and for sure it had been painful. On the other hand, Adrien had given me no real reason to think he was waiting for anything other than the right girl to walk into his life and was still waiting even after I'd walked back into it. I crossed out "where I am trying to figure out our relationship."

"This comes to you from darkest Provincetown," I wrote again on a fresh sheet of paper. "Darkest" was cute; Adrien didn't like cuteness; I crossed out "darkest."

"This comes to you from Provincetown," I wrote for a third time. "Shit," I muttered, "the postmark will tell him that." I crossed it out.

Now I was left with "Dear Adrien!" But the exclamation point was working too hard to be cheerful, and I knew I couldn't sustain it anyway, so I changed it to a dash. "Adrien" was silly because he knew perfectly well what his name was. "Dear—" I wrote. As I could think of nothing else to write after that, I put it in an envelope and addressed it and stamped it. "Remind me to mail this in the morning," I said, shattering the sense of isolation we had both been indulging in.

"You ever wonder how Bernard is doing now?"

"Sometimes," I answered, feeling my way into the conversation.

"Why didn't you marry him?"

"He didn't ask me," I said. "Plus, if you want to know the whole truth, he had some very bad habits."

"Like?"

"He was entirely too punctual. He was a great believer in motives. Most of all," I said, warming to the subject, "he wouldn't allow me to be misunderstood. How would you like it if somebody was convinced he knew everything there was to know about you and knew just how you ticked! Tock?"

"I'm asking you to be serious with me," she said.

I said I was. I was.

"Jonathan Zucker doesn't have any bad habits," she said. "Not so's you'd notice them. What would you say if I married him?"

"Why didn't you just ask me that?" I asked. "Why did you pretend to talk about Bernie? You know what I'd say. I'd say you only met the guy a few weeks ago!"

She sighed. She was wearing one of the sweaters we'd bought her on our first trip up. She took it off and pulled a flannel nightgown over her head. "I figured that was what you would say, man."

"Max, has he *asked* you to marry him?"

"He will if I conclude I want him to ask me that. Take a tip. You could do the same for Adrien."

"Let's leave Adrien out of this," I said. "But I want you to know this comes as something of a shock."

She climbed into the bed, toes pointed toward the crotch of the vee. "Wow," she said, softly, "wouldn't I like to be five years old again. Tell me a bedtime story, Tennessee."

"Did the doctors in Bellevue ever talk to you about this Cinderella Complex?"

She threw the book she'd taken to bed toward me and it landed on my half. "How about 'Yellow Bird'?" she said. "It's by your namesake, after *all.*"

I opened the book to "The Yellow Bird" by Tennessee Williams. "What makes you so *sure,* Max?" Indeed, that confidence was very unlike her; and gloomily I wondered if she was right to feel it. No man was wholly dependable. Look at Bernie. Look at Adrien. Look, lord knows, at the first date I'd ever had. Chuck Pryor. I had sat in the living room on the couch, wearing my new navy satin skirt, ruffled blouse, and seed pearls, my father in the big chair, my mother in the smaller chair, sister out of sight around the corner. And sat and sat. The next time he was supposed to call, my sister went on to bed, my mother and father stayed in the kitchen figuring out the tax forms, and I waited alone in the living room, red coat hanging useless and rejected from the coat rack next to the door. Later I found out I had been part of his fraternity initiation. Some first date. But I didn't think my experience had been all that different from anyone else's, and couldn't reconcile it with this new sureness of Maxine's. "Come on, Max, what makes you so sure?" I pressed.

She sighed.

I said her sighs seemed excessive of late.

She said, "Sometimes, I feel like we're just cruising around the way we all did back in the fifties, looking to pick up someone for the ride." I said she hadn't been old enough for that. She said she might as well have been. We went on talking for a little while about this and that, mainly about where we were going and whether it was ever possible to know where you were going and what kind of life would we have if we ever arrived at the Kingdom of God or were ever able to translate heaven into earthly terms. "You never answered my question, though," I said, wanting her at least to acknowledge that I wasn't all that easy to put one over on.

"I got a right to change, you know," she said.

I snorted. "Feel free."

"You too." Her voice was slowing down, she was getting drowsy.

I sighed. "Not I," I said.

"All you have to do is get out of that crazy place."

I thought, Maybe so. But Lulu Carlisle could change too—and not only from "the changes." Her personality was no more static than anyone else's, even given that the changes which took place in it took place furtively, slowly, beneath the bland blue eyes and monologue of complaints, and until I knew whether change was for better or for worse, I wasn't free. I didn't want to burden Max with this—I might in the morning, but not when she was half-asleep. "I thought you were going to read," she said.

The light from the night table bathed her weak arches in a halo; her face, at the bottom of the bed, was in darkness, but I could tell from the evenness of her deep breathing that she was asleep. "Alma was the daughter of a Protestant minister . . . ," I said to the unhearing, recounting the tale of the thirtyish daughter who finally kicked over the traces and left home for a good-time house. Almost everybody liked Alma, in spite of or because of her wild wickedness, and those that didn't weren't worth fretting over. And when she was an old lady and lay in bed, her best, dead lover, father of her son, "appeared, like Neptune out of the ocean. He bore a cornucopia that was dripping with seaweed and his bare chest and legs had acquired a greenish patina such as a bronze statue comes to be covered with. Over the bed he emptied his horn of plenty which had been stuffed with treasure from wrecked Spanish galleons: rubies, emeralds, diamonds, rings, and necklaces of rare gold, and great loops of pearls with the slime of the sea clinging to them.

" 'Some people,' he said, 'don't even die empty-handed.' "

But that meant, I thought, letting Maxine's book slide to the floor and turning out the light, that others did.

6. SUPERSEX, OR WHAT TO DO TILL NORMAN MAILER COMES

Adrien answered my letter: "Received yours and was moved by the brevity of it to reconsider our relationship. (These questions are always questions of duration; how long will it last?) Naturally I went for a walk while doing this. I was walking along the Delaware River and, hearing my footfalls thud softly in the March mud, got to counting all the women in the world. (You know how one rhythm will set up another.) There were my mother, my cousin, Sarah and Sal, Letitia, Dr. Hartly, Lana Turner, and thou, O Tennessee. (Dr. Hartly taught freshman biology at Vanderbilt; she was an ungainly giraffe of a woman five inches taller than I was then and smelled like a candied yam but I swear I was in love with her.) That's not very many (of course I counted only the ones that counted), and I sort of feel there ought to be more but that's not a statement of desire but of obligation. Obligation to whom? I asked myself, there on the bank of the Delaware River in the early March morning that was crisp and chilly around the edges but really rather sweet and liquid in the center."

Adrien had crossed out "in the early March morning that was crisp and chilly around the edges but really rather sweet and liquid in the center." That made me proud of him.

"I'm too Catholic to feel obligated to myself in the current mode (self-actualization, development of my potentiality, etc.) so I wondered if I owed it to God. (The extension of the list through love of mankind.) Obviously I owed God *something,* though what that something might be is something that has had me buffaloed for years. But if Christ died for my sins, then I'd never paid in full for them myself, and nobody ever gets something for nothing, at least not in America, where we've all been taught that if bad luck befalls you it's because you've done something to deserve it and if you die it's because you've sinned, originally or otherwise. Remember the wages of . . . ? Grace does not sit well with the American conscience. At that point—sitting beneath a willow five miles out of New Hope—I realized that I thought Christ was pretty damned presumptuous in usurping my sins when I'd prefer to deal with them myself. But what could I do about it? I could write a pretty little poem every now and then and in that way take my mind off these weightier matters but they were still there and still burdened me with guilt and frustration. I think, Tennessee, that you had better step lightly where you go, and watch your step, lest I dump my load on you when you're not looking. Meanwhile, there's a frog in the river, and he's got a song like a redbird's, but if you can't hear it, I can't quote it. Love, Adrien."

I called Maxine on Long Island, wanting to read the letter to her and solicit her opinion of it, but her mother said she was out on a date. "Oh," I asked, "who'd she go out with?"

"I think his name is Jonathan? Joshua? Jeffrey? Would my own daughter date a Jeffrey? Jonathan, I think."

I called Veronica but her answering service answered. I left a message.

Adrien had never signed off "love" before; on the other hand, when he was telling me that he didn't want to lay his problems on me, the point seemed to be that he didn't want me to burden him with my sundry desperations. Without Max or Veronica to convince me differently, I felt rejected. And this in spite of the fact that my article was now on the newsstands, me, the famous author. But I didn't have anyone to celebrate with, and it was really beginning to eat on me (the spleen first) that I didn't: Lulu wouldn't care, Max wouldn't understand; and while my parents would be pleased when I presented them with a copy, the timing didn't strike me as too terrific. As for Adrien, well, he was the one I wanted to tell, but if I wasn't exactly sure of his affections as things already stood, I didn't dare risk them on a stupid article. He would probably dismiss me along with all those underground poets and Pearl Buck. Thinking about it, I felt more rejected than ever, and decided to take a bus ride down Fifth Avenue, past the Hare Krishna kids chanting and dancing in front of St. Patrick's, past the stop for Ohrbach's, all the way down to the Village; then I started walking back up, which is the best therapy there is for an out-of-towner in New York. There was a suspicion of spring in the air. . . . I decided to go see my old friend Peter, who lived, obstinately, in the west 40s. By then, it was twilight. I was walking past the Forty-second Street Library when I saw, approaching from the opposite direction, my long-lost lover and his wife (I assume she was his wife but perhaps he has a mistress now, or even a female friend), and relapsed immediately into a cold and angry mood all the more virulent for having been almost shaken off. Bernie was wearing Western boots and working-class clothes (but he had come closer to enlisting in the Army than he had to digging ditches) and kept waving his cigarette around like a piece of chalk against an invisible blackboard to illustrate the point he was making, and I knew he was making a point because his flinty little eyes were shooting hot little sparks the way they did whenever he had a point to make. "Hey, Bernie!" I shouted, scaring the bejesus out of myself but prompting him only to raise his head slightly so that his eyes now met mine straight on. I thought with violence how viciously he had seared me. I saw him frown—and thought it was a self-righteous thing to do, as if to say that I, having been rejected and *informed* I was, had no right then to reappear so inconsiderately (bold as you please) precisely here, proximate to the Main Branch. "Hey, Bernie!" I yelled again: "Getting much?"

I ducked into the subway entrance and hid in the ladies' room, leaning against the wall of the cubicle I locked myself into. Yes, I thought, thinking on what I'd just done, that would've swelled dear Peter's heart, and lightened Adrien's, and just thinking on it made mine flutter like a leaf in early spring. "Is you all right, honey?" a voice said from the neighboring stall. "You ain't sick, is you?"

"No, ma'am," I said, "I'se fine."

"Seems to me," Willa Mae said when I got home, "the water's done traveled 'neath the bridge long 'nuff now that you should start to look *a*round now." I was sitting on the stool in the kitchen, drinking coffee and watching her prepare long-grain rice for supper. "What you want is a real man, no more of them hippie-student-types."

"That's all right, Mrs. Wood," I said, "but where do I find one?"

"I don't know, hon, I don't know. It's for sure my Estelle can't help you out there none." She laughed. "At least Stella don't *want* a man. But this house, lord, this house sure does seem to me to cry out for one. I ain't jivin' you, I ast my Doak would he want to come over here and—don't go gettin' on any high horse now—I ast my Doak could he calc'late comin' over here and servicing the women of this poor house."

I fell off the stool.

"It's Mrs. Carlisle I gives the deepest thought to," she went on. "That woman! She jus' like a baby sometime, not knowin' how to get what she want."

"Okay," I said, "I'll call Rosie Jones."

Willa Mae shook her head, diamonds swinging from the earlobes hidden beneath the wig. "That ain't what I had in mind and don't tell me you ain't knowed it, Tennessee. A white lady need a white man!"

I put my question as tactfully as I could. "Since when's Doak changed color?"

"Doak's Doak," she said. She laughed and laughed. "He a rainbow all by hisself! You better believe it!"

"Maybe Rosie is too," I said, in glum defense, not knowing what rainbows had to do with anything.

"Oh yeah? Well, let me tell you, girl, that it be my firm 'viction that that there Rosie have a heart black as the rest of him."

"What's your basis for saying that? You don't have any basis at all."

"I gots lots experience."

"In what?"

She winked. "In th' *ways* of the *world.*"

"Rosie is my friend, Mrs. Wood!"

"But is he the madam's?"

"Talk about prejudice!" I said, slamming my cup down on the counter so hard it spilled. In my head, I told Willa Mae to clean it up: *she* was the housekeeper. The coffee was spreading over the counter, growing slowly and equally on all sides like some brown fungus, like a liver spot. Willa Mae said, "I'll clean that up!"

I was watching her clean it up.

"Isn't you got studyin' to do?" I admitted that I had—Growth and Development. "Ha!" she said, looking at me in much the way Roberta had. "Too late for that!" I was searching for a reply. "G'wan," she said, "don't study *me,* I done growed a long time ago." She was rinsing out the rag. "Growed and growed up," she said, her back turned finally to my face. . . . And so she sent me out of the kitchen with the feeling that I was somehow irresponsible. Because, unless I made messes, would Willa Mae have to clean up after me? At least, I thought, that's what she'd *like* me to think. Out of spite, then, I called Roosevelt Jones and asked him to join Lulu and me on Friday, but, remembering Willa Mae, called him not without trepidation. "Look, man," I said, "you've got to promise me you won't give her a hard time. She's shy."

"So's Rosie, baby," he said. "Iffen I weren't so devilish black you'd *see* how much I blush." Only, he'd been drinking, and what he really said was "how mush I bluch."

"You won't forget?"

He said he wouldn't; but just to be on the safe side, I called Peter and invited him too. Between the two, one would remember.

"But are you sure you don't mind?" I asked Peter, apologizing in advance for the company they would be keeping that night (they were in danger of rape). Of course he didn't mind; he was curious. "Besides," he said, "somebody has to help you celebrate." Bless Peter! As for Rosie, he was old enough to enjoy himself no matter how bad the scene. I, however, dreaded the evening, and almost got the still powerless—impotent?—vibrator out of the closet just to work off that anticipatory tension; instead, Veronica returned my call and I set up an official appointment. She would see me at three o'clock on Wednesday. I got off the bus —in the vicinity of my old haunt—at Ninety-sixth and Broadway; it was unseasonably warm. I was wearing my winter coat, from the pocket of which a copy of *The Male Bag* protruded. Like most members of my background and generation, I knew nothing of weather except what could be deduced from the observation of human habits, and the way I knew it was warm was by seeing how the old men and women out for their daily walks to Riverside Park or the benches on Broadway had opened their coats and let their mufflers fall free and by observing how the sunlight glinted off the specks of mica mixed in the sidewalk cement. I knew it was *not* summer because the hydrants hadn't been opened. I decided to walk down Broadway to Veronica's place on Eighty-second and bought myself a Styrofoam cup of coffee on the way, which was a wise move because I soon discovered that Veronica did not feel I was entitled to kitchen privileges when I was no longer seeing her at six-thirty in the morning before work. "How have you been?" she asked.

"Let me see your new shoes," I said. She lived next door to a

Thom McAn and spent all the bread she got from me on clodhoppers and denim platforms. "Nice," I said, commenting on the open-toed sandals.

"How have you been?"

"I was thinking," I said, and I had been, "as the result of a letter I received from Adrien, that Christians are responsible for . . . guilty of the death of God. I mean, willy-nilly guilty."

She smiled and yanked her hair out of her coffee; I pried the lid off my cup, carefully, so as not to spill the stuff. "Couldn't you think of something pleasanter to think of?"

"Veronica," I said, striving to keep the edge off my voice, "life is not only a question of interpersonal relationships, whatever Harry Stack Sullivan may say. There are other relationships, such as one's relationship to the past, to the future, to one's work, to oneself, and to God. There are probably others that have slipped my mind. Oh, yes, country. Patriotism."

"I see."

My father never said "I see"; he said "we'll see," which, if it held less assurance, was, looked at another way, certainly a more democratic statement than the authoritarian "I see" head doctors, even including Veronica, were prone to. I wondered suddenly whether I liked Veronica at all; but maybe I was simply envious of her new sandals. I decided to give her a fair chance. "What," I asked, "disturbs you about that?"

"Well," she said, agreeably, "let's start with patriotism."

"You don't like the notion of patriotism?"

"It's not that," she said. She thought. "Simple," she added.

I nodded. Whatever she was going to say, I knew nothing was ever as simple as I liked to make it out to be.

"The word 'patriotism' smacks of blind allegiance." She giggled. "I'll never forget the time in high school when I had to lead devotions in the auditorium. 'I pledge allegiance to the flag of the United States of America and to the republic for which it stands, one nation under God, indivisible. . . .' Why shouldn't it be divisible? What makes a nation? How are the boundaries drawn?"

She was a secret secessionist! but I didn't want to upset her by telling her that. I said, in that unobtrusive tone which she had sometimes used on me, as if I were merely—offhandedly—giving body to the embryonic ideas that populate the less frequently visited chambers of our minds, "What constitutes an entity? . . ."

"That's the question," she said. "It's the biggest question of all. What makes a person an entity?"

I tossed the word "integrity" into the conversation. I muttered something about "getting yourself together."

"I used to think I'd go out of my head trying to figure out how it was defined—"

"How your head was defined—" I repeated, encouragingly.

"Yes, because if it isn't separate from all the other heads, then it's not *yours.*"

"Eastern," I said, hinting broadly at Buddhism, Taoism, Confucianism, and so forth.

"I guess so, and I had an Occidental reluctance to accept that kind of cosmic conglomerate." *I* called it the Grand Blur Theory. "My ego was just strong enough to wish it was stronger. Funny," she said, leaning back in her chair, "I even remember going to my father, once, with this problem—once when I was feeling particularly stumped by it. He told me not to worry. All things resolved themselves in time."

"Your father was a religion professor?" I asked.

"He was an electrician," she said. "Why do you ask?"

"Just curious. It's interesting that certain viewpoints crop up in certain fields and not others. Plumbers, dope addicts, and grass-roots politicians, for example, prefer the cyclical view of history." My father always said that at the very least Hegel was more amusing (as a puzzle is amusing) than Nietzsche; my mother said they were both cowards who whistled in the dark to keep their courage up.

"Well," Veronica said, "don't you see that's a selfish, sadistic thing to tell a daughter? She should wait and things will take care of themselves! Meaningless! Children don't have enough of a grasp on the concept of time."

"Sez who?"

"They've established it in the laboratories."

"I see," I said.

"*Act*ually," Veronica said, "there was very little communication between my father and me." She had forgotten that her hair was in her coffee again, and stared off into space for, oh, a full five seconds. "Actually."

"That's bad," I concurred.

"You can't live with someone you can't talk with," she added, as if to justify—to herself—what she'd done.

"So you moved out?"

"When I was eight— No, the truth is I was nineteen. I put myself through college waiting on tables."

"Rough. That's rough. But you feel pretty good now, do you?"

"Damn right," she said, focusing again, and fishing her hair out, and slinging the lank, dank strand back over her shoulder. "I only wish he could have lived to see me where I am now."

"So, he died?"

Her eyes had taken on a pinkish hue that eerily echoed the twinkle of polish peeping through the open-toed sandals. "Last year, before I passed the final exam. You'd think," she said, "that the lousy bastard could have held on for one more year, but he had to go and have a heart attack while wiring Mrs. Frisby's rec room. You see," she continued, reconstructing the scene of the crime, for herself if not for me, "he was wearing old shoes that he'd had resoled so they would last a little longer, and slipped— skidded—" Her voice caught.

"Skad," I said helpfully.

"—on Mrs. Frisby's freshly waxed rec room floor. His hand grazed against the live socket, and the charge shocked his weak heart into stopping dead. After all, he was a pro*fess*ional. He'd never expected to slip on somebody's fool *floor*. Talk about life's little surprises! It couldn't have been more than a tiny little charge."

I waited.

"Don't you see? Shock . . . heart . . ." Clearly, she didn't trust her own capacity for understanding, much less mine. "Go ahead, laugh!" she said. "I know it's a very funny way for somebody's father to die, people always want to laugh when I tell them about it."

"That's terrible," I said, looking around the room for a way out. Not being a trained psychiatrist, I didn't know what to do next. I looked around for something to do. There was a box of Kleenex on the small table next to my armchair. "Here," I said, handing the box to her, "would you like a tissue?"

She daubed at her eyes.

"I brought you a copy of the article I wrote in reply to Norman Mailer's," I said, "so you could get to know your patient in all her ramifications." She was sniffling. "Or something," I said.

"That's a good idea."

"Yep."

"Do you want me to read it now?"

"I think my time is up," I said, turning around to look at the clock she kept on a shelf behind the chair in which I sat.

"Right you are," she said.

"Yep."

"Maybe next time—"

"Yep. I mean, I'll call. Soon. *Arrivederci* for now," I said, easing myself from her office as quickly as I could. There would never be a next time. Then Veronica shut the door behind me, leaving me alone in the anteroom. I opened the issue of *The Male Bag* to the page where my article started and left it prominently displayed on the bench that had to serve as sofa until Veronica's clientele graduated from med school, law school, Columbia grad school, or got promoted to full-fledged city planners, and could pay her what *she* had gone to school to qualify for. (Each generation did its own little bit for inflation.) The title looked pretty swell, though the picture of a young woman in glasses and lab coat and stethoscope, and nothing else, on the facing page, detracted somewhat from my byline. I wondered if anyone would think she was me. I could hope! Meanwhile, anyone visiting *this* doctor's office would receive a pertinent lesson which I knew Veronica would appreciate.

SEXUAL INMATES: A CELLULAR STUDY

The Man says, "Women are the most mysterious and devious of nature's accomplices. They have been tipped off to the times of the high and low tides."

I am one of nature's accomplices. Speaking as a stool pigeon (squealing), I may say that there's a lot he could learn. Just the other afternoon, while I was riding the long armpit, or axilla, of the subway,[1] I realized I was commencing one of my three distinctive functions. (The other two are gestation and lactation.) Time and tide wait for no woman.

Naturally, I was torn between pride in this continuing confirmation of my femininity and sorrow at the loss once more of that precious endometrium which might have lodged a future justice of the Supreme Court, or pickpocket. That night, what restlessness. Finally I fell asleep, only to wake to a choir of gentle cries issuing from my womb. "Come," they called, but they didn't mean anything funny ha-ha or even funny peculiar by it; they meant that they were yearning after the particular fulfillment which Norman Mailer had promised them, and said they would find. I was sore as hell at being wakened and figured that if they knew as much as Mailer said—all about time and tide and how to flag down the grooviest of the sper-

[1]It is my duty (and pleasure) to point out that I am not responsible for this image, which originated with Guess Who, but I have taken the liberty of refining a layman's language.

matozoa—they could handle the problem on their own without further ado by me. Someone wants to know who "they" were? That someone is most certainly not Norman Mailer, since he is not concerned with such details as whether or not the egg(s) exist(s) and is (are) accessible or whether it is only the chicken who is crying. (But think for a minute how happy a man is who is only potentially impotent and you will have a measure of the difference between the definition of woman and a woman.)

I need my rest because I am a medical student, and, as such, subject to constant shock. I was messing around in the clinic not long ago, picking up pointers on how to develop a friendly, medical manner which I might or might not also use at my bedside. . . . The patient is a high-school dropout and she's scrunched down at the end of the table, her feet in the stirrups, and the doctor is taking a Pap smear and trying to be sociable. "When is the wedding?" he asks, because he's glanced at the card the nurse gave him and knows this is a prenuptial examination. "Next month," she says. "And you're marrying one of our own orderlies, right?" "Yes, sir," she says, "how can you tell?"

. . . Let us now be serious for just a moment. The Man says that women are rotten logicians, seem disgustingly able to function adequately without calling upon the justification of a world view or metaphysic, are either practical or impractical, as the case may be, and show very little aptitude for nonsense. I am not going to deny these charges (that would be nonsense) but even the male sex had better plead guilty to being fallible, unless they want the book thrown at them. . . .

We are all sentenced to death. Why, think of the company on this Death Row! I tap love notes to Norman Mailer on the bars of my cell but all he wants to do is argue. He'll be arguing with the hangman. He thinks that by doing this he can get his sentence commuted but that is a delusion which was programmed into his genes to encourage him to function adequately without calling upon the justification of a world view or metaphysic.

Meanwhile the only response to my lovesick tapping is the clanging of an iron door as the person to my left starts the longest mile.

I can't stand morbidity, actually. It really gets under my skin. So I'll go back to what I was saying before: what we don't know about steroids is probably what's killing us. . . . Any woman who has ever felt unmanned by the dicta of lovers and the circumscriptions of unambitious critics, usually husbands (that term is descriptive), knows what I'm talking about, and if we are to pay any attention to Dr. Freud, all women feel that way right from the, uh, word Go. . . . The Man says, "Anatomy is destiny."

Maybe not, but it sure is hard. . . .

Etc. etc.[2]

I left feeling as though I'd done a good deed, and spent the rest of the week happily sneaking copies of *The Male Bag* into the library at school, my dentist's office, and the clinic, until Dr. Goldberg stopped me in the hall to ask me *exactly* how I was paying my way through school. His voice carried. I shrank. "I've got your number now," I heard him yelling, and when I looked back, he was waving the magazine in the air and all the kids who happened to be in the hall were pointing at me and laughing. Little did they know. My personal life was so clean it was driving me crazy. I even tried Peter again—to no avail—and finally broke down and started bawling, late Friday night, after Rosie and Roberta had gone and Lulu was asleep downstairs. "You're the one," I told him then, sniffling, "you're the one who ought to be doing this. Crying. As I was the one who should have been crying on Wednesday. Everything is all screwed up." I apologized for my unfortunate diction, telling him about Veronica.

"No sweat," he said, referring to my diction. "As for Veronica,

[2]The rest got dirtier. I asked Mr. Winters to print it under a pseudonym (i.e., my real name).

she doesn't sound like a successful mother-figure to me." But I explained that that was why I liked her: Veronica was so ordinary, so similar and accessible, that, seeing her manage, I began to believe in my own potential for self-government. "Then what are you complaining about?" Peter wanted to know.

I said, surprised: "Nothing."

"You don't need her any more," he said, wiping my face with his thumb, but, recollecting the immediate reason for my tears, I suggested that *she* could help *him*.

"I'm cool," he said, zipping himself up. He had on brown corduroy trousers and what seemed to be an Aztec Sunburst shirt. Also desert boots, wide doubleknit tie, and a side-vented sports jacket. Peter, in case I neglected to mention it, over the past few months had gone increasingly Mad. "Cool," he insisted.

"Since when."

"It dates from the divorce," he said. He meant his trouble. He drew a comb from the leather purse he carried—the jacket didn't admit pockets—a small, silver-plated comb with a long stem, and began to drag it through the handlebar moustaches. "You must have sensed something was wrong," he said. "Why do you suppose I kept turning you down?"

I hoped this was not why Adrien had turned me down.

"Doesn't it bother you?" I asked.

"Not really."

I accused him of putting me on, pulling my leg, kidding, razzing, teasing. I didn't want to think he might be telling the truth. Shaven but shadowy, his jowls, though plumped up by the smile, seemed to adhere to their curvature too rigidly, and yet the skin had plainly lost its snap, was slack, as if the discrepancy between structure and design, base and arch, inside and outside, was fatal. I wanted to tell him to pull himself together. Smug hypocrite, I thought, horrified to be thinking so. Aging and wasting, out of work: where was the friend and lover who had done so much for me, sent my essay to Winters, executed my cat, held my hand through the worst with Bernie, advised me about Adrien?

"Peter!" I called, prefatorily—but I didn't know what should come after that. "Let's be frank," I said, efficiently. "You must be able to do . . . to get it. . . . What I'm trying to say is, it's just me, right? You have all those other chicks, so it must be—" I was ready to commence crying all over again.

Peter loosened his tie, undid the collar button—two things he had not done before, signifying that only now was he really relaxed. "You should know," he said, "how desperate the women in this city are."

"You mean—" Were they content with a platonic escort?

He said, "Yes."

I said, "Gee, Peter, I didn't mean to put you on the line. . . . All those times when I was propositioning you . . ."

"That's okay," he said, magnanimously.

"But it's not okay," I cried. "What are you being so doggone calm for!" I wanted to cure him.

He had gone prowling in his purse again, and this time came up with a flat, folded-over rectangle of Reynolds Wrap. "Coke," he said, unnecessarily.

"Count me out."

"Oh, come on."

"Peter," I said, "that's not the way I wanted to get off!"

He slipped the cocaine back into the purse. "All right," he said. He finished up the wine and set the bottle back down on the table. "Don't be too harsh," he said. "I can't even find a job. Do you know what that feels like?" I put my hand on his knee, trying to console, but it merely reminded him of his other failure. "Now you know why I've been keeping my distance, you don't have to hate yourself any more," he said, faith, hope, and charity—his—conspiring at once to acquit him of the accusations I had silently made, returning him once again to that state of friendship where I now desired with all my heart he would remain forever, stable and unsullied, secure from the vicissitudes of larger passions. Thus, rather than tell him that it wasn't so easy as all that—my opinion of myself wasn't so intimately connected with him as he evidently liked to think—I agreed and told him he could stop worrying now.

"I can take care of myself," I told him, watching relief take hold of the expression on his face and turn it into one which was much more open and likeable.

"I'm glad to hear that, really glad to hear that." He paused. "Really glad," he said again, "to hear that." I knew that during the pause he'd thought of Lulu and how she seemed unable to take care of herself.

"She'll be okay in the morning," I said; "we didn't do anything wrong—not you and I."

"Too bad," he said, "about her." He was settling back on the bed with a flask he hadn't brought forth when Lulu and Rosie were still with us. I told him he drank too much. He said he kept the flask hidden because it was Rosie who drank too much.

"You may be right," I allowed. Rosie had already been soused when the evening started, but that didn't stop him from accepting the grass Lulu brought up to my room and passed around. "Now where'd you get this fine stuff?" he wanted to know. He passed the roach to me; it was too tiny to grasp and I waved it on to Lulu, who, feigning indifference, sucked on it and collapsed in a coughing fit. I slapped her on the back.

"I'm not used—" she started, but had the grace to stop when she saw the look in my eye. "It comes from Vietnam," she explained, "via Mrs. Wood." Rosie asked who Mrs. Wood was. "Willa Mae," she said, lighting a new stick with an avidity I found off-putting. The attempt to portray herself as a pharmaceutical virgin had fallen away almost as soon as the smoke went to her brain.

"Willa Mae," I said to Rosie, "is Lulu's housekeeper."

"The maid?" he asked, innocently.

"The housekeeper," Lulu repeated, firmly. I explained to Rosie that we were the Radical Chic. He laughed. He said we weren't the Radical Chic he had heard tell of: they all gave parties (what was this?) and talked phony ("phonier"). I said we were the *real* Radical Chic. He said, touching Lulu's hand very quickly and tentatively, "If that's so, I gotta revise my thinking, you know?" Lulu said, as I was afraid she would, that she didn't know. "My sympathies are with *you,*" he said. "Look to me like we Panthers —oops, them Panthers—they be doin' an outstanding con job." He was nervously squeezing the squeegee that he'd brought with him from work, not having gone home first, in and out, in and out. Lulu, losing herself in the argument, unthinkingly took the squeegee from his hands and began to squash it up herself. She said the Panthers were his only chance in the long run. He said he didn't like to think all his eggs were in that one particular basket. "Besides," he said, "if your Willa Mae makes a living as a maid, more power to her!"

Peter said, "Housekeeper, Rosie."

"Right on," Rosie said. "You know what they say! A dandelion by any other name . . ." He was stoned out of his skull and went off into a little dance in which the main action was sniffing at his axillae. Lulu started to giggle. "Um-mmh!" Rosie said. "Willa Mae has got some fan*tas*tic connection! Willa Mae is a right clever woman, if you ask me!"

Lulu's face darkened. "Mrs. Wood is married," she said, "and I believe she has a boy friend named Doak."

I believe?

"Too bad!" Rosie said, and I couldn't tell whether he only meant to fire Lulu's sense of competition or whether he really regretted, for a moment, the fact that he would probably never come to know Willa Mae Wood. Who knew what visions could leap up in an instant, even in the mind of a window-washer? I asked him what he was thinking about.

"I was thinking," he said, grouping us with his gaze, "that neither of you has got a husband, and you don't act to me like you got a lov—a boy friend, either." He chuckled.

"Where do *you* get off being so cocky?" I asked, reaching for the sponge Lulu had set aside.

"That's right," Peter said, only very lazily entering the conversation; "what's got into you, man?"

"Besides," I said, swallowing some wine myself—too much—and answering before Rosie had a chance to, "it isn't true. I do have a l—a boy fr—a fi—er, a pen pal."

There was a lull while everyone felt embarrassed for me, as if they were all doing me some kind of big favor because I didn't have the sense to be embarrassed on my own account. Finally Lulu said, *"I* don't."

"Well, I sure *do not* see *why not,"* Rosie avowed, fervently. "A good-looking female like you. Shucks, I'd be honored."

I thought he was laying it on a bit thick. Maybe, had we known that this would be Lulu's last "affair," we wouldn't have thought so, but then, Lulu seemed to think so too. She started making a lot of brisk, miniaturized movements. She wrapped the cheese in its cellophane and brushed bread crumbs from her lap. "I don't see why Tennessee is such a pig," she said. "It's so easy to keep things nice and neat."

Peter, acting the good guest, helped me collect the glasses. Now we had crumbs on the floor, an eyesore of a small hill of glasses, and neat cheese. I asked Lulu if she was happy. She said she was hot. I thought she said "not."

"H-h-hot," she said, the extra breath a subtle ornamentation, a sultry breeze over a mysterious country, whether she intended it to seem so or no. Peter smirked. Rosie inched himself in her direction. "I mean," she said, rising, "it's too *warm* in here."

"But it's winter!" I argued.

Rosie said it might be the body heat that was bringing up the room temperature.

Lulu fanned herself with a copy of *Cosmopolitan.*

"All right, all right," I said, and got up and turned the air conditioner on low. Even Peter was chilly, but none of us quite dared to refuse: it *was* her home. Peter turned up the collar of his jacket. Rosie shivered. I put a sweater on. Lulu noticed nothing. "Does anyone want to see the view?" she asked.

It was freezing out there. "I've seen it," I said, but under my breath, of course. Rosie jabbed his elbow into my ribs.

"I'd be most appreciative," he said, "if you'd show me the view from this fine luxurious duplex apartment of yours." I thought, If he's going to skirt sarcasm that closely, it will serve him right to freeze to death. I also resented the reminder of my status, since I had come to enjoy thinking of the penthouse terrace as mine. He got up, ready to follow Lulu out, but she, when she saw Peter and I hadn't budged, sat down again. We waited for her to tell us why.

"Oh, well, if no one wants to come . . ."

"I do," Rosie said, quietly.

"It's cold," she said. "Out there."

"I'll keep you warm." Rosie *would* know that with a woman in her fifties he could get away with a line like that—it was obvious from his bearing, aggressive, leading with the shoulders, barely balanced on the balls of his feet. But then when Lulu, in response, hastily produced a regular cigarette, tamping the tobacco down against the nail of her index finger, and lit up, he dropped back into himself, relaxing his stance and sending all that energy headlong into his eyes, which widened and popped as they came to focus on her nervousness. "White women!" he said. I asked him to embellish that, if he would. He laughed—Rosie was too old to lose his poise easily, but he was angry, all the same. "You're all cowards, baby," he said, nuzzling my neck, while peering over my shoulder at Lulu, who kept her eyes on her cigarette as if it might suddenly of its own will start to blow some very informative smoke rings. "I've never known you to be this . . . crass," I said to Rosie.

"There's a lot that you don't know," he said.

I couldn't deny that.

"Ever ask yourself how come you ain't known me more intimately?"

Peter said, nonchalantly, "Shut up and drink, Rosie."

I asked Rosie how come I ain't.

"*Be*cause," he said, "you are white and I am, as you will observe, black."

"I didn't know you were politically-minded," I said, friendly-like.

"Politics," he countered, with a pomposity he had begun to develop only with age, and girth, "is a big word for human relations." He was putting on his coat.

"What kind of relations did you say?" There was one kind in particular I would like to discuss.

"Human!"

I now noticed, sewn onto the side pocket of his windbreaker, a small patch with sky-blue embroidery, which read: "Help Fight Pollution—Eat a Pigeon Today."

"You wouldn't do anything like that, would you, Rosie?" I asked sorrowfully.

"If you were a window-washer," he snarled, "you wouldn't be so hot on birds."

"Think about that," Peter said to me. Then he asked Rosie if he were going.

"Don't go!" Lulu said, rosebud lips unfurling, torso inflexible as the wire stem of a fake flower. She jumped up, holding herself erect, but crossed the room and begged him to stay.

"Why?" he asked. "You dig the color of my tax deduction?" Lulu flinched. "That's just dandy."

"Dandy schmandy," Willa Mae said, when I related this part of the story to her. "Mark my words, that there nigger is just out to rip off whosoever will let'm."

"Boy," I said, "youall don't even trust each other!" We were back on speaking terms, but I was trying not to let things get out of hand. "Rosie makes people happy, Mrs. Wood . . . some people."

"Maybe he does and maybe he don't. But a woman oughtta be able to make herself happy 'cause yo' can't trust a man like that to do it for you." She sat on the kitchen stool, crossing legs clothed, callipygous as she was, in ski pants.

"How come you know so much about what makes a woman happy?"

"I knows," she said, "one big bunch 'bout what *don't.*"

I asked her what don't.

"Heron."

"I'm sick of hearing about drugs," I said. I was smoking more and enjoying it less.

"You ain't half as sick as my Stella."

"Oh?"

"Lockjaw," she said, nodding her head. The diagnosis simply confirmed what she'd suspected all along, that her daughter had been mainlining.

But Estelle could die from that, from tetanus, from "the real thing." I wondered if my wisecracking around had worked the wrath of God on poor Estelle. "Naw," Willa Mae said, "she be okay. In a way, it was a good thing, this trouble. Now they'll fix her up."

"Who?" I asked.

Willa Mae leaned heavily on the counter. "The welfare folks," she said. "She was hanging out in the Village wi' Jewel. Hell, Harlem's safer'n the Village."

"You going to miss her?" I asked, stupidly. Willa Mae was kind enough not to get tough with me; she just let the question linger in the kitchen until I realized even the onions smelled sweeter. "I mean, I guess you're going to miss her." Willa Mae shrugged.

I drilled a little hole in an orange and sat at the counter in the kitchen, sucking the juice, remembering the previous evening, not all of which I related to Willa Mae. "You going to miss me?" It was Rosie's reply to Lulu's spontaneous "Don't go!" The way he said it was hurt, hurtful and a lie.

"She's shy!" I had interjected, wanting to say more, to explain that Lulu was afraid that if she said she would miss him he would assume she meant she was ready to take him to bed—and he *would* have assumed that, and she wasn't ready for it; and I wanted to tell Lulu that when he asked her if she would miss him he kept his tone sardonic because he was afraid that if he asked it seriously he would have assumed that *position* of beseechment which had too long been the relation of black to white.

"I'll bet she's shy," he said to me, as if she weren't standing between us. "So shy she just can't stand to be touched by no *brownie.*" He turned to thrust his other arm into its coat sleeve, and as he did so, the light behind his profile seemed a nimbus, and I was reminded of the gentle Roosevelt Jones who liked nothing better than a good bottle and some crazy talk and an opportunity to lay a little soulful advice on me now and again. His feelings are hurt, I thought, startled. "I'll tell you about crass," he said, "I got more of you chicks than you can shake *a stick* at." It was true. It was so true that I couldn't believe he really found it necessary to make such an issue out of it.

"Hey," Peter said, "wait up."

"I'm late already," Rosie said, altogether enigmatically, and stormed out. A few months later, when Lulu's presence would be forever a thing of the past, Rosie and I would spend an afternoon analyzing this evening, wondering whether his display of temper had acted as a kind of green light for hers, had signaled to her that it was safe to go ahead and let it all out for once. We would be drinking in the Recovery Room, near the barber pole that the owner had installed, presumably to remind us of the surgeon's humble origins, or maybe just to hint that we should all get our hair cut. Rosie would plunk down the silver for another drink and wonder why he had had to choose that particular evening to decide he was being discriminated against. He thought it must have had something to do with her money: "Rich people *owe* the rest of us a certain amount of tolerance," he said, carefully fitting his glass to the ring it had made on the table. I said Lulu wasn't guilty of racial discrimination: she just couldn't get it on—be easy—with a man of any color. "I know," he said. Then why had he gotten so angry that night? "I don't know," he said; "she made me feel like I was in the wrong."

"In the wrong?" I asked.

"Place," he said.

"You drink too much, Roosevelt Jones."

"Shucks," he said, "I bet you say that to all the boys on the block." Swiftly he pulled a long face. "My psychoanalyst says I have a White Lightning Complex."

I giggled, but we went one more round in recollection of Lulu. "Do you remember—" I said . . . that Rosie, storming out, had slammed the door to my room behind him. We waited until we heard the elevator arrive and leave. Then the door to my room opened again, and Rosie reappeared, winningly, with Roberta Rodriguez beside him like a portable pinball machine, gum popping, eyes blinking, and the nervous leg just itching to be pulled.

"Lookit what I found," he said, putting his arm around her.

I made introductions. Peter perked up. Rosie took off his jacket again. Lulu said nothing and her stare seemed uncomprehending (she was very stoned by that time). I tried to pretend nothing much was going on, nothing that wouldn't be going on in any med student's apartment on a Friday night. For all I know, nothing was, but I doubted it. As it turned out, I had an ally in Roberta's ambition to be the coolest chick in the city. She acted as if any apartment she visited on a Friday night would have to be reeking of marijuana (and again, for all I know, it would have to). "What kind of grass is that?" she asked, knowledgeably.

"Blue," I said, doubling over with laughter; I too was rather high, in spite of trying not to inhale deeply.

She didn't ask to be included, and Peter and Rosie had the sense not to hand her anything. I figured she didn't want to run the risk of being turned down instead of on. "Is Cameron here?" she asked then, and one couldn't help realizing she would have felt a little more comfortable if there'd been another kid her own age there—even if she wouldn't want that kid to know how she felt. But I had to tell her Cammie was back at school. I asked her if that was why she had come over, to see Cameron.

She said yes, shook her head no, giggled, frowned, and took out her chewing gum and asked me if I had a Kleenex. When I said no, she put it back into her mouth. Rosie told her he liked the way she chewed her gum. Peter asked if she had another stick of it. She said no. I asked her again why she had come.

"I got to talk to you, Miss Settleworth."

"My daughter told me about you," Lulu said, abruptly, sepulchrally, in a voice which seemed disembodied because it wore none of the usual clothing of context.

"She did? What'd she tell you?"

I said, "Cam thought you were pretty okay."

Rosie pulled her down onto his knee. "She looks pretty okay to me," he announced. "Let's see your teeth."

"Hunh?" she queried, while Rosie clamped her cheeks with one hand and held her mouth open. I explained to her that in his youth down south Roosevelt had had a lot of experience with horses.

Pale Rider spoke again. "Played them, probably," she said.

"You know what Sir William Osler said about teeth?" I put in quickly.

"What did Sir William Osler say about teeth," Peter said.

"Osler said, 'The single most important thing . . . is the hygiene of the mouth.' "

"Who's Osler?" Roberta asked.

"Don't talk," Rosie said.

"I got to talk to Miss Settleworth."

I asked Roberta what was on her mind.

"It doesn't matter now," she said.

"You go right ahead and tell Miss Settleworth what you came to tell her, chickadee. Rosie see no evil, ain't gonna say no evil, and most of all he don't hear no evil." Rosie made a series of monkey faces that put Roberta in stitches.

"Very funny," Lulu said.

Roberta was growing bolder the faster Rosie bounced her on his knee. "What's wrong with *her?*" she asked.

"Nothing's wrong with me."

I held my breath. I had never had the courage to ask her that myself, and wished just then that Roberta had shared my tendency toward abject servility. But Lulu merely looked surprised, as if she had had no inkling that someone might ever have found her a bit touchy, or moody, or remote. Frankly, I doubted whether the surprise was real: that seeming innocence granted her a sort of social immunity which let her say things which other people would have been hooted at, shot down, or just plain shot, for. "I just don't think Mr. Jones is very funny. Or anybody who makes faces. Why do people think it's funny to look like that? Freakish."

"He was only teasing me!" Roberta looked wholly bewildered, and for a moment both legs, one on either side of Rosie's right, rested in a state of suspended animation.

"That's all right," Lulu said, "you don't have to worry about looking like a freak."

Everybody knew what everybody was thinking but nobody dared to say it. I said we could all play cards. Or go for a walk. Or go downstairs and watch television. Nobody wanted to do any of those things.

"You had something you wanted to tell me, Roberta," I said. "You can whisper in my ear."

"Mine too," said Rosie. "Anytime."

"Good God," said Peter. "Would you like another joint, Mrs. Carlisle?"

"I don't know why," she mused, "now that I think of it, why my encounter group hasn't tried blowing pot at one of our sessions."

"Or my Lib group." I observed that Lulu was acting as though Rosie and Roberta were not in the room. But Roberta wasn't about to leave.

"Are you really into the Women's Movement, Miss Settleworth?"

"Call me Ms.," I said, huskily, and let my fingers wander meaningfully over Peter's chest.

"Cut it out, that tickles."

"Do I believe in the Movement?" I asked. "You better believe it. I believe in the Movement the way a drowning man believes in a floating oar. Rowing is not the point."

Roberta stuck the tip of her finger in her mouth to moisten it and then used it to press down a strip of false lashes that was curling up at the inside corner. Then she shrugged, as if to say she couldn't possibly be expected to think and fix her face at the same time, and fixing one's face took precedence. "Phy*si*cians," she said, as if that were a statement complete in itself.

It was getting late. I pulled her away from Rosie and took her outside the room, where we could talk in privacy at the top of the stairs. "What's the trouble?" I asked.

She was tapping her foot on the floor. "It ain't anything much."

"Yes it is."

"It's just that . . . hell," she said, "I shoulda known better than to come over here."

I sat on the top step.

"The doctor," she said, "said he wants me to go off the Pill for three months."

"How long have you been on it?"

"A couple years. Since I was twelve and a half."

"Then it's time for you to go off it. Just for a while. Just to make sure everything's okay with your system."

"Yeah, that's what the doctor said."

"What's the trouble?" I asked again. "Come on, spit it out." That was what my mother would tell me to do.

"You *know* what the trouble is."

"Roberta, *you* know that if you use something else for a few months it doesn't mean spirits are going to occupy your body."

"Yeah, I know."

"Then," I asked again, growing exasperated, *"what* is the trouble!"

"The trouble is, I know but I don't know. You know."

She had lost her cool, and, without it, looked almost as helpless as Cameron. I tried to reassure her. "Well, look; will it help if I promise absolutely positively no spirits are going to slip in alongside anything else? That's the truth," I said, crossing my heart. "No mean spirits or demons." I rose from the step and patted her on the head. Just then Lulu opened the door.

"What's so secret?" she asked, brightly. "Is this a party too?"
Roberta clammed up.

"We were just having a little girl talk," I explained.

"I'm a girl!"

Roberta darted past her, back into the room. "Kids," I said, as
if by excluding Roberta I could make Lulu feel she was included.
She didn't buy it. Entering the room, she saw Roberta dancing
with Rosie. The space was so small that the dance was closer to
the Dirty Boogie than to anything contemporaneous (in the olden
days, say around the start of the New Frontier, the mating dance
was still that, not pole-vaulting). Peter's gaze was riveted to
Roberta's hips. Without a word of warning, Lulu went over to the
hi-fi and yanked the tone arm away, and the scratch of needle on
record seemed the shriek she would have uttered if she had ever
been able to say exactly what it was she wanted. "Like daughter,
like mother," I said, thinking back to the fit Cameron had thrown
at Christmas.

"What do you mean by *that*?"

"Nothing. I'm stoned."

"You *all* are."

Nobody reminded her that she was too.

"I'm not stoned," Roberta said, in the silence that had followed
Lulu's accusation.

"Oh, you—you—*slut*—" Lulu hissed, the words uncoiling from
her throat like a whip; and then, although Roberta's face, always
so full of flash and shine, had already gone off, blank and negative as a DINE-sign with the N bulb burned out, Lulu reached out
wildly and latched on to my hair dryer, and with a terrible inrush
of breath that seemed to suck our souls out from our bodies (but
it is necessary to remember that I was in that condition of height-
ened sensibility which is a part of being stoned), as if *we* were
the dope she got high on, were mere weeds with the useful prop-
erties of being more or less malleable and altogether consum-
able, she hurled it at Roberta's head. It smashed into the wall

where one of the mirrors used to be, an oblong field of pansies somewhat pinker than those elsewhere scattered over the paper. Once I saw Roberta wasn't hurt, I had a ridiculous urge to applaud, but Rosie was furious. He put his jacket on and held Roberta's out for her. "All I got to say," she said—and at her age it must have been instinct that told her where to hit with the hypo in order to draw the most blood—"is, I sure do pity that poor kid Cameron!"

Lulu was standing at the other side of the room. When I realized she wasn't going to say anything, I asked Rosie if he would see that Roberta got home all right. He said he'd put her in a cab. Peter got up from the bed to go with them, but I pushed him back down. We heard Rosie and Roberta walking across to the Sun Room, and when their footsteps stopped, knew they were waiting for the elevator. "It's not fair," Lulu said, softly, in that kind of wry whine which meant she was herself again. "Probably not," I said, "but you weren't exactly fair to her, either."

Then I waited for her to tell me to move out, but she didn't. We heard the elevator arrive and leave. I poured myself another glass of wine. Peter rolled himself another joint. Lulu put out her cigarette, said "Ohhh," and fell to the floor.

"She's fainted!"

"You're going to be a great doctor."

"Well, get some water or something."

He trickled wine onto the squeegee and sponged her face with it. She began to come to.

"I didn't know she was that wrought up," I said to Peter.

"There's a lot—" Lulu said, opening her eyes.

"I know, I know. A lot I don't know."

She closed her eyes again, as if to agree. "Here," Peter said, handing me an arm and insinuating himself under the other. Dazed, she still succeeded in working her weight to my side of our threesome. She shivered—and I knew *she* wasn't cold. It was almost as if her skin crawled under Peter's touch until it reassembled itself under mine, where it could feel safe and sound again. If she was afraid of men, I could soon have told her that Peter was not the threat Rosie was. We got her downstairs and into her bed, where she sat up long enough to say, "I don't know what I'd do without you, Tennessee," and to ask for a sleeping pill. I gave it to her. Under the sweet-smelling covers, Lulu curled up for the night like a flower that might, with luck and sunshine, bloom another day or two. Peter had gone on back up and I rejoined him in my room. "I wish she wouldn't say things like that," I said.

"I guess she means them."

I said he was a big help. He said he was glad. I said if he really wanted to help he'd strip right then and there. He said, "What the hell, maybe it'll help."

"Help what?" I asked.

"You'll see," he said, ominously.

"Oh no," I said then. "When did this happen?"

"Since the divorce," he said. I started to cry. He turned off the air conditioner and loosened his tie and undid the collar button.

"It's not fair," I wailed. "Well, you can stop settling in because you sure can't stay the night. Why should I let the doormen look down on me for doing something when I'm not even doing it?" I shoved the squeegee into his purse and reminded him to return it to Rosie.

"Right," he said, stepping onto the elevator. "Hang loose," he added, which, so far as Peter was concerned, was making a virtue of necessity.

"Right," I said, waving good-bye. Then I went into the bathroom and threw up. When I called Maxine, her mother said that she'd gone out with Jonathan Zucker again. "Do you know what time it is?" she asked. I apologized for calling at such a late hour. Then I called Veronica but realized, when her answering service requested one, that I had no message to leave that I hadn't already left. I didn't dare call Adrien in New Hope since he might feel pressured, as men are apt to. I had called Dial-A-Prayer in the morning and knew the tape wouldn't have been changed yet.

So I called Bernie and purposely hung up when he said hello. Then I threw up again and came back to the bed and put the phone out of reach and lay down and fell asleep. This is the dream I had.

I dreamed I was in a small fishing village called Provincetown. This town was in the province of New Hope. I was wearing a pea jacket and bellbottom levis and stood under a black tree in front of a house on which a cold moon shone. There were sounds of argument coming from the house, quaintly couched in the third person: "Then Norman thought to himself that he hated that woman with the finest part of himself." I hid behind a tree, the better to hear. At once, the door opened and Mailer pitched out, and his wife followed like a prize bitch on his heels. She had a knife at the end of her upraised arm, a bright and pointy fang gleaming in the moonlight. I thought, Oh, Norman, please watch out, you think it's all in good fun but they are out to get you. At that point a door across the street opened, and a man in a night-shirt (he may or may not have been my father) stepped out onto his stoop. "God damn it," he shouted, "there are some of us who have to get up before dawn to set the goddamn nets in the sea. Will you for crying out loud pipe down so we can get a little SHUTEYE!"

Ms.—all right, Mrs.—Mailer dropped the knife; Mr. Mailer picked it up and turned it over in his hands, rather wistfully, but then relented and put it in his hip pocket. I saw them look at each other and shrug and sigh and saw Norman pout. That's okay, I thought—and I really did think that in my dream. Better to go back on inside, I thought, where no one would get hurt, even if it *was* a darn shame that everyone had to stop playing now and go to work in the morning. I slept peacefully for the rest of the night, knowing Mailer was out of danger. The joke—I'll bet one of you out there has already guessed this—the joke was on me, as usual. In the morning, I received a letter from Adrien, telling me, with detectable satisfaction, that he'd just learned from the literary grapevine that somebody was writing a novel in which the "hero" murdered my Norman Mailer. My Norman Mailer! Just like that! Dead! Finished! Done with! Not even one's dreams were safe, I thought, shaking: they could be perverted into nightmares in a moment, no advance notice. One might as well wake up. Face reality. Set the nets. Go to work. Just like that!

7. ON THE MOUNT OF OLIVES

The nurses at Mount Sinai were taking classes in karate. We lived and worked in Muggers' Heaven, islanded by El Barrio, East River, the dark park and Penthouse Row. The nurses wished to be able to defend themselves. Women wanted to protect and control their own bodies. They wanted abortion on demand. My own Lib group invited a soft-spoken, chubby-cheeked Communist to demonstrate the ease with which self-examination of the pelvic region could be performed. She shed her clothing strip by strip, a subconscious tease, but kept her lashes pointing downward as she climbed the six-foot door-top table that the Fourth Woman used as a base on which to construct her Joseph Cornell boxes. Speaking of which, when it came time for each of us to copy our leader, it developed that Fourth Woman was harboring an infection. Our guest of honor recommended unpasteurized yogurt. "Good show," I said, applauding her prescription, but felt compelled to add that a vaginal suppository obtainable on a doctor's signature would be both more efficient and safer. Second Woman groaned. It was true I was averse to some of what was being said, but I had nothing against self-examination: nobody could have, as long as it didn't take the place of the gynecological check-up. The only equipment our guest lecturer had was a sterilized speculum, a flashlight, a mirror, and a set of slides, and although I already knew that the os was the "hole in the doughnut," and the cervix was the "doughnut," I was as curious as the others to see the differences in our various doughnuts. But then she began to explain that the darkening of the cervix to deep red was a sign of pregnancy, and I knew we were going to get a talk on the "new" technique for period extraction which was supposed to revolutionize the world: with a Karman cannula and a vacuum syringe, the menses could be extracted in a few minutes, abbreviating the period the way abortion abbreviates pregnancy. If the woman happened to be pregnant at the time her "period" was being extracted, then she was in fact having an abortion. Done at home under less than ideal conditions, the procedure, in the opinion of nearly everyone whose comments I had read or heard, was dangerous. Happily, our lecturer could only describe it to us. When I raised some objections, the Fourth Woman told me to "knock it off and get your ass up on the table." I'd been afraid she was going to say that. Thinking fast, I said that as a med school student I couldn't see—at least I couldn't advocate—subverting the American Medical Association. "Looked at from their point of view, it's a rip-off," I said, slinging a little slang as a smokescreen to block my exit from *their* view. But what did I really care about the AMA? I should have stayed with my sisters. I should have supported the nurses at Sinai. Instead I was stepping out with Maury Goldberg.

He called me up in the third week of March and asked me to have dinner with him. I was weary but still wary. "Is this a professional—make that work-related—dinner?" I asked. He said no. I said no. He said that in that case it was a professional, if not work-related, dinner. I informed him that I was no more inclined to play around with married men than I had been but that after more than half-a-year of brown rice and steamed vegetables I couldn't object to a chance to eat well (for free, I meant). He told me to meet him at the bar in the St. Regis Hotel.

Naturally, I arrived first (I learned never to do that again). The waiter, too solicitous for my comfort, led me on a tour of the bar: we made a rapid-transit circle around the outer edges, waiter in the forefront, Tennessee in tow, and arrived back at our starting point in less time than it takes to say Jiminy Cricket. I was short of wind. He looked at me pityingly. I couldn't decide whether he thought I was a whore or just a loser whose date had stood her up. "Look," I said, "I'll wait in the lobby."

"If that is your preference, *Liebchen.*"

"Don't get fresh," I said. He pursed his unexpectedly red lips and went off to wait on someone more worth his while.

I was therefore already on the defensive by the time Dr. Goldberg showed. He was not in the least apologetic. "You're early," he said, wonderingly. "How marvelously naïve." I swiveled my head upward to lock glances with the goateed giant.

"Down South," I said, "we are always on time."

"Of *course* you are," he said, gently, "and it probably makes sense down there, but this is New York, and we are going to have to teach you a few things."

He ordered Scotch for himself and a Bloody Mary for me. "To start with," he said, "we'll have to get your hair shagged. Not too much. Say, to right about here." He rubbed his thumb along the curve of my jaw, as if cutting along the dotted line.

"Easy," I mumbled, "I recently had a joint problem with my jaw."

When he let that pass, I knew that whatever his proclivities were they were not such as to enlighten me. I no longer minded. I didn't mind being in the dark so long as all these men would keep their problems to themselves and let me alone. "Your clothes," he was saying, in the manner of an American Higgins. "We'll put you in something with a little sophistication, a little *chutzpah.* Pleated skirts."

Pleated skirts? Shades of high school. Sue Carol had worn pleated skirts. I began to wonder what this was all about. Meanwhile, he finished off his drink and asked me if I'd like to turn on. I thought of registering out front for a room upstairs. I said no. "Don't get uptight, baby doll," he assured me, "I am not going to spirit you away. We can snort right here."

"You're kidding."

He reached into his pocket and pulled out a glassine envelope and set it on the table. "Omigod," I said, "someone will surely see it."

He smiled the way he would when he was at the head of the classroom, challenging us to come up with any questions that he didn't know the answers to. A smile pinned back tight against the ears. "All you have to do," he said, "is, hang loose." All men must think of me as uptight, I thought.

I hung loose; indeed, my arms felt as though they were suspended in only the most casual of ways from my shoulders, and my legs, loosed, seemed so ready to run away from me that I had to cross them under the table to keep them down where they belonged. My eyes darted frantically about the dim, impassive room and returned to rest on the envelope that I could have sworn was sending out signals saying, "Look at me, look at me!" No one did. The doctor ordered another drink and the waiter took his glass and never blinked an eye. Goldberg put the dope back in his pocket. "See what I mean?"

"Aren't you a little old," I queried, "for games like this one?"

"Old?" he said, suddenly unscrewing the smile from his face, but hamming up the voice like a comedian in the grand days of radio. "She thinks I'm old! Why, I was blowing pot when you were still a babe in the frigging manger."

"I thought that was what I said," I said.

"Maybe it was," he admitted. "Did you think I was listening?"

"How naïve of me," I murmured, delighting him with my quickness, so that in an inexpressibly brighter mood he took me on to the Oyster Bar in the Plaza Hotel for dinner. The place was overstocked with women wearing pearls, although one hopes they didn't do it intentionally. I couldn't believe the prices on the menu. "Go ahead," he said, "whatever your little heart desires." Perversely, I chose the lobster. He pinched my thigh. I moved his hand away. "Aw, come on," he said, "let an old man have a little unsophisticated fun." Some old man, I thought. "I have trouble doing two things at once," I said.

"That's the trouble with you young people today. No versatility. No tolerance for contradiction. You are all fascists and don't know it." He explained that he could help me overcome this problem if I'd let him set up a little thing *à trois.* "To promote intellectual flexibility," he said. "I have in mind an older woman. Loverly!"

"No." I already had one.

"Righto," he went on, undaunted. "How would you like to be my summertime mistress?" Dipping a forkful of flesh into the pot of melted butter, I asked him what that would involve. "Our wives," he said—he made it sound like a club—"our wives go to the Hamptons after Memorial Day, and naturally that leaves us looking up a few, hmmm, boss ladies around town." I choked. "Not for sex!" he said quickly, replacing his hand on my knee as if he merely meant to convince me and certainly didn't intend to do anything *wrong.* "Just for company." He sighed. "For comfort, solace. Where are those qualities more completely come by than in a woman?"

"Why me?"

"Why not?"

Hurt, I stiffened under his frankness and told him that I didn't relish the thought of being thrown out into the cold when winter returned. He promised to buy me a fur. "You could stand a little sprucing up anyhow," he said. If he'd put it any way other than that, I might have taken him up on it. (I say that by way of illustrating just how good the lobster was.) But he didn't, so I told him I was going to be busy studying all summer long. He asked me why I wanted to be a doctor anyway. I didn't want to reveal everything. I told him there was no special reason. "An impulse toward the wholesome in life," I told him.

"Hah! So you admit there's something else that moves us!" My face was growing hot and sweaty from being stuffed with food so fast, and my glasses slipped down my nose, halted only by the upturn at the end. Dr. Goldberg's hand was working its way in the opposite direction as if in a hurry to meet my glasses. I addressed myself to his question. At fifty, he was curiously unclear. I had the feeling that he left himself open to various interpretations partly because it amused him to see how other people, defining him, defined themselves. Two could play that game, I thought, and when he said, "I am speaking of . . . darker forces—" I rushed in with an answer I was sure would dampen his ardor.

"A death wish?" I asked, archly. "No," I said. I slapped his hand. I explained at length what a waste of time it would be to wish for the inevitable.

He said he was beginning to get an idea of how serious I was. I was "deep-thinking." I asked him what it was he was plumping me up for.

"Let's go somewhere where we can really talk," he said.

I was suspicious. "Another hotel?"

He seemed to find that very funny. "Another bar," he said, as if my caution showed I was anticipating attack more eagerly than he was. I didn't like being laughed at and told him so. "I'm not a kid," I objected.

He sighed. "How old are you . . ."

I tried to be honest without being specific. "Old enough," I said, "so that I've started investing ten bucks a month in mutual funds. I wouldn't want to be a burden on anyone in my old age."

He used his napkin to wipe the butter from my chin. Then he said: "I wouldn't want this to get out around town, but do you know I'm dying?"

"No," I said, "I didn't know that. Actually."

"So it's no big deal, you understand. I've been dying for years. It's a muscular degeneration process which for some reason was spontaneously arrested. No one knows very much about it, but it could start again at any moment."

I thought maybe he was trying to seduce me with sorrow.

"That's sad," I said, moving a few inches away from him on the leather seat.

He seemed to have forgotten I was anywhere around. "I don't think about it very often," he said, "and sometimes when I do, I kind of like the idea. To die, to sleep." I was doubtful whether death could deplete his energy in any significant measure: he had too much of it to begin with.

"You're just telling me this," I said, "to play on my sympathies."

"You don't believe me." He stroked his goatee. "That's good. The fewer people who believe me, the less certain death seems."

I refused to believe him. He wasn't dying any faster than I was. "But in time it's inevitable," I pointed out.

"Nothing's inevitable, I may have myself frozen. I may find myself resurrected in the twenty-first century."

"I hope not."

"Just because I put my hand up your dress, that much you hate me? Wicked chick! Evil little girl." His eyes, in the candlelight, had taken on a dull golden sheen, like the fabled eyes of Satan.

I was flustered. "I mean," I said, "that I imagine that death is a good thing, if you look at it from the broader viewpoint. Which of us is good enough to live forever?"

"You have an inferiority complex," he suggested. "But who doesn't."

I was earnest. "If the wages of sin is death," I said, "and I'm going to die, then it means I'm sinful."

"There's a flaw in your argument."

Of course there was; I knew about syllogisms. "Logic is not the issue," I said, admittedly supercilious.

"Who said anything about logic?" The eyes were dark again, a few white hairs had strayed into the goatee, and both his hands were on the table. "I thought we were discussing history. The flaw is that you aren't sinful because you *don't* die. I am the Christ-killer. You, little one, receive eternal life." He laughed. "Over my dead body." Then he sighed again. "Let's get out of here," he said. He signaled for the waiter. "American Express okay?"

The waiter very pleasantly brought the check and Goldberg signed it. "Don't tell anyone," he said to me, "but this is going to bounce. If credit cards bounce."

I whistled through my teeth.

"*Ma naïve,*" he said, the smile, for once, relaxed. "Do you know how many ex-wives I gotta pay off? What the current one costs? Do you know what it costs to be a hotshot society physician? Oy, the overhead!"

"Can we *afford* a cab?" I asked, still not knowing how seriously I should or shouldn't take him. We were standing in the crescent drive in front of the fountain where dumb, doomed Zelda had baptized herself on the spur of the moment fifty years earlier.

"Do you think I'd make you take a bus home? Your lack of faith," he said, "appalls me." He hailed a cab and we climbed in. But he was silent on the ride home. When we got to my place, Lulu's place, on Park Avenue, I looked at the preoccupied stare on his shadowed face and touched his coat sleeve and asked him if he wanted to come up. "Dr. Goldberg?" I began.

"Maury," he said, "the name is Maury."

"Would you, well, do you, that is, would you care to come up—" I started to forewarn him that I had in mind merely a cup of coffee, but he seemed so sad that I thought I might be able to come up with something more. The man, it had turned out, was even more cynical than he knew, and it was probably my fault that he was so depressed. "Maury," I added.

He shook his head. "No," he said, patting my arm, "our talk seems to have tired me. I think I'll go home and read." By the time I'd got out and looked back, he was already sunk in thought, the head bent, the little beard resting on his chest like a beloved pet held close. I went upstairs alone.

❧ From medicine to literature is no great jump, as any number of writers and doctors have proved. But Ace Winters felt I'd landed at the bottom of the gully. Winters was the editor who, not without a sales pitch from Peter, had accepted *Sexual Inmates: A Cellular Study* for *The Male Bag,* monthly magazine for hip highbrows with dirty minds. Buoyed by that success I'd sent him another article, this one titled "O Come All Ye Sons of Art; or, The Peter and the Wolf." It was a confessional exploration of the way in which the advent of the Album had served to shape and re-shape our personal histories. Whole lives, I thought, were given new direction by whatever disc happened to be on the record player when Uncle Louey came home after doing his time for tax evasion or when Sydney took her first double shower with Elliott or when Rowena, having snipped the jingle-bells from stuck-up Large Marge's sneaker-laces, went home and lay down on her mother's bed to reconsider what she had done. There was a moral spin-off from music that I was sure Purcell could not have foreseen but Prokofiev's reputation might yet benefit from my thinking on the subject, if only it were made available. It wasn't going to be. Winters returned the article with an impersonal note. For days I was unable to do much besides mope around the penthouse; I could have used some extra cash for a terrifically stunning slide rule in a burnt-orange case. Strictly a luxury item, and I never got it. More urgently, I needed bread for books. Fi-nally, at Peter's bidding, I called Mr. Winters' office, and when his secretary answered, I asked to speak with Ace. Though I felt funny about using the first name I'd begun to realize no one went far in this burg without being a little bit pushy. Ace agreed to meet me at Elaine's. At least I was dining in style these days. "Guess what," I said to Lulu, "I get to go to Elaine's tomorrow. If I'm with Winters, she won't dare throw me out."

"That's nice," Lulu said, absently. "About your social calendar . . . is the twentieth all right with you?"

"All right for what?"

"For our trip! I thought," she said, "we'd make it Nassau this time, since Cam has only a week for spring vacation." I had not planned on any kind of spring vacation and didn't want to spend a whole week ever again on an island alone with Lulu and Cameron. "Well," I said, stalling for time, "I'll have to check things out with Winters."

She gave me a quizzical look. "What does he have to do with it?"

"He may want me to do a series of articles for him. See? On what Women's Liberation means in terms of your average big-city playboy."

"I don't see why you can't write in Nassau." Her voice had assumed its most adamant whine. I mumbled something about "research," bade good night to Brinkley, and went upstairs. In the morning I dressed fit to kill, choosing a sophisticated black midi in memory of my one night with Dr. Goldberg, and walked to Elaine's. Ace Winters was waiting for me at the bar. I liked his looks. "Hello," I said.

We moved to the table he'd reserved and when he asked if I wanted a drink I said yes because I felt I needed fortification. "Against what?" he asked.

"Well, you didn't like it," I said. "I guess that's what I'm here to have you explain to me."

"I don't like anything precious," he said. He put his hands on his hips and I thought he was, unconsciously of course, making sure I saw just how straight a shooter he was.

"I thought your magazine specialized in preciosity," I said, demurring with "if you don't mind my saying so."

"Of course I don't mind." But for all his nonchalance of tone, the small blue eyes were jabbing at my glasses. "Why should I mind? We do, we do specialize in preciosity." He paused. "Of a certain kind."

I drank my drink. He stretched his legs under the table; his tie was askew. Twenty pounds heavier and slightly shorter, blue eyes, his hair gray where I was used to black, he reminded me of Bernard I. Stein. Fierce. Impetuous. "It has to be a *felt* preciosity," he was saying; "otherwise it's meretricious. You were not committed to this article the way you were to Norman Mailer."

"Mailer's dead," I said. "And naked."

He laughed. "Go tell Mailer," he said. I said someone already had. He said, baffled, "Look, I saw Norman just the other day and he seemed fine to me. He's working on *Marilyn.*" I should have known I never had a chance. Personally, I preferred to think that he was out of commission than that he was romancing the Monroe myth—and not me. He might as well *be* dead, for all the good his existence was doing mine.

"You only think you saw him," I said, growing bolder by the drink. "You probably overwork your imagination as it is."

He glanced at my glass and cocked one brow, saying, silently, "Well, Glass, we know what the trouble is, don't we." I was pleased that the glass didn't answer. He turned back to me. *"Male Bag* is a magazine for men. It's the kind of magazine it is because I believe in the audience for that kind of magazine."

I blinked. "Pornography?"

He was not as amused by my lack of sophistication as Dr. Goldberg had been. "There is nothing wrong with pornography," he said, "it fills a very real need. But no, that is not what I meant. I mean that my magazine is a reflection, an accurate reflection, of the unspoken but hardly inarticulate philosophy of a great many men, intelli*gent*sia if you will, and I will not allow any essorant eidolology to distort what at my age I am confident in saying are very fundamental dynamics in the ongoing process of life."

"Oh," I said. "You didn't like it when the wolf ate the peter." At least he *was* straight.

"I did not," he said, chewing on his lower lip in a pretty cute way.

"You talk beautifully," I said, regretting it immediately after, when it became clear that he was merely warming to his subject. I asked him to order me another drink.

"Women," he said, "have certain advantages over men. Ahhh," he groaned, impatient with his own verbal shortcomings (the way an emperor castigates himself for forgetting to cut off so-

and-so's head), "I shouldn't say advantages. But they have their own capabilities and talents and bring considerable joy into the world when they content themselves with the cultivation of their own gardens."

"Silver bells and cockle-shells," I agreed.

"You can be flip, if flip is what you want to be." His eyes were as bright as stars, as bright as stars that stand out in the daytime. I made a wish on them. (A drunken wish.) "But what I'm saying to you now is something that should have a rather profound influence on the course of your life if you're smart enough to grasp it." I hated being threatened. Again I drank my drink.

"Tell me," I said, "what *are* these profound differences between men and women."

"We'll start with the simplest. Men," he said—and here he looked at me in a way which made me feel far more optimistic about my life than I had in quite some time, "are polygamous."

I covered my mouth with my hand, Japanese-style. "Are you polygamous?" I asked.

But he wasn't that simple after all. He leaned back in his chair. "By nature. What you don't understand is that equally cooperative in the definition of a man is the sense of power he achieves in surmounting nature."

"Why can't a woman want power?"

"She can," he admitted, "but then she's making a grave mistake. A woman's power lies in her willingness to serve."

"That kind of power," I said, thinking once more of Bernie, "is exhausting."

He wouldn't let up. "Birth and sustenance are never easy," he said, joyfully pontifical; "neither are death and transfiguration. But both offer an opportunity to legislate meaning into the order of the universe."

"Suppose," I said, speaking slowly to avoid slurring my words, "just suppose the meaning to be found in birth and sustenance is determined by its relation to that universe of discourse which you have said belongs by right only to the male sex? Death and transfiguration!"

"Precisely!" His hand zipped across the table to close on mine. "The philosopher-king is always a man."

"And his fount of speculative wisdom is his handmaiden."

"What's wrong with that?" He seemed genuinely stumped.

I decided to hop all the way in. "It's all right," I said, "if Yeats transforms himself imaginatively into Zeus, the god of gods, and preys on us women for his symbolic sustenance?"

"You bet," he said. "All life-affirming statements must be symbolic. The truth is we all have to go. Transfiguration's necessarily symbolic."

"I don't object to that," I tried to explain. "What I resent is your disinclination to admit that women might want themselves to seek an affirmation of the worth of life in a symbology of men."

"You don't," he said, wrapping his fingers around mine, "like men very much, do you?"

I wondered what I could say to that. If I said no, he wrote me off as a dyke; if I said yes, he would demand evidence. Either way I lost ground. I started to challenge him with the assertion that I liked some men and not others, but the waiter, setting still another drink at my elbow, interrupted me. "Look," I said, eager to get it all over with, "what I don't like about your system is that Leda gets screwed."

He smiled. "You're an arrogant little thing," he said, making me feel I was about three feet tall.

"But you *do*," I went on, "want to go to bed with me?"

He laughed again. "Don't get too arrogant. Didn't you hear anything I said? I have a wife." He withdrew his hand.

"Then you're faithful," I said, "by virtue of your will only."

"Did I say I was *suffering* by not going to bed with you?"

"Well," I said, "if you're not, and considering that *I* would go to bed with *you*, maybe I'm the one who's polygamous by nature."

"Oh, you would, huh," he said. "Why would you go to bed with me?"

"Ace—" I began.

"My name is Winters."

"Yes, Mr. Winters. I would go to bed with you because it's been a very long time since I went to bed with anyone." I tried to stand up and fell against his shoulder. I was never any good at quitting even when I was ahead. "A girl," I explained candidly, "doesn't get much chance to, in a city full of bankrupt physicians and uninterested fags. Not to mention the ones who would like to but can't."

"Then you are generally pretty discriminating?"

How could I tell him it was I who was discriminated against? I had too much pride to let him know everything he would have to know in order to realize just how arrogant my disappointments were making me: the story of my life. I sighed. "I guess so," I said, "I guess you could say that."

"There." He took my hand again—and shook it good-bye with professional efficiency. He was beaming. "You've proved my point," he said, and walked away. At least I'd made one man happy.

❦ Lulu came upstairs to ask me what Winters had said. "You can take Cameron's portable along," she offered. "It's very light." I knew there was no way out of it; if I pleaded a series of articles, she would read *The Male Bag* every month, and, every month, would ask me when my articles were going to appear. "I called Cammie at school today," she said. "She won't go unless you come with us." I thought that was a hell of a note; they'd got on together for about fourteen years before I entered their lives, and surely they'd shared vacations at some time or other. But Lulu looked at me with tears in her eyes and anger in the set of her painted mouth and I said yes, I would go to Nassau on the twentieth of April.

"You shouldn't have let her browbeat you," said the First

Woman when I went to our weekly meeting.

I said: "What could I do?"

SECOND WOMAN: You could have told her the truth. That you don't want to go to Nassau.

(But I was curious to see what Nassau was like.)

I: It isn't Nassau I object to, it's going there with her.

THIRD WOMAN: You could have told her that. *(She didn't really think so; she was nervously spreading cheese on a triangle of rye bread.)*

I: Oh come on.... How do you tell someone you just can't stand to be in her presence?

FIRST WOMAN *(hugging her chest in intense sympathy):* Sometimes you just have to. My parents— *(The Fourth Woman stopped her with a sharp glance.)* I mean *(obediently),* pity is a poor substitute for love.

I: Well, it's second-rate, but I wouldn't say it won't do in the absence of anything better.

THIRD WOMAN *(talking to me but looking at the Fourth Woman):* You may be right. On!

SECOND WOMAN: But I think the truth is always better than a lie. That's what we're asking from the men, isn't it? The truth. Without whitewash or softsoap or underplay or punch-pulling or black or white lies.

FIRST WOMAN *(sincerely):* Wow.

I: Well, cripes. You have to be pretty sure of yourself to think you have the truth always on the tip of your sassy little tongue.

FOURTH WOMAN *(rising, sweat shining on her face like stigmatic beads of righteousness, as she entered our conversation):* But in this case you knew the truth. You knew it and you blew it.

I: There's a poet on the floor. Kill it quick, before it propagates.

FOURTH WOMAN: Now if I were you, I would have said, "Mrs. Lulu Cameron Carlisle, I will not be going to Nassau with you on the twentieth of April."

THIRD WOMAN: It doesn't have to be that . . . blunt.

FOURTH WOMAN: The hell it doesn't. If it didn't, Tennessee

wouldn't be here. You know that as well as I do. *(There were daggers in her eyes.)* Mary Settleworth, we think you should stop coming to this particular consciousness-raising group. We no longer want you.

THIRD WOMAN: You *don't* have to say it like that. It's just that, well, Tennessee, we all feel that you would be happier in a different kind of group.

SECOND WOMAN *(worried):* You can dig it, can't you?

FIRST WOMAN *(tearfully, not wanting to believe she'd been roped into this so quickly but unable to cut herself loose):* They don't really mean it, Tennessee, it's just an example—

I *(stalling till I found the proper stance):* Example of what?

THIRD WOMAN *(Fourth Woman was letting them do all her work):* An example of, that we don't think you're serious enough about what we do here.

I *(now rising also . . . and with enormous dignity looking Fourth Woman straight in the, uh, not in the eye, exactly. She still wore see-through shirts):* Gee, girls, what can I say, but *(I blushed)* right on!

"Exactly," Max had said when I told her what had gone on at the last meeting. "So what's to feel hurt about? Your consciousness is raised high enough anyway. So now you can do something sensible and get married."

To whom? Besides, she should talk.

"You better believe it," she said. "Jonathan and I"—she was folding her hands, which, however, never hurt her any more, in the lap of her dress with an uncharacteristic, and, I hoped, fleeting primness—"like, Jonathan and I are eloping in June." Then I remembered I'd seen that primness coming on, like a bad cold, back in January.

❡ The way she rested one hand in the other mirrored my mother's posture in the booth of the restaurant at Kennedy Airport. As if the topmost hand were tired and required the support and companionship of the lower. As if neither expected to be held by any one other than each other. But my father, next to her on the leather seat, put his arm around her. "She'll be all right," my mother said about my sister, "but it will take a long time." I was having trouble tearing the paper off the cube of sugar and finally gave up and plunked it into my coffee anyway. There the paper drifted away and surfaced so that I was able to spoon it out. "What about Octavio?" I asked.

My mother said, turning both hands inward so that I could now see the liver spots on the back (but I had never before known she was old enough to have liver spots), "Tiger won't marry him now. She says she won't marry until she is whole and well again. He's a nice boy but he could be gone with the wind by then."

I was wondering whether my sister was really as independent as she seemed to be or if not marrying Octavio was a form of martyrdom. If she did want to marry him, why shouldn't she?

"I don't see why she won't go ahead with the wedding," my mother continued. "You young people. You think we're against free love and living together and so on because we're square but we really just want to be sure that somebody will be looking after you when we're gone."

It was too late in the day now to make jokes about when they went. I said: "How are the retirement plans holding up?"

She said they were going to try to retire sooner than they had planned. "In fact, if we can"—she knocked on the wooden rail that ran around the wall—"we'll sell the house and move to Paris right away."

"Paris?"

She started to cry.

"I guess your mother and I," my father said, "are getting old." He laughed quietly. "It seems we no longer have the energy to sustain us in our set ways. . . . After a certain age, you don't fight back any more, you just roll with the punches." I hadn't known my father could speak so secular a language. But he was silent now, idly, almost absent-mindedly, patting my mother's shoulder. At least, I thought, watching their plane lift off for Knoxville, at least I could rest easier, knowing she had somebody to look after her.

❡ The afternoon was gray and misty. I was miserable enough to feel it warranted a taxi back to the city. There I retired to my room and waited for Adrien and summer. Cameron wrote that she had a new old-fashioned teacher who was making her do all kinds of dumb studying and I sent Cameron my congratulations. But I spent my spare time, such as it was, reading *Cosmopolitan* cover to cover and eating candy bars. Downstairs, in the big bedroom, Lulu spent her days reading circulars from the NAACP, SNCC, CORE, and the Black Panthers; she ate candy bars too. Late at night I'd sneak down to the kitchen to snitch one from the refrigerator, and the next day at supper, she'd say, "I've got to stop eating so much candy; it just seems to disappear." Then she'd stumble to her chair at the patio table and knock over her milk and mumble, "Let them drink wine," while Mrs. Wood and I averted our eyes, she in a pretense that Lulu's behavior was normal, I in avoidance of any implication in the disappearance of the candy. I'd been mistaken to think that Lulu's outburst that one evening in mid-March was something to be heartened by. I had thought it might be some kind of psychological break-through, but, instead, afterward her withdrawal was more pro-found than ever, as if her divisive desires had been so basic that atonement, as their equal and opposite reaction, was now using up every last erg of her energy. She had her attorney arrange with Mr. and Mrs. Rodriguez to send Roberta to the school that Cammie used to go to, on a scholarship she herself established, and then, for good measure, called her bank to make a donation to the Young Lords. I imagine Roberta was in her element in Cam's old school and never thought of it as a hand-me-down; I imagine she was busy getting accustomed to the society she had, incredibly, overnight, succeeded in climbing up to. Anyway, she stopped coming to the clinic, and I never saw her again. Her name was no longer mentioned in the duplex on Park. But Lulu's expression, when it wasn't tranquilized out of existence, took on a glow of satisfaction, that was, however, still too feeble for me to risk a request for a new hair dryer, and soon I began to realize something strange about that glow: it came not from reflecting upon good deeds done but was almost a preternatural anticipation of accomplishment, like the flush of a lover confident of conclusion, only the end in this case could not be union—not earthly union. I, lacking that eerie confidence, absorbed only her sense of anticipation, and began to feel we were on the edge of something—and felt bored and edgy. When Lulu went out to therapy, I called Bernie again for the pleasure of hanging up on him, which was sometimes even greater than the pleasure of hearing his voice. "This has got to stop," I told myself, flipping the pages of my magazine and throwing the posthumous works of Norman Mailer out unread. I called Dial-A-Prayer. "Thank you for calling the Fifth Avenue Presbyterian Church," said my favorite voice. "We are sorry to tell you that our Dial-A-Prayer service has been temporarily disconnected. If you are in spiritual distress, please call . . ." So much for my hot line to God. I wasn't interested in strange numbers, I wanted the comfort of familiar things. It was Easter, and Easter is a time of new beginnings only for sentimentalists. It was also Lulu's birthday, and I didn't want to sit around being morbid with her about that. I left her present with a card on the table in the downstairs hall where I usually placed her share of the mail. Thank God, at two o'clock the telephone rang.

"Adrien?" I held my breath, it lingered in my lungs like the aftertaste of chocolate in my throat. I brought it up in one big puff and expelled it in an exclamation: "Adrien!" I said. I combed my hair.

The dogs, sensing something was up, began to bark; I shut the door to my room to keep them outside and him in. With the windows open, the birds' chirping carried through the screens. Summer had come—had nearly come. And Adrien?

"I didn't know," he said, "whether you were willing or not,

since we never really settled it, but just in case, I rented us a house. In New Hope, of course. It's got more rooms than my old place. You wouldn't believe so many rooms were available in the state of Pennsylvania." He had on a soft gray monk's sweater, hood in back, pouch in front. He looked . . . uncompromising.

Suddenly I thought: This is more definite than I thought. Think how lonely Lulu would be! How lost, Cameron! But if Cameron came home for the summer, she would know her way around well enough, and Lulu would not be lonely. So much, I said to myself (harshly), for that as a reason for hesitating. The real reason had more to do with Adrien's blue eyes and the way they examined me. Under his gaze I grew clumsy and self-conscious.

"When will it be ready?" I asked, playing for time.

"You don't have to stall for time," he said. "The house is ready now, I'm living in it." He set the knapsack on the table. "I'm just not sure I'm ready," he said (but he wasn't able to keep on looking at me while he said *that*). He opened the knapsack, releasing oranges, apples, pears, bananas. Adrien was a veritable cornucopia. Looking again at all those storeboughten samples of a Whole Earth, I, child of the twentieth century, had the feeling I was watching an old movie being run backward. But it wasn't funny and I wasn't laughing.

"Why aren't you sure?" I asked, reaching for an apple.

He asked, "Did you miss me?"

Did I miss him! But how could I tell him how much I had? Think what control over me he would have then, when as it was I agonized over every single thing I said and did, not knowing how far he was willing to put up with me. The trouble was that I didn't *know* to what extent I could be honest with him. Maybe he missed me—up to a point; maybe he'd been disappointed in love and was looking for a sidekick around the house till hope, new or not, sprang again; maybe it gratified and amused him to be missed (I'd known, come to think of it, several men who were pathological in that way). I didn't even know whether he would recognize my sex this time, or render it its due, or tolerate it, or not. The birds' chirping now had a sharper edge to it, as if, all this time, they had been honing their song on the breeze. The breeze itself was keen as a knife, intensified, and then lightning sparked and jumped across the sky and we realized it was electricity that was charging the wind and the birds. I was afraid of thunderstorms; I put Adrien between me and the window. The room was dark. One minute there was plenty of sunshine managing to circumvent the potted plants on the penthouse porch and then it was so dark that Adrien turned on the desk lamp. I moved away from the lamp. I was ashamed to let him know I was afraid of being near the lamp while it was lightning, so I sidled away as if I always sidled away from lamps. Feeling foolish, I sat down on the bed with my apple and tried to talk with Adrien the way I would talk with anyone else (he was *human*, after all).

"Have you been writing?" I said.

"Yeah."

"May I see something?"

"Nope."

"Why not?"

"There isn't anything to show."

"But you said—"

"I write in my head now. It's ecologically unsound to write on paper, when you consider that I'm my only reader."

I was hurt. I thought I was his reader too. He had no right to denigrate his poetry like that. Then I was angry. He seemed to think it was okay for *him* to behave like a spoiled brat, but if ever I was sullen or taciturn he acted like I'd let him down in some terribly fundamental area that only a half-wit woman, petty and self-seeking, could fail to define as clearly as he did. That, I knew (I had been taught), was sexism. It really was, and if he wanted to fight, I had a right to fight back. "You don't honestly believe that," I said, "or you'd stop writing letters too."

He let my words hang in the air. The air was hushed, still, but only for a moment; and then the rain came down all in a rush. It was falling straight so I left the windows open.

"Did you put your bike in the basement?" I asked.

He said he came by convertible.

"Not yours."

"No."

"Hitchhiked?"

"Not exactly. A friend gave me a lift."

"Anyone I know?"

He said she was a blonde with a Greta Garbo face and an almost intimidating figure. I asked if she dug poetry. "Ah," he said, "don't you see, it isn't her." He stood up and stretched his arms and legs. "It's just—" I asked him just what it was. "It's just that I'm not sure it's being fair to you to ask you to patch me up—"

"After what kind of accident?"

"—after the blonde in the convertible." He grinned. "Tennessee," he said, "you *know* you expected me to say that."

"But what I *want* to hear you say," I said, "is the plain long simple truth."

"The truth is," he said, sitting down again, "I could use some patching up."

I demurred; I was no good at that.

"You could be. It wouldn't hurt you to gain some confidence in yourself as a healer."

I had an idea. A brainstorm in the rainstorm. "Hey," I said, "I can be a faith-healer, I can turn you on to some mighty fine miracles." I looked at his face to see whether he'd go for it—that is, again, since it was the same old idea I always fell back on—but needn't have worried; Adrien shared the belief in drugs with the rest of us, and if some of us—like myself—thought that it was not true that all revelations were equally desirable, we were willing to be told that if we kept trying we might yet receive the ultimate wisdom that made up for the bum trips. So I got out the hash, shaved some paper-thin slices for burning, and stoked the cool, polished, four-ninety-five stone pipe. Adrien was eating an apple (it was just a little thing he did). "What do you see?" he said.

I was embarrassed. "Nothing," I said.

"Don't lie to me!"

"I see you eating an apple."

"I see you not eating an apple," he said. I had finished mine.

"That's impossible." Even in the first nutty exuberance that pot induces, I did not lose track of logic to the extent he had.

"You think you know what's going on, don't you," he said. "Better than I do. That's what comes from reading too many books, that sense of superiority. When—if—you come to New Hope, I'll show you how to read the Latin names of English herbs and the spoor of small animals."

"Adrien," I practically screamed, "please don't teach me anything." This was a man with an inferiority complex?

"All right," he said, instantly agreeable. "What do you want me to do?"

"Come sit by me." I moved toward the wallflowers to make more room on the bed.

Approaching, Adrien took my hand. "By," he said. "How by is by?"

"You're stoned."

"That's not answering my question."

"What do I want you to do?" I wanted him to like me better than the blonde. The raindrops, slower now, descending to an unvaried, dependable beat, drowned out the rusty grinding of my mind's wheels while I tried to figure out how to tell him that. "Well," I said, "I want you to streak my hair. Peroxide."

He was disbelieving. "Why on earth would I want to streak your hair?" he asked. "It's got bolts of lightning in it already." He was only being poetic, I knew; *his* hair caught fire every time we turned on—and hers too, no doubt—but his hair, being yellow—like hers—was combustible to begin with. Mine was the color of wet clay. I told him I wanted to streak my hair so I would be a beauty and could play a little havoc with his life.

With both hands, he clutched my throat, a little too tightly if the truth be known, and kissed it. "You would go for that, wouldn't you," he said. "Figures. I never knew a woman who wasn't a snake in the grass."

Beneath his hands I pictured myself long and slinky and snaked my arms around his back stealthily. "Like a snake," he said, "you have no sense of restraint, O Lady of the Urgent Passions." He was whispering in my ear. "Maybe more urgent," he said, tickling himself, "than passionate." I thought it was rude of him to be amused at my expense, and would have got up then and there if I hadn't been hypnotized by the exotic sensation of his breath on my ear, his sly whisperings hissing like the fangs of a snake sawing through the heavy air. I was afraid I was going to lose myself in those strange sounds and sinuous reeds and snapped my face away and Adrien laughed. Nor was it a real laugh: he forced it out of himself as if it were an advantageous laugh. But it was inauthentic, and I didn't believe him any longer. "Don't then," he said, admitting that he was inclined to be a bit melodramatic even when straight; "but you *are* a snake." I was fuming. "You are a cobra," he insisted, "and I am the mongoose."

I said I was not; I was too disillusioned, and, frankly, too old, to offer myself up so willingly, much less humbly, to someone's private mythology. (Banal mythology, I thought, but I didn't say that.) Adrien wouldn't know or care that the serpent and staff were symbols of the ancient art of Aesculapius—Adrien operated out of typical twentieth-century attitudes. "I'm not going to be any guy's stupid sex symbol," I said; and then, reflecting, got the giggles. It was super grass. But I wasn't far enough out of my mind to sit still for the kind of rap Adrien was trying to pin on me: that Serpent and I, sharing the intimacy of an infamous meal, were one and the same, co-equally evil, co-evally equivocal. I wanted to tell Adrien that this was all nonsense, there was nothing of the temptress about me, he had nothing to fear from me. But dope had tied my tongue. "Adrien," I said, but there the dope stopped me, sad to say, because if it hadn't, I might have gone on to explain what I found loathsome in all this, and hearing me explain, Adrien would have seen that I didn't know that the relationship, classic and incontrovertible, of the cobra to the mongoose was one of victim to executioner. If Adrien had said I was his victim, I wouldn't have been in such a stew: no mortal man was going to eat me up (alack), I was too tough for that. What's more, I wouldn't have had to accuse Adrien, even silently, of being banal. But I thought, rather, that he meant I was his executioner, and not wishing myself to be once again made to believe my body was filled with that poisonous Guilt with a capital G that Bernie had felt I infected him with, I declined the honor of any mythical role at all and said to Adrien: "Oh, Adrien, you don't mean you take all this stuff and nonsense seriously." Of course he said he did, because he did; and even I knew it was only people with too little money, or people with so much money that they had plenty to fool around with, who could afford not to take seriously all the things that middle-class people can only pretend, by playing cool, not to take seriously.

Now I had angered him. I hadn't taken him seriously enough. He was moving away from me, rising from the bed, the light in his eyes so lucid that if sacrilege didn't send chills up my spine I'd have said Adrien's upgetting was easily as spellbinding as the first Ascension had been. "Aren't you going to sleep with me?" I asked, biting my tongue as soon as I realized I had asked him that the last time.

He said no. I asked him why he wouldn't. If the old notion about the pineal gland had had any truth to it, that the pineal gland was where mind and body became one, I would have sworn that was the organ Adrien lacked. His other one seemed willing, which confused me: "Don't you want to?" I begged. He said it was just an exercise that he did. What was? Sleeping with someone was an exercise? Or not sleeping with someone? Sagely I said, as if I knew which he referred to, "It's an exercise we all do. From time to time." But I could tell by the immobility of his features that he knew I didn't know what he meant and he was being kind by going along with my pretense that I did. How superior he must have felt then! "I didn't mean to annoy you," I said, frightened. "Where are you going?"

"To put a record on." But after he'd gone through the cabinet and chosen one, he sat on the floor, disc in hand, and spoke to me from the opposite side of the room.

I said, harking back to our earlier conversation, that since we'd known or at least been acquainted with each other for so many years, about five, it shouldn't be necessary to romanticize each other. He said, "speaking as a Catholic," that he wished I had some other brand of flower on my wallpaper. "Pansies," he said, "put me uptight."

"You're just stoned," I repeated.

"Stoned! *Just* stoned," he said. "Tell that to Saint Stephen. Can't you see"—he banged his fist on the floor—"that this is a truth drug, and I'm giving you a little piece of the truth? All I have been trying to do all along is make sure that you know what you are getting into." He got up and started to gather up the apples, oranges, pears, and bananas. The apples and oranges and pears kept rolling away on the table so I got up from the bed to help him and together we stuffed them back into the knapsack (minus one green pear which I found later under my pillow). This time the wooden spoon was at the bottom of the knapsack. If we'd ever lived together, I was going to ask him what good a wooden spoon was when he always cooked his oatmeal in a metal pot. "One thing I know," I affirmed, stubbornly, blood-bugs creeping out into the open as my face turned red and I started to cry, "I know that there are things I have every right to refuse to get into, and myth is one of them."

He raised the hood of his sweater over his head. The Gray Inquisitor. "Well," he said, voice gentled (he had had to calm it down), "I'll write to you when I get back to New Hope."

"Don't."

"You're sure?" he asked.

"Yes," I said, amazed at how we seemed to have arrived somewhere when all along I had not known we were going anyplace. I sat down again, cross-legged on the bed, while this man, this poet I'd counted on all winter, collected himself and got ready to walk out on me. A whole winter of waiting! and one afternoon— Easter—defeated the purpose of it. Just as he was leaving, he turned back. I didn't want him if he didn't want me. "Good luck," I said, to show him that I held no grudges.

The angelic chin went up, he made a little snort of disgust and left. I heard the dogs pester him until the elevator came, heard Adrien get on and the elevator door clang shut behind him. I sat on the bed, picking at my dehydrated lips, wondering why my cheerful Godspeed warranted his condemnation. But of course I knew why, it was because it was androgynous and therefore dishonest. I could have cried. I didn't know why I couldn't simply open up and be free with Adrien. Whenever I was with him, my own ardor inhibited me, because I knew it was stronger than his, so that I didn't dare let him see clearly who I was and what I thought and felt. It was as if I relinquished my critical powers to Adrien and to Lulu, letting both of them think for me because they might be offended or even disgusted if they knew what I really thought. But I thought Adrien ought to have allowed for the fact that he had left me no choice but to do the best I could with what little face he'd let me save. I paced the room. Passing back and forth in front of the table, I noticed the old issue of *The Male Bag,* which I'd never shown Adrien, squeezed in between two textbooks, and burst into tears again, not from a welling-up of fond literary memories, but because it suddenly struck me that now Adrien would never publish any poems about me. He probably would never even write one of his invisible poems about me. (I fancied myself a doctor, and a muse on the side.) It was hard to believe it was over, but I supposed everyone, including Bernie Stein, would know the whole story soon. If this was the whole story. I went over and picked up the record Adrien had left lying on the floor and put it on my hi-fi. It was Beethoven at his most laborious, striving with Teutonic determination to nail the ever-elusive Christ with a chord. How tiresome, I thought, to think that Jesus and his Apostle Peter would be found raising their steins and their voices in a Viennese beer hall just as any two hard-working men might elsewhere. I lay back on the bed, turned my face to the wall, traced the flowers on the wall with my finger. Despite my mood, the rain had stopped, the sun was breaking through again, in bits and pieces, shards of light, and all the heaviness in the atmosphere rose up as if it had grown wings and flew from the room. And then Lulu came tearing in, unannounced. That was unlike her, but she didn't have a birthday every day.

I asked what was wrong.

"The roses," she said. I had brought her three from the florist around the corner. "When I took the paper off to take them out, to put them in water, the heads fell off of two."

Her face was pale with distress; the words she was saying ran together in their haste to communicate her plight. "But *I* didn't do anything to them," I said, immediately defensive. "I just carried them around the block."

"I know that florist. He once refused to let me cash a check there—"

I supposed I was supposed to boycott anyone who didn't do business the way she wanted to.

"—and he must have given you two rotten roses on purpose."

"Maybe it was an accident?" I followed her to her bedroom.

"Look," she said, laying the roses out in a long-stemmed row on the chaise longue by the doorway. She showed me how the heads of two of them had been severed, but I couldn't tell whether it happened naturally or not. "I think you ought to call him up right away and insist on your money back." I lied and said I didn't know the name of the store. She ripped it off the paper the flowers had been wrapped in and handed it to me. "You can call from here," she said. So I went around to the other side of the other chaise longue and sat on the edge of her bed to dial from the white princess telephone.

"Lady!" said the florist. "You're imagining things. You must have cut the heads off yourself."

"Why would I do a thing like that?"

"I don't know," he shouted, "but if you're crazy enough to think we'd cheat you on a measly sale like that you are crazy enough to do anything."

"I'll report you to the—to the Better Business Bureau," I said.

"Yeah, lady, you do that."

I looked at Lulu. "Well?" she said.

I said I was sorry. I wished I had completely forgotten her birthday. How was I to know she'd never have another? All I knew was, if I hadn't brought her a present, I wouldn't have to feel guilty that it turned out to be a loser. "I'm sorry," I said.

She was placing the single rose remaining in a narrow silver bud vase. The set of her mouth was rigid, as if she had to restrain herself from telling me what she really thought of me—and my present. Then her shoulders drooped, and in the split second between anger and resignation I saw shock: the state of shock that a young girl suddenly grown inexplicably old might, dazed, continue in forever, unable to accept this odd new texture of her skin, the astounding loss of color from her hair, this realignment of bone and skin and fat, because all these things had happened before she was ready for them to. "I'm sorry," I said, yet again, to Lulu. Her hands fluttered around the flower.

"These things," she answered, resigned, as though such things happened to her every day of her life, "happen."

What things? Which ones? I wanted to yell. Because she did *not* have to withstand the constant barrage of the mean and the boring and the pesky that she liked to imply I, and Cameron and Willa Mae Wood and Rosie, were representative of. I stalked out and stomped up to my room. (But outwardly I was sweet.) I turned the volume of my hi-fi up. I was furious, and it wasn't until much later, after I had left Park Avenue for good, that I realized that I'd picked up all the anger I felt toward Adrien and dumped it onto Lulu. At the time, I remember, I was only angry with Lulu for making like such a martyr. I happened to think martyrdom was a coward's kind of suicide, which furthermore caused all around to feel uncomfortable. Christ on the Mount of Olives praying: "Let this cup pass from me; nevertheless, not what I will, but Thine," laid the responsibility on God; and God, saying, "The curse remains on man until atonement is made by shedding blood," passed the buck back to me. "When this debt is paid, man will live forever." We tried to erase original sin with the Christian Martyr of martyrs—but two wrongs do not make a right. It was like being trapped in a double bind. Either Christ was a suicide (and that didn't sit well with the Creation of Life, or Man in the Image of God, or the Golden Rule; in fact, it was irreconcilable with any of those), or else his death is on our hands. No one should be expected to live with that on his conscience! No wonder we had had to invent the Jews. But I didn't see why I should have to be the murderer of the Jews or of the Jew. I jerked my chin up and gritted my teeth and thought, rather wickedly (I remember!), that if I had been fooled (and even that was only temporary) into feeling responsible for the ways in which everything existed—that is, haphazardly, awkwardly, and briefly—well, others had been fooled too, as this music proved. I took some consolation in knowing that even Beethoven could miss, so full of health was he, even with his glorious genius not quite capable of reconciling his scale to its subject or of subordinating himself to a system. Until, then, the soprano-seraph appeared on the scene, and in her clear, clean, liquid, unadulterated voice sang: *Er stirbt für euch aus Liebe, sein Blut tilgt eure Schuld. O Heil euch ihr Erlösten!*

I didn't know German either, but I knew music, and knew enough to know that when there was an angel singing in your room you should shut up and listen, as old Beethoven, not having yet been badgered into deafness by a world full of ugly sounds, had done: had listened, marveling how beauty could come from a celebration of blood and loveliness issue from threat. "You *will* let this man die or die yourself." It was, was it not, the law of survival tricked out in garb of our choosing. But what a raiment, what a raiment religion made.

8. THE STONED FIRE

The naked truth, though, was that we have only one choice: live or die.

I would have been at my Women's Lib meeting, if consciousness-raising still obtained in my life as a way of life. Instead I was in my room, packing for Nassau, trying to talk Maxine into turning on. I needed to relax. Earlier, I'd taken Cameron, and Lulu's charge card, to Bloomingdale's, rendezvous for the swinging singles of the Upper East Side (the daily *Times* had told me that), to buy clothes for *her* to pack for Nassau. (Nothing had ever been said about replacing the hair dryer; I had told myself to forget about it, washing my hair at night so it could dry during my sleep.) It was slow going. We'd take the three possibilities allotted to us at a time, try them on, discard them, get dressed in our jeans, and go back in search of three more. Cam had trouble standing for long periods of time and got tired and cross. When we'd finally selected three or four dresses and some hip-hangers and tops, we presented Lulu's charge card, the one I'd been clutching tightly all day. The clerk called upstairs and then turned to me and told me I had to go upstairs and receive a pass slip. So we went from the basement to the upstairs and then waited in line half an hour until a genial-faced woman who gave herself away by speaking through clenched teeth assured us it was all a formality but she would have to call Mrs. Carlisle for confirmation (she was controlled by unseen forces). "Why?" I asked Lulu when we got home at five o'clock with our packages. "Well, *I* don't know," she said. "The Republicans are taking over New York."

She was spaced out, her little red head seemed as precariously attached to the stem of her neck as the rose's (a different one) to its stem in the vase on the nightstand. "Dresses," she said, opening the packages. "You know Camisole never wears anything but blue jeans."

"I do too, Mama! Jesus please us!"

"I'll believe it when I see it."

Cam slammed the door of her room. I went up to mine and shut the door of mine. At seven I called Maxine and asked her if she felt like coming in to town. The Fiat had broken down for good; she took the train in and planned to stay overnight. At eight, Cammie joined us. "How's school?" Max asked her.

"Stinks," she said.

"Shhh!" I said. The phone was ringing. Slightly above the static, I could make out someone saying "Paris."

"This is Tennessee," I said, and then kicked myself.

"New York?" queried the operator. "Have I got New York on the line?"

"Non, non, non," the party said, talking French as haltingly as he was obviously going to talk English. *"C'est correcto."*

"Am I talking to Paris?" I yelled.

"This is Octavio. Octavio Santos?"

"Yes!" I agreed, wishing I could leap headfirst into the telephone and follow my voice overseas. "What is it? What—"

"Your sister is much—how you say—improved, Miss Tennessee. She would like me to convey to you her response to the cable you have sent her some time, I believe it was, ago."

I waved my free hand at Cameron and Max; the static was bad enough without having to contend with theirs at the same time.

"Tiger wishes me to tell you that you are not to be anxious about her." He laughed. He seemed very happy about Tiger's message, whatever it was. "Tiger wishes me to tell you that *music hath charms to soothe the savage beast.*"

"Breast!"

"Oh, yes," he said unperturbed, "Poland! I regret to say I have not been there."

I screeched: "No, no, no, what do you think this is? Some kind of game? Word association?"

"*Sí,* most weird," he agreed, "but I assure you I will do my utmost to care for Tiger."

"Are you going to be my brother-in-law?" I asked him.

"Music," he said. "Bassoon!"

"Soon!" I said, and rang off.

"Everything okay?" Max asked.

"Why shouldn't it be . . ."

"It's not o-k-k-kay with me," Cam said.

I asked what was wrong.

"Nothing," Max said. "She's got this teacher who's making her work. High time."

"Max is getting fat," Cameron said.

I told them I couldn't listen to them both at once. "You got any books we ought to be taking?" I asked Cam, considering the suitcase open on my bed. She dimpled and admitted that she did.

"Everybody wants to educate me," she complained to Max.

"That's the price you pay for being ignorant," I said.

She clapped her hands. "The price I p-pay," she said, "is ten dollars an hour."

I felt absurdly proud of her. Then she trained big brown expectant eyes on me as if I ought to paste a gold star between them, but there was something unsettling about her eagerness to please. When I said she was an apt pupil, she laughed excitedly, in spite of her professed disregard for Western culture, and clownishly shook hands with herself, losing her balance in the act. She looked up at us from the middle of the floor. "Okay,

okay," I warned, "calm down before you get into a state. Where's the book?" I shooed her out the room and down to hers. Descending the stairs, she planted one foot down and then brought the other down to meet it before she advanced to the next step, her left hand clinging to the rail, her right arm outstretched for balance. I went back inside. "Cam's right," I said, "you are putting on weight." I told her she'd better get back on her low-carbohydrate diet or the grapefruit one.

"What do you know from diets? You were born skinny, and anyway—" She was pouting, not something I'd often seen Maxine do. I had read articles which said that a lot of people overate because they felt misunderstood.

"Is it because you feel misunderstood that you overeat?" I asked her, folding my drip-dry underwear. Deliberating, I packed the bra, but shunted it underneath so Cameron wouldn't notice it.

"Maybe I *will* turn on," Max said.

I couldn't believe her. She was supposed to be clean, but then I remembered she wasn't getting her acupuncture treatments these days.

"It's only grass," she said. She was angry. "You think it's a joke, my being misunderstood. You should only know."

"Know what?"

"Knock, knock!" I went to the door and opened it.

"Who's there?" I asked.

"Hump," Cam said. Child's play! I thought smugly, casting back in my mind for memories of nursery rhymes I had known and loved.

"Hump who?" I asked, going along with the game.

"Hump whom, you ignoramus!" she said, falling on the bed in a fit of giggles. Maxine, tapping pot into the cradle of cigarette paper she held between her fingers, was giggling too.

"It's like riding a bicycle," she explained, "you don't forget how." She handed Cam the cigarette and the matches. I made a face, picked up the anthology and reading list Cam had tossed in my direction, and said, "Well, I'm glad you've got a teacher who's making you learn something at last." Even Matthew Arnold's name was on the list.

"Tennessee," Cam said to Max, "doesn't really know I'm n-n-not a baby any more." The dimple disappeared. "She's just like my mother, she *patronizes* me."

I asked her what that meant. "Just what do you mean by 'patronize'?" I said.

"It just means they care about you," Max said to Cam.

"Well, I don't want to be cared about. It's bad luck to be somebody's d-d-daughter."

I said that placed us all in a pretty horrible fix.

"You don't understand!" she cried. "I don't mean bad luck for us, I mean being a daughter is bad luck for my m-m-m-old lady."

"I *don't* understand," I said. "Who told you that?"

She looked at me with pity and contempt. "Nobody."

"I didn't think so," said Max. She was hunched over the roach, her *zoftig* shoulders, in one of our Provincetown purchases, rising and falling, the knit midriff not now as becoming as it had been. She was wearing her hiking shoes.

"If you're going to smoke," I said, "you might as well make yourself comfortable while you're doing it."

"Groovy," Cameron concurred. "Let's put some sounds on too!"

I went to the turntable and put *Christ on the Mount of Olives* on. "Tennessee," Cam said, "I can't stand all those crazy people singing that crazy shit." She said she was going downstairs to get something to eat and to call her when we felt like playing the Jefferson Starship again. Meanwhile, my mood shifted with the shift in music, the paranoia that was an unavoidable part of every trip (like the Holland Tunnel out of the city) lifting (as if music were sunshine scraping the mist off a stream). I asked Cammie to close the door behind her as she left so I could turn the volume up even louder. I wanted Max to listen to the seraph.

"I hear someone screaming," she said, sitting up and looking at me. The dark, defined brows were pulled together over the bridge of her nose.

"Screaming?" Stupidly, I thought at first that she must have noticed a scratch in the record. Or she was being sarcastic, because she preferred jazz and resented being made to listen to Beethoven.

"It could have been a cat." She leaned back again. "But Lulu Carlisle doesn't have a cat, does she?" She sat up again.

It seemed to me that she was speaking very slowly and that the changes on her face were as total and incomprehensible as changes of weather: an expression would affix itself to her face and she'd hold it and it would be absolutely there, complete, a season unto itself, and then suddenly the climate would undergo radical alteration and that expression would melt and a new one would take its place. The current one peered at me through black eyes dulled with dope, and the corners of its mouth drooped. I too was often close to tears lately and felt that there was a precipice I walked along the edge of, and that below there was that slough of despond my father used to caution me against, following along the curve of the cliff like a distant but ever-present reminder of the dangers of self-pity and exercising the same kind of sympathetic pull as the tides of despair do. Why should I let Max bring me down? "Oh," I said, "she does have a cat. Clio." I lit another joint. "You never saw her," I explained, "because the dogs usually keep her up against the wall." The dogs had been taken to the kennel where they would stay while we were in Nassau.

"That explains it, all right," Max said, sarcastically. "It was a cat screaming?"

Why not? I could still hear The Prune's screams rattling around in the back of my head, where I had stored them. "You can't dwell on these things," Peter told me, echoing Max. "Accidents happen."

I had gone to see Peter to ask what he'd like me to bring him in the way of duty-free items. I looked around for the dark-skinned girl friend. She was gone. In her place was a Nordic model with tight sunny curls, not to mention the tiny purple decal, in the shape of a star, stuck to the lobe of her left ear. "Meet my new friend," Peter said to me, his old one. I shook her hand. "What do you think?" he asked.

"Terrif!" I said. "Super! Magnifico . . ."

"I don't need anything," he said. "Thanks for the offer but"— he put his arm around the model—"I have everything I want."

"What shall I bring *you?*" I asked Maxine, who'd been lying on the bed, behind the suitcase, following her own train of thought.

"I could use a Pepsi," she responded, misunderstanding my question. I got up to go across to the icebox in the Sun Room, and opened the door of my room, and then as soon as I opened the door, the smell of smoke slapped me in the face. I tore down the stairs, calling Cameron, and wondered afterward why we didn't wake the dead, because Max was calling after me to ask if every- thing was all right, and from Lulu's bedroom, Cameron was call- ing for help. She was kneeling on the floor by the television set, bending over her mother, screaming, "She's dead!" But it was obvious "she" wasn't because the red head was moving to and fro a bit, as if in response to a faint breeze, and she was mumbling. But there was no time for that. The chaise longue she'd been lying on was in flames and going up fast and anyone could see that if the fire wasn't put out right away it was going to block the doorway and seal off Lulu and Cameron with her. "Water!" I shouted to Cameron—and I wasn't too dim-witted to notice even as I was beating at the burning blanket with the end of the blanket that hadn't yet burned that in the end my language was as elemental as anyone else's. Cam ran down the hall to the kitchen, hopping at full speed on her good leg, and returned with a small glass jar of water. "Omigod," she said, throwing the jar over her head back into the hallway, "it's not enough." She ran back to her mother. I leaned over the lounge and started beating with my bare hands; nothing was left of the blanket by now and the throw pillow atop the lounge was spitting flames two feet into the air. I grabbed the pillow and ran with it to the kitchen, dumped it in the sink, turned the faucet on, grabbed a dish towel from the rack, ran it under the water, and ran back to the bedroom to beat the towel against the lounge. The most frightening flames had been damped with the pillow in the sink, but the lounge was still burning, and the colors alone—pink, red, yellow, blue, green, white—were enough to set your head spinning. A low voice behind me said, "Wow!" I looked over my shoulder and saw Maxine, late to arrive because as a guest she hadn't wanted to interfere with whatever family matter was being conducted downstairs; but finally, she said later, she smelled something peculiar and thought Cam might have burned herself cooking up a snack. With this notion clogging the gears of her brain, she stood at my shoulder, saying, "Oh, wow!"

"Water!" I shouted.

She shot off toward the kitchen while I went on beating the devil out of the couch and Cameron tugged at her mother without success.

"You got a screw loose?" I snorted, when Max returned.

At least she had the presence of mind to be embarrassed, and gave a little laugh. "Sorry," she said, "it was all I could find."

She'd filled the inside of a percolator with water, and ran back to me with it, gripping the contraption by the stem that poked through the coffee-holder. The water, such as there was to begin with, dripped through the holes before she got it to me. "What's the point in sprinkling the hallway?" I asked her. But as it turned out, there was a point.

The fire seemed to be over. I propped myself against the doorjamb to catch my breath while Max got to work helping Cameron move her mother out into the hall. The stench of smoke made all three of us sick to our stomachs. "Air," Max said.

Happy to be following orders rather than giving them, I opened the front door and rang for the elevator. When it arrived, I yanked the operator, a young Puerto Rican whose English was as minimal as ours—"Air! Water!"—yanked him into the apartment and made motions with my hands meant to indicate window-opening. He nodded his head up and down as my hands went up and down, and when I'd concluded, he stopped and said, "Fire var*rooom?*"

Lulu lay at our feet, legs outstretched in a broad V, back propped against the wall, where Cameron and Maxine had got her. "No," she said hoarsely, "nobody know." But she seemed to be saying it in her sleep.

I took the elevator man by the hand and led him into Cam's bedroom and pointed to the windows, which were sealed. This time he nodded more vigorously and began to take the windows out. When he finished, I shook his hand and said, "Thank you very much," and showed him out the door.

"Do you think he could tell we're stoned?" Max asked.

"How could he?"

"He could smell—"

As incense had disguised the smell of pot, the smell of pot had at first masked the smoke. But now it was the other way around, and now that we stopped to think of it, it smelled as though it was getting worse. "I don't think this is out," I said, quietly enough; and then pulled the mattress from the frame of the chaise longue just as the fire started to erupt once more. I was unwilling to carry it into Lulu's bathroom, though that was closer, because the bedroom was carpeted, so I pulled it on end down the hall to Cameron's bathroom. Fiery chunks of mattress stuffing fell out onto the hall floor, but luckily the floor was wet. I threw the mattress into the shower—surprised to see that there was no tub—and turned the faucet on. The mattress wouldn't fit all the way into the shower. I tipped the hotter end in and hoped for the best. The mattress was still on fire inside its cover. When the thing seemed to be only smouldering, I left it and went back to the hall. "Nobody," Lulu mumbled, "see me." Her nightgown was tucked up around her hips like a loin cloth—or a diaper. "Nobody saw you," I said, resolved not to mention the elevator man, because what good would it do? Then she slid to the floor and lay with her head in a puddle of water. Cameron and Max and I, pushing and pulling together, dragged her back into the room; we were all barefooted, and the charred stuffing from the mattress, mixed with the water in the hall, caused us to slip and slide like three clowns in a circus act, but eventually we got Lulu into her room and into bed. We had just got her tucked in when Cammie screamed: "Water!" I thought it was starting all over again. But what she'd remembered was that I'd forgotten to turn the shower off. We slid down the hall to her bathroom, now flooded ankle-high. . . . But the fire was still eating away at the inside of the mattress, and I, having gotten the idea from the fear I felt when Cam had shouted, was afraid it would start to go up again all of a sudden and send sparks out to ignite the wooden shelves next to the stall. Maxine was more worried about the water seeping down to the apartment below. "If anyone comes up," Max plainted, "we'll all go to jail."

Cameron, thinking quickly, gathered a scatter rug from her room and laid it out on the floor of the bathroom. As it soaked up water, she stood on top of it and moved it around with her feet. "Look!" she said. "I'm rug-skating."

Max made it clear that she thought such highjinks were un-called for. "If you were B-B-British," Cam told her, snickering, "you could call it rugby."

"Move over," I said to Cam. The mattress was still on fire and I had grown to hate it. I thought by now it was refusing to be not on fire, was on fire out of spite, and I thought I'd better get a knife and open it up so the water could reach all of the flaming foam. I waded into the kitchen and approached the pantry; the knives were ranked on the back of the pantry door. There were a big knife and a little knife and a middling knife, a bread knife and a butcher knife, a paring knife, a blade for the electric knife, and even a jackknife. I reached for the short knife with the sharp edge, but then, feeling the butt cold against my palm, hesitated. In my mind I saw my cinematic Caligula, malnourished but long-limbed, sweet but sick, pathetic and vicious, presenting his audience with the head, as if it were a corsage, of the flower of manhood. What heads would I gather and rearrange if I left the kitchen with that knife in my hand! I put it back in its slot, went back to the bathroom, and used my hands to rip open the brocade covering. Fire had eaten a seam down the middle, which made it easier; and I pulled out more huge chunks of fire. But though we'd reached the point where we could have relaxed, I was unable to. The mattress was my enemy and I couldn't rest until we were sure it was dead. Out. I dragged it from the shower to the maid's bathroom on the other side of the dining area and dumped it into the tub there. Then Max and I ripped it the rest of the way open. Two billion little balls of synthetic foam burst from the opening; where fire had not reached them, they were not fused into the chunklike condition I'd thought the whole mattress was in; but once released, they expanded and popped all over the little room like popcorn. Max began to laugh. Her laugh rose and rose, following the flight of the popping corn, until it reached the highest pitch I'd ever heard it at, and, fearful she'd become too hysterical to control or would wake the neighbors, I tried to find out what was so funny.

"My father," she said, "used to run the projector at Loew's."

I worked a concession stand (I swear it) at the circus one summer, lying about my age (it was a long time ago), and knew what she meant: the way the corn swelled, climbed, sank and snowed, accumulating in crunchy, salty mounds. "Max! I hadn't realized your father was ever in show business."

"That impresses you," she said. She had my number now.

"Yes," I admitted, thinking of my kid sister and her connections with the concert stage.

"You worry too much," she said, "if you ask me, about keeping up with her."

I pointed out that my sister was in a hospital and that I had just done my best to keep out of one. "To keep us all out," I said, and then discovered that Cam wasn't with us. I rushed back into her bathroom. She wasn't there. "Camera?" I called, keeping my voice gay. But I was scared to death something had happened to her.

"Here," she answered. She was trying to climb the stairs to my room, her arms crammed full with a sleeping bag and night-gown. "I'm not sleeping down here tonight," she said, firmly. "Not on your life."

⟨ Max and I went over everything again to make sure there wasn't one spark still alive. Then we went into Lulu's bedroom, because it had just occurred to us that as she had certainly been blowing pot and popping pills, she might have popped too many. Of course neither Max nor I had any *concrete* idea what the symptoms of overdose were: the crowd Max had once upon a time hung out with were careful not to O.D., and when they graduated to hard stuff, moved into another crowd; and I, as a med student, knew more about the theoretically proper administration of drugs than about their possible improper effects. A good deal more, since from February on, the second-year class received a series of lectures on pharmacology. But no one, least of all my-self, had expected that I would be doing homework on the subject of barbiturate poisoning. So I crept up to Lulu's side to listen to her breathing, and when I couldn't hear anything and had to put my ear next to her chest, Max turned white. "Whaddaya think?" Max said, backing away.

I listened. Then I grabbed Lulu by the shoulders and shook her and slapped her face. I asked Max to bring some ice from the kitchen. Cooling her forehead, droplets of water trickling into the crevices of her crepy skin, I felt a thrill, as if I'd won some exotic competition and held the prize in my hands. But then she moaned and fell back against the pillows. I took her pulse; it was slow and irregular but functional. We went upstairs then, but the windows downstairs were still open, we couldn't seal them up ourselves, and the wind kept making strange sounds. Cameron and Max were still high and kept saying, "I'm afraid, Tennessee; someone's downstairs," and I'd go downstairs and come back up to report that the wind was knocking the cord of the venetian blinds against the pane, or the wind was flapping against the loose corner of a rock-band poster in Cameron's room; but once I was scared enough to make Max come down with me, and Cammie came too, preferring not to be alone even if it meant being downstairs. I looked at the kitchen clock: it was two in the morning. Finally the dope wore off and Cameron spread out her sleeping bag in the middle of the floor and zipped herself up and went to sleep. Max washed her face. I put some unguent on the burns on my knees, on my stinging hands—and a little Vitamin E cream too, just in case it worked. I asked Max: "You haven't turned on in lord knows how long, you know. What got into you?"

She was amused. "I am pregnant, Tennessee. I thought I needed . . . like, a final fling. This final I could have done without."

"So you did—"

"What?"

"In Provincetown. With Jonathan."

"It was an *ac*cident."

"Like everything else?"

She ignored me. "At this rate," she said, examining her waistline, "I am going to turn into a lousy blimp by the time we do our thing." She referred to their elopement.

"Who ever heard of planning an elopement like this?" We were paddling comments back and forth across the room like a slow-motion ping-pong ball, until the ball stopped in mid-air and hung there.

"How else," she said, "would I get a caterer? Besides, Aunt Mina is too old for surprises." Rubbing sleep from her eyes, she donned pajamas and spread out her own sleeping bag on the side of my room nearest the door. I got up and tiptoed over Cam and Max and out to the terrace, where I could breathe freely again; I could've said there was smoke trapped in my throat. The lights of the city blinked nervously in the distance; though I couldn't see the park itself, there were clouds over Central Park, moving, scudding across the horizon, turning the city lights off and on. I felt something cool pass over my face: the wind, and something warm with life against my leg: Clio. Purring, as if nothing had happened, or as if she knew what had happened and was glad to see me. "Here, kitty," I said, touched by her concern. I picked her up. We stood there together, one head atop the other, looking out over the city, until she turned herself around in my arms and began to knead her paws against my chest. When I tried to stop her, to keep her from tearing my shirt, she hissed and scratched my arm. I was angry with her for not letting me cuddle her. I put her down and told her to scram. I licked the scratch on my arm. That reminded me that I had half a candy bar in the pocket of the shirt and I got it out and ate it. I was standing there, chewing nougat, looking out over New York, when that reminded me of a passage from the Matthew Arnold I would be reviewing with Cameron: something about the world and how it . . . lies. . . . I went back in and looked it up in the book which lay on top my bathing suit in the Harvard bookbag. For her tutor, at least, it would be groovy to get back to the Old Standards.

> . . . the world, which seems
> To lie before us like a land of dreams,
> So various, so beautiful, so new,
> Hath really neither joy, nor love, nor light,
> Nor certitude, nor peace, nor help for pain;
> And we are here as on a darkling plain
> Swept with confused alarms of struggle and flight,
> Where ignorant armies clash by night.

❡ At six A.M. the alarm clock went off. Max left by the upstairs elevator—she seemed to be walking in a dream and wanted to get home before she awakened to a clear recollection of the night before—and I got dressed while Cameron went down to rouse her mother. When I joined them, she said: "I understand I missed all the excitement last night!"

I collected all the suitcases and the typewriter into a pile in the front hall while Lulu left a note directing Willa Mae to see that the super fixed the windows while we were gone. "Willa Mae Wood," Lulu said, "isn't going to jump for joy when she sees this place."

I apologized for not having had time to clean it up.

The elevator man—not the one of the night before, this was the old man (there were many)—escorted us downstairs to wait for the airline limousine and then returned to bring our bags down. Checking in at Kennedy, I put the typewriter on the scale, but Lulu said it was too likely to get damaged if we let it go with the luggage. I was still carrying bag and purse (bookbag) and books and Cameron was carrying nothing, so I asked her to take the typewriter. "I don't see," she said, "why *I* have to carry it."

"*I* don't see," Lulu said, "why we have to take it along at all." We didn't really, since the second article hadn't panned out and no one had asked for a third; but if I told her that, I'd have to tell her all about Ace Winters and that would probably encourage her to talk about Rosie Jones or ask after Adrien, and I had been learning, over the months, to want to keep my private life private. Who, I was wondering, was playing parasite to whose sucker of a host? (Hostess.) I was getting tired of hunting up reasons to enlist in the service of all the pity I felt I owed her in return for room and board.

"All aboard!" I said, chipper-like, to Cammie, pushing her on. Lulu continued her bitching as we took our places in the line of passengers waiting to board. As we approached the officer who would check our tickets, she noticed that hand luggage was being searched. "They're looking for hardware," I explained, though secretly I thought it might be exciting to be hijacked to Cuba. But that was not what was on Lulu's mind.

"Here," she said, in a loud, frantic voice, and reached into her purse and pulled out an envelope which she passed to Cameron: "Hide this!"

We must have been the only Americans ever to smuggle pot into Nassau instead of out, and if we had been caught, Cameron would have taken the rap for possession. But maybe Lulu reasoned that Cammie, as a minor, risked a lesser penalty, or that since she wasn't carrying a purse she wouldn't be checked. In fact she wasn't. I held my breath until we got through, and, when we were on the plane, didn't dare say anything for fear I'd tell Lulu she was crazy and could go straight to hell for all I cared. "Tennessee is certainly uncommunicative today," she said, when we were over water. Cameron laughed and said Tennessee was being sulky. I found it difficult to answer to the third person and settled down to read a month-old edition of the *National Observer.* Cam fell asleep and Lulu looked out the window. We were in Nassau shortly after noon, but had a long cab ride to the hotel. All the way to the cab, and then all the way to the hotel, Lulu kept saying: "It really is inconvenient to have this *thing* along"; "Watch the typewriter! It's likely to get damaged"; and "I *don't* see why we had to bring that thing at all." Then when she went to sign us in (that being something she had to do), Cam said, "Oh, look at the ugly people," meaning the boys in short hair and the women in stretch slacks, her tone infuriatingly innocent of any unpleasantness. The bellboy showed all of us to our rooms: two rooms. "I want one to myself," Cam said. She dimpled and brushed back her thick, protein-treated tresses. She had a dusting of freckles across the bridge of her nose. "If I meet any boys, I have to have a place to bring them, don't I?"

"You could let *them* worry about where to take *you,*" I suggested.

"That's stupid," she said after a bit.

"What's stupid?"

"Playing games with p-p-people."

"You just don't like the idea of losing."

"I don't know what you mean."

We were standing a little apart from Lulu.

"Okay," I said, backing down.

"If you mean I should play hard to get," she said, "I think that's really d-d-disgusting. Ick!"

"Disgusting?"

"Uh-huh! Lying is for the birds."

"You mean flying."

She wasn't in a mood to fool around and seemed to think I badly needed instruction. "I m-mean if you pretend to be what you aren't, you aren't going to know whether he's really in love with you."

"Who is?"

"It's not *my* fault," she said, "if you and Mama don't have any boy friends."

I should have spanked her, except that, as always, she looked as though she'd long ago been punished unjustly—and didn't mind. I said, speaking of boy friends, "If I had any, I sure wouldn't feel I had to entertain them in my hotel room."

Before I could apologize, pleading fatigue, she showed me her dimple again. "I'll take them for a *walk* along the b-b-beach—"

But the two rooms were not the ones Lulu had asked for, and they hadn't been made up. Swearing, she went back to the desk. Cameron and I stood in the hall. "Jesus please us," she said, "if you only knew how sore my arm is from lugging this t-t-type—"

"If you don't stop complaining," I said, "I'm flying out of here this afternoon."

She started to say something and then changed her mind. I thought (until I learned otherwise) that maybe she was at last learning something from me (what?). "No way," Willa Mae said later, talking about me—and I could have said the same about Cameron; "ain't no way yo' goin' to teach a new dog old tricks." That was right after I'd told her I didn't think I ought to move out.

"After all, Mrs. Wood, you were the one who thought I ought to stay on!"

"It's my purgative, honey, to change my mind any time I damn well feel like it. How was I 'spose to know the madam goin' to burn the place down? Jus' don't you be in it!"

I thanked her for her concern.

She put both hands on the patio table in the dining room and lowered herself into a chair. (Her bursitis was acting up.) "Sure thing," she said. The diamond pears swinging from her ears caught the overhead light, toyed with it, threw it back. "What I am tellin' you, Tennessee, is you got to look out for yo'self." But it was precisely that event which might have given me the strength to move out—the fire—which ensured that I wouldn't. I couldn't leave Cam to deal with her mother alone. I half-wondered if Lulu had figured this all out in advance, but I knew she was too constantly stoned to calculate in such fine detail the risk she took. "Day's goin' to come when The Man, he catch up wi' all us."

"What did he do to Estelle, Mrs. Wood?"

"I ain't complainin'. Stella, she be straight now. Course, they done took her away. Give her a job. You know them *wel*fare workers. They always workin' and *wel*farin' in ever'one's business." She said that now that she didn't have a family any more, she was going to move in with Doak. "You got a brain in yo' head," she said, "you move on out. Now go do some of that studyin' you be all the time doin' anyway so's I can fix my wig up nice for when I tells my husband the news." As I left, she reached up to remove the beehive, as if it were an extra, unneeded head, or as if the old one were molting to be replaced by the new. Only it was the other way around, new giving way before the old as her iron-gray unstraightened silhouette came into view. Plebeian nimbus! Hard-earned penumbra! She was slipping—she wouldn't use to have let me see how old she really was. I felt like a snoop. I jerked my eyes down and left the room. "I have studying to do," I said, going to my room.

Lulu and the bellboy were coming back down the hall. We watched him gather all the suitcases under his two arms (I would have required several) and followed him upstairs to another two rooms. Throwing the keys on the glass-topped dresser, Lulu said, "It's so *hot,*" and turned the air conditioner up. I lay down on the bed on the far side of the room while Cam went to claim the adjoining room. I closed my eyes. "Camelot," Lulu called, a sudden urgency in her voice. I opened my eyes. "Tennessee is going to sleep." I shut them again and pretended to be asleep. Cameron came into the room.

"You've got to help me keep her awake," Lulu said, laughing, and Cam, humming, began to lay out her fortune-telling cards. I rolled over. "Don't let her go to sleep," Lulu commanded.

I sat up. "Why?" I asked. "Just, *why not?*"

There was a moment in which Lulu and her daughter, linked along some line that I could travel only parallel to, looked at each other and arrived at an agreement. Then Lulu turned back to me and said, her querulous voice listing dangerously like a ship at sea: "Well, *Tenn . . .* if you take a nap now, you'll be wide awake after dinner, and you'll want us to *do* something tonight. Discuss. Play cards. And I really *would* like to get a good night's sleep tonight."

❡ One day twenty-some years ago, when we were living in the old neighborhood, next door to the little mongoloid, Tiger had come home from school with a stomachache. By the time I'd got out and got home, her fever was a hundred and five. They had her lying in a tub of cold water but she was burning up: the fever refused to go down. The doctor admitted that he didn't know what it was. His guess was that it was Rocky Mountain Spotted Tick Fever, and when my father pointed out that there weren't any spots on Tiger and we lived in the Smokies, not the Rockies, the good doctor shuffled his feet and said, "Well, yes—" but that was just the way it was, so to speak, unless we had any better ideas? We weren't medical doctors, and didn't. "The thing is," he said, "not to let her go to sleep now, you hear?" So began our vigil, the three of us (for the doctor went home) watching by her bedside, spinning stories and cracking jokes, and once dashing for the bed manually (manfully) to persuade those long-lashed, delicate-veined, practically pellucid eyelids open. By midnight the fever had vanished as inexplicably as it had come. I remember being both exhausted and elated.

❡ Lulu was right: I was wide awake. They were both asleep later when I sneaked out via the porch to go down to the beach (not Dover). The moon was full but there was a chill in the air. Ambling along the shore, I stumbled over a dead starfish the tide had cast up. (The newlyweds I spied in advance and was careful to steer clear of.) It was the kind of happenstance my religion-professor father, as susceptible as most men to the seductive lure of symbol, would jump on and never let go. Indeed, I reckoned Christianity herself was a romance my father still courted (but he has always had the sense to keep his wooing of her a little less than wholehearted). Her skirts were wide enough to conceal all ambiguities and a certain amount of hanky-panky too, including the violence that was at the base, the birth, of our civilization and had been our heritage ever since, recurring in each of us, man or woman, like a dominant and unshakable gene. Take Lulu. Pitying her, I endowed her with martyrdom; or maybe, sacrificing herself, she solicited my pity. But did she deserve it more than anyone else? More than the rest of us? Every death created its survivors who were burdened with the responsibility for it—for burying it. Shoot. I was damned if I was going to bear the responsibility for her suffering any longer! nor should I let anyone assume mine for mine. I would dare to define myself—and to elect my own debts.

The Passion was a paradigm, which, all-encompassing, lacked that specificity necessary for moral statement. . . .The Passion, acted and re-enacted over and over, was unavoidable, and was consequently rightly contained within the realm of necessity rather than that of free will. . . . The Passion was a circle describing two indistinguishable arcs, heaven and hell, mount and vale, life and death, and both sides of the coin my father was wont to flip when all else failed. If running around in circles confused one, the answer was to get back to the beginning—to the center which, like some rare *topological* flower, generated petals concentrically until the very odor of earth was freshened and made sweet everywhere. There was the aroma of hibiscus, the tang of sea-spray.

But I am my mother's daughter too, and looking back, must admit, that if the former way was too astringent or too proud or too theological for a pretty night in Nassau, there was a more prosaic way of summing up my thoughts as I looked again at the stiff, unfortunate starfish that lay at my feet. Whatever a person's philosophy might be, I thought eagerly, excitedly, even, almost, hungrily, it would all, as my mother had so often with great and evident satisfaction said, "come out in the wash."

PART THREE

Heb. 12:29 For our God
is a consuming fire.

9. THE BURNT OFFERING

There was a hitch: there was a difference between declining, however wisely, to suffer vicariously and plain long letting a middle-aged woman burn herself up. She was going to. "Move the furniture around, put your new chaise longue against the far wall, hire a full-time nurse," I told Lulu, naming thirty-odd steps she could take to stave off what I nonetheless knew was inevitable. The paradox was that the only way she could go on living was by denying that she wanted to die. She insisted she wasn't going to. "I'm not worried," she said, "it won't happen again." But I was worried—I was afraid—and would've moved except that Cameron's bum leg would inhibit her from running for help and to call for help she'd have to run to my room since the telephone in Lulu's room was on the other side of the chaise longue she refused to move. If before I wouldn't leave, I now felt I couldn't leave. "Go on and get yourself out of here," Willa Mae said, pounding fish fillets with a mallet; "a li'l girl like you is ain't goin' to teach an old dog new tricks at this late date." But Willa Mae went right on supplying Lulu with grass from Southeast Asia and Colombian Red, and the chemotherapist went on writing out her pill prescriptions. "I'm going to call her shrink," I said to Cam, but Cam said I had no right to and to quit worrying: *"Que será,*

será." She said I reminded her of Chicken Little (but that I was cute); so I kept my worries to myself, reminding myself that if Gladys Brunner had known of Lulu's penchant for semiconscious arson, moving out had not saved *her.* I figured I always had the back staircase to count on in an emergency, and took the few precautions I could think of that were within my province: I quit using any kind of dope at all, always wore heavy levis that fire would have to saw through, and every evening stacked Bernie's old letters (they were beginning to be priceless from age alone, those chicken-scratched communiqués in which he analyzed his reasons for not marrying me), the issue of *Male Bag* in which my article had appeared (also an antique), my mother's mother's jewelry, and my purse in a pile on the floor by the door to the back staircase; and opened the door to my room every hour on the hour every evening until the silence and darkness downstairs revealed that Lulu was asleep for the night. Then I waited another hour before I went to sleep. Sometimes late at night I would succeed in getting some real studying done—I especially enjoyed Genetics, which we'd already gotten into the previous year and now explored more thoroughly—and when the time came I passed the National Boards (the Doodler didn't), and passed them with plenty of room to spare. The school let us out two weeks earlier than the previous year, expecting us to use that time to study for the Boards. I did. But then I had nothing to do. I had no plans for the summer. I spent a couple of days just hanging around the hospital. One morning I bumped into Fran Dabrowski and asked her how come she hadn't gone away for the summer. She said she had to stick around because she had seven cats that she hadn't been able to find homes for, and now they were getting too big to appeal to anyone. She asked me if I would like a cat. I said no but said I would like to see them sometime. "It's too bad we didn't get to know each other better," she said. I said maybe we could do that next year. The magnifying lenses of her new glasses were even thicker and set up an odd sensation of distance or obstacle between viewer (her) and viewed (me).

We parted on Madison and I went home. Sometimes late at night I called Max just to talk for a while and calm down, because she would no longer visit me in my penthouse, and, anyway, was preoccupied with the details of her elopement. Less than two months after she and Jonathan did elope, heading north to Harvard in a Volkswagen bus that her parents, never grudge-bearers, had given them, she produced a premature baby boy and sent me an announcement scrawled on a postcard depicting the Boston Commons in summer: "Father and son doing fine. *(Signed)* Mother Zucker." She said she wasn't ever coming back to Fun City. Everyone else was out of town for the summer, including, of course, Adrien, who was out for the summer and the winter and who wasn't ever coming back either. Our correspondence had ceased. Then one day toward the end of July I got a call from Bernie Stein: "May I speak to Tennessee Settleworth," he said, and three things went through my mind. I'll bet he wanted to speak "to" me; when had he ever spoken with me? Did he really not recognize my voice? And what was the point in making such a big deal about my maiden name?

"You still aren't quite sure that you didn't marry me, are you?"

He wasn't going to let me play *my* games. "Adrien is in a hospital near New Hope," he said, unsettlingly serious, "and wants to know if you'll come down to see him."

"Is— Is it—"

"No, Tennessee, it is not serious." He said it was a broken leg. His voice was even and dispassionate, as if he were discharging a duty he found unpleasant but not mean enough to rail against. With some surprise, I discovered that I understood exactly how he felt. "Time heals all wounds, I guess," he said, weightily, when I told him. He seemed relieved to think mine might have been repaired by the agency of time (since he hadn't done anything to help).

"Well, when it doesn't *cause* them. Wounds." Actually, I was thinking of Lulu; he thought I meant I was still angry about the years I'd spent on him, when I might have been having children or becoming a famous (precocious) gynecologist.

"You think I like placing myself in a position of being vulnerable to your paranoia? It just so happens that believe it or not Adrien is a friend of mine and he wanted I should call and let you know. Christ."

"Talk about paranoia!" I asked him to give me Adrien's number. Then, duty done, he said good-bye.

"Forever, I would think," he said. No doubt his life-calendar was already booked solid with plans for organizing (his wife) and picketing (anyone).

"Yeah, well, thanks a lot, Bernie Stein," I said, reflecting idly that bedfellows make strange politics.

But Adrien wasn't in a laughing mood. "Even though I know it hardly rates, compared with what your sister's been through." He'd fallen off the bike carting groceries home to his house in New Hope, where Bernie had happened to be visiting for the weekend. I took a bus down. To the hospital. Adrien's face was as white as the cast his leg was in, and his yellow hair fell back from his forehead against the pillow, leaving the lovely profile so helplessly exposed as to render me noticeably uncomfortable. It—the whole scene—seemed to call for a degree of solicitousness that I hadn't been accustomed to expressing, at least not openly. Blushing, I managed to assure him his suffering was as significant as any I was acquainted with. He perked up in spite of my pomposity. Maybe because of the TRIUMPH tee-shirt I was wearing. "Relax. I'd feel *great*," he said, "if they would just cut out the pain-killers so I could *feel*. Deliver me from drugs! I'm sick of them." Though I didn't say so, I was pleased to hear this declaration of independence (from his father). I said I knew how he felt.

"Do you . . ." His hands were taped too, around the palms, but his thumbs were free, as if he were wearing snow-encrusted mittens on the hottest day of the year. Sweat dripped down his neck. I sponged his face. "I didn't mean to hurt you," he said. "I never wanted to hurt anyone. Especially not you."

"That's okay, Adrien, you go ahead and hurt me." The longer

he lay there, dependent and defenseless, the surer I began to feel about myself. "I can take care of myself," I said; "I know how to roll with the punches."

"Every girl"—he corrected himself—"every woman I care about I corrupt."

Bless his soul! I thought, now that I was seeing everything anew from this unusual vantage point (above). Then the Shortcoming Theory, to which I and others had subscribed, was wrong. So much for Bernie's analysis. Adrien really did feel as superior as we'd all, male, female and academic dean, led him to believe *we* felt he was. If he labored under the delusion that he was dangerous for me, I myself was still slowed—my decisions were slowed—by its opposite, compelling me to check out all my ideas and feelings before I could believe in them or act on them because they adhered to the wrong sex. "Even if that's true," I said, still allowing therefore for the possibility that he might be right in principle, "you can't corrupt me." So what if I was less experienced than I led him to imagine? What he didn't know wouldn't hurt him. Besides, I meant it; but of course I also knew perfectly well that he would read it as a challenge, and even if men were stupid to, they persisted in being titillated by challenge. Indeed I had turned the light in his blue eyes back on. I decided then to go all the way. "If you ask me," I said, "I think you can stop feeling sorry for yourself now."

"Who asked you?"

He had me there. "But you must have wanted to see me pretty bad," I countered, "to take this risk of being at my mercy." He was in traction.

"I wanted to see if you would come down. . . . Aw, come on, Tennessee, you know what the hell I mean."

In spite of Adrien's apparent impatience, his remark carried undertones of self-doubt: it seemed, I thought in some disbelief, the distant relative of a plea. But how could Adrien be so self-sufficient and at the same time feel the lack of my company? To the best of my knowledge, he had not felt it before. I decided he was playing with me. "I mean," he was saying, "I just wanted to see."

"So now your curiosity is satisfied."

He wriggled his thumbs, motioning me closer. "I still don't know," he said, "whether or not you miss me."

The delicate tip of his finely articulated nose took on a high sheen, as if all his bottled-up feelings were concentrated there (or maybe he had a touch of telangiectasia).

"You're blushing!"

"Well, hell, I'm embarrassed!"

"But why, Adrien? You know how I feel about you—"

"That's why, that's why!"

"You mean you don't feel the same way about me—"

"I mean I don't know what I'm getting into if I let you go on feeling the way you do. I don't know what your feelings mean in terms of what you might or might not be willing to do about them. That's what I keep trying to find out, don't you see?"

"In your own way," I said, "you're sort of a shy guy."

He got really angry then; I thought I had blown it for good. "I take it back," I said, "I apologize!"

He just looked at me.

"You wanted to know whether or not I miss you up there."

I waited until he indicated that he still wanted an answer.

"You want to know whether I miss your letters."

"Not my letters," he said. "Me."

I said I did. Then rushed on: "But of course I'm busy a lot of the time, I don't really spend all my time missing you or anybody. I gotta study."

His eyes dimmed.

"But"—heaven help me if I'd overdone it—"I don't have to stay at Mount Sinai."

"You wouldn't quit school?" I was happy to hear the note of disappointment . . . whether it meant he wanted me to quit or wanted me not to. As always, I didn't know which it was.

"No," I said. "I could transfer to another school." I waited for him to ask where. He didn't. "In New Jersey, for instance," I said, nonchalantly. "Maybe even Pennsylvania," I said, bravely. I explained that my classwork was pretty much completed, and in my third and fourth years I would be rotated through a series of clinical clerkships from OB/GYN through ophthalmology, with a stop at each major specialty along the way. I didn't have to do this at Mount Sinai, however much I might miss the place; though if I did plan to transfer, I'd better see about it right away, and might lose a little time. . . . I was used to transferring anyway, and considering the time I'd lost before I ever started med school, a little more wasn't going to mean the end of the world. That was something I could be sure of now: one thing my year with the Carlisles had done was teach me what medical school was all about (sickness) and I knew clearly now where my sympathies lay (on the side of health). What I had become less sure of was my commitment to gynecology. Adrien was looking at me expectantly. "I've been thinking of switching to pediatrics," I said.

"It doesn't surprise me."

"Of course, I'll still learn something about obstetrics and gynecology. Someday I'll deliver a baby! At least one." Every med student got to do that. "The thing is, I really don't have to make up my mind yet."

"I know you don't."

"The thing is, I really do like kids. Even when they're not my own." I was thinking of Cameron. "Maybe even especially when they're not my own. I don't expect you to understand that."

"I said I wasn't surprised."

"Why aren't you?" He ought to have been. I was!

"You really do like kids," he said.

"Take Cameron," I said. "I don't see how I could, well, it's a stupid word but I don't see how I could commit myself to any child of my own more than I have to her. Anyway, do you know that every twenty-four hours somewhere between one and two

American children are fatally abused by their *parents*? That is no exaggeration. Those children could use a medically qualified sentimentalist."

"You don't have to convince me."

"But Bernie said—" If it was sentimental, my response to kids, it was also—aha!—indiscriminate. "I never told you what Bernie said—"

"Don't," he said. "Forget Bernie. You were never even married to him. Though sometimes you seem to think you were."

"We lived together for a long time. He's the only man I ever lived with," I said, pointedly.

"It's not because you haven't been asked," he replied, just as pointedly.

I reminded him that he had apparently changed his mind about that.

"You misunderstand, Tennessee. I didn't change my mind, I just wanted you to know that I can't give you— I'm not the kind of man who— It's undoubtedly a defect in my character but it's the way I am—"

"What is?"

"Look," he said, "I'm not in love with you the way I think I'm supposed to be." Quickly he added: "Don't take it personally! I've never been in love with anyone that way. I probably never will be."

I wanted to tell him he was lucky. I also thought he was probably healthier than those of us who had succumbed to that kind of love. But something else I'd learned as a second-year med student is that nobody enjoys feeling that he hasn't experienced pain as severe as somebody else's. I just said, "I haven't exactly heard any bells ringing." He knew I was lying.

"And I'm not going to fall apart if you decide to split. Do you see, Tennessee?"

"Me neither." That was only a half-lie.

"It's just," he said, "that I don't feel like I've got it all together when you're not around. I guess I sent you some of it in those letters." He drew a deep breath.

"You're really worried about what I'm going to say!"

"Don't be stupid. I'm tired, that's all. Lying in this bed all day would wear anyone out."

Nonetheless, he had as much as said that he needed me. A little time, a little patience, and that need could grow into love: light, airy, leafy, full of songbirds better than the dull bells of thralldom. If it didn't . . . if it didn't, I had nothing to lose except the love I hadn't yet won. And the stability of my digestion, which was contingent upon a steak and candy-bar diet. "If you want me to eat that health food and stuff," I warned, "you'll have to do the cooking."

"It's all right with me," he said, "if you want to liberate me."

In my mind I could hear what my dear old friend, the Fourth Woman, would have replied to that. I thought it over. She had managed to teach me something. "No," I said, "you'll have to liberate yourself. I've got too many other things to do." Thinking of them brought Lulu to my mind. "Is the fall okay with you?" I asked then.

"Why not now?"

"Why the rush?" I tried to phrase my question casually but tightened up inside, afraid that Adrien would accuse me again of backing down. But I had to work something out—I couldn't just pretend that Lulu didn't exist or even that she could take care of herself, or that she wasn't endangering her own daughter, or that Cammie, try as she might, could take care of her unhappy mother. She needed me more than Adrien did. And if Adrien and I were going to be liberated, we had to admit that we'd been separated long and often and ought to be able to get along without each other for a little while more while I tried to work things out with Lulu. I had no idea how this might be done. "I have to work things out with the school," I explained.

"Okay. The fall."

We didn't know what to say to each other then—though it seemed something ought to be said to commemorate the occasion. "Hey," I said, "don't you want me to sign your cast?"

"Go ahead," he said, "sign it." I picked up the ballpoint from the nightstand and clicked the point down and approached the cast.

"Mary or Tennessee?" I asked.

He didn't answer. I signed it. "Which did you decide on?" he asked.

"Settleworth," I said.

He started to giggle and reached for my hand with his thumb, and I, holding his thumb, started to giggle. The good feeling which had always been bewilderingly absent suddenly swelled up and surged in and filled up the space between us, like water diverted from a useless course and returned to its naturally intended riverbed. Adrien was giggling too, and I knew everything was going to be all right, even if it was going to take a long time getting there. "Everything?" I asked myself, riding the bus in to Port Authority late that afternoon. "Not everything." Because of course there was everything, and then on the other hand there was everything else. I drew my hand across my forehead. The sun was shining in my eyes.

⟨ After supper Willa Mae brought our coffee into Lulu's bedroom and then left. Lulu was in a good mood. Brinkley reported the case of a man who'd walked into Bellevue, pulled a gun on the receptionist, and demanded to be admitted. The receptionist had told the man he had to wait his turn in line, whereupon he shot her. Lulu found this hilarious and said it just went to show how insane the world was. I agreed that it was just like Vietnam, wasn't it, and asked her if she'd heard anything more about the headmaster who had absconded with twenty-five thousand of her dollars. She thought that was hilarious too and said no, and then, putting on a maternal expression, said that the school was now being run by fine people. "Has Cameron called?" I asked.

She was on a camping trip in Canada.

"Not yet," Lulu said, "but she will. Her birthday is next week." The mention of birthdays made us both pause. "Remember the roses?" she asked.

The hum of the air conditioner, Dave Brinkley's lazy voice, Lulu's high spirits ("I bought a dress today"; she showed it to me) were working on us with a nostalgia for a kind of communication we had never really shared. "I'm not unhappy," she said, during the commercial. "I have my vibrator and my daughter." I thought it was an odd pairing but didn't want to violate the confidence by questioning it. I nodded. I did venture to ask again whether her daughter might not be better off in a more traditional school. "What difference does it make?" she asked. "Cameron won't ever have to work for a living. I only hope"—she sighed—"I live to see her married off." I nodded. The news was drawing to a close and I wanted to get upstairs before the mood changed or before she asked me to stay downstairs and watch a movie with her. "Don't you date any more, Tennessee?" Her blue eyes betrayed nothing but her hand shook as she stubbed out the cigarette in the ashtray.

I said no.

She found that hilarious too. "No man is worth it," she said, and before I could ask, Worth what?, she thumbed her nose at the television and said, "Good night, Dave." I took our coffee cups out to the kitchen and called good night from the hall. There was no answer.

❡ Upstairs in my room I sat for a while at my desk, scanning stories in search of one to study with Cammie when she came home for summer vacation (she had to, sometime before it was over, though she seemed to be putting it off as long as possible). About nine or nine-thirty—I'd never gotten around to replacing the Timex that quit on me when I accidentally wore it into the water in Jamaica a year ago—I closed the books and lay back on my bed to listen to music. With Lulu so cheerful, I thought it would be all right to turn the music up full blast. Whether it was rock or classical is something I can't remember now, any more than I can remember which stories I had been reading through earlier. When the dogs started barking—they may have been for some time, though—I turned the music down and went to the door and opened it. Everything seemed to be all right, so I decided that the dogs were only barking after the cat, and closed the door again. But when they kept it up, I went downstairs and looked out the peephole of the front door to the apartment next door. Lulu's own door, just to my right, was open, and again everything seemed to be all right. I thought maybe the dogs were responding to a noise I hadn't heard. Then a third time they began to bark and this time I stood at the head of the stairs and noticed that Lulu's door, which had been partly open, was shut. She's moving around, and everything is all right, I thought. I went back into my room and turned the music up. If anything bad was going to happen, it always happened on the third time (I was still superstitious).

I don't know how much time had gone by when I realized that the dogs were making a racket again, but this time the little one wasn't barking—he was making a queer little noise from the bottom of his throat like a muted siren. I ran to the staircase and as soon as I opened the door the stench hit me. Oh god, I thought, it's happening all over again; and while I wasn't surprised, I couldn't help feeling it was unfair. Twice was too often, even if the first time had forewarned you of the second. I ran down the stairs but all the lights downstairs were off and it was pitch black and I couldn't find the light switch. I was talking out loud to myself, asking myself, "Where's the light switch? Where's the switch?" until my hands bumped into it and the hall lights came on in answer. I threw open Lulu's door. I don't know what it was I had in mind to do—but it was a shock to discover that there was nothing to do.

Lulu was in bed on the far side of the room. The lounge nearest the door was swimming in a pool of water. No flames, no smoke.

I had turned on the light in her room and she stirred, a diminutive figure under the sheets, and raised her red head. Half-sitting, she said: "I did start a fire, Tennessee, but it's out now. Please turn out the lights and close the door and go upstairs." I picked up the pillows from the lounge and felt them with my hands, feeling for fire as I might check myself for untoward lumps, and smelled them, and put them back on the lounge. I raised the mattress of the lounge and looked all around, but there were no signs of sparks, only damp ashes and a drowned butt. I pocketed the butt. "Will you let me get to *sleep?*" she said again. The dogs were quiet now, the little one had curled up on the bed with her. If it had been my own mother or my father or my sister, I would have dragged the mattress into the shower as before, sensible, I am sorry to say, of how it could smoulder and blaze up when you were most unaware, but Lulu was my employer, or was more closely that than anything else, and I had no right to rip up her furniture without so much as a by-your-leave.

"Are you all *right?*"

"Dandy," she said, disappearing under the covers. "Sleepy."

I turned out the light in her room but not in the hall and left her door open, planning now to go sit at the top of the stairs for a while just to be sure that the smell of smoke was in fact weakening; but at the top of the stairs, when I sat down, I suddenly started to cry: my whole body was sobbing, I was shaking all over. Of course I knew it was a delayed reaction to the first fire, but knowledge wasn't sufficient to stop the shaking. The first fire, I'd had two panicky people to keep in line; this time there was only myself, and I had to give the orders and take them, panic and tell myself not to panic. I stood up, walking stiff-legged to keep my knees from bending out from under me, and went into my room and sat at my desk. The only sound was the hiss of the record spinning pointlessly on the turntable. I moved the needle over to the side and turned the machine off and reached for a cigarette. As the sulfur of my match flared, so did the stink of damp stuffing. The little dog was whining louder now, and the big dog shot past my door on his way out to the Sun Room. I crushed my cigarette in the ashtray. Where there was that smell, there was smoke, and where . . . Maybe I should have gone downstairs again, but if the lounge was already in flames, I wouldn't be able to get to Lulu, and if it wasn't, wasn't yet, and I got to Lulu, I wouldn't be able to get her out before it went up. I jumped for my telephone and dialed the operator. It rang—and rang—and rang— The smell was stronger now, there was smoke in my room. I slammed the receiver down and ran across to the Sun Room to the elevator entrance on my floor and leaned on the buzzer (but I don't know how my legs got me there). Later I learned that the doormen and elevator men knew, from the Puerto Rican boy, what was probably happening, and had begun when they realized the ring wasn't letting up to mobilize the house fire extinguishers. But the boy that came up wasn't the Puerto Rican; he was a young Irishman, nineteen I'd say, a strapping-big kid with left-tackle shoulders. "There's a fire," I screamed up at his face, "and Mrs. Carlisle is trapped in it."

"Oh, my god," he said, and beelined past me to the staircase. "Please come back," I called after him, recognizing even at the time the forlorn note in my voice. But he vanished down the stairs, and I, looking after him, saw that her doorway, which minutes before had been dimly shadowed by the hall lights, was a solid sheet of bright flames, and yet no time at all could have elapsed from the time I'd tried to reach the operator. I leaped back toward my room and tried again, dialing O as the newspaper had said to do "in case of fire." No answer. The room was filling up with black smoke, I could hardly see, and the stink of smoke and mattress and (as one of my friends delightedly explained later) flesh thickened like a bad batter. I didn't know whether I was going to throw up or suffocate, and giving up after giving O three more chances to come up with the right answer, lost my head and grabbed the things I kept on the floor by the back door and unlocked the door and in a rush of indecision ran to the apartment that backed mine. "Let me in," I hollered, pounding on the door; but all was silence, not even the strains of *Lieder* reached me through the thick back wall. "Let me in!" I shouted again, thinking that surely Lulu and the Irishman were both toast by now, and that an alarm had not yet got through; but my unknown companion had deserted me, or thought she was some smart not to open the door to lunatics. I ran on down the stairs, ringing doorbells as I went, knocking against closed doors, screaming: "Please let me in so we can put in an alarm, there's a *fire* in this building." I was polite as you could please, but in a hurry, and after shouting I would run down another flight of stairs, and then think, Of course no one answered, I didn't give anyone time to. Then I'd turn and run back up and knock again and run back down. Once, near the end of the eighteen flights I traveled thus twice, I tried a doorknob and the door opened. "Isn't *any*body home?" I pleaded, but the apartment was dark. I moved inside a ways, trembling, and stumbled against something in the dark, a chair or a stool, but it was enough to frighten me, and I closed the door and continued my flight, knowing that at any moment the nineteen storeys—give or take a few—above me were going to cave in on my head, which the firemen told me afterward was not so farfetched a notion as it might seem: I'd left the back door to my room open, and with the air conditioner in Lulu's room urging the fire out and up, the long staircase down the back of the building would act as a funnel to draw the fire down after me. Then when an eternity had gone by I found my-self at the foot of the stairs, and thinking, Free and clear!, turned left to leave visions of hellfire and brimstone well behind me. Irony of ironies, I'd never had occasion to use the building stairs before, and never thought to ask where I would come out. I came out in front of a heavy crosshatched wire door in an iron frame that reached from floor to ceiling. I tugged at the latch—and nothing happened. I could hear voices in the distance. *Endure,* they said. *Endure! Endure! Endure! Endure!* I wanted to—I wanted to answer. "Oh, won't somebody please let me out of this stairwell?" I called, very cleverly letting them know where I was and that I wanted out from there. But nobody answered. I thought everyone was going to leave me without ever realizing that I was there, and started walking in circles, circumscribing the stairwell as pointlessly as a record spinning on a turntable without being listened to, and reckoned, thinking of Lulu sprouting flames like a flower in hell, that my bones burned white would be just retribution for failing to see that an angel could adopt the guise of a martyr and might expressly choose that pose as the one least likely to be seen through. Wearily, I stopped spinning and sat on the bottom step. My bones, I thought, would give me away: my teeth and my wire eyeglass frames. If I only suffocated to death and they put the fire out before it reached me, my mother's mother's jewelry would identify me, and the police could have a good laugh over my connection with *The Male Bag,* and the *Post* could write a touching feature based on Bernie's letters. Then I was put out with myself for bringing his letters with me instead of saving Adrien's (but at the time I was preparing my pile, I thought it would serve Adrien right if his poetic correspondence was lost to posterity), and decided to go back up for them, but rising from the step, decided to try the wire door one last time. It opened, and I stepped out into the lobby, and fell straight into the arms of my Swedish super and the Irish elevator operator I'd last seen plunging toward the fire in an excess of Christian love for the long-awaited Apocalypse that was now so vehemently upon us. "Hi," he said.

❡ "When I saw I couldn't get out the front door," he said, "I ran back up. Your door was open, I mean the back door, and I figured you'd gone out the back way. It was a good thing, too, on account of I was about to pass out, what with that godawful smoke and all, and if I had to have stopped and carried you out, Miss Mary, I don't know if I would have made it? So I made it back to the elevator and went down to the floor below you, Mrs. Carlisle's floor, and warned the folks in Eighteen-A. Dr. Krickovic? He's the one that got through to the Fire Department." He patted my shoulder; his hair had been badly singed and as he talked flecks of it fell on my shoulders. "Dr. Krickovic is up there now with the firemen." To the right of the lobby I could see Mrs. Krickovic in her nightgown, and Baby Krickovic in the arms of her mother's maid. *"Va falls,"* the super said, "impossible she should live."

"Have they got her out?"

"Not yet," said my Irish friend, heartily. "But they will, don't you worry. Miss Mary," he added, as if hearing my name would be a comfort in itself. The firemen were rushing past me, going up, going down, some just standing around, it seemed; I heard a siren, and then another flock of firemen breezed through the lobby. But the super was shaking his head, pushing his lower lip out to disparage my new friend's optimism. "Never," he said. *"Va falls,* no. Never, yes."

"What happened? What happened?" Mrs. Krickovic was tugging at my sleeve.

"What happened," I repeated, and sank onto the couch and burst into tears.

◖ One of the firemen bummed a cigarette from me and stood there smoking it, his face smeared with grime and sweat. "You lived on the top floor?" he asked. I nodded. "What a place," he said.

"Have they got her out?"

"It's hot as hell up there," he said. "We're doing our best."

"How old is she?" This from a policeman clutching a clipboard.

"Fifty-three," I said. "Not long—"

"Relatives?"

I explained her situation. There was no way to get in touch with anyone unless I could find names and numbers upstairs. "The paper said to dial O," I said, "but the lousy operator wouldn't answer."

The fireman looked at the policeman. The policeman nodded. "I read it in the paper myself," he said. Then he turned to me. "Next time," he said, "dial 911."

While I was wondering whether there would be a next time, the fireman and the policeman moved a little away from me. I heard the fireman laugh. "You boys," he said, punching the policeman on the arm, "don't always answer either. Tell d' troot!"

"Easy, easy," the policeman hissed, motioning in my direction. Then he turned back to me. "You look like you could use some sedation," he said. "Don't you think you ought to go to the hospital?"

I said no and took another cigarette out of my purse. I was out of matches. I looked at the fireman. "Can I have a light?" I asked.

❡ Mrs. Krickovic said: "She must have been crazy. Think of the danger she was placing my baby in!"

I said I had thought of it.

"Poor child," she said, though I was certainly older than she was. "It must have been terrible to live with a woman like that."

"I was the governess," I explained.

"Well," she said, "my husband will have to do something about this. We can't have a woman like that living here and endangering the lives of all of us. Think of my baby!"

The baby began to cry.

❡ The super said: "They got her out, already, but believe me, she's dead." I began to cry again. The Irish boy said, "No, she's alive." I cried some more. It didn't seem right that no one should know whether she was dead or alive: how removed she was from the world! That was the worst thing. Then they wheeled a stretcher down the hall, and from where I was on the couch, I could see Lulu's red top bright as blood against the white sheet. If she was dead, wouldn't they have covered her? But I didn't go see—it wasn't the same as an anonymous cadaver, after all. (I shouldn't even have to say that, except I did say it to myself.) As the stretcher disappeared through the front door, the policeman asked me again if I didn't think I should go to the hospital. I thought of Lulu in the hospital, and how no one—no one who knew who she was—would know she was there. She deserved better, a keener witness to the most dramatic event in her life. But who else would have done what I did now? (I ask myself.) "No," I said, "I've got to go upstairs." He took me to the elevator and we rode back up to the eighteenth floor. The hall inside the apartment was black, paint and plaster dangling from the walls and ceiling like stalactites in a cave. It looked like a cave. The policeman guided me into her bedroom (Adrien said he would have thought of Dante touring the Inferno, but I did not), telling me to be careful where I stepped. "Exposed wires." It was too dark to see clearly. I bumped into the frame of the chaise longue, which the firemen had propped against the wall. The policeman found that the light in her dressing room still worked and turned it on. The nearer half of the bedroom looked like a battlefield. The Aftermath of Armageddon. I looked around. "But the bed—" I said. *It* had not burned. The policeman explained that the air conditioner had driven the fire out of the room. "It was concentrated in the doorway," he said, "which was why it was so hard for the firemen to get in." Then maybe she wasn't burned? "She was burned, all right," he said; "she evidently woke up and tried to get out and collapsed in the area of concentration." I said, "Oh," and began my search. Finally, on the stand on the far side of the bed, I found what I was looking for, an address book, charred, damp, and dirty, on top of an old magazine open to *The Prisoner of Sex* by Norman Mailer. Real funny. I put the address book on top of the things I was carrying and went back out into the hall. I felt I was walking in a trance. I followed the trail of hose upstairs—they had snaked it in through the back door to my room—and looked in, but nothing made any sense, came together, or jibed. I shivered. Then I realized how cold it was, where it had been so unseemly hot before, and realized that all the windows had been axed wide open. I went to the Sun Room and stepped out on the terrace to let the cold air dry the sweat on my face. "Clio," I purred, seeing the cat. Then I remembered the dogs. The big dog was shaking like a leaf behind the potted plants outside the window to my room. The little dog wasn't there. "We found him in the bedroom," the fireman said, when I got back downstairs. "He must have stayed with her during the entire incident." I shifted my load of purse and papers and reached out to pet him: he was trembling, body vibrating like a little motor, and his breath gurgled in his throat. The fireman had wrapped him in a blanket. "If I were you, miss," he said, "I'd leave him be. He's going to go by morning." I nodded and stood up. We were in the living room, about twenty or thirty firemen and the policeman and the super and Dr. Krickovic and myself. The firemen were sprawled on the sofa and on the floors, breathing hard, their shoulders slumped. A hush fell over all of us; it was a gauze net trapping us into self-consciousness. I wanted to thank them, but saying, "Thank you," after what they'd done, seemed not only innocuous but patronizing. I walked toward the center of the room, to speak to them, but the center of the room moved away from me. I took another step forward, and the room receded even farther. Dr. Krickovic asked if I had anywhere to spend the night. I said I had to make a phone call, and he took me by the elbow and led me across to Eighteen-A.

❝ The Krickovic maid met us at the door. She was big and quiet with an attractive smile. "You just set yourself down right here, hon," she said, pointing to the phone. "Wouldn't you like a nice shot of som'thin'?" I said I'd like a cup of coffee. Mrs. Krickovic came darting in, a robe over her nightgown, her finger over her lips. "The baby's asleep," she said. "Oh, *Ora,* why haven't you put newspaper on the floors?" I took off my shoes but my hands were still filthy, and after I'd reached Willa Mae on the phone and recited the names and numbers of Lulu's relatives (her long-lost father, he who had looked like Marshal Dillon, was still listed), tried to clean it, but the receiver wouldn't come clean. Mrs.

Krickovic sent me to the bathroom. "Don't wake the baby!" she cautioned, and then set my coffee cup in the sink although I wasn't through with it.

Alone in the bathroom, I tried to collect myself. I washed the soot from my face and neck and hands and then tried to wipe the sink clean, but the only towel I could find bore a large portrait of Donald Duck, and I was nervous about using the baby's things, so I ran water into the sink and tried to clean it with toilet paper, but the paper shredded and when I tried to pick the pieces up they stuck to my hands. I forgot to turn the water off and then I heard Mrs. Krickovic knocking on the door and telling me I was going to wake the baby. I turned the water off, but, wiping my hands on my jeans, palpated a small cylinder in my pocket: it was the butt I'd retrieved from Lulu's chaise longue before . . . before. I hadn't been able to get my hands very dry without a towel, and now the dried-out butt, redampened, began to crumble, tiny brown bits sticking to my palms like a nicotine pox. I wiped them off on the inside of my tee-shirt. From the outside, it looked as though I had rust stains on it. I turned off the light and opened the door to Mrs. Krickovic. She showed me to the couch in the study and Ora brought in a blanket. There was now a pathway of newspaper from the study through the living room to the kitchen to the foyer to the front door, and I knew I wasn't supposed to stray from the straight and narrow. "Now you just make yourself comfortable," Ora said, and Mrs. Krickovic said, "If you need anything, you can talk into the intercom." She pointed at a speaker on the wall. "We have one in every room and leave them on all the time, because of the baby," she said proudly. Then they left me alone and I went through Dr. Krickovic's medical books looking for articles on burns until the wind outside suddenly blew up and it began to storm and I had to spend the night crouched behind the couch where the lightning couldn't get me.

❦ Dialing as quietly as I could, I called the hospital at dawn. They said she was satisfactory, and then half an hour later they said she was critical, and then half an hour later they said she was satisfactory, and then I gave up and called Willa Mae. When she arrived, she rang the doorbell of Eighteen-A to pick me up, and when I got to the front door, following my newspaper path, Ora was whispering to her. Willa Mae had the little dog in her arms and Ora was stroking him. "What in heaven's name is going on?" Mrs. Krickovic demanded, appearing at my side. "Don't you know that animal is bringing *germs* into this apartment?" Ora winked at Willa Mae and I thanked Mrs. Krickovic for putting me up and she closed the door on us and then Willa Mae and I looked at each other and she said, "Well, Tennessee, I am now going to take this nasty little animal that was so loyal to our madam to the *vet,* 'cause he might make it *yet."* She said they had located Cameron through the school but that the consensus was she should not come to the city to see her mother, at least not just now. "I was jus' over there," Willa Mae said, "and that poor lady!" Then the old man brought the elevator up and she got on it and I went into *our* kitchen and poured myself a glass of Minute Maid from the main icebox.

❡ The first day I went to the hospital, the doctor didn't want to admit me to her room because I wasn't a relative, but after I pleaded my case, mentioning my med student status, he allowed me two minutes. She was covered to her neck but the face was severely burned, blotched red and black, one eyebrow completely gone and the other raised forever in an unanswerable question. "Hello," I said.

She laughed. "Well, Tennessee, I really did it this time, didn't I."

"Yes, you did."

"Are the animals all right?"

"They're fine," I said. "Mrs. Wood took them to the vet, and they're going to be fine." The little dog's mind would never recover from the shock, but he was going to live.

"I don't want Cammie to see me," she said.

I didn't answer.

"I must look like hell," she said.

"You look fine. How do you feel?"

"I just wish they would leave me alone. They keep doing things to me, and I wish they would leave me in peace."

"They're just trying to help," I said.

"Does my hair look all right?"

"You look fine," I said. Then she closed her eyes and went to sleep. The doctor told me she had seventy percent burns and that it would be touch-and-go for six months, if she lasted that long. There was the danger of infection, the danger of fluid accumulating in the lungs.

❡ The second time I went to the hospital, she was asleep. A sister-in-law from Arizona had arrived and was sitting at her bedside. "I brought these," I said, holding out the flowers: camellias. The nurse appeared from behind the open door and whisked them away. "Not allowed," she said.

"Who are you?" the sister-in-law asked.

"Mary Settleworth," I said.

She looked blank.

"Tennessee."

"Oh, yes," she said, "I've heard of you." She turned back to face Lulu again.

"When she wakes," I asked the nurse, "will you read her the card that's with the flowers?"

It said: "Guess what florist these *don't* come from! Love, Tennessee."

❡ All my friends in the city knew what had happened. Rosie Jones even wrote her a sympathy letter, but she never got to read it. The third time I went to see her, she was in a coma. It was very early in the morning and no one else was there, except the doctor and the nurse. Then they left the room too. Her breathing seemed to have stopped, but I knew it hadn't because there hadn't been any change from the way she was before the doctor and the nurse left the room. Slowly her face began to darken. Sunshine was spilling in through the slats of the venetian blinds and I didn't know why her face was getting darker. I stood up and leaned over her and felt dizzy, as if I were being pulled to the floor by that same force that was sucking the blood down in her veins. As I caught my balance with one hand against the night table, the expression on her face changed slightly . . . ever so slightly. Then the doctor and the nurse came back in and said that was it.

❡ I went home to the duplex on Park Avenue. It was still only about nine in the morning, a bright, cheerful August day that was going to get insufferably hot by noon. It was a year almost to the day since I'd moved in—not quite a year since the very day I'd moved in. I went up to my room, picking my way past the glass and plaster and charred wood. Nothing had been cleaned up since the fire, and there was glass everywhere—my own room was barely functional. Even the pink pansies on the wall had turned black with soot and dust, as if neglect might have wilted them. The windows had been boarded up, of course, against wind and rain, and it was no longer possible to go out to the terrace. I thought that was a pity, as I would have liked to have another look at Park Avenue from the nineteenth floor, but there was nothing to be done about it. The view had never really belonged to me anyway. So I listened to the next-door *Lieder* for a while, and thought for a while, and after thinking, rang for the elevator, and when it came up, the Irish boy came up with it. I told him that Mrs. Carlisle had died that morning and asked him to notify the super. He said he hoped I wasn't upset. I said I wasn't.

In my room, I began the job of sorting out my things. The clothes had to go to the cleaner's, the books had been knocked from the windowsill when the firemen opened the window and there were bits of glass in between all the facing pages. I picked up the books and binders one by one and shook the glass out of them. At noon I went out for a sandwich, and when I returned, the super stopped me. "Do you know"—he stopped to form the words carefully—"a Gladys Brunner?"

I asked him why.

He said, "So-and-so"—he named a relative—"said she was in the last will Mrs. Carlisle had—had—"

"Drawn up," my Irish friend said.

"Will?" I asked, beginning now to understand the drift of the conversation.

The super smiled.

"Gladys Brunner," I said, "died last summer."

❡ On the elevator again, my Irish friend told me, "If I were you, Miss Mary, I'd clear out of here as soon as I could. You know? There's going to be a lot of gold-digging and money-grubbing and ripping-off going on around here."

I said I was going to do just that, but wondered if any of the relatives would think to tip him. Did saving the lives of tenants come under his job description? He patted my shoulder again and I waited while he closed the elevator door and I heard it descending. As the sound of the elevator disappeared into the depths of the building, I became aware of the silence in the Sun Room. But there wasn't any sun in the Sun Room because of the boards over the windows and the glass doors. Back in my room, I went on with my work. I found a half-melted fire mask next to the closet and threw it into the trash basket. I found a ball of cord in the kitchen downstairs and started tying up my records into piles of ten each. When I had finished that task, I started packing my papers, including the ones I'd saved that night and Adrien's letters, and found the prayerbook which I'd forgotten to save. It was months since I'd written anything in it. I leafed through it for a while. "Dear God," I'd written, "it looks to me like one little child isn't all that much to ask? I'll forgo the husband, if I have to. And it's not as if I were merely seeking self-gratification, is it? Or asking for something that would cause anybody any hurt. So why not? Amen." But I'd learned since then, late-bloomer that

I was, that it wasn't very smart to try to wheedle God into giving you what wasn't meant to be yours, because even on the spiritual plane you never got something for nothing, which, if you wanted to be really honest about it, just went to show you where the spiritual plane was. I didn't like the rarefied atmosphere there; and anyway, before being liberated on any level at all, however low or lofty, it was necessary for the body—my body, any body—to survive. That struggle was the earliest and most profound and perhaps, no matter what the Fathers of the Church would say about the Son, the only testament of faith there was. I threw the prayerbook into the trash basket. Just as I did so, I heard the elevator climb and stop at the eighteenth floor and the door downstairs open. I went down to see who it was, but Willa Mae, entering first, held up her hand to stop me on the steps. Behind her was Cameron. I waited until Cameron had gasped and turned into her mother's bedroom, and then I moved a little farther down the stairs to look in. She was limping through the room, disappearing into the dressing room and then coming back out, touching things, turning over char and rubble with that peculiarly disinterested movement of the wrist which we have seen the war orphans of Vietnam and Europe exercise on the evening news.

"Today's her birthday, isn't it," I said.

"Leave her alone by herself," Willa Mae whispered; "she'll be all right when she's done being alone." I nodded and went back up the stairs to my room and closed the door. Then I picked up the phone and called New Hope.